BEFORE December

JOANA MARCÚS

sourcebooks
casablanca

Originally published as *Antes de Diciembre*, © Joana Marcús, 2021.
Translated from Spanish by A. Nathan West.

Published by Sourcebooks Casablanca, an imprint of Sourcebooks
1935 Brookdale RD, Naperville, IL 60563-2773
(630) 961-3900
sourcebooks.com

Originally published as *Antes de Diciembre* in 2021 in Spain by Montena, and imprint of Penguin
Random House Grupo Editorial. This edition issued based on the paperback edition published
in 2022 in Spain by Montena, an imprint of Penguin Random House Grupo Editorial.

Cataloging-in-Publication Data is on file with the Library of Congress.

Printed and bound in the United States of America.
PAH 10 9 8 7 6 5 4 3 2 1

For every Jenna who is still learning to love herself;
For every Ross who is still learning to accept himself;
For every Naya who is still learning to care for herself;
For every Will who is still learning to relax;
For every Sue who is still learning to open up;
And for every Mike who is still learning to forgive himself.
This book is for you.

1

AN OPEN RELATIONSHIP

"An…open relationship?"

"Yeah. Exactly."

My boyfriend was beaming. I wasn't. Not in the least.

"What's that?"

"Jenna, I think the name kind of gives it away."

He had to be joking.

Or should I say: he'd *better* be joking.

He had just dropped me off in front of my dorm! Literally! I hadn't even had time to get my suitcase out of the car, and already he was thinking about changing everything about our relationship.

"Monty, do we have to talk about this right now?" I grumbled. "How did you not get around to it before?"

"Uh…I just didn't."

"Are you serious? We've spent the past two days together."

"I know, but…I just didn't know how to bring it up. It never felt like the right moment."

"Oh, but I guess now is just perfect?" I asked.

"Jenna, don't be like that. I've got to go, and I had to tell you before leaving. It's not something you'd want to talk about on the phone, right?"

"No, it isn't."

I sighed and decided to relax a little bit. I was nervous about college, out of my comfort zone, and it wasn't right to take that out on Monty. Especially when he was about to leave. Being angry at each other the last time we were together... I didn't like that idea.

But what was I supposed to tell him? I looked at him awhile, dwelling on that innocent smile of his—too innocent for the person he really was.

Then I realized I hadn't really thought about what would happen to us when I stayed here and he went back home. He was finished with school. Or at least that's what he told himself for now. Our town had a NBA development league team, and he was going to focus on that. He only liked one thing, really. Playing basketball. All day long.

Me, though... I'd been so busy getting ready for college, wondering what life in the dorms would be like, that I hadn't even considered that we wouldn't see each other for a long time. Too much time, I guess. He had to train and I was taking a full load, so daily contact was going to be a hard ask. Plus, it's not like I had money to go see him all the time, and I doubted he'd want to come out here to see me. I could already hear the excuses: *Babe, I just had practice and I'm beat...*

At least we'd see each other for Christmas. But December was so many months away.

I tried to focus again on the conversation when I realized he was waiting for an answer.

"I don't know what to tell you," I admitted. "I'm not even sure I understand what it means to...have an open relationship. I just don't know what one is."

"It's simple. Look, you and me, we're a couple, right?"

"I think so," I joked.

"Perfect. So we love each other, we appreciate each other, we respect each other, but...we've both got our needs."

"Our needs?"

"Yeah."

"What needs, Monty? Like eating?"

"No, Jenna."

"Drinking?"

"Not exactly..."

"Sleeping?"

"Jenna, I'm talking about sex."

"Huh?" I blushed and looked around, wondering if there was someone nearby who could hear us. "S-s-sex? Are you...?"

"Could you stop looking around like we're plotting a murder? We're just talking about sex."

"I don't like talking about sex," I said.

"I know." He rolled his eyes. "Still, though. Sexual needs are real needs, right? I mean, I don't know about you—you're kind of asexual—but me..."

"Do you even know what it means to be asexual?"

He ignored me. "I do have my needs."

"Wait." My voice went three decibels higher. "Are you telling me you want to sleep with someone else?"

"What? I'm not..."

"I hope this is a joke," I said.

He held my face in his hands and told me, "All I'm proposing is that if at some point...you know, like if we feel the need, we can just do it."

I pushed him away. "And might I know why you'd ever feel the need to sleep with someone who wasn't me?"

"I don't. Not now," he said, looking almost offended.

"Oh, you don't. Then should we go back over what you meant when you described an open relationship to me just now?"

He knew what I was getting at, and he tried to cover it up by touching me again, but I dodged him. I could tell he was upset. I lowered my head.

"I'm sorry," I murmured. "But I'm really nervous and…"

"I know." He relaxed and took a breath. "I know it sounds weird," he went on, "but open relationships are a thing now. And scientists have shown that couples in open relationships stay together longer."

"I'm sorry, who are these scientists?"

"And I'm not even saying I *do* want to do it, but…how long are we going to go without seeing each other? Three months?"

"Almost four," I said. "But you're ducking the issue…"

"I don't think it's good for the body to go that long without doing it, Jenna."

I scowled. "I went seventeen years without doing it with anyone and I was perfectly fine."

"Yeah, but when you're a virgin, it's different. You don't know what you're missing, so you don't suffer when you don't have it." He grabbed my hand and pulled me softly toward him. "Come on, babe. You know I love you, right?"

"Yeah, Monty, but…"

"And you know that won't change. No matter what happens. Or who happens." He laughed at his own joke. "You get me. That's why I'm with you, why I love you, because you've always understood me perfectly. And you know I have my needs, Jenna. So…what's the problem if I give a little love to someone else when you're not around?"

"That's a very fancy way to avoid the word 'cheating,' Monty."

"It's not cheating if both people consent to it."

"Right. So you're asking for my consent for you to sleep with whoever you want."

"Hey, it's not just me. If you meet a guy, you can sleep with him, too."

Honestly, I didn't find that very consoling. "Did it ever occur to you that I might not want to sleep with anyone else?" I asked.

"Great! Then don't. But at least you've got the right to change your mind, you know?"

"So you mean that if I walk into the dorm right now and meet a guy and I like him and I want to sleep with him, you don't care? You know you don't believe that."

"That's not what I'm saying, Jenna."

"What are you saying then, Monty?"

"We don't even have to sleep with anyone. It's just, with us having a long-distance relationship, we could have the right to...you know...be in situations, and if a person's there and we're super-attracted to them, then fine, we can do what we want with them. Without resentment, without reproaches, without jealousy."

He was still holding my hand, and I wanted to pull it away. I didn't like what I was hearing at all. "I don't know, Monty. It sounds a little weird."

"Come on..." He smiled and gave me a kiss on the lips. "It'll be fun. Plus, we can have rules."

"Rules?"

"Of course. To make you more comfortable. Like, every time one of us does something with another person, they have to tell. That would be best, I think."

"I don't want to know what you do with other girls," I told him.

"OK, fine. We won't enter into details. We'll just let each other know it's happened."

"Monty..."

"Now it's your turn to set a rule."

"I never even said I wanted to do this," I argued.

"Well, let's imagine you agree. In that case, what rule would you pick?"

I turned it over in my head a moment while he looked at me expectantly. "Well...no friends. I don't want you hooking up with any of my friends. And I won't hook up with yours."

"Sounds good."

"Are you actually telling me you don't mind if I sleep with other people?" I asked.

"Jenna, if it's just sex, then I don't care." He cupped my cheeks again. That was a thing he did when he was trying to convince me of something. "That's what an open relationship is. You might sleep with someone else, but you know you love the person you're actually with. And that's how strong our relationship is. Cool, right?"

I wasn't sure *cool* was the word I'd use to define the situation, but he wasn't going to give me any peace till I said yes, so finally I shrugged and responded, "If that's what you want…"

He smiled and grabbed the back of my neck to kiss me. I let him, even though I wasn't feeling it. Then he took my suitcase out of the trunk and left it on the ground next to me.

"Great, well we'll…"

"I'll take it from here," I told him. "You should go. Otherwise you'll be home late."

Surprised, he asked, "Do you really want to go inside alone?"

"Yeah, I really do."

"Jenna, I don't mind lending a hand."

"I've got it." I gave him a peck on the cheek and he smiled, and I told him to call me when he got in.

"And you text me and let me know how things are," he said.

To tell the truth, I'd expected a more emotional goodbye. But instead I got a pat on the cheek and he hopped in his car and took off. I saw him wave as he hit the gas.

For a moment, I regretted telling him to go. But it was better that way. I needed to absorb the fact that from now on, I'd probably be spending a lot of time by myself. I had to get used to it, and the sooner, the better.

I turned toward the building and started dragging my suitcase, stomach tight from my frazzled nerves. I felt like a soldier headed out to fight her first battle.

My dorm was close to the Humanities, where I'd be studying. Looking at the worn redbrick façade, I thought it probably hadn't changed much in decades. There was a huge poster hanging on one of the walls that said something about women's rights. That made me smile as I took the stairs inside, huffing and puffing because my bag was so heavy.

Inside it was packed. The place itself looked old-fashioned, but there were so many people there, I forgot about that right away. I had to glance around a moment to find the reception area. There was a blond guy in huge glasses behind the counter, not much older than me, and he seemed stressed as he shouted something to a young man who was leaning against the wall. I wondered why he was there. It was a girls' dorm. Maybe he was someone's brother or cousin?

Anyway, it wasn't my problem. I stood there behind him, waiting for him to finish.

"Ross, I can't let you go up there," the guy behind the counter said. He sounded tired, as if he'd already repeated this several times. "On day one, only family members can go up. And no guys. You know that."

"'You know that,'" the other one repeated mockingly and grinned.

The blond guy turned red in the face. "Could you take me seriously for once in your life?"

"Could you give me a break for once in your life?"

"Ross, this is a girls' dorm—"

"Thanks, I didn't notice—"

"And you're not a girl."

"Neither are you, and you're working here."

The guy behind the counter got angry and groused, "Look, I'm here because this is my job and I'm trying to do it to the best of my ability!"

"Perfect. Then you can be the one to go tell Naya she has to take her own suitcase upstairs."

The guy behind the counter froze. "No. You tell her."

"Me? I don't think so, buddy. That offer's expired. I tried to be a gentleman, but you won't let me." He shook his head. "I guess it's going to have to be all your fault, Chrissy. Too bad. I liked you. But no worries, I'll come to your funeral to tell you goodbye, OK?"

The blond guy—what kind of name was Chrissy?—looked at him as he decided what to do. "Let Will do it," he said. "He's her boyfriend. That counts as family for my purposes."

"Do you think I'd be here if Will could come?"

"No," Chrissy said. "I guess not."

"Bingo," the other one replied.

"Why couldn't he come?"

"Our dear friend Will is busy and thinks I'm his errand boy."

The receptionist asked if whatever this Will was doing was more important than his girlfriend.

"What do I care?" Ross replied. "I literally just got up twenty minutes ago. I slept two hours. Maybe less. I'm dying to go back to bed. And this suitcase is like a ton of bricks. And I'm hungry, Chrissy. All I want to do right now is go home and eat my cold leftover pizza from last night and sleep away the next decade."

Ross paused and then leaned over the counter. "So will you let me take Naya's suitcase upstairs so I can get on with my life, or are you going to keep telling me no?"

Chrissy was flushed. He seemed to be having some kind of short circuit. Was it really such a big deal to let a guy go up to one of the rooms? With all those people in there, who'd even notice?

"Fine," Chrissy murmured, defeated. "But get a move on! If someone sees you…!"

"I'm a discreet man. You know that," Ross said, smiling from ear to ear.

The blond guy seemed to finally realize I existed, and his face turned serious once again. He nodded his head toward me and said, "Look, Ross, as you can see, people need my help, so…"

Without even looking at me, Ross picked up the suitcase and started making fun of him again. "Yes, I can see you're a very busy man."

"How can I help you?" Chrissy asked me as his acquaintance wandered off toward the stairs. I tried to look friendly and said, "Sorry, I didn't want to interrupt…"

"I wish you had," Chrissy replied. "He's unbearable. Anyway, what's up? You're staying here?"

"Yeah. My name's Jenna. Jennifer Michelle Brown." I showed him my license, which he stared at for a moment.

"Jennifer Michelle. Strange combination." He tried to find me on his list.

"My parents are very imaginative," I murmured.

I'd always hated my second name. My family loved to call me by my middle name to tease me, but I usually kept them in check. I knew how to hit back. Still, it was there on my birth certificate. I'd never entirely escape it.

"Let's see, then… Oh, yeah. Here you are. Hmm. That's a coincidence," Chrissy said.

"What?"

"That suitcase Ross was just taking upstairs belongs to your new roommate. Good luck. You're going to need it."

Somewhat frightened, I asked why I'd need good luck.

"I'm kidding," he said with a nervous chuckle that hinted he wasn't kidding at all. "Your roommate is Naya Hayes."

"You know her?"

"Yeah. She's my little sister."

His tone was strange, and I asked, "Is that…bad?"

Slightly louder, slightly higher-pitched, he replied, "Well, uh, no. I mean…" Then he tossed a key on the counter. "Second floor. Room 33. You can't miss it."

Just then, Ross reappeared empty-handed. "I need the key," he said. "Your sister's not up there."

"Where is she, then?" Chrissy asked.

"I don't know, bro. She's your sister, not mine. Why don't you tell me?"

"I don't have another key, Ross."

"Great, then I'm leaving her shit in the hallway where some creep can steal all her panties."

I tried not to laugh.

Chrissy looked at me and said, "How about you chill for a moment and I'll make an official introduction here. This is Jenna. She can open the door for you. If she doesn't mind, of course."

I felt a little uncomfortable as Ross looked at me and said, "Sure, no problem."

"Good," Chrissy finished. "Then welcome to the dorm, Jenna. If you need anything, my name is Chris, and I…"

"He's the head of making sure guys don't enter without permission. Or so he wishes," Ross cut him off.

Chris pretended not to hear him: "I'm the person who keeps order around here. I'm in Room 1, first door on the second floor. If you need anything and I'm not here, that's where you can find me."

"Otherwise he'll be down here playing *Candy Crush*," Ross added.

"I don't play video games during working hours," Chris said, trying to maintain his composure. "Anyway, Jenna, try not to come to my room unless it's an actual emergency. I mean like if the building catches fire. If you drop your phone in the toilet and you don't want to fish it out because you think it's gross, that's your problem."

"Do lots of people come knocking?" I asked.

"More than I'd like," he assured me. "If you lose your key, you can get another one, but there's a ten-dollar fee. You can have visitors during the day, but if they're coming at night, we need at least one day's notice. And your roommate's got to be OK with it. There are shared bathrooms at the end of each hallway, but I think your room has an en suite. Anyway, they're always open. Anything else…? Oh yeah, this."

He fished around in a drawer and pulled out a little basket full of plastic squares. "Safety first," he told me, and I saw they were condoms. "It's a welcome present from student health services. One per. My recommendation is the strawberry flavor. That's the one most people ask for."

I was red with embarrassment as Ross peeked over my shoulder and grabbed a handful and Chris reminded him he'd already taken one. As Ross dropped them all, I picked up a blackberry one. I slipped it into my pocket, feeling hellishly uncomfortable, and said, "Thanks…"

Chris wished me a good day and reminded me I could come to him for help whenever I needed. Then he shouted, "Next!"

I almost twitched, his voice was so loud, and another girl immediately took my place. Ross asked me, "So, you have the key?"

Clearing my throat, I showed it to him and said, "Yeah, unless they gave me the wrong one."

"Great," he replied. "I'll give you a hand."

He grabbed the handle of my suitcase and I followed him upstairs, just carrying my backpack. All around were weeping families saying goodbye and hugging and lonely-looking girls. I thought of my mother and what a scene she'd have started if she'd come. It was better that Monty brought me. It was better that he'd left, too.

Ross dropped my suitcase next to the purple one I'd seen him with earlier and stepped aside to let me open the door. Even with the key, I had to give it a good nudge. That depressed me somehow. But I tried to put a happy face on it, saying, "It probably just needs a little oil in the lock."

"It could always be worse," Ross replied. I looked around inside. The room was simple. Too simple, maybe. The walls were green and white, and there was a window over each bed, a desk with a chair and a lamp, and two small closets. I'd clearly not been the first to arrive, because the bed on the left already had my roommate's stuff on it.

"So you know my roommate?" I asked Ross.

"Me? No, I just love lugging around strangers' things. It's my passion, actually."

Of course he knew her. Why did I say so much stupid stuff when I felt awkward? Was it because he was handsome? I hoped not. But obviously I had noticed. I don't know if it was his brown hair, uncombed, or his bright eyes or his welcoming smile. Or maybe it was that old sweatshirt that made him look like one of those guys who doesn't care what anyone thinks. I don't know. He seemed like a joker type, and I usually hate that. Those kinds of men bore me. But why was I even thinking about all this?

"She's my best friend's girlfriend," Ross said. "Her name's Naya."

"Is she, uh…" I didn't want to sound scared. "Is she nice?"

"When she wants to be. She can also be… What's the word? Persuasive."

"What's that supposed to mean?"

"You'll figure it out when she has you doing stuff you don't want to do and you don't even know why," he replied. Then he pointed at the door and said, "Listen, if you'll excuse me, my work as a mover is done."

"Yeah, sure. Thanks for helping me with my suitcase."

"It was a pleasure," he said with a smile, then turned around and walked out.

I sat on the bed, but jumped back up when I heard it emit an awful creak. I obviously hadn't chosen the luxury dorm. For the next hour, I put away my things. Then the door opened again. The girl who appeared was a blond with clear eyes and a pointy nose. She looked sort of airheaded. I could tell right away she was sizing me up.

"Hi," I said.

"You're Jenna?" She looked more enthusiastic than I'd expected. "Cool! You don't look like a weirdo. I'm hoping you aren't?"

I blinked with surprise.

"Honestly, I would consider myself pretty normal."

I probably should have said boring.

"Cool! My parents had me freaking out about this whole roommate idea. I was terrified about having to spend the next few months with a stranger. But then, I'm kind of weird myself. I admit it. By the way, I'm Naya. Nice to meet you."

She spoke so fast it was hard to understand her. I watched her sigh and fall back on her bed. Hers creaked, too, but she didn't seem to care.

"I hope you don't mind me picking this side," she said. "I'm happy to change."

"Not at all. Your bed doesn't seem much more comfortable than mine."

"I actually tried to take a nap and couldn't." She frowned. "We'll have to get used to it, though. What else can we do?" She looked over, saw her purple suitcase, and shouted, "Did my boyfriend come?"

"Some guy came, but I don't think he's your boyfriend. He said his name was Ross."

"Ross? He sent Ross?" She sounded confused and indignant. "I hope he wasn't a pain in the ass."

A pain in my ass? I mean, we hadn't been together long, but he seemed like a pretty nice guy. He'd helped me with my stuff even though we'd never met.

"Not at all. He brought my suitcase upstairs."

"Ross helped you?" She seemed confused. "It must be the summer heat. It got to his brain."

She stood and opened her bag and dug through her things. I did the same, asking her as I laid my favorite boots in the closet, "What are you going to study?"

"Social work." She smiled as she folded a sweater. "I really want to help dysfunctional families when I get done."

"That's so altruistic," I said.

"I don't know. It is a job; you do get paid for it. What about you?"

"English," I confessed.

"Oh, cool. Do you like poetry?"

"No."

"Theater?"

"Not really."

"Novels?"

"No."

"Anything else? You must like reading?"

"Ummm…"

Confused, she asked me, "You do know that studying English means lots of reading, right?"

I admitted that I hadn't known which major to pick.

"Oh. Well then." She must have been confused about what to say next. "Maybe you'll learn to like it."

"I hope so." I smiled. "Otherwise, the next four years are going to be long."

Or not. My parents hadn't wanted to let me move far from home, but I'd managed to convince them to let me do a trial semester away. In December, I'd find out if I would stay there or go somewhere closer to them. For now, I was certain I didn't want to go back.

Naya and I talked for a while, and that made me feel good. She was a sweetheart. I didn't understand why her brother had wished me good luck. We were soon chatting about our families and how they had cried when we'd left and how we were going to miss them. We lost track of time until she looked at her phone and realized it was nighttime.

"Shit!" she shouted. "I'm going to be late."

I wanted to ask, but I wasn't sure because I didn't know her well. I couldn't resist though: "For what?"

"My boyfriend is living close by with his two roommates. He wants to show me their place, and... No! I've only got five minutes till he picks me up!"

She was yelling so loud I was worried the neighbors would complain as she dug hysterically through her closet and began tearing off her clothes. "Dammit, I need to get changed right now!"

"You look fine," I murmured, looking at the blue blouse and jeans that fit her like a glove.

"You're kidding, right? I look like an Oompa Loompa. I've been waiting forever to see him again, and he's been waiting to see me, too."

As I watched her jump up and down, trying to fit into her impossibly tight pants, I said, "Well, I'm sure you two will have fun." I took out my phone. Monty obviously hadn't gotten in touch. One day... He couldn't keep his promises for one day. Some romantic he was. Naya threw on a blue sweatshirt so fast it almost tore, then walked over to the mirror hanging on my closet door and touched up her mascara.

"Maybe you could use some eye shadow?" I asked.

"Mine's buried in the bottom of my suitcase somewhere!"

"Here," I said, "you can use mine."

"For real? THANK YOU!"

I shrugged. It was just eye shadow. I tossed it to her and she caught it in the air. Then she gave me a stare so strange I had to ask her what she wanted.

"Nothing, just...you want to come with us?"

I hadn't expected that, and I wondered aloud, "Who? Me?"

"Is there anyone else in the room?"

"No, but...are you sure? I mean, I don't know your boyfriend."

"Yes, I'm sure, dummy! I can already tell I'm gonna love you. And so will the guys. Besides, you met Ross and you said you liked him, so that's one down already."

I didn't know what to say. I wasn't usually good at making friends, especially my first day somewhere. But maybe it would do me some good to try to fit in. After all, my brother Spencer *had* given me a long, boring lecture about how I needed to be more social. And he'd made me promise I'd stop saying *no* so much.

I was already about to say yes when Naya begged me, "Come on, they're nice. Plus there's free Chinese food. Spring rolls and fried rice with shrimp." *Jenna does not say no to free Chinese food*, my brain reminded me just then.

"Sure!" I said. "I'm there."

"Cool!"

I grabbed my green jacket and threw it on as I watched her fixing her hair. I was interested in meeting her boyfriend. If he was like her, I'd like him. Naya picked up her key and said, "Come on, he's probably waiting."

We walked down the stairs together and Naya nodded at Chris, but he was busy handing out condoms to the new girls and didn't notice.

"Poor Chris," Naya remarked. "He's so stressed out."

"Doesn't he have any coworkers?"

"I don't think so. But he seems fine! For the most part." She smiled. "We don't have a lot in common."

"No, it seems like you don't."

"He can be a little bit of a pain, but he's really a sweetie." She looked outside. "Hey, there's Will!"

Will was tall, dark, handsome, and very peaceful looking. He was waiting outside with his hands in his pockets. Naya ran out of the building shrieking so loudly that Chris shushed her. He was angry, but she didn't pay him any mind. I dillydallied a second to give Will and Naya some privacy while they kissed, and when Naya heard me open the door, she separated from him.

"Hey, babe, this is my roommate. She's goofy, right?" she said.

I was dumbstruck, and Will smiled as if to apologize for her. "My name's Will," he said. "It's a pleasure."

"Jenna," I replied. "Likewise."

"Will, do you mind if she comes with us?" Naya asked.

"Of course not. Go get in the car before the other two eat everything."

I got in the back seat and put on my seat belt, rubbing my nose, which was chilly, while Naya told Will how her brother was mad at her because she had lost the keys to her room five minutes after moving in and had needed to use his copy of the key. And that meant Ross couldn't borrow one. Will shook his head and smirked. I guess he was used to this kind of thing happening.

Naya looked back and caught me glancing at my phone.

"Waiting for your mom to call?" she asked with a smile.

"Huh? No. She's only allowed to call me once a week. We agreed on it. But of course, we both know she won't stick to that."

"My mom doesn't even bother calling," Will said. "Once you've been away for a year, she'll get used to it."

"Who are you waiting on a call from, then?" Naya asked.

"My boyfriend," I replied. "He told me he'd call."

"Oooh, you've got a boyfriend?"

"Yeah. A forgetful one."

"He's probably busy," Naya replied, as if it weren't important. "And now it's time for you to get distracted and forget about him."

"Will, are your roommates our age?" I asked, not wanting to talk about Monty.

"No. All three of them are sophomores. We're the babies there," Naya answered.

"Sue's a junior, actually," Will reminded her.

"Oh yeah, Sue. I forgot I was supposed to care about Sue."

"Don't be mean," he responded.

"Will, you know I'm right."

"Babe, Sue doesn't come out of her room when you're there because you two don't get along."

"We don't get along because she's unbearable."

"That's what Sue says about you," he told her.

"See?" Naya crossed her arms. She was angry, but she got over it instantly and turned back to me, changing the subject. "So this hand-some guy here and I have had a long-distance relationship for almost a year. Until this moment. Now we'll finally see each other every day again!"

The light turned red just then and they stole a quick kiss.

"I heard long-distance relationships are hard," I ventured, trying to be heard over their sucking sounds.

"Not for us," Naya said. "We've been together for seven years. So there's a lot of trust there."

Good lord. Seven years. I'd only been with Monty four months, and it felt like an eternity. "Jeez," I responded. "That's almost half your life."

"I know!" they both said in unison.

"But it's like we met yesterday," Naya told me, and Will nodded along as she explained. "We were boyfriend and girlfriend when we were little kids. Like, too little even to do anything physically. I remember the first time Will kissed me, I tried to slap him. Didn't I, babe? He stuck his tongue in my mouth and it was so weird. I didn't know people even did that!"

I laughed as they argued gently with each other. Will turned onto a little-trafficked street of apartment buildings and closed shops, and half-way down, he pulled into the one empty space in the garage. I got out and stared a moment at a black SUV with movie and music stickers all over the back. I passed my thumb over one of them, curious.

"Shall we?" Naya said, breaking the spell.

"Huh? Oh, yeah."

I followed them to an attractive building lobby, and Will pushed the button on the elevator for the fourth floor.

"Are you sure your friends won't mind that I came?" I asked, twiddling my thumbs and trying to tell myself to hide my insecurity.

"Of course not," he assured me. "Ross will be especially happy to see you again. He liked you."

I'm sure my surprise was evident as I asked, "He mentioned me? We were only together for a couple of minutes..."

"Yeah, but he said you seemed nice. And that Naya would probably make you want to kill yourself soon enough."

Naya rolled her eyes and said sarcastically, "Yeah, Ross, he's just the best."

On the fourth floor, there were two units and a closed window in the hallway. Will took out his keys and opened the door on the right. The scent of Chinese food immediately made my stomach growl. Will pointed to a coat rack. "You can leave your jacket there."

Naya had never been in the apartment, and she seemed almost as nervous as I was. I followed the two of them into a simply furnished living room: two easy chairs, a coffee table covered in bags of food, a huge TV and various video game consoles, a shelf by a window, and a wide hallway that seemed to lead to the bedrooms. A tiny window opened onto the kitchen.

Oh, and one other detail: there were two couches, one with two people sitting on it.

"Finally!" Ross shouted. "I was dying of hunger."

"Happy to see you, too," Naya said.

There was a girl there, too—Sue, I assumed? She frowned at me and then looked away. Ross smiled at Naya malevolently. As they bickered,

Will threw his jacket in Ross's face, eliciting a laugh. Ross threw it across the room into one of the chairs, and Sue, who clearly found the whole scene annoying, tried to focus her attention on the bags of food in front of her. She looked a bit like me. Soft tan, brown hair, the same color eyes. But she was thinner and her eyelashes a bit longer. She was pretty, even if she covered it up well with her constant grimacing.

Ross looked at me. "I'm impressed you haven't taken off running yet."

"Don't frighten her," Naya told him. "She's my roommate and I don't want to lose her yet."

"What's that supposed to mean?"

"That you're annoying, Ross." Naya grabbed my hand. "Here, Jenna, come join us." Will had made me a place on the sofa next to him, and Naya sat on his other side.

"She just got here, and she's already insulting me," Ross said.

"You're trying to scare my roommate!" Naya shouted.

"I'm not trying to scare anyone, and stop shouting! Anyway, if she's going to live with you, she needs to know what she's in for."

"How so?" I asked.

"Wait till they keep you up all night for an entire week with their noises. Then we can have this conversation again."

Will butted in. "Ignore him, Jenna. We've all learned to."

There was a brief silence when all I could hear was Sue unwrapping her chopsticks. When she saw I was looking at her, she scowled. She didn't introduce herself, so Naya did for her. As I got my own chopsticks, Ross told me how Ross was actually his last name and Jack was his first, but since his dad had the same name and Jack Ross Jr. was too long, he ended up going by Ross. I grabbed a spring roll as Will asked, "So, Jenna, are you from around here?"

I swallowed quickly and responded, "No." I nearly choked, but then I managed to get out, "My family's like seven hours way."

"Did you drive here?" Naya asked.

"Yeah. Well, I rode. I actually slept the whole way."

"Why here, then?" Ross wondered. "Is it the air pollution that drew you here? Or the convenient location near a bunch of depressing gray factories?"

"The schools are better here," I replied. "Plus I actually wanted to get away from home."

"Ahhh," he said. "The fledgling leaving the nest."

"Home was no good?" Will asked.

"It wasn't bad. I mean, I was fine at home. But I'm from a small town: always the same people, the same places… It's so repetitive. I wanted something new."

They kept asking me questions for a long time about home, my studies, my boyfriend. I got a little upset, though, when I recounted the story about Monty from that afternoon. I'm just that type. I can't keep my mouth shut even when I barely know someone. Naya seemed never to have heard of an open relationship, so I tried to explain it. "I'm not sure if he made it up, but he says it's when two people love each other but they can sleep with other people."

Ross said, "I'll never get two people acting like they want to stay together forever." Then, looking at my egg roll, he asked, "Are you going to eat that?"

"It's all yours."

"Hey, I like this girl!" he said.

Will told Naya, "Hey, maybe we should give an open relationship a try, babe?"

"Sure! If you want me to kill you in your sleep," she warned him. "I could never relax if I knew Will was sleeping with someone else."

"But she said it's not someone you love, right?" Ross said.

"I guess that's the idea," I responded.

"Yeah, but what if you do end up liking them?" Naya shook her heard. "Sorry, that's a no go for me."

I hadn't thought about it, but Naya was right. What if he did like the other girl more than me? What would I do then? It was best not to think about it. Not then, anyway. I didn't want to freak out over something that hadn't even happened yet. I leaned back against the cushion, trying to get comfortable, but then I straightened up when I heard what sounded like a shrieking cat. It was no cat, though, it was Sue, who was crucifying me with her stare.

"Mine," she said, snatching the cushion away.

"Eh, sorry," I mumbled. "I didn't know."

She hugged it to her chest hatefully. "Sorry's no good."

As I tried to figure out what to say to her, Ross burst out laughing. "Don't take it personally. She's crazy."

"I'm not crazy, dumbass."

"OK, sorry, you're not crazy. You're off your goddamn rocker."

Sue flipped him the bird. Will and Naya were so busy making out that they didn't notice. So they were one of *those* couples. But the worst part wasn't the kissing; it was the noise. It was impossible to talk over. Ross was grimacing at them, disgusted.

"You want to go, Jenna?" he asked me.

"I exist, too," Sue said irritably.

"OK, Sue, you want to join us?"

"I'd rather die."

"There you have it then. Jenna?"

Since Naya had apparently forgotten about me, I said, "Yeah, let's go." Better that than watching the soft-core porno movie being acted out in front of me. Ross thanked me for not being boring.

I followed him through the front door and he opened the window in the hall. "What are you doing?" I asked him. "It's cold out."

"Do you know a better way to get on the roof? Come here, help me."

"Help you what?"

"Just come."

When I walked closer, I saw there was a fire escape outside leading upward. "Are we really taking that?" I asked.

"It's safe," Ross replied with a smile. "At least, I've never seen anyone die on it."

"With my luck, I'll be the first."

I looked down and froze and then took his hand and we hopped out through the window frame and grabbed the handrail. He told me to go up first and followed close behind me. We had to climb two floors before reaching a flat roof, covered in gravel, with a couple of giant tubes that I guessed pumped air through the building. You could see the college from there, and the park that was next to it. And most of the city, too. I wished it wasn't so cold. I rubbed my hands together and put them in my pockets.

"Not bad, right?" Ross said.

There were four camping chairs up there, plus some thick blankets and a dorm fridge. They'd thought of everything, it seemed.

"What do you do when it rains?" I asked.

"We run up here and cover everything."

"And if you don't make it in time?"

"Then we wait for everything to dry off. Are you thirsty?"

I nodded and he tossed me a beer. I hadn't had one in forever. Monty hated the taste of beer and wouldn't kiss me if I'd drunk one. The first sip reminded me of how much I liked it, and I licked my lips as I covered myself in the thick blanket Ross passed me.

"Your neighbors don't mind you being up here?" I asked.

"They've never come up here."

"So they don't know."

"So they don't care," he corrected me.

"And what if they do, what's your plan?"

"Give them a beer and ask them to join us."

"If that doesn't work?"

"Toss them off the roof," he said with a laugh, raising his beer. "No witnesses, right?"

"It really is gorgeous up here. Apart from all those abandoned factories back there," I told him.

"If you pretend they're forests, it makes it nicer."

He dug around in his pocket for something. A pack of smokes. I watched him light one and as he put it in his mouth, I imagined the look of disgust on Monty's face if I... Dammit! Why couldn't I stop thinking of him? He hadn't even called me.

I asked Jack if he'd known Naya a long time as I tucked my face down inside the blanket.

"Since high school. She was already going out with Will. Seven years they said they'd been together, right? Jeez, time flies. It makes me feel old." He took a sip of his beer. "When did you meet her?"

"Two or three hours ago?"

"Wow! So you know how to fit in."

"I wish. I barely even had any friends in high school." *Congratulations*, I thought to myself, *you just blew your chance to look cool.*

"That surprises me," he said.

Since I couldn't be cool, I'd have to be sincere. "It was a weird place. It's not like it had a lot of friends to even choose from. Like, there were a couple of popular kids, a couple of losers, a bunch of invisible people..."

"Wait," he said, "let me guess. And there was a very bad, but very pretty girl who put down all the girls she thought were inferior."

"Yeah," I replied. There was one of those. "She never messed with me, though. I didn't exist for her."

"And there was a guy who skipped all his classes and mouthed off to the teachers, and of course all the girls liked him."

"All of them but me," I said.

"And a theater club, and a band, and those were for the losers."

"If so, that makes me a loser, because I did band."

"No way." He laughed. "What did you play, flute?"

"Um, not exactly."

"Guitar? Piano?"

Don't guess it. Please don't guess.

"No," I said.

"Well, what then?"

"I played the, uh, triangle."

He froze, stared at me, and turned beet-red as he tried to suppress a laugh. "The triangle?" he asked, in case there had been some confusion.

"Listen, it's harder that it looks! It sets the tune for the whole band!"

"Of course. The triangle is known to be a very complex instrument."

"Oh, shut up."

He continued, "With something so trying, I'm guessing you didn't make it long."

"No. Two weeks. Then I found another hobby."

"Choir?" he asked.

"If you heard me sing, you'd throw yourself off this roof."

"You danced then?"

"Yeah." I took a sip of my beer.

"Not hip-hop, I presume."

"You presume right."

"Please God, don't tell me it was ballet," he groaned.

"So what if it was?" I asked, irritated.

"Is that a yes?"

"Yeah, for a while." I crossed my arms. "And I was good at it, by the way. But I had to quit."

"Why?"

"My teacher told me I'd need to lose ten pounds if I wanted to keep doing it." The mere memory made me angry.

"I'm hoping you didn't do that."

"I didn't. That's not the end of the story, though," I said.

"OK, I'm all ears."

"Well, my mom found out and she got so mad she went down to the school to meet with the teacher and ended up throwing coffee in her face."

He laughed so hard he nearly dropped his beer. I thought it was pretty amusing, too.

"I like your mom," he said. "If you'd been my daughter, I'd have done the same."

That reminded me I needed to call her the next day so she wouldn't have a nervous breakdown.

"You're actually the kind of person who'd throw coffee in a teacher's face?"

"Depends. Maybe I'd have invited her up here and tossed her off the roof. I'm kind of itching to try that, now."

"So you're a bad guy?" I asked.

"I am. I've got a reputation to uphold."

I asked him if he had finished with his guesses about what my school was like, and he said, "No, not at all," then inquired whether I had been one of the invisible people.

"You could say so."

"Did your boyfriend go to the same school?"

"Yeah."

"He wasn't invisible, though, right?" Ross pinned me with his eyes.

"Nope."

"Probably the typical popular guy you'd have never thought would notice you, right?"

"You're pretty good at this," I conceded.

"And when you hooked up, the whole school was talking about it for a week."

"Actually two weeks."

"I was close," he said.

"Close but no bull's-eye."

"You're so negative!"

Looking at him askance, I asked whether his guesses were so accurate because his school had been like mine, too.

"No. Mine was boring. Nothing interesting ever happened. But I've seen lots of movies where the plot is like this."

"Stereotypes are often true," I said.

"I never said they weren't." He crushed his cigarette out on the ground. "So your life is basically a modern version of Jane Austen."

"Who's that?"

He stared at me as if he couldn't believe what I'd said. "You're studying English and you don't know who Jane Austen is?"

"I don't like to read," I murmured.

"Wait, let me get this straight: you're studying English and you don't like to read?"

"I have to pick a major, right? But I don't know what I want to study!"

"You're telling me you've never read *Pride and Prejudice, Sense and Sensibility, Northanger Abbey, Mansfield Park*? You never even saw any of the movies?"

"No, but I guess you like her," I replied, "because you know all the titles."

"My mother loves her," he admitted. "She has all her books and DVDs of all the film adaptations. I know them all by heart."

He shook his head in disbelief and asked, "OK, so you don't like books, you don't like movies, apparently, so what do you do with your time? Listen to music? Play dominoes? Stare at the wall?"

"Dominoes, no. Walls, no. Music I do like, but I'm choosy, so I don't listen to a lot of it."

He seemed stunned and asked what I did like, and I protested that I liked all kinds of things.

"Such as…?"

"I mean, I used to love ballet before the coffee incident."

"But what about now?"

Well, there was running. I used to do that before I met Monty. But he had this idea that a girl shouldn't leave the house alone—especially not in tight clothes—so I kind of forgot that and ended up sticking to things you could do around the house.

"I like reality shows," I finally admitted. "The more fights on them, the better."

He smiled, but I think he thought that was ridiculous. He tried to change the subject to movies, saying there was nobody who didn't like movies and asking me if I'd seen anything recently.

"Sure," I said. "*Finding Nemo.*"

"Well," he said, arching an eyebrow, "that's the summit of cinematic culture right there."

"Yeah, my boyfriend doesn't like movies."

"Yeah. I'm not asking questions about your boyfriend. I'm asking about you."

With a frown, I exploded, "I don't like movies, OK? They take forever to watch. It's just a bunch of people talking about whatever, and I hate the way they, like, show a building or a field from a bunch of different angles… Who cares!"

"You're not watching them right."

"How do you watch them wrong?"

He shook his head and asked me if I hadn't watched Disney movies when I was a child, and when I brought back up *Finding Nemo*, he said he was pretty sure that wasn't Disney. He regretted that I'd missed out on my childhood and I said he was exaggerating, but that my brothers had always hogged the TV to watch sports.

He started rattling off a list of movies I supposedly had to have seen: *The Lion King. Life Is Beautiful. Forrest Gump. Gladiator. The Pianist. Back to the Future.* Some of the titles rang a bell, but I had never seen them and had never felt the temptation.

"I thought I had a sad life," he said, and I objected that I was very happy.

"You're not, though, but you will be a couple hours from now, when we finish watching *The Lion King*."

He was already standing up to get ready. I set down my blanket and hurried over to the stairs with him, asking why it mattered whether or not I'd seen some dumb movie. "It's not dumb," he said, and when I apologized for offending the honor of his favorite movie, he went off. "It's a classic, for the love of God! You not even knowing the first thing about it is like... Well, it's like I'm talking to a person from another planet!"

When we were back in his apartment, he froze so quickly I almost ran into him and ordered Naya and Will, who were still on the couch making out, to cut the lovemaking because there were people coming through.

"What are you two doing?" Naya asked, looking up.

"Jenna's never seen *The Lion King*," Ross said in the same scandalized tone as before. "I'm about to fix that."

"You're kidding!" Will exclaimed.

"See," Ross said, "she's weird."

"And you're a little annoying," I told him.

But at least he wasn't stuck up. And he was funny. He guided me to the last door on the left and invited me into his room. The first thing I noticed was a giant poster for what I guessed was a famous movie. Then another. Then another. I had never heard of any of them. There was a sliding glass door that led out onto a balcony and a small window, an orderly little desk with a laptop covered in stickers, and a big bed with a notebook on it that he tossed to the other side of the room brusquely. Grabbing his laptop and sitting on the bed, he said, "Go ahead and take off your boots. And get ready to have your life changed."

I did as he said and walked around, looking at things while he tried to find the movie. That first poster that had caught my eye showed a girl with blond hair and a long sword in her hand. "What's with the sword?" I asked.

Disappointed, he replied, "It's called a katana, it's Japanese, and the film, as you can see from the poster, is called *Kill Bill*. It's a classic, one of my favorites, directed by Quentin Tarantino. I'm assuming you haven't seen it, either."

"No. I would, though. I'm curious now."

"I would recommend you begin your movie journey with something by Disney, which is a bit softer," he responded. "I don't think you're ready, psychologically, for Tarantino."

On his dresser, I saw photos of his family. His mother looked young, and he and his father shared the same features, except that his father had shorter hair and glasses. There was one picture of a younger Ross standing next to a basketball trophy smiling from ear to ear, and that same trophy, along with a few others, stood behind the photo frames. Passing a finger over it and thinking how much Monty had always yearned for his team to win a title, I asked, "Do you like basketball?"

"I used to. I think it's boring now."

"You were good, though?"

"I'm still good."

"And humble, too, I see."

"Humility's never been one of my faults," he said. "Now come here. I've got the movie."

Less than two hours later, I was watching Simba climbing up Pride Rock with swelling music in the background. As soon as the movie finished, Ross turned to me, awaiting a reaction, his expression like that of a child waiting on a piece of candy.

"It's good, right?" he said.

"It was...fine."

"What do you mean, 'fine'?"

His indignation made me chuckle, and I admitted, "Look, I liked it, OK? The music's fun. The characters were amusing. It was good."

He relaxed and said, "I knew you couldn't resist Simba's charms."

"Actually, I liked Pumba better."

He seemed unable to believe that, but I explained that Pumba seemed more tender to me. He made a dumb joke about how wild boar meat was tender and I slapped his shoulder and said, "How dare you talk about eating Pumba," and he offered me two options: going to see whether Naya and Will were still getting it on or staying there and watching another movie. I wanted to know what time it was, and he said it didn't matter, I could definitely stick around to watch something else. So after thinking it over for a second, I said, "Sure, put on another of those Disney movies."

And so there I was, at three in the morning, watching the end of *Beauty and the Beast*. We'd actually started with *Snow White*, but I thought it was corny. Ross wanted to know my opinion, and I said I gave it an eight out of ten.

"You like *Beauty and the Beast* better than *Cinderella*?"

"Sorry, but *Cinderella* goes against all my feminist principles."

"Yeah, that story's hundreds of years old. There was no feminism back then. You have to look at it from the perspective of the culture of the time," he said.

"It sounds like you should be the one studying literature."

"Maybe in another lifetime," he said. "I'm very happy with my major. Bet you can't guess what it is?"

"I just met you at dinnertime."

"OK, you got me. I'm studying film."

"Naturally. I guess I understand now why you got so offended by what I said earlier. That car outside with all the stickers on it must be yours, then?" I asked.

"Yep, that's my baby. You like it?"

"It's original. And I like original stuff. I feel kind of bland around you. I don't have a single poster in my room."

"Now you can put up one of Pumba," he said.

"Yeah, I'm sure Naya would love a giant picture of a red pig on the wall." Speak of the devil… Naya knocked on the door just then and peeked inside. "Y'all aren't doing anything indecent are you?" she asked, pretending to cover her eyes but peeking through a gap in her fingers. "Ah, good, Ross, I see you're behaving."

"Gee, thanks for sounding surprised," he responded.

She asked if I was ready to go, and Ross smiled maliciously and said, "Wow, you guys finally finished!" She told him to shut up and for me to walk down with her to catch our Uber. I slid on my boots as Ross yawned.

"Good night, Ross," I said.

"Good night."

"Thanks for the film class."

"Next time we'll watch something weird and gory," he joked.

I shook my head and followed Naya outside.

2

THE GIRL WITHOUT HOBBIES

"I was late to my first class," Naya complained, dropping her backpack on the floor in front of me. I was in the cafeteria eating a burger, which was passable, at least compared to the rest of the offerings there.

"Why?" I asked, chewing.

"Gross! Don't talk with your mouth full!"

"Sorry," I said, swallowing.

"Whatever. I slept in because we were over at Will's so late. That's why I didn't make it to class on time." She stole one of my fries. "It was worth it, though. I hadn't seen him in ages. Still, my teacher was pissed…"

"It can't be that big a deal. In my class there were so many people you couldn't even tell who was who."

"Same with mine. It's also me, though. I hate being late." She gave the soup she'd just gotten a sniff. "This smells weird."

"I'll bet it tastes weird, too."

"How do you know? Did you try it?"

It was just a guess, but it was a good one. She took one small spoonful of it and said, "Yeah, you're right," pushing it aside in favor of her turkey sandwich as she asked me whether I'd talked to my boyfriend.

"He sent me a message this morning like *Yo, what's up?* But that's basically it."

"You could do it over Skype," she said. "That's what Will and I used to do when we couldn't see each other much."

"Do it?" What was she talking about.

"Yeah, you know, cybersex. Hey, don't look at me like that! It's normal."

"Why is this what we always end up talking about?"

"Because sex is interesting, Jenna. Then again, you could just buy yourself a vibrator on Amazon."

"Great, that'll be my backup plan."

I returned to the dorms soon afterward and saw Chris sitting behind the counter playing *Candy Crush*. He looked up when the door opened and said, "Hey, Jenna. How was your first day?" He was much calmer than when I'd first seen him.

"Kind of boring, honestly. It was all just introductions."

"Tomorrow, you'll get into the material and it'll be more interesting," he reassured me with a smile.

"Or less interesting."

"Now, Jennifer, that's not the kind of positive attitude we like to see around here."

"You can call me Jenna, you know?" I told him. Back home everyone called me Jenny, but now that I was at school, I'd decided to make a change. "Even my mom only calls me Jennifer when she's mad."

"OK, Jenna it is."

He put his phone aside and commented, "Naya told me you two were getting along. That's good news. When people want to change roommates, it's always a major ordeal."

"Do they do that a lot?"

"You can't even imagine. This girl came to me yesterday and was telling me that her roommate kept a corkscrew hidden under her pillow and she was scared she wanted to stab her with it and she needed to move immediately. But of course, nothing happens immediately around here. Weirdly, she hasn't come back today."

"Maybe she's a victim of the Corkscrew Killer," I said.

"Maybe." He laughed. "She can poke her eye out with it for all I care, as long as they don't mess up the dorm furniture."

"I'm glad to see you're a man with principles, Chris."

He glanced over at his phone and yelped. "Shit! I'm out of lives."

I said goodbye to him, but he didn't even notice. On my hallway, a couple of girls were yelling at each other over a T-shirt, and I had to duck as I walked by to avoid being hit by a flying pillow. I'd been lucky with Naya, I thought. Once I'd made it through the war zone into my room, I sighed and looked around at what was starting to feel like my new home, now that I'd arranged my things. Staring at the wall, I wondered if a poster with a red pig on it might not be just the accessory I needed.

My phone rang as I dropped my backpack on the bed, and I saw my mother's smiling face on the screen. When I picked up, she screeched, "Jennifer Michelle Brown!"

I had to pull the phone away from my ear, her voice was so loud. I knew what mood she was in by what she called me. If it was *Jenna*, she was feeling good. *Jennifer Michelle* was reserved for when she was irritated. If she used my complete name, it was time to head for the hills.

"Hey, Mom. Missed you, too."

"May I know why you haven't called? You've been there a whole week already!"

"Mom, I got here yesterday."

"Well, it feels like a week. How is everything? How's your roommate? Your classmates? Your teachers? How's the weather?"

"I'm good. My roommate's name is Naya and she's nice. My classmates were all groggy this morning, same as me. The weather's good. It's cloudy, I guess it rains a lot around here."

"Well, I hope you grabbed your boots, then?"

"Yeah."

"The black ones and the brown ones?"

"Yes, Mom."

"I know you prefer the brown ones, and they are pretty, but they won't protect your feet. The black ones, though… You should use those when it rains. Don't try and be fashionable and end up catching cold. I assume you've got your raincoat? The green one? Jenny, I just don't know if you know how to take care of yourself! Are you eating enough?"

"I try. The food here's not as good as the food Dad makes."

"Well, do what you can. You finally put on a little weight this past summer, and it honestly suits you, so try not to lose it," she warned me. I looked at myself in the mirror. What she'd said was true, but I was able to pinch a little fat on my belly, and I wasn't sure if I liked that.

"My pants aren't falling off of me, so I think I'm OK," I said.

Since Mom was obsessed with food, she turned back to that topic. She must have been psychic, because right away she told me, "Try to stay away from junk food. I sure hope you didn't have a hamburger for lunch your first day there."

"Of course not," I lied, and she caught me.

"You lie just as bad as your father."

I heard Dad just then in the background. He and Mom argued for a minute before she finally passed him the phone and he said, "Hello, Jenny."

"Hey, Dad. Did Mom force you to talk to me?"

"You know how it goes. I hate talking on the phone. But I better be discreet. The sergeant's standing right here and I'm sure she'll chew me out as soon as I hang up."

I could hear Mom snap at him, and I laughed. "Try to hold out till I get back, Dad," I said.

"Oh, I will. How is everything? Did you make some friends?"

Naya walked in just then and waved at me as she closed the door. I pointed to my phone and mouthed the word *parents* as I told Dad how much I liked my new roommate and her friends.

"Well, that's just great," Dad said. "When I was in college, I hated my roommate and he made that whole year horrible. Probably that's why I didn't go back after that!"

"Yeah. I think I'll make it longer."

My father talked for a minute about how he hoped my brothers would *get off their asses* and go to school, too, and when I tried to scold him for giving them a hard time, Mom started blabbing about how she needed to talk to me some more, and I heard a thud that I assumed was her tearing the phone out of his hand. In a near-panic, she asked, "Jennifer? Hello? You didn't hang up, did you? Hello?"

"Mom, I'm here."

"I'm sorry to repeat myself, Jenny, but you need to listen to me: no more hamburgers. And don't eat chocolate every day either."

"Mom, I'm eighteen."

"And I'll still be telling you this when you're thirty because you probably won't have changed. And you'll always be my little girl, and I have a right to get worked up if I want to."

I was laughing, but I was also exasperated. I asked her what she planned on doing when I'd been gone a month if she was already acting this crazy after one day.

"You'll understand when you have kids, honey."

"Yeah, that's not going to happen."

"If you don't give me grandkids, I'll kill you!" she shouted. Then she excused herself and said of course it was my choice, but she knew I'd change my mind. When I reminded her that she already had a grandson and asked if she'd forgotten him, she said she loved him a great deal, but that didn't mean she didn't want more.

"Why don't you put more pressure on one of the boys?" I asked.

"Because they're a bunch of layabouts. Oops, I shouldn't have said that. Steve is right here in front of me." I heard my brother protest, and my mother told him to hush before continuing. "I need to go. We're going to go see your sister and Owen."

"Tell her I'll call in a couple of days."

"Sure. Love you, hon."

"Love you, too, Mom."

She was shouting more nonsense into the phone about my diet and how I dressed as I hung up on her, looking at Naya. She grinned and said, "Your parents sound amazing. I'd love to meet them."

"That would be a mistake on your part," I assured her. "Being stuck with the guys at home is probably going to put an end to whatever sanity she has left."

"Who are the guys?"

"My three older brothers and my dad."

"Three brothers?" she seemed shocked.

"Yeah. There's a sister, too. She's the oldest of all of us, but she's got a kid and she lives with him in her own place."

"My brother, Chris, and I fought all the time. I can't imagine what I'd have done with four other siblings." She reached into a bag of gummies, pulled out a handful, and ate them.

"Oh," I said, "there were fights. Trust me."

"It must have been fun, though, right? When you take away the fights and the arguing?"

"Sure." I smiled. I actually missed them already. They were so… I don't know, they just put themselves out there. Shannon especially. If she were here, she'd already have a whole group of followers. I wouldn't have talked to anyone if it hadn't been for Naya. Even though I'd promised myself I'd be more outgoing. It even felt weird not having anyone here to pick on me or make fun of me.

Naya asked me what I was doing that night, and I told her I had no idea. "Lie back on the bed and watch the world spin, I guess."

"Wow, that sounds like some plan. I'm probably going back over to Will's."

"Making up for lost time?" I asked. She tossed a pillow at me and I batted it back, laughing. "You guys must really be in love."

"I know I am," she said with a smile.

I thought of Monty and me as she dug back into her gummies. Did anyone think we were in love when they saw us? I wasn't exactly affectionate with him, but he wasn't with me either. And that was OK, right? You didn't have to make out all the time to show that you cared about someone. I asked Naya how she met Will.

"It was simple," she replied. "My dad's friends with his dad. My parents got divorced, and we all met in a restaurant, and while the two men were talking, Will and I were kind of left to ourselves. He asked me for my number, I gave it to him...and the rest is history."

"And it's been smooth sailing since then?"

"Not exactly. I mean, Will's never been the problem. Not exactly. It's a long story. But before I came here, I was part of this really close group at my high school: Ross, Will, me, and this other girl. I liked her a lot, but we also had out disagreements, and when there were problems with her, I always took them out on Will."

"It's hard to imagine you guys fighting," I told her.

"You should see us when we get mad. But we always make up after a few minutes. What about you and...what's his name, Monty? Do you guys argue much?"

"Eh…sometimes." Lots, actually. Every time we saw each other. But I didn't want to admit that. She asked if we'd been together a long time.

"Is four months a long time? Because that's the longest I've ever been with a guy."

"Four months isn't long, but I know it can feel like it. When you're with the right guy, though, time flies… How corny! I must have had too much sugar," she said.

I laughed as she grabbed her phone, which had just started buzzing: "Yeah? Hey, babe… Yeah, I'm in my room… For real? You're the best! Hold on."

She asked me if I wanted to go see a band Ross's friends were in. But before I could answer, she got back on the phone and said, "Jenna's in. An hour…? Perfect. See you soon."

I tried to protest, but she cut me off. "Jenna, even Sue's coming. And they only manage to pry her off the bed a couple of times a year."

"It's not easy to tell you no, is it?" I asked. "Fine. I'll go take a shower."

"Almost impossible. Now hurry up. I need to go in after you."

If we were going to see a band, I guessed it would be in a bar—though I wasn't sure, since I'd never been to a concert. Fuck, Ross was right. I'd literally never done anything. Naya showered quickly after me, to my surprise, and when she came out, she helped me pick my outfit: ripped jeans and a sweater. She opted for a black skirt. I had to wait around while she put on her makeup and checked herself out in the mirror in my closet. Even when the knock came on the door, she wasn't ready. I opened up and saw a bored-looking Ross standing there.

"I'm not trying to rush you guys," he said, "but Sue's getting cranky. And I don't want to be responsible for whatever she does to Will in my absence."

"Jeez, Ross, I'm just putting on my makeup!" Naya shouted.

He leaned his head on the doorframe. "Why do I feel like I'm having déjà vu?" he asked. "Oh, yeah: because this happens every single time we go out."

She told him to shut up, but he peeked his head in and said, "Listen, if you're not ready in five minutes, we're going without you and Will can check out every chick in the bar because he knows I'll never tell."

Naya turned toward us with an innocent smile. "Ready!" she announced. Then she hurried past us and halfway down the stairs before turning around and saying, "Come on, guys, we're going to be late!"

Ross shook his head.

I asked him whether he'd ever considered being a teacher. "You're really good at establishing authority."

"I'd rather die," he said.

I was slipping on the jacket I'd draped over my arm as we walked toward the front door. Chris had just enough time to look up at Ross and scowl. "You said you'd be right down!" he shouted.

"Chrissy, short visits aren't against the rules," Ross replied.

"Stop calling me 'Chrissy.' Also, it's dark out. That means it's nighttime. That means no visits. I hope you're listening too, Jenna."

Like it was my fault he was so miserable! I mumbled that it had just been two minutes, and he shot back, "Rules are rules."

"'Rules are rules,'" Ross said in a joking nasal voice, and I couldn't help but laugh. As we hit the lot, I saw Sue's head emerge from the car window and she asked, "Can you guys speed it up?" She and Ross and I sat in the back seat. I saw what she was really angry about: Will and Naya were already making out as if none of the rest of us existed.

Ross told them, "Hey, whenever you guys are ready, we can go. No rush. We're only running half an hour late."

Will apologized, started the car, and said hello to me.

"Hey," I said, then remarked to Naya, "So you spent twenty minutes fixing your lipstick just to mess it up in a few seconds."

"It was worth it," she said with a glowing smile.

The bar was close to campus, but it was rainy, so it was best that we drove, especially because parking was easy to find. Inside, everyone was staring at the stage, where a singer with a shrill voice and a bunch of zits on his face was screaming into the microphone while some guy was abusing a guitar and another was banging the drums like he'd lost his mind. The music wasn't very good. Actually, it was terrible.

"So…you're friends with these guys?" I asked Ross.

"Yeah!" He smiled proudly. "They're great, right? They practice all the time."

"You can tell," I lied. "They're very…original."

"Probably you've never heard anyone like this, right?"

I sure hadn't. Ross stared at me across the high-top table and then cracked up laughing. "I've got no idea who these guys are, but if they plan on doing this for a living, I'm afraid they're going to starve," he confessed.

Embarrassed, I shouted, "Why'd you do that? I was trying not to offend you."

"Jenna, I doubt you could ever offend me."

I asked where the band he knew was, and he said they were up next. I sat down and he sat next to me. He was clearly staring at me, and I could feel it. He told me I was a bad liar—the same thing my mother said. Was I? *Yes*, my brain answered.

Thanks, Brain.

Will complained about the openers still being onstage while we all ordered beer except for Naya, who asked for a cocktail, and Sue, who ordered nothing, taking a bottle of water out of her bag. I assumed it was one of those places that didn't ID you. I asked Sue if she liked beer, trying not to shut her out of the conversation, and she made a weird remark about how I'd better not ask her for a sip of her water that made me realize I should have just left her in peace.

Whatever. I turned toward the stage when Naya said the headliners were about to come on. Once again, it was three guys. The openers and a few bar employees helped one guy set up their keyboard and drums while another plugged in a guitar and the last one, long-haired and wearing short shorts and a jean vest with no shirt, took his place behind the microphone.

"Interesting choice of outfit," I said to Ross. He didn't seem particularly impressed, which I found weird since they were supposed to be his friends. As soon as they started playing, I stuck my fingers in my ears. It was all just yelling and banging, and the rest of the clientele didn't seem to appreciate it any more than I did. Luckily, after twenty minutes, they took a break.

Will seemed amused at my reaction and asked me what I thought. I couldn't even formulate a complete thought before Ross jumped in. "Just say it. They're horrible. Everyone's thinking it."

"Not everyone," Naya said, pointing at the front row, where five or so girls wearing T-shirts with the lead singer's face on them were clapping and shouting the names of their songs while the band members pointed at them. Then they went to the bar for a drink and a regular soundtrack came on, to our gratification. Everyone seemed tired of the group after their first short set. Or almost everyone.

"I liked them," Sue blurted out.

We all turned to her with the same confused expression, and Naya asked what exactly she had liked.

"I like things that are ugly and terrible and suck."

Two members of the band went to talk to their groupies while the singer came up to Ross. I saw he had a tattoo of a heart on his thigh. "What do you think, bro?" he asked. "Great, right?"

"Fascinating," Ross responded.

"How about the rest of y'all?" he asked our little group with a smile. I

Will and Naya froze, then nodded. Sue frowned. I tried to smile and said, "Oh, it was great."

"And you are?" he asked.

"Yes, I am," I said, eliciting a grin from Ross. The singer turned, and I thought he was angry, but instead he dragged over a chair and shoved it between Ross and me, putting his arms over our shoulders.

"The name's Mike," he introduced himself. "I'm this idiot's brother."

I'm sorry—this was Ross's *brother*? But now that he said it, I could see a certain resemblance. Ross was taller, and less uncool—from what I could tell so far—and his hair was shorter, but they had similar eyes and similar features.

"Alas, he's not lying," Ross said.

"Don't worry," Will said. "They're very different."

Mike asked my name again and Ross told him not to worry about it, and that he'd done his duty by coming to see his brother perform so Mike should tell their mother he was off the hook for another year.

"How can you talk that way in front of my new fans?" Mike asked. "You should support your brother more."

"When you give me something to support, I will," Ross said.

Mike chuckled and asked, "Is she yours?"

Seriously? What century was this? "I'm nobody's," I said, "except maybe my mother's, because she gave birth to me."

"You don't have to be rude," Mike said, "I was just asking."

"You were asking rudely, and you got what you deserved, Mike," Naya said.

Mike fired back, "What would you know? You're in college and you've been with the same guy forever. You two should try to enjoy life like me. Look over there. I've got a whole line of chicks wearing T-shirts with my face on them. I'll take one of them home with me tonight. Or maybe two or three, if I get lucky."

"How charming," Naya said, taking a sip of her drink.

"Yep. Charming, that's me," Mike told her before asking me if I'd like a signed shirt.

"Nobody wants a signed shirt," Naya answered for me.

"They do!" Mike pointed back to the groupies. "Speaking of, pleasure talking to you guys, but I've got to get back to my real fans."

"Jesus, I can't stand him," Naya said. "I'm sorry, Ross, but…"

"I feel the same way you do," Ross replied. "But I promised my mom I'd see him at least once a year."

Will asked how his parents were, and Ross answered, "Same as always. Good, I guess? Mom's still painting lines on canvases and calling it abstract art, and Dad is still reading books to keep from dying of boredom."

That surprised me. I used to love painting. My parents even sent me to lessons for a while, but then I had to give it up because they needed to give my brothers money for their garage. It was exciting somehow to know someone related to a painter, and I said so, but Ross tried to play it down. "Painter is what *she* calls herself. I can't speak for how good she is. One thing's evident, though. As Mike has shown, artistic talent doesn't run in the family."

Ross drove us back to the dorm so Will could get in the back and make out with Naya. I called shotgun, which meant Sue had to sit back there and frown and groan every time they accidentally bumped her. When Ross parked in front of his building, the two lovebirds and Sue got out, and he asked me if I wanted a ride back to the dorm. I hesitated, but I definitely didn't have enough money for an Uber, and I had no idea how far a walk it would be. Plus, he seemed to want to drive, and that amused me, even if I didn't want to admit it.

"Do you mind?" I asked.

Instead of responding, he just sped off. He was one of those drivers that made you long to set foot on solid ground again. I tried not to get nervous every time he passed a car, took a corner at top speed, or ran a yellow light, but it was hard. Monty drove like a tortoise, and I was used to that. I tried not to let him notice as I reached up for the hand grip, but he asked, "What's up? You OK?"

"You drive like my brother," I said.

"That's a good thing, right?"

"Yeah, in a demolition derby, maybe."

He smiled but slowed down somewhat, asking, "How was your first day of class?" Miraculously, he started using his turn signal and respecting the traffic lights from then on.

"Fine, I guess. Introductions. The teachers all seem kind of boring. Yours?"

"We were able to skip the introductions. It's my second year, and we pretty much all know each other."

For some reason, him being ahead of me made me feel like a ten-year-old. He explained that it was a program with a focus on production, and after two years, you studied abroad or got an internship as part of your studies. It made me sad, somehow, that he'd be leaving after a year. I asked him if he had plans for the future.

"My plans for the future are to finish this degree. Then I'll make it up as I go along."

I liked his positivity and wished I could share it.

"And you, what do you plan to do after four years of English?" he asked.

"I hope I'll know by then," I said. "Worst-case scenario, I guess I'll be teaching fourteen-year-olds the different types of relative clauses."

"Now that's a bright future. Do you honestly not like anything?"

"Not really," I responded.

"That cannot be possible. Something has to excite you."

I thought about it. Painting and running weren't really life options. So again I told him *no*.

"What the hell have you done for the last eighteen years then?" he asked me.

Knowing how dull it sounded, I said I'd been trying to make good grades, survive my brothers' harassment, and keep my mom from yelling at me. It sounded so boring. He encouraged me, saying there was something for me but I just hadn't found it yet, and when he dropped me off and I unbuckled the seat belt and threw on my jacket, I thanked him for taking me back.

"No problem, Miss Girl Without Hobbies. By the way, you look good in red."

It wasn't even my sweater. It was my sister's, but I'd stolen it before I left. I didn't usually wear things that flashy, but now that he mentioned it, I did look pretty good.

"Good night, Ross," I said. But before I could get far, I had the overwhelming urge to turn back. He was still there, watching me. It felt strange, and I forced myself to come up with a question: "So, when's our next cinema lesson?"

He smiled. "You tell me."

"The next time Naya drags me to your apartment, then?"

"I'll be waiting with bated breath," he said.

I smiled and turned around, and this time, I made it inside. Chris was no longer at his desk. It was late, though. Probably he had gone to his room. When I climbed the stairs and entered the hallway, I froze as I saw Mike, the singer from earlier, stepping out of the room across from mine with his shorts around his ankles and arguing with a girl who was pushing him before throwing his vest in his face and screaming, "Get out!"

"Whatever!" he replied. "You're not that hot anyway!"

She closed the door in his face. Mike bent over to pull up his shorts and looked up. When he saw me, he smiled.

"Hey, you were with my brother, right?"

He sounded actually normal, but I needled him, "Yeah, and you're the guy who just got tossed out of some girl's room!"

"Some people can't take a joke," he said. "I just told her she didn't look as hot in real life as she did in a photo she had in there. I didn't know it was her little sister! Some people just go through life pissed off."

I walked past him, shaking my head, and turned my key in the lock. By the time I cracked the door, he was leaning against the wall and smiling at me maliciously.

"And why are you here all alone?" he asked.

"To go to sleep."

"Already?"

"I've got class tomorrow."

"You don't want some company?" he asked.

"Nope."

"You never told me your name."

"Jenna."

"Jenna, you're a little bit off-putting."

"Great."

"I'm…"

"Mike. You already told me."

He seemed to have forgotten that, but then his phone buzzed and he lost track of what we were talking about as he saw a girl's face appear on the screen. He grinned and said, "Well, nice to meet you, Jenna, but I've got new plans. Your loss."

"I'll be crying about it all night."

He winked and strolled off, and I shook my head and walked inside.

3

SUPERHEROES

"Superheroes. Really," I said, looking at the book in my hands.

Ross took it away and frowned. "I'm sorry, why the snotty tone?"

"What snotty tone?" I asked.

"Listen," he said, "I have to tell you I like you a little less now that I know you think superheroes are stupid."

"Jeez," I replied. "And I wanted you to like me so bad!"

"I do still. It just happens you've got bad taste."

"That must be why I like you," I joked.

That made him chuckle. He showed me the comic again and said, pointing to a guy holding a big hammer on the cover, "Anyway, this isn't just any superhero, it's Thor."

"So?"

"So he's powerful. And he's not a superhero. He's a god. A Nordic god."

"Oh my," I said. "Tremendous. I'm feeling lightheaded."

"You should show a little more respect. You never know when a Thanos might show up in your life."

I didn't know who or what a Thanos was, but my assumption was it was some kind of villain. I kept walking around the shop, looking absent-mindedly at the books. Naya was sifting through the action figures. I didn't recognize any of them except Spider-Man.

It was my second week already, but it felt like I'd been there two days. Between class and homework and just life, I'd barely had a free moment. I'd hardly talked with my family or Monty. And funny enough, I was over the moon about it. Sure, I missed them, especially the family, but I was having fun. With Ross in particular, even if I wouldn't tell him that. His ego didn't need the boost. All of them were great, though: Will, Naya… I mean, Sue was an exception. But at least she'd stopped grimacing at me. That was something, right?

"Are you into this stuff, too?" I asked Naya.

"When I started going out with Will, I pretended to like it, but then you sort of get into it, you know?" She showed me a blue female figurine. "This is Mystique. What do you think?"

"Nice," I said. "Very blue. Probably should see a dermatologist."

"Don't be mean." She nudged me with her elbow.

Since Will was talking to the cashier, I decided not to bother him, instead watching Ross as he ran his finger across the spines of the books. I had to say, he didn't look bad from behind. Not that I should be thinking about it. Did he have a girlfriend? I wondered. He must. But I didn't think about it as I walked back over to him. He frowned and said, "Are you back to make fun of me some more?"

"Ross, dear, I'd never make fun of something you cared about."

"I like that 'Ross, dear,'" he said.

He had just set aside a comic. I picked it up and said, "Green Lantern? What's up? You don't like this one?"

"I've already got it."

"How many do you have?"

"Too many. I collected them as a kid. Now I just read them. They keep me entertained."

"I could think of other ways to entertain you," I said.

"So can I. But I'm not sure you'd go along with them."

I ignored the implications of his remark and told him how Shannon and Spencer used to spend all their money on that stuff. But I don't really remember which ones. "Who are your favorites?"

He thought for a moment, set aside a Justice League book, and as I picked it up and scrutinized it, said, "Thor, Batman, and Spider-Man."

"Thor's handsome," I told him, pointing at one of the books.

"Don't make me jealous of my childhood hero."

"Come on, Ross, let's be realistic. You can't compare yourself to a Nordic god."

"True. It wouldn't be fair. For him."

I grinned and flipped through the book. Then I asked, "Is there really only one chick in the Justice League?"

"Yeah, Wonder Woman."

"How do you think she fights in that outfit without one of her boobs popping out?"

Ross admitted he'd never really thought about it. I said maybe I'd come back and buy the comic one day and find out, and he said he'd get it for me as a welcome present. When I reminded him I'd been there for two weeks now, he said, "Just pretend I gave it to you on your first day. It'll be our secret." Then he hurried to the register before I could protest.

I walked outside, where it was raining—that's why we'd gone inside— and looked at the window display. I didn't mind being out there. I liked the rain because it reminded me of the wet summers back home. Once we were all together again, Will said we should go to his apartment to eat. Sensing that people were waiting to see what I'd say, I agreed. I'd had a couple of meals in my room alone, and it was depressing.

I was soaked when we got there. Everyone else had thought to bring a raincoat. Ross had tried to wrap his around me a bit, but it didn't help. I asked for a towel. But instead of getting it, Ross stood there chuckling at my misfortune.

"Get her a towel, you jerk," Will said.

While Ross left for the bathroom, I stayed with everyone else in the living room. Everyone else but Sue, that is. She must have been in her room. I have to admit I was starting to really wonder what her deal was. When he came back, Ross tossed me the towel, but it landed on the floor and he started laughing again.

"You want a dry sweatshirt?" he asked.

"Yes. Please."

I went to his room, stripped off my soaking-wet one, and tossed it into a corner, then dried my hair while he looked around in his dresser.

"If my mom could see me, she'd be losing her mind," I said. "She always tells me to dress for the weather, and I always tell her I'm an adult and don't need her advice. But apparently I do." He glanced back with a sarcastic expression and I said, "Don't make me dry my hair on your sheets. Because I will."

"OK!" he said, laying a sweatshirt on the bed. "The way you talk about your family makes it seem like your mom's a hysteric."

"Nah," I replied. "At least she's not diagnosed. But she worries. A lot. Too much."

"Is that bad?" He put two more sweatshirts on the bed. "Take your pick. Those are the smallest ones I have."

"No, it's not bad," I said, "but it can be a pain. Does your mother call you all the time to ask how you are?"

When he didn't say anything, I looked over and realized he was standing there in a trance, gawking at me. And it dawned on me that my undershirt was so wet that he could see straight through it. At least I had on my favorite bra. But still. As I caught his eye, he didn't look ashamed. I'm not even sure he noticed that I'd busted him.

Remembering what our conversation had been about, he said, "What, my mom? Nah, she doesn't call much. She never really was that type."

I had the feeling he didn't really care for the topic, so I looked at the sweatshirts he'd offered, picking up and discarding a blue one. I wondered if he'd look at me again. The idea didn't displease me. Finally, I settled on the red, and he said, shaking his head, "I don't know why, but I figured that's the one you'd pick."

In the center of it was an illustration of Pumba.

I waited for him to leave the room so I could change, but he just stood there grinning with his hands in his pockets and asked what I was waiting for.

"For you to leave so I can change!"

"That's exactly why I'm still standing here."

I shouted at him to get out and tore off my wet top and bra as soon as he did. The soft, warm fabric was comforting, and as I pulled up the sleeves, I realized his scent permeated it. And I liked that. A lot more than I would necessarily admit aloud. Walking back to the living room, I smiled at Sue, who was eating pizza in an armchair with a depressed look on her face while Will and Naya talked on the couch. Obviously, Sue didn't smile back. I sat next to Ross on the other sofa. I examined the options on the coffee table and picked up a slice of barbecue pizza.

"That is literally the grossest flavor," Ross said. I looked straight at him and started chewing with my mouth open, eliciting a smile.

"How dare you insult my favorite pizza flavor," I said.

We started arguing back and forth about who had worse taste until Naya interrupted us to say, "Guys, nobody could be happier that y'all are getting along so great, but I have a problem, and you're ignoring me!"

"What is it?" Ross asked.

"Tomorrow's the birthday of this girl who was like my sworn enemy in high school, and she invited me to her party for some reason, and I don't want to go!"

"You should, though," Will said. "You need to make peace."

"Yeah, but what if she wants to humiliate you in front of everyone and traumatize you for the rest of your life?" Ross inquired with a smile.

Salty, Will said to him, "You're not helping."

"No one asked me to help," Ross said.

"No one asked your opinion, either," I butted in, and he told me, "Yeah, but I give it out for free."

Naya told Will that even Ross agreed with her and that she'd decided she wouldn't go. This irritated Will, who reminded her that she and the other girl had barely seen each other in the past three years. During their last years of school, they didn't have the same classes. Probably the girl had changed a lot.

"Doubt it," Naya said.

"Why?" he wanted to know.

Naya asked me if I had ever known any stuck-up popular kids at my school. I laughed and said I had—my boyfriend.

"That's different," Naya objected. "This girl used to constantly make fun of me and try to get under my skin. And I don't want to go to her party. I don't even want to see her. I hardly remembered who she was. What should I do?"

Sue piped up, "Put a dead rat in her mailbox."

Nobody else showed the least surprise at this morbid remark.

Stuffing more pizza into his mouth, Ross said, "I'd skip it. Stupid people never change."

When Naya responded, "That's pessimistic," he told her, "I'd rather call it realistic."

My turn came afterward, and I advised her to go. The worst thing that could happen was she'd get bored. "Or they'll humiliate you," Ross interjected. But I reminded her she could always leave if she had a bad time. That wasn't so hard, was it?

She resigned herself to going, but tried one more time to convince

Will to go with her. He said he had a lot of work to do and would be too tired to go to a party afterward. "I'll make it up to you, though," he added.

"You sure will, Will."

Then they started making out again, and Sue and Ross rolled their eyes in unison.

The next day, I opened my closet to get out my pajamas and saw Ross's sweatshirt hanging there. I needed to give it back before the temptation to keep it forever became too strong.

Naya walked up behind me and looked at herself in the mirror. I could tell she was nervous.

"Are you sure you don't want me to go with you?" I asked.

"No, it's best if I go alone. Plus, I can tell you're not into it."

I tried to tell her otherwise. She had been so nice to me since I'd gotten there that I couldn't leave her hanging if she needed me. But she said it was fine, and she already needed to be downstairs anyway. Her Uber was waiting.

"If you get bored, call me," I said, just before she walked out the door.

Slightly depressed, I looked into my closet again, and after considering the moral implications of doing so, I decided to put Ross's sweatshirt on again. It was just for one night. That didn't mean anything, right? It was really just because it was so soft. And no one would know.

I can't say I looked beautiful in my cotton shorts and thick rainbow socks, with the sweatshirt hanging off of me. Even Monty had never seen me in such a state. I grabbed my laptop and went through some of my notes while I listened to music. Then I settled down on the bed and decided to watch that *Thor* movie Ross had talked about. I liked it. Not just because the hero was handsome. Though, of course, that did count for something.

Then I put on *Captain America*, and with the end credits rolling, I was already looking for another. I don't know how many superhero movies I watched that night, but when I checked, it was two in the morning. I didn't have anything else to do that day, but I couldn't just keep going until dawn. So I took out my contact lenses and lay back to sleep, but just then, I saw the bag from the comic shop and pulled out the book Ross had bought me.

Surprisingly, it wasn't bad, and I burned through it before turning off the lights. I fell asleep thinking of masked musclemen and women in outfits too tight and too skimpy to kick ass in.

I opened my eyes again at four. I heard something—what was it? Trying to focus, I reached for my glasses and saw my phone buzzing on the nightstand next to my head. Unknown number. I cleared my throat and responded.

"Hello?"

"Hey. Can you come get me?"

It was Naya. She seemed to be crying.

"What happened?" I asked, throwing on my boots. I knew I couldn't say no.

"Just…just come, please. I don't want to go into the whole story now. I'm right by the bridge, next to an ugly yellow building." That was a half hour away by car. It was going to be expensive. I wasn't sure I had the money in my account to get me there and bring us back. But I couldn't leave her hanging.

"What about Will?"

"Don't say anything to Will, please." She groaned. "I don't want him to worry. And the same goes for Ross. I'm begging you, Jenna."

"I won't," I said, hoping I had gotten better at lying. As she thanked me, I told her not to move, that I'd get an Uber, and I asked her to call me if anything else happened. Then I scrolled through my contacts, looking for Ross. It took me a second to find him; I'd forgotten I'd saved him as *Errand Boy*. I hoped he would answer. I'd never called him before, and

I wasn't sure if he had my number. But if he didn't pick up, Will was the only other person I had to turn to.

"Who is this?" he grumbled in a groggy voice.

"I need your help," I said.

He took so long to respond that I thought the line had gone dead. Then he said my name. "Jenna?"

"Yeah, it's me. I need a favor. Naya called me and she's crying and she needs me to come get her, and she wouldn't really explain what was going on, but I was wondering if you'd come with me."

"Why didn't you call Will?"

"She made me swear I wouldn't tell him anything."

"Do you know what he'll do to me if he finds out I'm keeping a secret from him?"

"The same thing Naya will do to me if Will finds out something," I said.

He sighed and argued with me a little longer about Will's right to know, but I cut him off with the words, "Ross, please," and he agreed, telling me he'd be at the dorm in five minutes.

I exhaled all the air I'd been holding in my lungs, and said, "Thank you, thank you, thank you. You're the best."

"We already knew that, though," he replied.

I smiled and hung up.

In exactly five minutes, a black car pulled up next to me at the dorm's front door with Ross inside. He still looked half-asleep.

"Taxi service," he said, and I thanked him again.

"It's not like I had anything else to do. I mean sleep, but…"

"Come on, you're a superhero fan," I reminded him. "This is your chance to go rescue someone."

Any improvements I'd noticed in his driving the last time we were together had gone out the window. But if Naya was in danger, I wouldn't complain. He asked me what had happened, but I had no idea, and I had no idea why she wanted to hide it from Will, either. When we hit a red light, I saw him glance over at me and grin sarcastically.

"Interesting outfit you've got on," he said.

I realized then I was still in my pajamas…and that I still had on his sweatshirt. *Well, this is a good start*, I thought.

"Sorry…" I said. "I was in a rush. I'll wash it and give it back to you."

"Just keep it. It's too small for me. It looks good on you. Take good care of it, though. It was one of my favorites."

Since he didn't want to argue about it, I didn't try to convince him to take it back. He yawned a few times. I was wide awake, though, staring out the window and wondering what Naya had gotten into. My nerves were frayed as I saw the bridge. Ross parked and we got out as I looked around for the yellow building. He followed me, his hands in his pockets.

"Jenna, now would be a good time to tell me exactly what we're looking for," he said, staring at a group of young people drinking on the other side of the road. All over were similar groups, and badly parked cars, and the muted thumping of music. The guys were in polo shirts, the girls in dresses—rich kids, I figured. I told Ross there was supposed to be an ugly yellow building nearby and waved for him to follow me. Some guy said to me, "Nice socks," and I tried to ignore him, but Ross said, "Nice face. If you want to keep it intact, you'll shut your mouth," and the guy fell silent and stared at the ground.

"Don't tell me you're a bad boy," I said to him.

"Bad? The worst. A danger to public order."

"You actually sounded scary. Even to me."

"Great," he responded. "Now you know my dark side."

I doubted he had a dark side, though. We kept walking a few seconds more and finally saw what had to be the place. Ross rested a hand on my shoulder and pointed at Naya with the other one. She was sitting alone on the sidewalk, hugging her knees, soaking wet, which was weird because it hadn't been raining. Her makeup, so carefully applied, was all smeared and running down her cheeks. She stood as we approached.

"Ross," she said, and I could see the word *traitor* in her eyes as she looked over at me. "You'd better not have…"

"She made me swear I wouldn't say anything to Will," he assured her.

Naya froze for a moment, then ran to me and hugged me tight. She clearly needed that hug, so I held her as firmly as I could.

"What happ—"

"I shouldn't have come," she said. "Everyone made fun of me. The chick I was telling you about asked to see my necklace, and I let her because I didn't know what to do, and she kept it, and then when I tried to get it back, a bunch of people threw me in the pool. I had my bag on me and now my phone's not working right. I could access my contacts but I couldn't make any calls. Thank God this girl let me use her phone to call Jenna…"

She was about to cry, and I said, "Oh, Naya," which was the only thing that occurred to me. And to think I'd been the one to tell her to go! She must have been freezing, soaking wet like that. I was already cold and I'd only been out there five minutes. I offered her my jacket, and Ross said, "Don't bother with that now. Let's just go. I've got a spare jacket in my car."

She agreed with him. "I don't want to be here a second longer."

Ross passed his arm over her shoulder and she smiled with gratitude. They started to go, but I remained nailed to the spot and asked her, "Why did they do that to you?"

"This girl… She's one of those people who like to laugh at others. I guess it makes her feel better about herself."

I shook my head and looked back at the building. The music was still booming. "It's not fair," I said. "What about your necklace? Was it special?"

She lowered her head and nodded. "It's the first present Will ever gave me. For my birthday."

"Did she break it?"

"No, she's wearing it."

"And you didn't say anything to her?" I asked.

"Jenna, it's not that easy. Everything came back to me, how small and insignificant she used to make me feel in those days, and I just kind of froze up, you know?"

I guess I did. But I knew it didn't have to be that way, either. I remembered the time my brother Sonny came home with a black eye. He said he got it playing football, and all of us believed him except for my brother Spencer, who kept pressing Sonny until he cried and admitted there was a classmate who wouldn't stop bullying him. Sonny had tried to have it out with him, and it hadn't turned out well.

Spencer didn't need any more details. He didn't even care if Sonny had done anything wrong. He just walked out, hopped on his bicycle, and took care of it. I don't know what exactly he did, but I know no one ever messed with Sonny again. And even if Sonny never thanked Spencer, I knew how much it had meant to him. Funny enough, Sonny started boxing lessons soon afterward, and he could probably pound Spencer into a paste now if he wanted.

Looking at Naya now, I remembered Spencer, and I didn't care if the girl who'd been harassing her had any justification. It didn't matter. I didn't like unfairness. And I might not have been like Wonder Woman—I sure as hell didn't look like her in that outfit—but I had to do something. No one deserved to be treated like that.

"Wait here a minute," I said.

"For what?" Naya asked.

"I'm going to get your things." Ross wanted to come along, but I told him to stay with Naya.

"Sorry," he said, "you're not going in there alone."

Naya hesitated, then nodded. The closer she got to the place, the more I could tell she was terrified, but she guided us inside. She didn't ring the doorbell, but no one seemed to care. She guided us to the backyard. I saw her wet purse on the ground next to a tall, curly-haired girl who was smoking a cigarette, holding her drink, and laughing with her friends. I recognized the necklace around her neck.

"Wait here," I said.

Like Thor waving his hammer, I approached the girl. Everyone turned and looked at me. Ross was right behind me. The girl asked me, "Excuse me, were you invited?" She seemed to be chuckling at my rainbow socks and brown boots.

"No," I said, crossing my arms. "But you invited my friend. Her name's Naya. Maybe that rings a bell. And it appears that you're wearing her necklace."

With a quick glance at Naya, she replied, "So what? Are you her body-guard? Because honestly, you're not very scary."

Trying to be the voice of reason, Ross asked, "Why don't you just give the necklace back and this can all be over?"

A guy friend of hers walked over, short but stout and mean-looking, and said, "You know what, buddy? If you're smart, you'll get the fuck out of here."

Ross didn't look impressed.

"Why should I give it back?" the girl asked me.

"Because it's not yours."

"It is now. Possession is nine-tenths of the law. Plus, this is my house. I can do what I want here. And honestly, this is getting boring. So why don't you fuck off?"

"Not without the necklace," I said.

Ross seconded me. "We're not leaving without it."

The short guy decided to jump in, asking, "What, she can't speak for herself? If the dumb slut wants her necklace, tell her to come over here and get it."

That was it for me. I nudged Ross aside, and he didn't put up any resistance. The short guy got ready to mock me, started to say, *Ooh, I'm scared*, but before he could get the phrase out, I sank my feet into the ground, twisted at the waist, wrapped my thumb around my fingertips, and gave it to him right in the nose. The same way Sonny had taught me.

I'd hit him hard. Hard enough to make my knuckles ache, though I wasn't about to show that. The guy stumbled backward, covering his face, and said, "She just punched me, the psycho bitch!"

"Try me and I'll do it again," I told him. Then I turned to his friend. "Now hand over the necklace," I said. She froze briefly, then took it off and tossed it to me. I could tell from Ross's and Naya's expressions that they couldn't believe what I'd just done.

"Shall we?" I asked.

Ross grabbed Naya's wet purse and they followed me out. I was scared we'd be followed, so I walked as fast as I could while pretending to maintain my composure. When we were outside, Ross said, "Man, you looked like Ronda Rousey out there."

"It wasn't that big a deal," I responded. "You should see my brother Sonny. He was a real boxer. He's the one who taught me how to throw a punch. This is the first time I've put it in practice, though. I'm going to have to tell him."

I looked at my knuckles. They were glowing red.

Naya's glum mood suddenly changed. "Holy shit!" she said. "That was incredible! I can't believe you did that for me! Did you hurt yourself?"

"A little," I said.

"I'm not surprised," Ross said. "But you can move your fingers, so I assume nothing's broken."

"There's an ice machine at the dorm," Naya said. "I'll get some ice for you. It's the least I can do."

We didn't talk much on the drive back. Naya put on her necklace, I rubbed my knuckles, and Ross hummed along with whatever was on the radio. Naya thanked Ross when we arrived at the dorm and walked off quickly, presumably to bug Chris for ice, though I'd told her ten times there was no need to.

"Ross, thanks again for coming," I said.

"I'm glad I did now that I know what happens when someone pisses you off, Jen."

"Jen?" I said. "Is that what we're calling me now?"

"Since five seconds ago, yeah."

"I guess I'm OK with that. It can be our thing. Good night, Ross."

He smiled.

"Good night, Jen."

4

THE CRAZY NUN

For a year, I'd been sitting on my ass instead of going for a run in the morning. Well, that was over, I decided. It was a Friday, and I was getting back in the driver's seat. I hurried downstairs, fully motivated, waving at Chris on my way out.

It took me five minutes to regret it.

Right around the time I started wanting to cough up my first lung from the effort.

I'd been good at track and field when I was a kid, when going out for a morning run was something I had to do every morning for school. Now I could barely peel myself off the bed, period.

But I forced myself to keep going. My heart was like a freight train when I stopped to catch my breath, resting my hands on my knees. Yeah, I needed practice. I tried to imagine the look of disappointment my former coach would give me. Or Spencer, who was a gym teacher and had helped me train in the old days. If he knew I was wheezing after half an hour, he'd be shaking his head…

I was hyperventilating by the time I walked back into the dorm. Chris smiled as soon as he saw me.

"How was it?"

"Awful. I should have stayed in bed."

He laughed as I climbed the steps to my room, where Naya was asleep and snoring. Nothing but a grenade going off would bother her, so I hopped into the shower without a second thought.

When I came out, I saw her stretching lazily and yawning and said, "Good morning."

"What time is it?" she asked.

"Eleven."

"So early?"

"Eleven's early?"

"On a weekend? Hell yes, it's early."

As I dried my hair, I asked whether she was supposed to be getting breakfast with Will. She sighed and pulled herself upright.

"Yeah." Struggling to organize her thoughts, she continued. "I'm just going to shower at his place. Half my clothes are there anyway. You coming?"

"Nobody invited me."

"So? Come. The more people who are there, the less weird it is to have Sue grunting to herself. Plus, I'm sure Ross will wonder where you are otherwise."

"You think?"

She arched an eyebrow and stood. "Just put on a T-shirt so we can go."

We took the light rail out there, and she kept yawning and groaning and adjusting her sunglasses as if she was returning from the party of a lifetime. She was just as groggy when we reached Will's door.

Sue opened the door for us and asked with her usual good cheer, "Back again?"

"Happy to see you, too," Naya said as she walked past her.

Sue went back to whatever she was doing and I closed the door behind me. When I reached the kitchen, I saw Will and Naya kissing and Sue scowling at them.

"Morning, Will." I smiled.

"Oh, hey, you," he said.

"Where's Ross?" I asked. It was strange not to see him wandering around there teasing people.

"He's asleep."

"Still?"

"I can see you don't know what it's like to live with him," Sue said.

"I'm gonna go wake him up," Naya announced malevolently and walked off without waiting for anyone's approval. A few seconds later, I heard her open his door and scream. A pillow flew out, and not long afterward, Ross emerged, rubbing his face, very clearly in a bad mood.

"Who let her off her chain?" he asked, leaning against the kitchen bar.

"I'm not a dog," Naya protested.

Trying to change the subject, I asked, "Aren't we having breakfast?"

"Sure," Ross responded. "Take your pick. We've got cold pizza, warm water, and beer. All the nutrients you need to face the day with energy. Oh, and I think there's ice cream, but it's Sue's, so don't try it unless you've got suicidal tendencies."

"Ross, go get us something," Will said.

"Why me?"

"Because I always go," Will replied.

"What about Sue?" Ross objected.

She responded, "I'm having ice cream for breakfast."

"Whatever." Ross stood up straight, walked to his room, and changed clothes. He left, complaining that people were using him. With nothing to do while Will and Naya made out and Sue stared at the TV, I started to drift off until Naya asked, "Hey, I think your phone was buzzing last night. I meant to tell you, but I didn't want to wake you up."

I usually didn't pay much attention to my phone, but I reached into my bag just then to check. My heart skipped a beat when I saw that Monty had called twelve times.

"Shit."

"What?" Naya asked.

"It was my boyfriend. He's probably mad I didn't get in touch. Will, do you mind if I go call from your room?"

"Sorry, Jenna. This is the only room that gets decent service."

This was getting better all the time. Everyone watched me dial and raise the phone to my ear. I was nervous. Monty answered on the first ring.

"Oh, so you're alive," he responded bitterly.

I knew that tone. I tried not to get angry, because it would only make things worse. "Sorry," I said. "I didn't hear my phone."

"Oh. I didn't know you lived in a mansion where you can't hear a cell phone that's right next to your head."

"How do you know it was next to my head, Monty? How do you know I didn't have it on Do Not Disturb?"

"I was worried."

"Count to ten," I told him. "It's fine. I'm fine."

Just then, Ross opened the door holding two bags of food, which he dumped on the bar, saying, "Who's your daddy?" Naya and Will tore them open while continuing to stare at me.

"I knew you'd do this to me," Monty said.

"What? Would you mind telling me what I did?" I asked. I didn't know if I was more pissed off or confused.

Chewing on a piece of toast, Ross watched me as Monty responded, "Blow me off. Just like you said you wouldn't."

"I'm not..." I began, trying to sound calm so everyone wouldn't think I was crazy, though nothing would have made me happier than lightning striking Monty right then. "Can we talk about this later?"

"No. You haven't even called me in a week."

"You neither!" I couldn't stand it anymore. "Why am I always the one who has to do everything?"

"You're the one who decided to leave!"

"Monty, I'm at college. It's not like I decided to take a sailboat around the world! Can you relax? Also, you wanted me to go to school!"

"Yeah," he said. "That doesn't mean I didn't want you to call me for three weeks."

"You just said it: three weeks. What are you going to do when it's a month? Two months? Are you going to come kidnap me?"

"Maybe I should. What did you do last night?"

"Nothing!" And that was true. I had stuck with my new routine of watching superhero movies and reading comics. Well, I'd gone to rescue Naya too. And had punched some guy in the face. But that was none of his business.

"Liar." He kept on about how he was sure I'd heard my phone, how I'd ignored him on purpose, how I didn't care about him, how I was just making excuses. Then he hung up on me. I was shocked. I liked the guy, but he could be such a loser… I wondered why he'd gotten so angry all of a sudden. I hadn't done anything wrong. Unless fantasizing about Thor was wrong, but I was pretty sure it wasn't.

When I looked up, I saw everyone staring at me for a brief moment before they pretended to be focused on eating. At least I wouldn't have to explain anything, I thought. Ross passed me a bag of food, but I told him, "Thanks, but no thanks. I never eat breakfast."

"You're telling me you go hungry till lunchtime?" he asked.

"That's correct," I replied, trying to sound nice and not succeeding. I felt bad. It wasn't Ross's fault my boyfriend sucked. So I took the bag and said, "I'll make an exception this time."

Will changed the subject, asking the group, "What are we doing tonight?"

Neither Naya nor I felt like going out. Monty had taken it out of me. Will proposed a movie, and Ross said he was in. Naya shrugged, and the three of them looked at me, making me feel uncomfortable. Then Ross understood and blurted out, "Please God don't tell me you've never been to the movies?" He laughed when he realized he was right and said, "It's honestly like you've come from a parallel universe. Like, I'm not trying to be a jerk, but can you please explain how it's possible that you've literally never been to the movies?"

"I don't know, man. My brothers weren't into it, and it kind of just never came up." I felt awkward admitting this. It was almost like I had only ever done what my family did, like I'd never had an opinion of my own. This was dawning on me more and more, and I didn't know how I should feel about it. Thankfully, Naya jumped in with a smile:

"Well, this will be your first time. But we can't do it till later. I have a ton of work."

"Me too," I said.

"I've got stuff to do right now myself," Ross added. "I'm a busy man. I'll see you all tonight. Someone text me the when and where."

With those words, he walked out the door.

Later that day, I worked on a group project with some classmates, and I didn't get back to the dorm until five. Chris was behind the desk. He said hello without looking up from his game.

"What's going on, Jenna?"

"The usual. I've got to say, it kind of freaks me out that you knew it was me without looking up."

"I spend a lot of time here. I've developed a second sense."

"You're in a good mood," I said.

"Yeah, my mom sent me her lives." As I shook my head, he paused the game and said, "Naya told me you were getting along with her friends. I'm glad. It's hard to start from zero."

"They're nice, yeah."

"I hope Ross isn't giving you a hard time. When Lana lived here, it was chaos."

Lana. Who was Lana? I didn't remember Ross mentioning any Lana. No, he never had. Was he trying to hide her from me?

"Is that his girlfriend?" I asked, trying to play it cool as Chris picked back up his phone.

"Not anymore, I'm pretty sure," he replied, not relieving me especially. "They used to go out, but she's gone now. I think she went to France. Or somewhere. Honestly, I don't know. She probably went to a better school. She was smart. One of the smartest students here."

"Interesting," I replied, tapping my fingers on the counter.

"She was all right," he said. "But she didn't say hi to me when she passed by like you do, so I like you better. But then, hardly anybody does. You're one of the only people who actually stops to talk to me."

He smiled and went back to his game. I wanted to ask more questions about this Lana, but I felt it wouldn't be appropriate, so I dropped it. I wanted to talk to someone, though, and my best friend Nelle didn't answer, so when I got back to my room, I wound up calling Shannon, who always gave me good advice.

She picked up instantly. She always did.

"Hey, stranger," she said. "How's everything?"

"Good. I'm bored, so I decided to call you," I said, sitting on the bed.

"Well, I'm flattered you were thinking of me, even if it was just because you're bored."

"That's not what I meant."

"I know, I was kidding. You should see Mom. She's out of her mind. I have to go see her every day because she misses you so much. Dad too. I don't know how they're going to hang on till Christmas break. I wish you could come earlier, but it's an expensive trip, and I honestly don't know if any of us could front you the cash to do it."

"Yeah," I said, "I guess you're right."

"Well, now that we've depressed ourselves talking about money and family, let's get down to the good stuff. Have you found any handsome guys to hook up with out there? Or girls? I'm not judgmental. Everyone's free to choose."

"Shannon, please. Have you forgotten I still have a boyfriend?"

"Who? The idiot?"

"He's not an idiot."

"He is, though," she said.

I told her about our argument, and I could almost hear her thoughts as I did so. She wasn't surprised in the least. When I mentioned how bad he always made me feel, she told me he always had, and I reminded her he'd never done anything to her to make her have such a bad attitude about him.

"Honey, him never doing anything bad to *me* is a pretty low bar when we're talking about *your* boyfriend."

"So what?" I asked her. "You want me to go out with Brad Pitt?"

"I wouldn't mind," she said, "but I'd try to steal him from you, and I know that violates the code between sisters. Then again: All's fair in love and war, right?"

I laughed and we talked for another hour, until the sky started to darken and she told me she had to go pick up my nephew, Owen, from his swimming lessons. As soon as I hung up, Naya walked in, looking bored from spending an entire day in the library.

"What's got you in such a good mood?" I asked.

"Oh, you know, just living my dream. Wasting a whole afternoon studying a bunch of shit I've already forgotten. I hate my life."

"You'll be fine, Naya."

"I hope."

Looking at the time on my watch, I asked when we were supposed to go to the movies with the guys. She told me we had half an hour and then added, "Why? Are you anxious for our double date?"

"Very funny," I said.

She grinned and responded, "I'm going to shower first."

She was in and out, and then I got in myself, taking with me the ratty old bathrobe with the pattern of tropical fish on it my father had given me when I was thirteen. I frowned when I saw the giant circles under my eyes in the bathroom mirror. I should have taken a nap that afternoon, I thought. I looked exhausted. When I was done, I opened the door and saw Ross lying there on my bed, looking at my photo album like he owned the place. Will and Naya were—of course—making out on the other bed beside him.

"Um…hello?" I said.

The two lovebirds were oblivious, but Ross looked over the album's cover and said, "Wow, nice robe."

"It's the only one I have," I said, embarrassed. "May I ask what you're doing with my photo album?"

"I was bored. It's not like those two were paying attention to me."

"Don't you have a phone?"

"Yeah. But I'd rather be nosy."

I grabbed the album out of his hand and saw he'd been looking at a photo of me with Monty, some friend of his, and Nelle. We were all smiling at the camera.

"Who is everyone?" Ross asked.

I sat down next to him.

"My boyfriend, Monty…"

"Monty? What is he, from nineteenth-century England?"

"It's short for Montgomery," I said. "It's a family name. That's Nelle, who's a friend of mine, or sort of a friend. It's kind of a long story, and not a very interesting one. And this guy is one of Monty's teammates. They had just won a basketball game that day."

"They're on a basketball team?" he asked, and when I nodded, he continued, "They look terrible."

"They were. They've gotten better." I dropped the photo album back on the bed and said, "I'll be ready in five minutes."

Ross told me he didn't mind if I went with them half-naked, and I thanked him for the suggestion but said I'd rather put on some real clothes.

"Cool," he replied, lying back. "I'm going to stick my fingers in my ears and see if I can ignore the sounds of Will and Naya."

I went back into the bathroom and got dressed quickly. When I came out, I found Will and Naya standing there smoothing out their clothes. Ross looked at them as if he'd observed this scene a million times.

I asked Naya, surprised, "Aren't you going to fix your hair before we leave?" It looked like a bird's nest. She checked herself out in the mirror and dragged a brush through it quickly.

We went in Ross's car. The guys rode up front and the girls in the back. I had to push their jackets out of the way to buckle my seat belt.

Ross pulled out without using his turn signal and asked where we were going. "The theater at the mall," Naya announced. "There's a war movie playing. I forgot the title, but that's the one I want to go see."

I didn't want to see a war movie—just thinking about war made me cry—and Will seemed to agree. Naya asked what the other options were, and Ross mentioned a horror film, "that one about the nun," he said, lighting a cigarette and driving me into a panic. I had grave doubts about his ability to smoke and keep a car on the road at the same time.

"Yeah, let's do that!" Will called out. Naya said, "No way!" and Ross responded, "Sorry, whose car is this?"

Naya whined that it wasn't fair, but there wasn't much she could do about it. I tried to back her up, saying, "It may be your car, but it's not your movie theater," and Will laughed, telling me I should come along more because not many people could get Ross to shut up. Ross looked back at me with an offended expression, and I shouted, "Keep your eyes on the road!"

"Whatever, it's straight!"

"You think no one's ever died on a straight road?!" I shouted.

After a bit more argument, it was decided: we were going to see the horror movie. Ross and Will smiled at the prospect. Naya and I huffed and puffed. There wasn't much more to say, so Ross turned on the radio. His driving was chaotic, and he moved his body frantically as he turned the wheel. When his sweatshirt slid down, I saw what looked like a tattoo below the back of his neck. I had one in almost the same place. I still regretted getting it. His was bigger, and I tried to see what it was. But I wasn't sure if I was comfortable with how much he intrigued me, so I tried to distract myself. "Why didn't Sue come?"

Ross blew a breath of smoke out the window. "Sue is basically fused with that easy chair. She doesn't like going out. Not with us or with anyone else."

"I feel like she doesn't like me," I confessed.

"It would be weird if she *did* like you," Naya reassured me.

"She just doesn't like people," Will said. "She's weird. But you'll get used to her."

"You won't," Ross declared. "It's my second year living with her, and I'm not used to her at all."

He pulled into the lot then. He had to park far from the entrance. When I got out, I was glad I had put on my coat for once. It was cold. Mom would be proud.

Will and Naya walked ahead of us arm in arm, and Ross complained, "I swear, those two make my blood sugar skyrocket."

"Aww," I said. "If you had a girlfriend, you'd be the same way."

He smiled and grabbed my arm. Ross paid for everyone's tickets at the window and we walked inside. The screen was massive. I couldn't believe it, and the spectators couldn't believe that I couldn't believe it and stared as they tried to walk past me. The theater was packed, so we had to sit up front, in the fourth row. I ended up sitting between Will and Ross, and Ross dug into his popcorn like a rabid dog.

"Are you always hungry?" I asked him during the previews.

"Always."

"And you never gain weight?"

"Never."

"I hate you."

He laughed. "No you don't."

"OK," I said. "But I definitely like you less than I did before."

"If I gave you some popcorn, would it fix that?" he asked.

I pretended to think it over and said, "Maybe." He turned the bag my way and I grabbed a handful and started eating. As I chewed, he bent over and asked, "Hey, have you ever seen a horror movie before?"

"No. Why?"

With an amused expression, he said, "You might regret coming when you're back home tonight."

I didn't know why he'd say that until thirty minutes later, when it was nighttime in the film and every five minutes the music would come on so dramatically that it made me jump out of my seat and grab whatever was next to me, normally either the armrest or Ross's wrist. He was having fun. Did he like to be scared? The main character of the film was stupid and kept doing stupid things, and that just made it worse. It was like she just wanted the stupid nun who was chasing her around to kill her.

"Why's she going in there?" I asked at one point.

"Because if she didn't, there wouldn't be a movie," Ross whispered.

"I know, but it's so dumb…"

Eventually, the torture—also known as the movie—ended, and I let go of Ross, who probably had bruises from how hard I'd grabbed him, though to his credit, he never complained. On my way out of the theater, I kept having to turn around to make sure I wasn't being chased down by a crazed nun.

"So now what?" Naya asked.

"How about you two come over?" Will said, though I was pretty sure the offer only really extended to Naya. I said I ought to get back to the dorms, but Naya protested with a frown. "Don't be like that. Come with. Please, please, please!"

"I can take you home after," Ross added. "I'm starting to adapt to my new life as an errand boy."

So, without knowing why, I said yes. Or maybe I did know why. Maybe I knew all too well.

The drive back seemed to take forever. Ross looked tired, too. The giggles and sweet nothings coming from the back seat were getting annoying, and at one point he asked me, "If I slam on the brakes, you think they'll go flying out of the car?"

"I don't know," I said, "but it's worth a try."

He laughed, and Naya swatted at me from the back seat, growling, "I can hear you, idiots."

We ordered a couple of pizzas and watched a home renovation show on TV back at the apartment. Sue never showed her face. When it was over, I went to Ross's room with him to put on a movie. But I couldn't pay close attention because I kept staring over at the closet, my nerves frayed. When he noticed, I tried to deny it, but I guess I was being pretty obvious. Finally he seemed to sense what was going on and said, "Look, if you're still scared after watching the movie, it's no big deal, but I can promise you, there are no monsters or possessed nuns in my closet."

"I'm not scared!" I said.

"Jen, you don't have to deny it. It's perfectly normal."

"Why aren't you scared, then?"

"Because I've seen like a million horror movies, and believe it or not, none of the villains have ever come out of the screen to murder me afterward."

Maybe that was true. But it didn't reassure me. It was nighttime, it was dark, and anything could happen. And to make matters worse, I had to pee. Bad. I bit my lip and asked, "Could you…uh…come with me to the bathroom?"

He stared at me and cracked up laughing. I scowled. "I knew I shouldn't have asked you, Ross!" I hit him over the head with a pillow and shouted, "You stupid idiot!" Then I stood and walked toward the door.

"No, wait!" Ross was still amused, but he followed me. "Of course I'll come with you." He grinned and threw an arm over my shoulders.

"I don't want you to anymore," I grumbled, but he responded, "Too bad, because now I want to. Maybe I can add bodyguard to my list of duties."

The bathroom was at the other end of the hallway fifteen or twenty feet from Ross's room. It looked like a long, dark passageway full of mystery and horror. When we reached the bathroom door, I pushed him aside and said, "You wait here."

"You don't want me to come in, too, in case there's a ghost in the shower?"

"Thanks, Ross, but I think I can protect myself."

"At your service."

I closed the door, peed as fast as I could, and started washing my hands. I heard a knock at the door.

"Hey! You still all right in there?"

"I think so," I replied. Moron.

"How do I know it's not an evil nun who's holding a knife to your throat and forcing you to say that?"

"Because I said so!" I opened the door angrily to find him there chuckling to himself. "You're not funny," I said. "I'm really scared."

"I am funny, and you might as well admit it."

"Whatever."

"You want me to hold you until sunup when the wicked nun can't come get you?" he asked.

I responded, "Up yours."

I walked back to his room with quick steps, and he jogged in behind me, flopping down on his bed so hard his laptop flew in the air, and I had to grab it so it wouldn't fall on the floor. I asked him whether a horror film had ever frightened him, too.

"Oh, when I was little, and I saw *The Exorcist*, that scene on the stairway terrified me for nights on end."

"So why are you laughing at me, then?" I asked.

"Because I was eight years old and you're nineteen."

"I'm eighteen!" I shouted as if that were an excuse. Just then, I heard knocking and moaning coming from Will's room. I blushed. Ross looked, if anything, bored.

"Here we go again," he said, right as Naya yelped.

"Are they always…" I began.

"So fucking annoying?" Ross said.

"I was going to say so affectionate."

"Yes," he responded, "they're always so affectionate. But no worries. Sue will handle it in 5, 4, 3, 2…"

Before I could ask what he meant, he pointed at his ears and I heard thudding footsteps in the hall, pounding on their door, and Sue screaming, "I've got to be up at six! If you want to moan and whimper, take it outside, losers!"

Instantly, the noises ceased.

"You know, I complain a lot about Sue," Ross said, "but she has her uses. Plus…" Before he could continue, his phone started to ring. On the screen, I saw a photo of a cute girl with blond bangs smiling.

"Do you mind?" he asked.

"Make yourself at home," I said. "After all, you are at home."

He stood and walked off toward the living room, where I couldn't hear him. I was tempted to follow him—I wanted to know what he was talking about—but I was a good girl, and I stayed there looking at the scene the movie was paused to and drumming my fingers until I got bored. Then I went to the kitchen. He had his back turned in the living room and was mumbling too low for me to catch anything. As I poured myself a glass of water, Will appeared there shirtless.

"You need to refuel before round two?" I asked him, passing him my glass.

"I would if it hadn't been for Sue," he said with a sigh. "Naya's asleep now."

"Yeah. It's late. Maybe I should go back to the dorm."

"You can always stay here."

"You don't have a guest room, though," I replied.

"You can use the couch, or you can sleep in Ross's bed. He's like a stuffed animal. Who's he talking to?"

"No idea," I said, though I was dying to say it was a girl and ask if Will might know who she was. But instead of taking the hint, he simply offered to drive me home. I protested that Naya was still here, but he reminded me she was asleep, and we both knew once that happened, there was no point in trying to wake her. "Give me five minutes," he said, and in exactly five minutes he was back, dressed and spinning his key ring around his finger.

"Shall we?" he asked.

As we were walking out, Ross turned to me pitifully and said, "Are you going? We're only halfway through the movie!"

"Yeah," I replied. "I'm sleepy, though. Maybe I'll watch the end of it back in my room."

"That's betrayal, that's almost as bad as watching half a series with someone and then finishing it on your own."

"You can come if you want," Will told him.

Ross smiled and said, "If you insist."

"I didn't insist," Will responded, but then they grinned at each other and the two of them walked out. Will's car was bigger than Ross's, and I felt like a child in the ample back seat, trying to lean forward to take part in the conversation. Ross was remarking on Will's new stereo, which Will told him was a gift from Naya. He didn't know why she'd given it to him, but I guessed it was to repent in advance if he found out she hadn't called him on the night of the party. It was rainy out, and droplets were splashing the windshield. I got lost in my own thoughts for a moment until I heard Ross utter my name.

"What was that?" I asked.

"Batman is obviously better than Superman, right, Jen?" he repeated.

Will asked him why all of his conversations revolved around superheroes, and Ross responded, "Because talking about the weather is boring. So Jen, answer the question."

"I don't know," I said. "I guess they both have their good and bad sides."

Will laughed. "She's saying that because she doesn't want to offend you."

Ross grimaced. Will argued it couldn't be Superman, because he didn't even have any special powers. Ross, offended, reminded him that Batman was a millionaire. As they went back and forth, I told them both I liked Wonder Woman. They froze a moment, then Will told me, "Sorry, Wonder Woman's boring." I told him she was the best, and Ross started making excuses: "It's my fault, bro. I showed her the movie the other day. I guess I shouldn't have started off with the feminist superheroes. Probably her brain wasn't ready for it."

"Hey! I like the Justice League, too!" I jumped in.

Will: "The Justice League sucks."

Me: "You suck."

"Look at you," Ross said proudly. "When you got here, you didn't even know who Batman was and now you're talking about the superheroes like they're your friends. How quickly they grow up. Isn't that right, Will?"

I couldn't let the Wonder Woman issue go. She had founded the Justice League! I was about to make my case again, but then Will tapped Ross on the shoulder, looking confused, and pointed to their right.

"Isn't that Mike?" he asked.

Mike, Ross's brother, was standing outside a bar. He looked like they'd just thrown him out. He was shouting through the glass door while a waitress flipped him off.

"Should we stop?" I asked.

"No," Ross argued. "I don't know if he still has a car, and if he asks us for a ride home, God knows what kind of trouble we could get into."

"Ross, he's your brother!" I said.

"Exactly."

I asked him how he could sleep easily knowing his brother might be all alone in the middle of town and he responded, "Trust me, I sleep like a baby." But after much arguing, and after me browbeating him, he groaned and nodded at Will, who cut the wheel, parked in front of the bar, and honked. Mike walked over beneath the rain and peered into the window, then smiled and shouted, "Hey, little brother!"

"Get in and shut up," Ross said unenthusiastically.

"Hey, Jenna," Mike greeted me as he did so. "I guess you guys came to rescue me?" He settled in beside me, smiling, while his brother glared at him in the rearview mirror. "So where are we going?" Mike continued.

"I'm going back to the dorm to sleep."

"The dorm? But it's Friday night! It's time to party!"

I told him I didn't like to party, and he said I would if I went out with him, and Ross told him not to bother me, and Mike told Ross not to bother him. Will found the whole thing amusing, but Ross was breathing loudly in frustration. Changing the subject, I asked Mike, "Do you get thrown out of bars often?"

"I'm good at pissing people off," he replied. "My brother can tell you that."

"That's the first intelligent thing I remember you saying in the last twenty years," Ross told him.

Mike thanked him sarcastically and told Will to put on some music, which he did, probably to keep from having to hear any more bickering. Mike belted out every song that came on full-throated while Will stared straight ahead and Ross scowled. It seemed endless. I was happy when we arrived, and I thanked Will for bringing me home as I threw on my jacket.

"Thank you, Will?" Ross asked, offended. "What about me, I'm just a mannequin?"

"And thank you, too, Ross," I said.

"Now that's better."

Mike asked if he didn't get a goodbye hug, and Ross told him to shut up, which he did, pretending to zip his lips.

5

THE NEXT LEVEL

I was wrapping up some homework when a videocall appeared on my screen. Monty. *Uh, thanks but no thanks*, I thought. I hadn't exactly enjoyed our last conversation. But I also didn't want to be mean. So after a moment's thought, I responded, and there I saw him, looking handsome with his innocent little smile, next to the lamp in his room. He looked tired. I assumed he'd been at practice.

"Hey, Jenna," he said.

"So you're not in the mood to shout at me anymore?" I asked.

Monty was good-looking, with short blond hair, buzzed almost, and a little earring in one ear that I'd always found sexy. He peered at me with his narrow brown eyes.

"How are you?" he said, ignoring my comment.

"Fine," I mumbled. But I wasn't good at holding grudges, so I tried to actually start a conversation. "School sucks, though."

"Really?"

"Yeah, they want me to read all these books and I hate them."

"Well, if it makes you feel any better, my training's going great. The coach thinks we can really win this game on Saturday, but he's been pushing us hard. We've had double sessions most days."

"I wish I could go see you," I said.

"I know." He smiled. His smile was goofy; it didn't quite suit him. "I'll tell you how it goes, though."

Feeling a little uncomfortable, I looked down at my fingernails and asked him whether he'd heard from Nelle. He seemed to find the question weird and said, "No, not really, why?"

"She won't call me back or answer my messages. I'm starting to think she's mad at me. I know she was sad when I left, but I don't think that justifies her not talking to me. Thank God I've got Naya and her friends. Otherwise I'd feel all alone here."

"You've got me," he said. "You know you always do."

Maybe. But I also knew that sweet as he was then, he could turn into a jerk at the drop of a hat. Why couldn't he just be normal? "I wish I was there with you," he added. Was he trying to make me feel worse?

"We won't have to wait much longer," I said with a sigh. "Just a few months."

He complained that it felt like those months would never pass, and I smiled, feeling discouraged as he continued. "At least you've got some friends. That's something. Right?" He seemed to want to add something, and when he just stared at me, I said, "What, Monty?"

"You've met someone, too. *Someone.* I can tell."

"Monty, I've only been here a month. I haven't even had time to meet anyone. Plus, you're the one who was all about this open-relationship thing. Maybe you have something to tell me?"

"I mean…I've had my eye on this girl, but nothing's really happened."

I didn't know what to say. So I asked what she was like.

"I thought we weren't going to go into details…" he replied.

I guessed it was better that way. Just the idea of my boyfriend sleeping with some girl bothered me. Putting a name and face to her would only make it worse. So I tried to change the subject. I tried to put on a seductive voice. Naya was gone, and I thought we could try some kind of *cybersex*... Wasn't that what it was called? But Monty didn't get it, and it went nowhere.

"Just forget about it," I said.

"I'm sorry, Jenna. Maybe if I was there, I'd understand you better."

"Yeah, but we might as well stop talking about if I was there or you were here because you haven't offered to drive up here and I don't have any money to go home." I knew that for a fact because I'd seen a message from Mom that morning. I didn't want to read it, but I could already guess it would be bad financial news. Monty didn't seem to believe me and said I could go see him if I wanted to. When I said I couldn't and things got heated, he apologized and said he was tired and he was probably taking it out on me.

"I'm going to get some sleep, babe. I'll call you tomorrow," he said.

"Sure."

"Good night. I love you, Jenna."

I told him good night, blew him a kiss, closed my laptop, and looked at my phone. On the small screen, I saw a message that said Call me NOW, Jennifer Michelle Brown. Just as I was typing, another one came through: If you don't, there will be consequences.

What was she, a mafioso? It was better not to prolong the inevitable, so I dialed, stood, and looked out the window. It was almost nine in the evening. She must have had her phone in her hand already, because she responded before the first ring was over, shrieking, "Jenna! I've been waiting the whole day for you to call!"

"I'm sorry, Mom. I didn't have time till now."

That was a lie, but I wasn't going to tell her that. I just hadn't wanted to hear what I knew she had to say. She began, "We need to talk..." and I finished her sentence for her: "About money."

"Yeah...you know your father and I haven't been doing so well, honey.

And Shannon needed money for Owen's school things. And your brothers... Well, their garage is a money pit, and I don't know how to tell you this, but..."

"You can't pay for my dorm."

I tried not to sound angry. I couldn't imagine why there was always money for my bumbling brothers but no money for my education. But I would never tell her that. She tried to make everyone happy. She failed at it, but she tried. And I didn't want to hurt her feelings.

"I'm so sorry," she said, sounding sincere. "I've tried to square the accounts, but the money just isn't there. If you like it there, maybe we can try again next semester."

"It's fine, Mom."

"You're so sweet. We're on a payment plan, you know, and the next installment was due yesterday, and..."

I cut her off, telling her I'd try to figure out something. But when I thought the call was over, she stayed on the line, and finally I asked, "What?"

"You know you could always just come back home, Jenna. You've had your little month away, but you could come stay with us again. We love you more than anyone in the world. Where would you be happier than here?"

"Mom," I said, "we've already talked about this a million times. I've got friends here. People who care about me. And I want an education. I don't want to just live forever in the town I grew up in and work some dumb job. I knew you were going to be this way, and I told you to leave me alone until December. And it's October. The beginning of October. I said I wanted to be independent and grow here without having you bothering me. You need to get used to the idea that I'm grown up now."

"I'm just saying, the offer's there. And I don't want you to have to get a job. It's so hard, working and studying at the same time."

"It'll be fine," I said. "It's not like I'm studying nuclear physics."

"Still, I'll try to come up with something. We should be in better shape next month and we'll be able to send you a little cash."

"It's fine, Mom."

But it wasn't, not for her, and she started back in on how maybe it would be best if I just went home, maybe we hadn't put enough thought into this whole college question. I started to suspect she was fine with money and had just cooked up this lie about the dorm payments to make me come back. Angrily, I told her I'd rather sleep on the street, and she told me not to get angry, and I swore I wasn't.

"Don't lie to me, honey."

"I'm not lying, Mom. I've got to go. Good night."

As I rang off, she was still blathering about how much she loved me and how I needed to bundle up and not forget to take my vitamins. I had already predicted something like this, I thought as I looked out my window. But I'd never imagined it would happen so soon. Regardless of whether my mother wanted me there and how that affected her attitude about paying for school, it was a fact that we were poor. We always had been. My parents had never had a cent to spare. So maybe it was time for me to get a job. Nothing major, just enough to pay for my lodging and take some stress off their backs. And maybe if I did so, they'd stop thinking about me so much and I could actually live my life.

But for now, I needed to figure out what to do for the next four weeks. I wondered: Would they evict me? Send the police up to kick me out? I didn't know, but I wasn't as excited about living on the sidewalk as I might have pretended with my mother. Scrolling through my contacts to see if there was anyone who could help me, I saw Ross's name and decided to call him. I was nervous. More nervous than I should have been over a mere phone call. He picked up right away.

"Hey, Ross," I said.

"To what do I owe this surprise?"

"Nothing, really." But I imagined him smiling as he heard my voice, and it warmed my heart.

"Jen, I can't believe you called just to hear my voice. You're turning awfully romantic on me."

"You wish." I started to blush. "Are you busy right now?"

"Why? Do you want me to come over?"

"I mean, I don't want you to have to…"

"I'll be right over," he said. Before I tried to tell him not to put himself out, he'd hung up. I shook my head and tucked my phone in my pocket. That had put me in a better mood, at least. I changed out of my pajamas and into some comfortable clothes. Looking at myself in the mirror, I kept trying to fix my bangs, which were pulling stubbornly to one side. Why did I care, though? I was just going to hang out with friends. Right?

Downstairs, Chris was playing with his phone. "Jenna," he said when I greeted him, "I'm glad you're here. I need to talk to you."

"I already know," I told him. "My payment's late. I'm trying to figure out what to do about it. Just give me two days, please. If I can't find the money, I'll go somewhere else."

"Like where?"

"I don't know."

He didn't seem to like that response and frowned, telling me, "I could pretend I didn't receive the notice and that might buy you a week. But the head of housing will start coming down on me after that."

"Thank you, Chris," I said, relieved.

"I just don't want to be responsible for you turning into a panhandler."

Chris was weird, but he clearly had a good heart. I almost wanted to cry from relief. It had been forever since anyone had done anything so kind for me. "You want a hug?" I asked him. "Because I sure need one."

But as I leaned in, and Chris stood and bent over the counter, I felt someone pulling me away.

"Now, now, no funny business, kids," Ross said. "What's up, Chrissy?"

"We agreed that you'd stop calling me that, remember?" Chris responded.

"You got it, Chrissy. What were you guys talking about? Was Chrissy telling you his favorite flavor of condom again?"

"It's not my favorite flavor, dumbass. I just tell people it's the most popular one. And no, for your information, we were talking about Jenna's financial problems."

"Wow," I said, "thanks for being so discreet."

"Sorry," Chris corrected himself, seeming slightly embarrassed. "What I mean was, yeah, we were talking about condom flavors."

"Good save," I added sarcastically.

"Are you having money problems?" Ross asked with concern.

I don't know why, but I didn't want to talk about that with him, especially not after seeing his expression, which didn't precisely radiate understanding. Chris pretended to focus on his *Candy Crush* game, but I could tell he was listening to every word we were saying. Since the cat was out of the bag, I figured there was no point in covering things up, so I told Ross, "Yeah, my parents are broke and they won't be able to send me any money for housing till next month. So I guess I need a job. If you know anyone who's looking for someone..."

"I don't. Sorry. I've got a better idea, though. You could just come live with us!"

"I'm sorry?" I asked.

"You heard me," he responded. "You're one of us now. Why not?"

"Ross, you barely know me. What if I were a serial killer?"

"I'm willing to take that risk."

"I don't know if I can accept that," I said.

"You already practically live with us anyway. It's just your things that live in the dorm."

"Ross, I'm broke. If I don't have money for the dorm, that means I don't have money for rent, either."

"Screw it," he said, almost offended. "If you don't have money, just don't pay. I don't mind. Now I know all the objections you're going to make, so let me cut you off now. The offer's on the table, no strings attached, and in your situation, I'd advise you not to hesitate for too long."

"Won't Will and Sue get mad, though?"

"Will would never get mad at you. If anything, you being there will mean Naya will come over more, and for him, that's a plus. We'll have to listen to them bumping and grinding more, but I'm willing to make that sacrifice if it means having you around the house. As for Sue, she hates everyone, so who cares what she thinks? I'm honestly just surprised she hasn't already murdered all of us in our sleep."

"Ross, I don't know what to say," I told him.

"Then say yes."

Chris stopped pretending he wasn't listening to us and butted in. "One thing, though. We can't just hold a room for you. Once university housing learns you're not here, that spot's marked as open, and there's always the possibility someone might transfer into it from another dorm. Obviously I'll see what I can do, but I'm just a peon."

That terrified me. That meant this was serious. I looked Ross in the eyes and asked him again, "Are you sure? Are you sure there's room for me? Where will I sleep? On the couch?"

"Of course not. You can sleep with me."

Chris choked on the water he was sipping and started pounding the middle of his chest. I could feel my cheeks getting feverish as Ross tried to ignore him and said, "Trust me, I'm a gentleman. I won't lay a finger on you."

"Sure," I said, giggling nervously.

"Unless you ask me to."

Dumbass. Now I was blushing for the second time in ten seconds.

"I won't," I grumbled.

He smiled, pinched the back of my neck, and said, "We'll see about that."

I wasn't sure about sharing a bed with a guy—a guy I had only known for a month—and it seemed strange to me that Ross was so chill about it. But he argued that his bed was huge and that he barely covered half of it. And he reminded me of what actually mattered in that moment: that it was better than a park bench.

"I don't know," I said. "I mean, park benches do have nice views."

"They're sure as hell not comfortable, though," he said, and I told him I didn't want to owe him anything.

"You don't owe me anything!" he grumbled, then said, "Come on, let's go get your things."

"You've still got another week," Chris said, but Ross ignored him as he headed upstairs.

I wondered if we should tell Will first and expressed my worries. When Ross asked why, I said, "I mean, it is his apartment, isn't it? He'd probably appreciate the heads-up."

"Sorry, babe, that apartment is mine."

"What?"

He arched an eyebrow and said, "Try not to act so surprised. I'm a responsible adult. I can have a place of my own. And I can open the doors of my humble abode to anybody I like. Or to my bed."

I'd heard that joke enough times by then, so I told him to hurry up and help me with my things. For half an hour, while he sat on the bed, I ran back and forth, stuffing things into a suitcase and trying to arrange them as best I could. But it was no use. The suitcase seemed to have shrunk since

I arrived. It didn't help that he kept pulling my clothing and keepsakes out to examine them.

"Why do you have so many clothes?" he asked. "You always wear the same thing anyway."

"That's not true!" I replied, offended.

"Don't get me wrong, you can wear what you want for all I care. Or nothing at all."

I threw a pair of slacks at his face, and he caught them, folded them, and laid them in the suitcase.

"So tell me something about your financial issues," he said. "Where did all your money go?"

"Mine, nowhere. My parents, though… They give every cent to my brothers and my sister." I tossed a pair of socks into the suitcase. "They think my brothers' stupid garage is worth more than my studies."

"How many of you are there?"

"Five in all. I'm the baby, then there's my three older brothers, then my sister. But she lives with her son, Owen, and her on-again, off-again boyfriend. He's not Owen's dad; he's just some guy she met a couple of months ago. They argue all the time and then break up and then get back together. The poor kid must be sick of it. But why do you want to know all this?"

"You've just never told me about your family."

For a moment, I stood still as I wondered why. Then I went back to folding clothes. "There's just not much to tell, really."

"I find it interesting," he said with a grin. "Kind of like these." He pulled up the pair of ratty panties I usually wore when I was on my period. "They're very fashionable."

I snatched them away and stuffed them under the rest of my things, embarrassed, telling him, "Don't touch my underwear."

"Yes, ma'am."

When I managed to get the suitcase shut, he lugged it downstairs for me.

Chris was kind enough to hold the door for us and tell me he'd be happy to see me back there if things didn't work out. "As for him," he said, pointing at Ross, "if he gives you any trouble, you have my permission to hit him."

"I'll keep that in mind," I said, laughing. "See you around, Chris."

Ross was already a few steps away, getting ready to load my suitcase into his car. Once I got in, I buckled my seat belt. I'd learned that was important with him, even if I was getting used to his driving to such a point that other drivers were starting to seem slow to me.

"Will's going to be so happy to see you!" he said. "Naya too."

"I don't know, maybe she won't like being alone in her room."

"She's never even there. You'll probably see her more than you did before."

"Why are you so pleased with this situation, Ross?"

He shrugged and smiled. "I don't know."

I poked his cheek, trying to get him to say something, but he just chuckled and said, "How about we put on some music?"

When we reached his apartment, he pulled out my suitcase and said, "This thing feels like you've got rocks in it."

"You carried it up to my room on the first day, and it's got the exact same stuff in it. Probably you're getting weaker in your old age."

"Oh, are you challenging me? Let's see how weak I am!" He bent down and grabbed me around the knees and lifted me, throwing me over his shoulder. The whole garage turned upside down and I shouted, "Ross! Ross! Put me down!"

"You shouldn't have provoked me!"

"*Ross!*"

He ignored me, grabbed the suitcase with the other hand, and carried us both to the elevator. I twisted and turned, but it was pointless, so finally I crossed my arms and waited, simply protesting. "You're going to make me pass out. All the blood's running to my brain."

"What brain?" he asked.

I hit him on the back, hard enough to get a reaction out of him, and told him he'd have another one coming if he didn't put me down.

"I prefer not to," he said. "After all, my head's right by your butt. That's motivation for me to give it a nice squeeze."

That thought hadn't struck me before, and I realized his hands were on the back of my thighs, dangerously close to it. "Put me down, you pervert!" I shouted.

"Booooring," he responded, setting my feet on the floor. I rearranged my hair and clothes while he stood there grinning. "I should have grabbed a big handful when I had the chance."

"You'll never have the chance," I hissed, and he said, "Are you daring me? Because I never lose a dare."

"I'm not daring you!"

"Imagine if someone opened the door right now," he said, "and they found you bright red, with your hair and clothes messed up. What do you think they'd say?"

"That you're a dumbass," I replied. He laughed, opened the door to the apartment, and let me through. Then he ran past me into the living room and cleared his throat, like a speaker making an announcement to a crowd:

"I left empty-handed, and I've returned with a new roommate!"

I dragged my suitcase in behind him.

"Excuse me?" Will asked.

"I'm going to live with you guys," I said, sounding a little too enthusiastic. "For now, I mean."

"She's just being shy," Ross said, throwing an arm around me. "We've decided to take our relationship to the next level. So I'd like to ask you all for a bit of privacy and respect in this moment of extraordinary happiness for us."

Naya was freaking out and kept saying, "Wait, what?" I had to tell her it wasn't true as Ross wiped a tear of laughter from his eye. "I'm just going to stay here for a while. If it's all right with you guys."

"Fine with me," Will replied. "You can't be any worse than the two roommates I already have. Do you know how to cook?"

"Yeah, a little," I said.

"Finally!"

Ross, looking offended, asked him, "Hey, what about my chili?"

"Your chili's disgusting," Will said.

"My chili's the bomb! Jenna, don't listen to them. I'm going to make it for you one day and you'll fall even deeper in love than you already are."

"What he means is you'll hate him even more than you already do," Sue murmured.

Everyone joined in making fun of him and the one recipe he knew, and Ross raised his chin and told them, "I'll pretend I haven't heard any of this because I know that deep down you love my chili, and anyway, I'm in a good mood. Now come on, Jenna."

"I'm coming," I said, lumbering behind him. Ross ran ahead of me and jumped on his bed like a happy child, pointing at a closet with a full-length mirror hanging on it and telling me I could use it. "The dresser is all the space I need," he added. "I'm a simple man, after all. Now you just make yourself comfortable, change clothes if you need. I'm going to go get us some dinner. What would you like?"

"You're letting me pick?"

I drew a blank. I wasn't used to choosing. Anything. Ever. At home, my brothers always decided everything. Among my friends, it was always Nelle. And if I was with Monty, he was the boss. That made me kind of sad, and I mumbled, "I don't know…pizza?"

"Sue's tired of pizza. But you know what? I just remembered I don't give a damn. I'm *your* errand boy. If it's pizza you want, it's pizza you'll get."

He took off with an energetic step while I stayed there unpacking again. I was halfway done when Naya knocked at the door and came in. Looking sad, she told me she was going to miss me.

"Ross is right," I reassured her. "We'll see each other more here than in the dorm. Anyway, I think it'll just be for the semester, and then I'll try to get back in."

She sat on the carpet next to me and helped me stuff my socks into a drawer. Soon malicious curiosity replaced her sorrow.

"So you're going to sleep in Ross's bed?"

"Yeah. So?"

"Nothing. I just think you guys make a cute couple. You look good together. Your personalities complement each other."

"Too bad I have a boyfriend, then," I replied, not really knowing what to say and preferring to make a joke of it as I kept putting away my clothes.

"Imagine if we went on double dates," she said.

"Yeah. Like I said, too bad I have a boyfriend."

Naya laughed and went on helping me, then left so I could put on my dumb pajamas with the slippers that looked like little stuffed dogs. I took out my contacts and put on my glasses. I hated wearing them, but my eyes were dry. I opened the door and found Ross there about to knock.

"The pizza's getting co…" He stopped midsentence, laughed, and said, "My God, you look beautiful. Especially your shoes. I'm going to need to get a pair of those."

I shook my head and said, "Just let me know when you're done making fun of me."

"I am, basically. I didn't know you wore glasses."

"I usually don't, because I hate them. But I needed to take out my contacts."

"I don't know," he said. "Glasses make you look like an intellectual."

"And what do I look like when I don't wear them?"

"That's a trap, and I'm not falling into it," Ross responded.

"Let me have another sweatshirt," I said, and he grabbed me a black one with the words *Pulp Fiction* on it and an image of a sexy woman. I threw it over my head. Instantly, I noticed his scent. I wondered if anyone had ever liked how my clothes smelled. I hoped they smelled as good as his.

"That used to be my favorite," he said.

"Used to be?"

"Yeah. Then I got the *Kill Bill* one. That's what I wear now."

This sweatshirt was bigger than the Pumba one, but it was comfortable and I liked it. We walked to the living room. Sue had already vanished, and Will and Naya were watching TV.

"What's on?" I asked.

"This radical makeovers program. This chick just got a nose job and it looks terrible, and now she has to go get a dress for some fancy ball." For a while, Naya was glued to the TV, but soon she and Will got up to their usual business while Ross and I stared at the screen and cracked stupid jokes. Then, the inevitable moment came: Will announced they were going to the bedroom and Naya took his hand, glancing back at me on her way out and saying, "Sweet dreams, Jenna."

Not long afterward, Ross got up, too, yawned, and said, "I think I'll actually do the same."

"Don't we need to clean up?"

"Leave it for Sue. She's like a magic fairy. When you wake up, none of this will be here. And don't think you should be nice and do it for her. There's a delicate ecosystem in this house, cleaning up is her thing, and I don't want her to attack you on your first day here."

I followed him down the hall, but turned off at the bathroom, where I looked at myself nervously in the mirror. I felt terrified, and I wasn't even sure why. It was just Ross, after all. Will had said he was harmless. *Like a stuffed animal.* I gathered my courage and walked to the bedroom, shutting the door behind me. Ross was standing there in pajama pants, finishing putting on his T-shirt. It looked good on him. Really, really good. But what did that have to do with me?

"Do you have a favorite side?" he asked.

"Honestly, I don't care."

"Cool, I'll take right then."

He flopped down carelessly while I stood there on the verge of panic. I undid my hair, took off my glasses, and rubbed my eyes. Then I tried to break the ice with a joke. "If you want to do something bad to me, this is your chance. I'm blind as a bat."

"I'll keep that in mind for the future," he said.

He stretched his arm out to turn off the light, and I lay back, looking at the ceiling in the darkness, hearing my own heart pounding. He yawned again, relaxed as ever.

"Good night, Jen." He looked over as he said it, and I held his stare for a moment. I was frozen. I often did that when I was uncomfortable. He noticed, and then I thought I should dig myself out of that situation, so I told him, "Good night, Ross," and turned my back to him, trying to relax and hoping I would fall asleep.

6

FORBIDDEN DREAMS

I woke staring at the ceiling, sweating, my heart going a mile a minute.

Had I really dreamed what I just dreamed?

It couldn't be.

I brought my hands to my face and cursed. No. I couldn't have. I couldn't have dreamed that I was doing it with Ross.

I looked over at him, sleeping calmly as an angel. He exhaled, gathered his pillow under his head, slid a hand under his cheek.

This wasn't right. I didn't *like* Ross. Why had I dreamed that, then? Was I losing my grip on myself after sleeping with him just one night? Did I feel guilty? But I hadn't done anything wrong! And even if I had, Monty and I had a deal. So what the hell was going on? Why did I feel so hysterical?

I edged over a bit and rubbed my eyes, trying to relax. What was I supposed to do now? Just stay there? No. That was the one thing that was clear to me. I needed to go. ASAP. Figure things out.

I threw on my workout clothes, pulled my hair back in a ponytail, and left the room. No one had gotten up yet, so I wouldn't have to explain why I looked so frantic.

The worst thing wasn't the dream itself. The worst thing was…I had liked it. A lot. Too much. More than I ever had with Monty. Not that Monty and I had really done it enough for me to know.

I wanted to pound my own temples with my fists. I went for a longer run than normal, trying to clear my head. An hour and a half I stayed out. I wanted to be exhausted so the next time I slept, I wouldn't have to worry about any sex dreams. When I was done, my knees and calves were aching. I stopped a moment at the door to Ross's building, bent over and panting.

Just then, my phone rang. My sister.

"Hey, Shannon," I said, trying to catch my breath.

"Somebody's panting. Were you out for a run, or is it something more interesting?"

"Running," I said.

"Spencer would be proud of you. Since he got that job as a gym teacher, he's obsessed with how everyone needs to exercise. Even me."

"Exercise is good for you, Shannon."

"Error. Exercising makes me tired. Being tired is bad for me. Therefore, exercise is bad for me."

"I can't question your logic," I said, shaking my head.

"I'm calling because Mom told me you were moving back home."

"What she means is she wants me to move back home. Obviously I'm not doing it."

"Yeah," Shannon replied. "I get the feeling they're not crazy about being at home with just the guys."

"You think?" I laughed.

My sister screamed at her son to stop running around before he fell and cracked his head open. Then she came back on and asked me what we were talking about.

"The thing with Mom, a.k.a. our financial problems."

"Are you going to get a job, then?" she asked.

"I haven't had time to look. But a friend offered to let me stay with him for a bit."

"Did you say *him*?" I'd hoped she wouldn't notice.

"Shannon, don't."

"What kind of friend are we talking about?"

I reminded her I still had a boyfriend.

"Oh, you do. May I ask why?"

My sister couldn't stand Monty. She had made that clear the first time she'd ever seen him, furrowing her nose and shaking her head. Nothing about her opinion had changed since, and I doubted it ever would.

"I like being with him," I said. "What do you hate so much about him?"

"To start with, his name."

"Everyone says that, Shannon. It's so stupid."

"I don't know. I think there's a lot to a name. Like your new friend... What's his name?"

"Ross. I mean, that's his last name. His first name's Jack, but everyone calls him Ross."

"See? That's a normal name. I can already tell he's better for you than Monty."

"Whatever, Shannon. I need to shower."

"Are you coming home for Christmas?" she asked. "I know it seems like forever from now, but two and a half months can pass quickly. And Mom's already freaking out about if everyone will fit and what she needs to cook and all that. And don't forget Mom's birthday. That's coming up soon and you really ought to be there."

"Shannon, I need a plane ticket to get there and I barely have a cent to my name."

"Well, figure it out."

"Thanks for being so supportive," I told her before ringing off. I walked inside the building at the same time as an old woman who smiled at me and held the door. I wanted to say something nice to her, but nothing occurred to me. She asked me if I lived there.

"Yeah. For now."

She smiled and said, "With the kids on the fourth floor, right?"

"You know them?"

"Yes, I've lived here for quite some time. They're very good people."

"Yeah, especially Ross. I guess he owns the place, and he invited me to stay there when I needed it. I doubt even my best friend would have done that for me."

As I said that, I remembered my dream and got uncomfortable again. I tried to reach for the 4 button, but the woman had already done it. I asked her if she was our neighbor from across the hall, and she nodded. I could tell she was sizing me up. I got nervous as I worried she might complain about the noise or tell me too many people were living there. But her expression was kind and gentle.

"Oh, when I was your age…" she said nostalgically. "I'd have loved to live with a couple of guys. I'd have set that apartment on fire, if you know what I mean. You can't imagine what we were like back then in the seventies. We did things you kids now wouldn't even dream of."

Would this elevator never stop moving?

"So what, are you doing the walk of shame?" she asked.

"No! I, uh…"

"You can tell me."

For some reason, I trusted her. Or maybe I was desperate, and I needed to tell the story, and I felt more confident with a stranger than with anyone I knew. So I told her about my dream about Ross, and how I felt bad about it because he was supposed to be just a friend, plus he was kind of my landlord and I needed to keep things professional, but she cut me off. "So how was he?"

Jesus, this old lady was spicy!

"Not bad," I said. "Better than my boyfriend. Who I feel like I just betrayed."

She laughed and said, "Well, it sounds like a good start to the day. If I were you, I'd take it as a sign. Turn those dreams into realities!"

Finally the elevator stopped, we both stepped into the hall, and she opened her apartment door, turning back quickly and winking. "Don't worry," she said. "I'll keep your secret!"

Before I could reply, Ross opened the door, looking surprised. "Did you go for a run?" he asked.

"Yeah," I said. "Not all of us can eat pizza four days a week and stay thin just because…"

Ross looked like he was going to say something back, but then the old woman called out from behind me, "Hey, Jackie!"

Did they know each other? I mean, she did say she'd lived there for a long time…

"Hey, Grandma," Ross said with a smile.

Oh no.

No, please.

Had I really just told a grandmother I was having sex dreams about her grandson?

I hoped my cheeks were red enough from exercising that no one could tell I was blushing. For the second time since the day had started, I wished the earth would just swallow me up. To make things worse, Ross grabbed me around the waist just then and pulled me close as he introduced us, "Jen, this is my grandmother, Agnes. Grandma, this is my new roommate."

"We just met," she said with a malevolent smile.

"Cool," Ross said, slightly confused. I was tongue-tied, too ashamed to move. But his grandmother salvaged the situation by telling us goodbye. "Well, I need to get some breakfast. You kids behave, now."

As she vanished inside, I pulled away from Ross and entered the apartment. How could I be such a loser? Trying to tell myself what had just happened hadn't happened, I overheard Ross say, "Man, you are drenched with sweat. It's kind of sexy, though."

"You're gross," I responded.

"Are you surprised?" He opened the fridge and took out a slice of cold pizza.

"Do you not have something healthier to eat?" I asked. "I've never seen a more depressing refrigerator in my life."

"What do you mean, depressing? It's got beer in it. How could a fridge with beer in it be depressing?"

"You know, a lot of people your age, when they have roommates, they keep a jar everyone puts cash into every week and then someone goes to the store and buys groceries for the house. It's a good policy, maybe you should try it."

He looked at me confused. "I don't know," he said. "I like pizza. I told you, I'm a simple guy."

"We're going grocery shopping, Ross."

"You and me?"

"Yeah. I saw a supermarket right across the street."

"Yeah, it seems like Will told me something about it one time."

"Ross! How long have you lived here?"

"A year and a half."

"You've lived here a year and a half and you've never gone to the supermarket. I swear. You can be so smart sometimes and then turn around and be such an idiot. Well, get ready for a new life experience, because I'm not going to eat takeout the whole time I'm here. Now, if you'll excuse me, I've got to go take a shower."

"Can I come?" he asked, his mouth full of pizza.

"No!" I set off down the hall.

"Boring!" he shouted.

"Pervert!" I shouted back, hearing him chuckle as I shut the door.

"Free-range organic chicken?" Ross read from the label, picking a package up and setting it back down in the cart before pushing it further down the supermarket aisle. "Why free-range?"

"Because that means it had a good life. Not cooped up in a tiny cage getting pumped full of chemicals."

"Does that change the flavor?"

I didn't know, so I didn't say, looking down at our items and counting them off: "Let's see, we've got chicken, pepper, oil, milk, cereal…"

"Beef for my chili…"

"And eggs and fruit and vegetables."

"Fruit and vegetables," he said. "Disgusting."

"Are we missing anything?"

"Beer. Laugh if you want, Jen, but that's a basic necessity in our place."

"You've already got enough beer. What we need is tomato sauce."

"There's never enough beer," he said. "Oh, tobacco. I need tobacco, too."

"You should quit," I told him. "It's toxic."

"I thought you said we had to get vegetables. Tobacco's a vegetable. Anyway, you've got to die of something."

"Have you ever kissed anyone who smoked?"

"Jen, are you trying to seduce me?"

I kept walking, ignoring him, and complaining that he didn't even have salt. I honestly didn't know how he had survived that long. Ross tossed a chocolate bar in the cart, and I took it back out and put it on the shelf.

"Why are you being so stiff? Shouldn't we try to enjoy life a little?"

"Yeah, and the way I enjoy life is not wasting all my money and then having to worry about where my next meal is coming from."

"Boooring," he said. This was turning into a mantra for him. "I have money."

"I don't need your money. And you should try to be less wasteful," I said, picking out a tomato sauce and looking into the cart.

"We still need…" he began.

"If you say 'beer' again, I'm going to strangle you."

He smiled and pinched his lips closed with his thumb and index finger.

I asked him again how it was possible that he'd never bought his own groceries, and he shrugged and said they had someone who took care of all that at his house. "For real? Are you rich?" I asked.

"My parents have money."

"I hate you. I've always been poor. And it sucks," I replied.

"If we got married, my fortune would be yours."

"But I'd have to put up with you all day. I'm not sure it would be worth it."

"Imagine saying that to the person who opened his doors to you," Ross said.

I stopped at the checkout line and started loading my things onto the belt. When I looked up, Ross had vanished. A few seconds later, he returned with two chocolate bars, a packet of gummies, and a bag of popcorn. I narrowed my eyes at him and he just smiled as usual. He put the junk food on his card and we carried everything outside. It was raining again, so I threw my wet coat in the back and he rubbed his hands together as he turned on the heat.

"Well, that was the last thing I'd planned on doing with my day, but it was OK," he said.

"I used to love going grocery shopping with Dad. It's weird, but it's just one of those things we did together, and it pops up in my mind a lot now that we don't live in the same city. I miss him. I miss all of them."

"You should go see them," Ross said.

"Ross, if I don't have money for the dorm, how am I going to buy a plane ticket home? I'm worried about it, too, because my mom's birthday's coming up and I can't go and she's going to lose her shit. I don't know what I'll do about Christmas. My sister was giving me a hard time about it this morning, but her scrounging money off my parents is half the reason they don't have any to give me. I'm sorry, I must be boring you…"

I wasn't used to anyone letting me talk for so long. I couldn't say more than five words to Monty before he started yawning and interrupting me to talk about basketball practice. At home, I could never get a word in edgewise. How did you know if another person thought what you were saying was interesting?

"You couldn't bore me if you tried," Ross reassured me. "Where did you say your parents lived?"

"About seven hours south of here."

He turned pensive, and I asked him what he was thinking, but he wouldn't respond, even as he started the engine and I pinched him on the cheek.

"You know," he told me, "this thing of pinching my cheek is turning into a habit. Now leave me in peace; I'm trying to listen to The Smiths. This is one of my rituals." Then he turned up the volume so loud he couldn't hear me.

We returned to find everyone in the apartment alive and moving. Sue was making some strange racket in her room, Naya was sitting on the couch, and Will was drinking a beer in the kitchen. He froze when he saw us carrying in the grocery bags, as if we'd showed up with a buried treasure or a rare animal.

"Ross, please tell me I didn't miss a news report about the apocalypse, because I can't think of anything else that would drive you to go to the grocery store."

"I had to drag him there," I said. "It was hard, but it was worth it. Finally there's something decent to eat in this house."

Ross had just taken out his bag of gummies and was about to tear it open when Naya leaped at it and tried to tear it out of his hands. "Hey, those are mine!" he shouted.

I told Will with disappointment, "He says he wants to make chili for dinner."

"Chili, again?" he sighed.

"Is it really that bad?" I asked.

"Let's just put it this way. I hope you like hot food."

Two hours later, Ross was playing mad scientist in the kitchen while I sat on the couch recopying my philosophy notes. Will was sitting next to me, flipping through the channels, while Naya was on the other couch asleep.

"So is it really true Ross's parents are loaded and they have people who buy him groceries and stuff like that?" I asked. When Will nodded, I said, "Jeez. I wish I'd been born rich. What do they do?"

"His father's Jack Ross, Sr." Will said. "Does that name not ring a bell for you?" I tried to think as I watched Ross opening and closing drawers, looking utterly baffled.

"No. And Ross hasn't really talked about him. I feel like he said his mom was a painter and maybe that his dad reads a lot or something."

"His father's a retired concert pianist. Like one of the best in the world. He travels all over. I think he played for the president or something. And his mom's not just some painter. She's a photographer, too, but she also sells art. I think she has five galleries in London, New York, and I don't know where else."

"Weird," I said, feeling stupid. "Ross doesn't act rich."

"Ross…" Will replied. "He's just Ross, you know." I must have had a look of terror on my face because he added, "I don't know what you're worried about, but you should relax. He's completely normal."

I tried to protest that I was relaxed, but he said, "Yeah, right," and turned back to the TV.

A while later, Ross started to shout for someone to set the table and we all jumped to it. *The table*, of course, meant the coffee table. God forbid there be a decent place to share a meal. When the scent of chili was too strong to resist, Sue came out and sat down without a word. Ross sat next to me. My stomach was grumbling.

"Not to be a show-off," Ross said, "but this turned out amazing."

"Let's eat!" Naya shouted.

Honestly, I thought it was delicious, but it was incredibly spicy. Ross didn't seem to notice, but Naya kept drinking more and more water, which only made it worse, and soon her face and neck were glowing red. Suddenly, a weird silence overtook the room. I looked at Will, who was looking at Sue. Her expression was grim, and since nobody had spoken to her the whole time, I decided to ask her, "Are you OK?"

I instantly regretted it when she responded, "Does it matter if I'm OK?"

"Uh, I don't know, I just…"

"Like what are you even doing here?" she grumbled. I wasn't sure what to say, couldn't understand why she was so mad, and felt too confused and embarrassed to speak.

"Don't be like that now," Ross said. "She was just trying to be nice."

"She might as well save herself the effort," Sue responded, and Will tried to comfort me, telling me, "Ignore her. She's just trying to get some attention."

But I couldn't. Before I could stop myself, I exploded, "Sue, do you have some kind of problem with me?"

"Wow, you're smarter than you look," she said. "Yeah, I have a problem. Literally no one here even knows shit about you, and all of a sudden you're living with us?"

"If that's an issue…" I began.

"There's no issue." Ross interrupted me, almost glowing with anger, then turned to Sue. "I invited her in here, so if you have a problem with her, take it out on me, not her."

"Oh, I will, don't worry about that. I live here, too, you know, and nobody even asked my opinion."

"Sue, if we had to ask your opinion, we'd never do anything. You're the most hateful, bitter person I think I've ever met," Will said. "Now can we just eat our meal in peace?"

But Sue couldn't quit grumbling about how no one cared what she thought, about how I was basically a stranger, how the last thing they needed was another person taking up space there, and Ross got angry. It was the first time I'd seen him actually angry. He kept telling me to ignore her, that I was welcome there, and the third time I repeated that I could leave if my living there was going to be a problem, Sue shouted, "Of course there's no problem. He wants to fuck you, so that means there's no problem with you being here."

That phrase hung there a few moments in the air. A few moments that seemed like an eternity. I felt ashamed, and I looked down into my plate. The silence was so dense, you could cut it with a knife. When I finally glanced over, I saw Ross staring at Sue with murder in his eyes. She dropped her utensils, stood, and stomped off to her room. Naya smiled nervously, trying to rescue the situation with a little joke. "Well, I guess Sue's not cleaning up tonight, so I'll get to this." She kicked Will under the table, and he added, "Yeah, we'll take care of this. Jenna, feel free to watch TV or take a shower or whatever."

I knew Ross was watching me, but I was too nervous to look back. So I stood and hurried off to the bathroom, stopping just briefly in front of Sue's bedroom door to curse under my breath and flip her the bird.

7

STUPID PERFECTION

I was nibbling the tip of my finger unconsciously as I looked like crazy for the answer to a practice test in linguistics on the internet. I couldn't understand how talking about language could be so complicated. And I was alone, so I couldn't call out for Will and Ross to come *help me*, which was the term I used when they did my work for me and I sat there watching them like an idiot. I mean, Will *was* home, technically speaking, but when he was in his bedroom with Naya with the music turned up, I knew what that meant. We all did. So there was no point in knocking.

I had virtually given up, crossing my arms in irritation, when I heard the doorbell ring. At last, an excuse not to do my homework! I opened the door a little happier than I should have been. But my smile vanished as soon as I saw who it was: a thin girl with blond bangs, a little shorter than me, dressed in fashionable and obviously expensive clothes. Everything about her was pretty, from her fine traits to her enchanting smile, which tugged downward a bit when she saw me. I guess she was expecting someone else.

"Hi," I mumbled.

"Hi," she said politely. "Is Ross in?"

I remembered: this was Lana. Naya had mentioned her. So had Chris.

And I had seen her face on Ross's phone one time when she called. But wasn't she supposed to be living in France?

Hearing Ross's name made me uncomfortable. After Sue's outburst at dinner, our relationship had become...weird? I mean, we still acted as we always had, but every time we walked past each other, accidentally touched, or our eyes met longer than they should have, we'd both clam up and try to pretend nothing had happened. Those attempts at avoiding each other made me realize how natural things had been with us before, how often we had poked each other or tickled each other, and...I missed it. It was weird not to just flop down on top of him on the sofa or curl up next to him when we watched a film. Not to rest my head on his shoulder...

Maybe it was for the best that we were a little less close? I wasn't sure Monty would like me doing all those things with a guy. Even if we did supposedly have a deal. What I knew for sure he wouldn't like were those dreams I kept having. My mind wouldn't leave me in peace. I had a bad habit of talking in my sleep, too, but as far as I knew, Ross had never heard me, thank God. I came back to reality when I realized Lana was still there staring at me.

"Sorry, he's not home." I cleared my throat. "But, uh, you can wait for him here if you like."

"Thanks!"

"I don't think he'll be long. He's done with class at..."

"Five, I know!" Was she always this bubbly?

I watched her walk in and wondered what she was doing here if she knew Ross wasn't home. She looked around and took off her jacket to reveal a clingy sweater I'd have never dared to put on. It would have showed my belly a little too much. She, of course, was rail-thin and looked dazzling in it.

I hated her. Why deny it?

So I didn't have a reason to. So what? I detested every single thing about her.

She put her hands on her hips and smiled at me for the umpteenth time.

"It's just as I remembered!" she said.

"So you've been here before…" At least I should try to make conversation, I thought.

"Oh, yeah, like a million times. Probably more than you have. I mean, I helped pick out most of the furniture."

Was she trying to one-up me? Something in her eyes told me so. And that threw me off. But she was talking so much that I couldn't really think about it too long.

"Were you doing homework?" she asked. "I hope I didn't bother you."

"Not in the least," I said, clearing my things off of the sofa and stuffing them clumsily in my binder. I was worried I was giving away how nervous she made me.

"Because if I am, I can just come back later."

"No, please, stick around. I was already finished."

She looked at my clothes—well, Ross's clothes, the ones I slept in—and I felt even stranger. Probably she wasn't being malicious, but she made me feel so goofy. Why was I wearing Ross's clothes, anyway? I looked like an idiot in them.

But I like the way he smells!

Shut up, brain! This isn't the time.

"I guess you're Jenny," she said, sitting down like she owned the place.

"Yeah. Jenna, actually. How do you know?"

"Ross told me a girl was living with him. He told me a lot about you actually. But I'm like his priest. I'm not allowed to repeat his secrets."

She laughed, and her stupid perfect laugh made me purse my lips to keep myself from screaming. Just then, Naya and Will opened the door and walked into the hallway, still pulling on their clothes. Naya froze for a moment and both girls screamed before running toward each other and hugging so tight they almost fell to the floor.

"I can't believe it! I can't believe it!" Naya screeched, not letting go until Lana pushed her away. She gave Will a hug, too, and said, "You better believe it! I missed you guys so much! This place is like my second home!"

Was I seeing things, or was she intentionally staring at me when she said that?

I stayed on the sofa, trying to think of an excuse to leave. I hadn't felt so out of place in ages, and I didn't know why. I finally pretended to be looking back at my homework just to have something to do. If all this wasn't bad enough, the door opened a few seconds later and Ross appeared, surrounded by the scent of barbecue pizza.

"Hey, Jen! Guess who bought your favorite garbage food? Oh…" He looked like a deer in headlights as he caught sight of Lana. "What the…?"

"Surprise, babe!" she shouted, jumping into his arms and hugging him.

Babe? Give me a break. But then, who was I to say what she could and couldn't call Ross? It wasn't my business. *Still, though. Give me a break.* I watched them long enough to know that Ross was looking at me, bewildered, over her shoulder, but I decided to wipe off the lenses of my glasses to pretend I wasn't studying their every move.

"Did you guys miss me?" she asked. "Because I missed you all tons."

"When did you get back?" Ross said. "You never mentioned anything…"

"This morning. I wanted to surprise you!"

"Are you staying?" Naya asked enthusiastically. "Like, staying-staying?"

"Not forever. But I don't have a return ticket, either."

Sue walked down the hallway and looked like she'd seen a ghost. I couldn't tell if her expression was one of horror or disgust. She, too, asked if Lana was going to stay, and Lana responded, "Hello to you, too, Sue."

"Cut the 'hello, Sue' bullshit and the fake smiles and answer the question," Sue grunted.

She seemed to hate Lana more than me. *Good job, Sue. I'm starting to like you*, I thought. At least I wasn't the only one who hated Lana. And that made me feel less alone in the world.

"Come on, Sue," Lana responded. "I know deep down you love me. But it doesn't matter, because I hear someone's sleeping in my spot." Again, she looked at me with that idiotic smile. I opened my lips to say something, but couldn't manage it. Naya laughed nervously and nudged Will to do something, while Ross turned pleadingly to little Miss Perfect and murmured, "Lana, look…"

"It's just a joke, babe!" she shouted. "Look at her. She thinks it's funny, too, right?"

She turned to me, and he smiled and shook his head, and for some reason, that made me angrier than anything that had happened so far. But I tried to play along and responded, "Yeah, of course."

Ross asked if she was staying for dinner. We had pizza, he said, but he could order sushi, too. He knew she loved that. In that moment, sushi sounded to me like the grossest food ever invented.

"You know I'd never say no to sushi," she responded with a cheesy grin.

Everyone went to sit down, and for some reason, I stood and walked over to the armchair next to Sue, who was still staring daggers into Lana. I liked observing that. It was better than knowing Ross was looking at me and trying to figure out what his eyes were concealing. Then I turned my attention to the pizza. I felt like a fourteen-year-old, unable to control my jealousy. Every time Lana spoke—which was the whole time we were sitting there—I wanted to throw a slice of pizza at her face. Whenever she laughed, Sue looked at her with disgust, and I felt our secret companionship growing.

"France is so amazing, you guys," she said. "You just have to go. The people are so cool, and every street is like a museum. It's just magical. I even learned to speak some French while I was there."

Wow! You actually learned to speak some French while living in France! Amazing. My brain could be nasty when it wanted to. But I didn't mind just then.

"I wish I could go to another country," Naya told Will. "But how could I leave my big bear behind?"

Sue stuck her finger in her mouth as if she were vomiting, while Lana went on. "And the parties... You just can't imagine. French people are crazy. And I'm so there for it."

It was then that I realized Ross wasn't smiling, either. He didn't even seem to be listening. He was just playing with his food and glancing over occasionally so no one could tell how distracted he was.

"But I had to come home for a while, you know. I missed my parents." She pushed her bangs out of her face, and I noticed her manicure was just as perfect as everything else about her. "Next year, though, I'll bet I'm going to go back to France. Probably. But you know, I wanted to see you guys, too."

She turned and gave Ross a strange look, and Ross looked over at Will as if to ask him for help. They had this kind of alien mind-meld; they never had to speak to know what the other was thinking. Will jumped in while I asked myself what exactly Ross was uncomfortable with.

"You should come over for dinner whenever you like," Will said.

I chomped on my pizza and monitored every movement of Ross's smile.

Placing her perfect hand on her perfect knee, Lana asked, "Sure... so...you guys don't have anything to tell me? I mean, I've been talking the whole time."

We know.

Will said there was nothing much new. I looked down at my plate. Ross said, "Same old, same old."

"How sad," Lana remarked. "But anyway, I'm having a welcome home party next week. You guys will come, right?"

Naya said, "I never miss a party," Will said he was in, Ross said he was in, too. Sue, obviously, said nothing, and then it was my turn. "Sorry," I said, "I can't make it."

"Why not?" Ross asked.

"Just because."

He had probably seen the bitterness in my expression. I didn't care though. At least everybody was pretending not to notice. I didn't want to talk, but that was probably inconceivable to Lana, who smiled *again*, revealing her gleaming white teeth and said, "Well, if you change your mind, let me know. It's gonna be at my sorority house. The girls are so cool. They organized the whole thing for me. And there's an open bar, so you don't even need to bring anything."

"I'm going to get soooo drunk," Naya said.

Lana talked more about France, about the other countries in Europe she'd visited, about her perfect grades, about every other stupid thing in her perfect life. And everybody listened like it was just the most fascinating tale they'd ever heard. The most irritating thing of all was the way she kept looking over and asking me questions like she wanted me to be a part of the conversation, and then, just as I was about to answer, she'd start talking about something else. When I couldn't stand it anymore, I stood and announced that I was tired and was going to bed.

"But it's only eleven!" Naya pleaded.

"Yeah," I responded, "but I've got to get up early tomorrow."

"It was a pleasure meeting you!" Lana called out in her singsongy voice.

"Same!" I said, thinking, *Whatever, bitch.*

Cursing wasn't my thing, but as I shut the door behind me, I let out a long string of them into my pillow, including the C-word, which would have made my mother's hair fall out. I didn't care; I was livid. The only thing that stopped my outburst was Ross coming in looking glum and confused. He shut the door and asked, "Is everything OK? You seemed like you weren't feeling good during dinner."

I sighed and shrugged. He could be so perceptive about some things and so blind to others. But why should he have guessed what I was feeling anyway? We were just *friends*. And it was borderline crazy to be jealous of someone because they had another friend. I was embarrassed at how unfair I was being.

"I…uh… Nah, I just need to lie down a bit."

I could tell he wasn't buying it. He knew there was something more. He reached over and put his hands on top of mine. I hadn't realized until then I'd been fidgeting. "Listen," he said, "whatever it is, you don't have to say. Just tell me you're OK."

I nodded, my face feeling hot, and said, "Ross, you've got a guest out there. You should go entertain her. I'm boring right now."

"You're not boring."

I wanted to ask him then, *Why do you always say that?* but I just nodded. He told me to let him know if I needed anything, and I said OK. Once the door closed, I felt like I could breathe again, and I turned to grab my phone. I called my sister. I needed her advice. Right now.

I walked around the room frantically trying to get a few bars, in vain until I reached one small corner of the balcony. It was freezing, and I'd closed the door so no one could hear me, so even the heat from the apartment didn't reach me. I dialed.

"Jenna," Shannon greeted me right away.

"I've got a problem, Sis. And I can't call Nelle because she's completely ignored me since I left."

"So I'm your plan B. Great," she said.

"Shannon, this is important. I've got a problem. I'm…jealous. I think it's really bad."

She sighed and waited a moment before saying, "Jenna, jealousy's not a bad thing as long as you understand where it's coming from and you don't cross certain lines."

"Sure. But the thing I'm jealous about…I'm not sure if it's right."

I could almost see her smiling as she said, "Let me guess: It's about the guy you're staying with? Now this is getting interesting. So what is it exactly you're jealous of?"

"It's a girl. His ex, I think. She came over and she's so perfect. You should see her. Her life's so interesting. She was living in France! I feel stupid and boring and ugly next to her."

"So why are you comparing yourself to her?"

"I can't help it! And everybody else thinks she's fascinating, too."

"You don't care about everyone else, though, do you?" She interrupted me. "The one you care about is dear old Ross."

"We're just friends, Shannon."

"Sorry, Sis, but you don't get jealous over *just friends.* So be honest, Jenna. Do you like him? It's a simple yes-or-no question."

Toying nervously with the cord of Ross's sweatshirt, I responded, "Shannon, I have a boyfriend."

She laughed so loud it scared me. "That isn't an answer! Not a real one, anyway. But it does clarify some things."

"I don't like him!" I shouted.

"Bullshit. I mean, listen, Jenna, if you need to tell yourself you don't like him, that's fine, and I'm happy to play along. But in that case, you're going to have to come up with a decent explanation for why you'd get jealous of a guy you don't like who's hanging out with his ex."

"I don't know… I don't know what's going on with me. And then there's this issue with Monty. Like, he said we could have an open relationship, but let's say I *did* like Ross and let's say I *was* jealous of him. Isn't that bad, somehow?"

"Trust me, I'm not defending Monty, but if you're worried about it, you should probably stay away from Ross," Shannon said.

"That's going to be a little hard. We sleep in the same bed. Not sexually or anything. But…another thing is, uh…" I was nervous, but I decided I might as well let it out. "I've been having sex dreams about him like every single night."

I felt almost feverish. I could tell when I touched my face. I couldn't believe I was confessing this to another person, even if that person was Shannon. For a moment, she didn't say anything, and I worried our connection had gone dead, but then she spoke up, "So…how was he?"

"Shannon! Do you honestly think that's what matters right now?"

"Was he better than your boyfriend!"

"Focus!"

"Oh my God, he was!" She started laughing. "I love this, this is soap-opera-level drama. Seriously, though, I don't know what to tell you. Maybe you should back off? Try to focus more on the friendship thing? Since you supposedly *are* just friends. And if it really starts to drive you crazy, tell your dumbass boyfriend to come up and distract you. I mean, it's not like he's good for much else. You know what I really think, though: I think this is driving you crazy because it reminds you of what happened with…"

My stomach turned, and I said sternly, "I don't want to talk about that right now."

"Jenna, it's been months. Maybe if you did let it out instead of keeping it all to yourself…"

"I said I don't want to talk about it."

"Fine. I know how you get when the subject comes up. I'm just trying to tell you not to freak out right now. I don't want to have to come pick you up."

"You're not going to have to come pick me up, Shannon. I'll be fine."

"If you're not, don't hesitate to call me, I'm always here for you. Besides, I like your gossip. It keeps me entertained."

"Thanks, Shannon. And thanks for the advice. Bye."

I hung up and walked back inside. I could still hear the laughter coming from the living room. I took off my glasses, but couldn't sleep. Eventually, I could make out Naya and Lana telling each other goodbye. Not long afterward, Ross came in and put on his pajamas. I had my back turned and closed my eyes. I wasn't in the mood for talking.

A few seconds later, he got in bed and asked me in a whisper if I was asleep. I didn't answer. He sighed, but didn't say anything else. I heard him turning, trying to get comfortable, and I wanted to cry for some reason.

After a while, I opened my eyes and saw he was still awake and rubbing his eyes. He must have known I was looking at him, because he turned almost instantly.

"Hi," I said.

"Hi... I thought you were asleep."

"I just woke up. How was the rest of the night?"

"Good," he murmured, seeming slightly confused that I had asked. "Are you feeling any better?"

I nodded and then came out with what I wanted to know: "Did you miss her? Lana, I mean?"

"Honestly? I don't know. It's been so long since I've seen her. I got used to being without her. What about you, though?" Finally he smiled again. "Are you sure you're better?"

"I said I was, right?"

"You're a terrible liar."

"I guess," I said, trying to come up with an excuse, "I miss my family a little."

That was true. And it felt even truer when I said it aloud. I thought of Mom and the fight we'd had when I left. Maybe she wasn't as hysterical as I thought. A few months really was a lot more time than it seemed. He reached over and pushed my hair out of my face.

"I'm sorry to hear that," he murmured, and his sincerity almost threw me off.

"It's OK. I mean, I'll see them again at Christmas. My mom and I made a deal. Because she didn't really want me to even go to school, you know? So I got her to agree to a semester. I'd come here for the fall, and then we could reevaluate."

"That's fine for your mom, but how do you feel?"

I didn't realize till then that his hand was still there, that he was stroking my cheek, running his thumb down my jawline. We barely knew each other, but the gesture was as natural as if he'd made it a thousand times. I held my breath. I don't think even he realized how unusual it was, that spontaneous feeling of being together. It was something I'd never known before, with Monty least of all.

"I don't know," I said. "I never really thought about it."

"But Jen, you're the one who matters here. Not your mom, not anyone else."

"If I go back, though… You guys won't forget me, right? You and Naya and Will, y'all will stay in touch, won't you?"

"For sure," he said.

But then I thought of Nelle, who had promised me the same thing and had ghosted me. He continued, "Besides, there's no need to miss your family. You've got a family here. We may be smaller, we may be weird, we may be a little dysfunctional, but you've got to take it where you can get it, right? And one thing I can promise you is that we do take care of each other."

He smiled at me, but I wasn't able to smile back at him. I was feeling something, a tingle in my fingers, that made me want to reach out and touch him, and I pulled myself close and wrapped an arm around his waist, resting my chin on his chest. He was very still. I could feel his halting breath.

"Jen, what are you…?"

"Do you mind if we sleep like this?"

I don't know how I managed to ask him that. I was never that forward. A silence followed my request. It was terrible, frightening. I closed my eyes, expecting the worst. But then he embraced me, too, got comfortable, and murmured, "No. Of course I don't mind."

Now I could breathe easy. One of my legs wove between his. I could feel his breath in my hair and his heartbeat against my cheek. His body was warm; my bare legs could feel the heat radiating from his sweatpants. Our skin wasn't touching, but it might as well have been. It was strange, but it was lovely, and I got gooseflesh when his hand moved up to my ribs and he caressed me distractedly with his thumb. I was a little embarrassed; I didn't know if he'd noticed how powerfully I reacted.

"Good night, Ross," I said, not wanting to talk again until the next morning. My vocal cords needed a rest. He told me good night, too. I could feel his lips against my hair.

I closed my eyes and tried to concentrate on the regular beating of his heart and hoped it would lull my own, which was still pulsating wildly.

And finally—I don't know how—I managed to fall asleep.

The next morning I put on some rock music, turned it up loud, and ran longer than usual. I was trying to cool myself down after waking up to find Ross's body and mine intertwined. I had told Shannon I just wanted to be his friend, and that had lasted less than half an hour. It was a disaster. It couldn't go on like this.

To get a little extra cardio in, I ran up the steps of the building, then stopped, closed my eyes, and tried to catch my breath. Once I was some-what confident I could pretend nothing had happened the night before—I mean, nothing had, right?—I opened the door and looked around inside. Sue was the only one awake. She was drinking a beer and eating peanut butter off a spoon. It was disgusting, but I tried to be friendly as I said, "I thought you usually had ice cream for breakfast."

"We're out," she replied as I poured myself a glass of water and drank. I could tell she was watching me. Finally she said something:

"You didn't like her, did you?"

"What?"

"That moron who came over last night. Lana. I can't stand her."

She was smiling—cruelly, but still, at least it was a smile.

"Honestly, I wasn't crazy about her," I admitted once I saw there was no one else there.

"People who act like they're all perfect are the absolute worst. And everyone else swallows it up and treats her like she's so special. Her coming over here has always been torture."

"For real," I said. "That dinner was the most boring thing I've ever done."

Sue looked at me sidelong and grinned. "You know what? You might not be so bad after all."

I wasn't sure how to take that, but I didn't have to worry about it for long, because she got up and walked to the sofa to finish her, um, "breakfast" on her own. I decided to take a shower. When I came out of the bathroom a little later wrapped in a towel, I found Ross in the hallway yawning. He gave me a once-over, and I tried to suppress my urge to take off running as I pulled up the towel to hide my cleavage and felt my palms starting to sweat.

"Good morning," he said. "The towel looks good on you. But if you feel like taking it off, be my guest."

We're just friends.

WE'RE JUST FRIENDS.

I couldn't force a smile, I was so nervous, so I just replied, "Good morning," and hurried past him. I could sense him turning around and watching me from behind, but I shut the door before the conversation could go any further.

I dressed and went to class, and fortunately, I didn't encounter any of my roommates on my way out. It was a long, boring day. I spent two hours in the library working on a group project. Half the group didn't show, and the other half was going insane trying to make sure everything was perfect. Plus I kept thinking about Ross. About the way he had looked at me that morning. And that made me so tense that by the end of the day I was exhausted.

On my way home, I found Mike smoking a cigarette and staring at the girls on campus, smiling at them and complimenting them and failing to get their attention. When he saw me, he said, "Look who it is! Funny how we keep running into each other. It's almost like it was destiny."

"Yeah, destiny," I said blandly.

"What's wrong, Jenna? Are you sad?" he said, putting on a fake frown.

"I'm tired," I corrected him.

"My brother's not taking good care of you?"

"Your brother treats me wonderfully. I'm actually headed to his place now. Probably you heard I'm going to be staying there awhile."

"I guess that means Lana's out?"

"I guess Lana's out," I said.

He laughed and made a clawing gesture before remarking, "I take it you didn't fall in love with her?"

"You could say that. So she used to live there?"

"Yeah, for a while. Then they broke up and she joined that sorority on the other side of campus." That made me feel worse, like I was taking someone else's place. I remembered how touchy-feely she'd been with Ross when she arrived. And the way Ross had held me the night before. Were they the same thing, or had last night meant something more? Had he liked touching her more than he'd liked touching me? They'd been together a long time. Comparatively, he and I barely knew each other. And that saddened me.

Mike continued, "I wouldn't worry about it, though. I always thought she was lame. I like you better. And I think my brother does, too."

A new doubt arose. "You don't think he invited me to stay with him just to replace her?"

"I wouldn't say that," he replied. "I mean, I don't really know the whole story of their breakup, what happened when she was in France or all that. And it's not like my brother and I talk about these things. You might have noticed he's not what you'd call wild about me. But anyway, I wouldn't sweat it. Now if you'll pardon me, I've got duties to attend to."

Just then, he turned toward a girl who had smiled at him and walked after her. I clenched my fists in frustration. My thoughts were driving me insane. I didn't know if the night before had meant too much or nothing at all. I wanted to cry, and I wasn't even sure why.

I got home and didn't need to even open the door to know that Lana was there. I found her standing in the middle of the living room in a slinky beige dress doing an impression that everyone was laughing at. They were having dinner. And no one had texted me. I felt like a complete idiot. Like someone who'd just been filling a hole until she got back. Everyone was in love with her. They had missed her. And now they didn't need me.

Will might have been an exception. Something about her seemed to grate on him. But he was obviously happy to see Naya enjoying herself, so I figured I couldn't count on him as an ally. Maybe I shouldn't have agreed to move in there. I barely knew my way around the place, and already I was starting to regret it.

"Hey, Jenna," Sue said, bringing me back to reality.

"Hey," I said, my voice a mere thread.

"We saved you something," Naya said, but to hell with that. I wasn't going to stay there with her around. No way. I threw my book bag to the floor with a thud and said, "Actually, I just wanted to drop off my things. I've got somewhere to be."

Will glanced at Ross, who looked down at the floor and told me, "Come on, stick around!"

"No can do," I replied. "Gotta go." I didn't give them time to change my mind. Out in the hall, I leaned against the wall and closed my eyes. I was an idiot. I had jumped into something, and now I had nowhere to go. My stomach was growling, but I'd have chosen starvation over sitting there listening to more of Lana's bullshit.

Before I could hit the elevator button, Ross's grandmother opened her door and smiled, almost as if she'd been waiting on me.

"Are you hungry?" she asked. I didn't know what to say. I stood there in silence until she finally prompted me, "Have you lost your voice?"

"Sorry, I just, uh…"

"Come in here. These hallways are freezing; you'll catch cold."

Her apartment had the same floor plan as Ross's. Just the furniture was older. And it was more orderly. On the kitchen bar she had a bowl of salad. On the TV was some gossip show.

"Is grilled chicken and salad OK for you?"

"Sounds great," I said. I was starving. Anything would have sounded great just then.

"Well, you just go ahead and take a seat." She served me a plate. The salad was delicious. We spent awhile watching TV together, with her laughing and sometimes looking over at me. When she was done, she asked me why I hadn't wanted to have dinner at Ross's. "They sure are laughing a lot. They must be having fun."

"Oh, they're having fun all right," I said.

"And you're not?"

I told her I didn't want to bother her with my problems, and she reminded me she had asked.

"The thing is, Ms. Ross…"

"Call me Agnes."

"Sorry, Agnes. I know it's stupid, but it makes me mad that they're having so much fun with her."

"With Lana? Why, dear?"

"I don't know. Like, for one thing, I don't understand half the stuff they're talking about. They keep telling jokes from when they were kids or when Ross used to go out with her, and they just leave me totally in the dark. And Naya used to be my roommate. She's supposed to be my friend, and now she's just slobbering all over Lana. Sue's the only one who doesn't seem just in love with her, and Sue, you know, has her own issues."

"So you're jealous?"

I hated that she had immediately drawn the same conclusion as Shannon. "I don't want to be jealous," I protested.

Agnes quickly responded. "Oh, but the problem is you think there's something wrong with that when it's actually totally natural."

I kept telling myself not to be jealous. *Don't be jealous, Don't be jealous, Don't be…* But that wasn't going to work. Agnes reached over, touched my shoulder, and said, "I know how you feel," which was weird, because even I didn't know how I felt. And then she hit the nail on the head. "But you're not a substitute for anyone."

I coughed, cleared my throat. She hadn't convinced me, but she'd touched me deeply.

"Listen," she went on, "if it makes you feel any better, I never cared for that girl. Especially not for my Jackie. She's not bad, but she's not right for him. Especially not after what she did…"

So it wasn't just Sue. My instincts were right. There was something wrong with that chick. "What did she do?" I hurried to ask.

Agnes started to explain, but then she said, "No, it's best if Jackie tells you. You're probably too embarrassed to ask him now, but soon enough you'll both figure things out and stop acting like you need to be embarrassed about your feelings. Now, would you like some dessert?"

I stayed there awhile longer, but she wouldn't reveal anything more about Ross, so we talked about the gossip show, which was one of my mother's favorites, too. Agnes was one of those people whose way of talking was so pleasant that even the dumbest thing in the world felt interesting. Time passed so quickly with her that I didn't realize until she started yawning that it was nearly midnight. She said, "Dear, if you don't mind, these old bones need a rest."

"Of course. Thanks for the dinner. And for the talk," I replied, standing up.

"It was a pleasure." She smiled. "Just hit the button to lock the door on the way out," she said.

I carried the dishes to the kitchen, and on my way out, I heard her calling to me one more time.

"Dear?"

"Yes?" I said.

She smiled enigmatically and said, "If my grandson asks, tell him you went to eat with a friend."

I walked outside, heard Lana's voice—that sweet, stupid voice—again, and composed myself before opening the door. I found everyone in the living room except for Sue. They all turned and said hello.

"How was the dinner?" Naya asked.

"Great," I replied.

Ross didn't look so pleased that I'd had a good time. Frowning and tapping his knee with one finger, he said, "Oh, yeah? Who'd you go with?"

Remembering Agnes's words, and noticing that Will was grinning, I started to find Ross's irritation amusing and said, "With a friend. Curtis. A guy from one of my classes."

At least there was a real Curtis. He was a good guy, in fact. Smart, a hard worker. Obviously we'd never gone out to dinner, though. An awkward silence followed, with Ross unable to stop staring at me, and to break it, I grabbed an unopened beer off the table and asked Will, "May I?"

"All yours," he responded.

As I opened it and took a sip, I noticed everyone was looking at me expectantly, and finally I said, "What?"

"Aren't you going to give us the details?" Naya asked. "I want to know everything. Is he nice? Is he handsome? What's he like? Do you like him? Are you going to tell your boyfriend about him?"

As Will told her not to be so gossipy, I looked over at Ross, whose mood was getting worse by the second. Lana said, "I didn't know you had a boyfriend!"

"Yeah." I felt more relaxed talking about Monty. I hated lying. "We probably won't see each other until December, though. He lives in the town where I'm from."

"It must be hard, spending so much time apart," Lana said.

"It is, but we still talk, so it's almost like he's around."

"I'll bet," Ross said bitterly. I finally caught his eye and I couldn't believe how angry he looked. He hadn't acted that way ever, not even the night before when Sue was trying so hard to get under his skin.

"They have an open relationship," Naya announced.

"Wow, what's that like?" Lana asked.

"Uh, it just means we can do whatever we want with whoever we want. But that doesn't change how much we matter to each other."

"Have you put it to the test?" Why was Lana being so nosy all of a sudden?

"No."

"Well, are you going to?"

I shrugged. Naya told me I should—maybe with the friend I'd had dinner with. I felt like I was under a microscope. Naya was grinning at me, Ross was clenching his teeth, and Will was looking around and trying to make sense of the situation. *At least Agnes would be proud of you*, I thought. Trying to break the awkward silence, Lana asked how my day had been. I would have loved to never speak to her again, but I didn't have many options for now, so I admitted it had been pretty dull. "I did run into Mike on my way home, though."

"Oh, Mike," Lana said. "I haven't seen him in ages." She smiled and looked at Ross as if expecting some reaction, but he just crinkled his beer can in his hand.

"Screw Mike," Naya said. "I want to get back to this Curtis. You didn't tell us anything. Do you like him? You're acting hella nervous, so I'm going to take that as a yes."

Just then, Ross stood so quickly the sofa seemed to rock under him and declared, "I'm going to bed." Without waiting for a response, he walked off. I wished I could go with him and tell him I'd been lying, but instead, I just stared at his perfect little blond ex.

"What about you, Lana?" I asked. "Have you got a boyfriend? You're so pretty…"

"Me? Thank you, but no. It's hard to find a decent man nowadays. Plus I'm always jetting around, you know. It's hard for a person like me to set down roots."

She was so nice to me, and still I couldn't stand her. I knew my attitude was cruel, but I couldn't help it. When she left, wishing everyone a good night, I knew it wouldn't be long before Will and Naya started making out, and to save myself the show, I decided to go to Ross's room. I found him there with his laptop in his lap. He didn't even look up at me.

"I've got to put on my pajamas," I said.

We'd made a deal. Whenever I needed to change, he'd step out into the hall. But this time, he didn't seem to care.

"Super," he murmured.

To hell with him, then. I'd change then and there. I turned around and undressed, and when I was ready, I got into bed and took out my contacts. I could see he was watching a video, but I didn't ask about it and he didn't explain. We remained there in silence until I fell asleep with him still playing around on his laptop.

8

THE DRUG SQUAD

When I was done with my exam, I was feeling rough…like really rough. I thought I'd done OK, but I couldn't focus. I had something on my mind and I'm sorry to say it wasn't Noam Chomsky and his damned universal grammar. I stepped outside, stared at the parking lot, felt sorry for myself, and took a breath. Then I walked to the light-rail stop. Before I reached it, I could sense someone was following me. Mike. Again. He smiled.

"I'm starting to worry you're following me," I said.

"How come you can't just be happy to see me?"

"Because you're depressing, and I'm depressed enough already."

He ignored my remark, which seemed to be his MO. Then I shook my head—I knew I shouldn't be so bitchy—and apologized. He was understanding.

"We all have bad days," he responded.

"And weeks," I said.

Because it had been a week now since Lana showed up on our doorstep. And things hadn't gotten any better. Ross and I were barely talking, and when we did, it was about stupid stuff: whose turn it was to make the bed, what time we'd be getting home. We were like strangers stuck in an elevator trying not to feel uncomfortable with each other.

"Are you going to Ross's?" he asked. "Me too. I'll tag along."

He spent the entire train ride picking at a sticker on the railing, so we didn't talk much. It wasn't until we were almost at the apartment that I asked him something I'd been wondering for some time.

"Mike, I was curious… Where exactly do you live?"

"I'm a free spirit. I sleep wherever I can."

"You don't have a home?"

"What for?"

"Like…to feel safe," I said. "So you don't have to worry about living on the street."

As I opened the door, I saw Sue in her chair reading a magazine. She waved at me, not at Mike, and Mike took out his tobacco and papers and started to roll a cigarette as he explained. "I've been on the street before. It's not so bad. But usually I find a girl to shack up with. And if not, there's always Ross. Or my parents."

I wished I could go through life feeling so relaxed.

"Excuse me, dumbass, but I don't know what you think you're doing." Sue interrupted him. Then she turned to me and said, "Tell him to stop."

I responded that everyone else in the house seemed to smoke, and she rolled her eyes and said, "That's not tobacco."

Mike pleaded with me, "Didn't you say you were having a bad week? Well, I've got the cure right here."

"Drugs!" I almost yelped. I didn't even dare to touch it. "Get it away from me!"

"It's not drugs-drugs," Mike said. "It's just a little weed."

"Isn't that illegal?" I cried. "Couldn't we go to jail for it?"

"Maybe in the nineteen-forties," Sue said. Then she walked over and told Mike, "I'll make a deal with you. You can smoke it here if you share with everyone."

"Are you crazy?" I shouted.

"Jesus, relax," Mike said. "Have you never broken the rules before?"

How many times had I heard that question as a teenager? From my sister, from my brothers, from friends. Then came a brief moment of reprieve. Then Monty started asking me the same thing. Were they right? No! I could be crazy when I wanted to. Couldn't I? Hell yes.

"Give me that," I said angrily.

Mike and Sue applauded when I flicked the lighter, lit the joint, and inhaled. It tasted strange, and the smoke burned my throat a little. I wanted to cough, but I tried to be tough and hold it in. I tried to pass it, but Mike and Sue found the scene so funny that they made me take two more hits. In ten minutes, we were all laughing like little children.

"Ross is going to be so pissed," Sue said, and Mike admitted that he'd never gotten high in his brother's apartment before. As they sat on the couch and I settled into an armchair, I looked up, my feet dangling off the edge. I can't say I felt good exactly. But I didn't feel bad. I was just...there.

"How is it, newbie?" Mike asked.

"Uh, nice..."

My voice sounded so weird! And that made me want to chuckle. I blinked, I felt relaxed, I almost felt like I was floating. I tried to focus on one point in the ceiling, and as I did so, I zoned out so much I forgot the rest of the world. My mind was completely blank until I started hearing a droning voice saying, "Hellooooo...?"

He laughed, I laughed with him, and I turned sideways on the chair, letting my head hang off and asking them, "You guys...why are you sitting on the ceiling?"

Mike suggested I needed another hit, which I took gladly, and then he asked me what had been up with me. "Didn't you say you were depressed or something?"

As I tried to pronounce the word *depressed*, Sue said lucidly, "She's depressed because she's jealous of Ross's ex."

"I am not!" I shouted. My indignation made them giggle, and then I had to giggle, too. But I struggled on. "The thing is just... Like, my sister was reminding me of how fucked up I was when I... Wait, what are we talking about again?"

"Your sister and your dark past," Sue said.

"Right... I was going to say, a few months ago, I had one of those... What do you call it? When you lose your shit and you stay that way for a while."

"Like a panic attack?" Sue asked.

"Yeah, one of those!"

"Why?" she and Mike asked in unison.

"You're going to laugh at me."

"We're already laughing at you," Sue said.

"So I found out my boyfriend, Monty, and my best friend, Nelle, had been sleeping together behind my back. For the first couple of months we were going out." There was a pause, and then everyone exploded, me included. I couldn't believe it! I had been so upset back then that I thought I wanted to die, and now I was laughing about it. And it had been a real panic attack. We'd gone to the doctor and everything. I couldn't see, I couldn't breathe, my legs were giving out. It was horrible. And now it might as well have never happened. I guess Mike was right about marijuana being my medicine.

"Your friend sounds like a bitch," Sue called out.

"Yeah," Mike said, belching. "And your boyfriend doesn't sound much better."

"You're right..." I mused, and Sue shouted, "Fuck them!"

"Fuck them!" we all chanted.

"I'm going to get some beers," Sue said. As I struggled to open mine and Mike and Sue poked fun at me, I heard the door open, though it sounded a million miles away. Ross entered, scowling, seeming to save the worst of his disapproval for me. And yet the only thing I could think was that I'd never seen him look so handsome.

"What the hell's going on here?" he asked his brother.

"What are you talking about, bro?" Mike asked and took a sip of his beer.

"You think you can just bring drugs into my house? You think I don't know what marijuana smells like?"

We couldn't stop giggling. Ross turned and looked at me, then back at the other two. "Did you get Jen high?"

Since they didn't answer, he came close and looked into my eyes. I smiled at him. He didn't smile back. He was pissed.

"We did it together," Sue said. "We're the drug squad!"

I tried to take a sip of my beer and spilled it down my shirtfront, and it startled me so much I fell out of the chair. As I stretched out on the floor, holding my stomach and trying to restrain my giggles, Ross took away my beer and said, "Jesus Christ, look at you." He grabbed my arm and pulled me up so fast that my stomach ached. I looked down at myself. I didn't see what the big deal was. I actually thought it was funny.

"Ross, chill out!" I said. Between cursing at his brother and reminding Sue that this was his apartment, he was trying to stand me up. But when he saw it wouldn't work, he wrapped his arm around my waist and lifted me up. Sue told him not to be a spoilsport, that they had some left for him, and the stare he shot back at her could have cut glass. I was up now but still wobbly, so I kept holding onto Ross's shoulders, but I admit there was an ulterior motive, too. He was so close to me that one of my feet was between his. He was looking at my soaked shirt and shaking his head. In my uninhibited state, I didn't mind. Flirtatiously, I told him, "Easy, big guy. My eyes are up here. And you know, I do have a boyfriend."

Jaw clenched, he said, "This isn't funny, Jen."

"It *is* a little funny." I reached up and tapped him on the tip of his nose.

Dragging me down the hall, he said, "You need to take off that wet shirt."

"I don't want to," I said, "I'm with my friends. You know what that's like, Ross, being friends with someone. Like you and me. We're just friends, right?"

He was getting steamy. But for some reason I just thought it was funny. "You aren't getting jealous, are you, Ross?"

"No, dammit," he said. "I just want you to take off that nasty shirt."

"Yeah, he does. To see what you're hiding under it," Mike shouted. He and Sue started chanting about Ross wanting to see my boobs until he finally shouted, "Enough!" Before I knew what was happening, he'd lifted me over his shoulder and was dragging me off to his room.

"Let me go!" I said. "I'm dizzy, and you're making it worse."

"Then you shouldn't have smoked that shit!" he said.

"It's a free country, Ross. I don't know why you think you can just barge in here and, uh…" He set me down and I grabbed his arm to keep from falling over and cracking my head. Then I realized I'd forgotten what I was saying, but I felt too indignant to shut up, so I continued. "And another thing: If you'd have come earlier, you could have had fun with us. I don't know why you're so bitter all of a sudden. You're acting like Sue. You should try to enjoy life. You've got lots of years ahead of you unless, like, a truck runs over you or something."

"Do you have anything on under this?" he asked.

"Look at it, Ross. It's a cheap piece of garbage. Of course I have something on under it. Otherwise it would itch."

"Fine. Lift up your arms."

"Yes, Captain." I chuckled.

I did as he said, and he lifted the sweatshirt over my head. I liked it. It almost felt like he was undressing me, especially when he brushed my hair back afterward. I was there in a sleeveless undershirt, chilly, and I rubbed my forearms. Ross tossed my sweater into the dirty clothes basket and looked back at me, clearing his throat and saying, "We ought to…"

But I cut him off. "I took off my sweater," I told him. "It's only fair that you take something off, too. That's called equality, and it's something we're all striving for nowadays."

I saw a mischievous gleam in his eyes as I rested both hands on his shoulders. The air seemed to get thicker. Especially once he grabbed me around the waist and his fingers touched a bit of exposed skin above my hips. My body temperature went sky-high. But then he closed his eyes and asked, "Jen, how much did you smoke?"

"A little too much," I admitted, edging closer to him.

"Don't do anything you'll regret tomorrow, Jen. Is it your first time?"

I was floored. How could he ask me that just then? But I was too stoned to think of anything snappy to say, so I answered honestly, "No, I'm not a virgin. I mean, technically I'm not. It's a long story, OK. The thing is…"

"I was asking if it was your first time smoking weed."

"Oh. Ha-ha. Yeah. Sorry. I thought you were getting pervy for a minute. I mean, not like I should be surprised. With that comment you made about me taking off my towel the other day, for example. Now that I think about it, you really are pervy!"

"Yeah, but I'm the sweet kind of pervert," he protested.

"Sure," I responded. "I'll give you that."

I guess he thought that was enough, because he let me go then and stepped back, and I hugged myself again to try to stay warm as he asked me what I wanted to wear. "It's kind of late," he said, "Maybe you just want to throw on your pajamas. Or you could go back to stealing my clothes. Even if you seem to have given that up, for some reason I wouldn't mind you explaining."

"Why do you care?" I asked.

"Because I do."

I narrowed my eyes. "It's just, you know…because we've been mad at each other, Ross. And so I thought you wouldn't like me using your stuff."

"*We* haven't been mad at each other. You're the one who's been acting weird for days now."

"Fine, then I'm mad, Ross."

"May I ask why?"

I sighed and fell back in bed. I wasn't in the mood to talk. I just wanted to lie back and relax. With him, if possible. Curled up together, if possible. I had liked it more than I'd been willing to admit to myself. Much more.

"Why did it take me so long to discover marijuana?" I asked.

"Because it's a drug. You shouldn't have even tried it. And I'm going to give Mike a piece of my mind about it."

"Mike's a good guy," I said. "Why do you dislike him so much? I mean I get he's not Mother Theresa or whatever, but he cares about you, right?"

His expression was cold. Calm, but not in the least amused. He even seemed to be gritting his teeth. I knew he didn't want to talk about it. At least not with me. After a few moments, he said, "Look, it's complicated."

"Sure. No worries. It's not my business. I get it."

"No," he responded. "It's not that I don't want to tell you, but…another time, you know? Preferably when you're not high."

He was crouched down looking for something, and for a second, I had the urge to jump on him, throw my arms around him, roll with him on the floor. But I didn't want to risk it. I said his name, and he looked up, and our eyes met, and I saw clearer than ever those brown irises with little green flecks around the pupils. I grinned.

"You OK?" he asked.

"You have very pretty eyes," I said.

I reached out and touched his chin, ran my finger up his jaw, felt the soft prickle of his three days' growth of beard.

"You could use a shave, though," I continued.

He grinned and said, "Thanks for the advice."

I wanted to touch his lips, but instead I traced a line down to his clavicle, uncertain whether he was tense or just holding his breath.

"I wanted to tell you something else, though," I said, my thoughts racing. "Have you ever dreamed something you weren't supposed to?"

He hesitated, then cleared his throat. "What, like, that I killed someone or something?"

"Not exactly."

"So...?"

I nearly told him. I was right there. But something stopped me. My survival instinct. So I faked a yawn and said, "Jeez, I'm tired." I know he didn't believe me, but he smiled at my attempt to throw him off and said gently, squeezing my knee, "No problem. I'll leave you alone so you can change."

The warmth from his hand stayed there long after he left. Lazily, I threw on a sweatshirt. Then I looked in the mirror, realized it was on backward, and took it off and turned it around. I had just pushed my head through the top when the door flew open. I rushed to cover my boobs, forgetting that I had on an undershirt, but it didn't matter. It was just Naya. I pulled the shirt the rest of the way down as she said, with a serious look on her face, "You and I need to talk."

"Now? I was just about to go eat something."

She sat on the bed and patted the place beside her, pinning me with her eyes. I sighed and sat down. The weed had pretty much worn off, I felt groggy, and I thought I heard my stomach rumbling.

"Is this going to take long?" I asked. "I'm..."

"I know, you're hungry. Whatever. Let's go get a bite. Otherwise you probably won't listen to me."

She grabbed my hand and guided me down the hall. Mike and Sue were still in the living room. Will and Ross were now there, too. Everyone watched me as I took out the chocolate bar Ross had bought. He didn't seem to mind.

"Hey, I'm hungry, too," Mike shouted. But then everyone scowled at him and he said, "Never mind. I forgot I'm on a diet. Starting today."

I flopped down with my head in Ross's lap and Naya sat with Will. Ross reminded me that I hadn't wanted to buy the chocolate, that he'd had to twist my arm. And I reminded him that I'd had to practically force him to take me to the grocery store. "So we're even," I said, and he grinned.

Unsteadily, Mike stood, took a look at his phone, and said he had to go. Then he looked at Sue and me and added, "Feel free to call whenever you like. I'm always up to do it again."

We nodded, and as soon as he was gone, everyone turned to me except for Sue, who broke off a piece of my chocolate and started chewing it.

"You want to tell us what the hell's been going on this week?" Naya asked.

"Wow! Why don't you leave her in peace?" Sue asked.

"I'm sorry," Ross butted in, "but do you want to tell me when you two stopped hating each other and became super besties?"

"When we both realized how lame you are," Sue said, and before I could dissociate myself from her, I started laughing.

"Don't listen to her," I said. "Have a piece of chocolate. It's a peace offering."

"That's *my* chocolate," he replied.

"It's all I've got, though, I said." He accepted, and I watched almost hypnotized as he broke a piece off and tossed it in his mouth.

"I'm sorry, can we get back to the subject?" Naya asked.

"I literally don't know what you're talking about," I said. Feeling uncomfortable, I looked over at Will, hoping he would rescue me. In that intuitive way of his, he understood perfectly and stood, pushing Naya's legs off of him and saying, "I'm going to grab a smoke. Jenna, why don't you come with me. I feel like you could use the fresh air."

I dropped what was left of the chocolate on the couch between Sue and Ross, where they fought over it, and followed Will out to the roof, where he lit a cigarette, stuck it in the corner of his mouth, and eyed me up warily. Digging his hands into his pockets, he finally said, "Look, I'm assuming you're not up here for the views. You've got something to tell me. So spit it out."

He was right. The air was helping to clear my head, though. The problem was, what I had in my head wasn't something I necessarily wanted to let out. So I hemmed and hawed and he interrupted my grunts with the question, "Are you going to the party Saturday?"

"What party?"

"Lana's party. She invited you."

"Oh, yeah. Probably not."

He grinned and said, "You know, it's actually funny how uncomfortable she makes you."

"She doesn't make me feel uncomfortable!"

"What is it, then?"

"I can't stand her!"

OK, now maybe I was being a little too sincere. But Will didn't seem alarmed. He just laughed and shook his head. "Lord, you've been cranky these past few days. At any rate, I'm sad to inform you that everyone adores Lana. Including Ross."

"I know," I responded. "Little Miss Perfect. Perfect grades, perfect hair, perfect smile. Sorry, I should shut up. I realize she's your friend."

"She's not, actually. I've never been especially crazy about Lana. But since Ross and Naya care so much about her, I've always tried to be nice to her. Our personalities kind of clash. She needs way too much attention, and that gets on my nerves. Plus, after what she did to Ross, I prefer to keep my distance."

I worried maybe he was just putting up with me, too, but I was glad he'd noticed she was an attention hog. I couldn't agree more. I wondered if

I should ask him what it was she had done to Ross. Probably he wouldn't tell me. But still.

Putting on my best innocent voice, I said, "What was it then?"

"He never told you?"

"I never asked."

"Well, if I don't tell you, I guess you'll just ask Naya, and she can't keep her mouth closed. Besides, everyone on campus knows. So this is what happened. She and Ross were friends, right? For a pretty long time, since high school. Actually the four of us were always together. I really think they started going out because they felt pushed aside when Naya and I hooked up. I never really believed they were in love. Especially not Ross. But they stuck with it. There was a problem, though. Lana loves to travel. She always did. Her parents have money, and there's nothing they like better than telling their rich friends that their daughter is in Switzerland or whatever. So she was always vanishing for weeks on end and wouldn't even call."

"Seriously?" I said. I was dying to hear the rest of it, and it felt good to have a new reason to hate her. Something that made her a little less perfect.

"Seriously," Will replied. "At first, he would try to call her. I don't think it was because he loved her so much; I think he just felt it was the right thing to do. He was busy, he was working on short films and taking classes and stuff, but he had a sense of responsibility. Eventually, though, he got the hint, and it reached a point where they'd go a month without talking. And weirdly, he didn't seem to miss her at all. And that was when Lana started to realize what she was losing out on. She's one of those chicks where she wants to be chased and she likes playing hard to get, but when you forget about her, she loses her mind and gets obsessed. So she comes back, she apologizes; of course Ross accepts her apologies. That's just Ross. He's too good to hold a grudge."

"So how did things go south?"

Will shook his head. "Well, they basically had this routine, and things had been that way forever: She'd go away, she'd meet some guy, they'd hook up, then she'd come home a few weeks later and Ross would be there for her. He never reproached her. He just told her that if she wanted to be with someone else, she should say so, and if she wanted to be with him, then she needed to stop talking to those other guys."

I couldn't believe his attitude had been so relaxed. When I had found out about Nelle and Monty, I'd wanted to die. It was basically the same thing, but I guess I was more sensitive.

"You can only do that so many times, though, right?" Will went on. "Then the person's feelings for you start to change. And I think Ross just didn't need her anymore. He'd gotten used to living without her. When he bought this place, he didn't even tell her. He ignored her, focused on his studies, and tried to earn a little money on the side. When Lana found out what he had here, she wanted to come live with us. But Ross said no. He wouldn't even let her sleep here. That was the beginning of the end."

That didn't sound like whatever Mike had hinted at, but I decided not to overthink it.

"Lana lost her shit," Will said. "She started acting like a child. She kept calling Ross, texting him, asking him if he was sleeping around... Ross got tired of it. And Ross is a patient man. But he just didn't feel anything for her anymore. If he ever did, which I'm also not sure of. So he told her they could be friends, but that was it. I remember when she told him she was moving to the sorority house, which is where she's still living now. She kept pushing him to get back together, and he finally had to get nasty with her. So she decided to get her revenge and do something that would hurt him. And I mean hurt him really bad."

"And that was...?"

"She slept with Mike. It was a low blow. Especially because it had happened before. Ross has only ever had two girlfriends, and he fell for Lana because she was basically a carbon copy of the first one. And that first one actually left him for Mike. He was fucked up over it. Not so much because of the chick but because of his brother. And then it happens again. So I guess you understand now why they don't get along so great."

"But…how could Mike do that to his own brother?" I asked.

"Mike isn't like Ross. He makes it the point of his life to get under other people's skin. And he's felt inferior to Ross forever. In their family, especially, that was a big issue. He's always been treated like the one with no talent. So for him, it was like an achievement to take Ross's girlfriend, a way of saying *Look, I'm just as good as you.* You must have noticed how flirty Mike is with you when Ross is around."

I got it now. I got why Mike made so many stupid comments to me, and I got why Ross always talked down to him. Maybe Ross and I weren't a couple, but there was something personal at stake there. Just seeing me with Ross meant there was a competition there for Mike. I hated that. I frowned and said, "Poor Ross."

"I know," Will replied.

"How can he even still speak to the two of them? How can he let them into his home?"

Will shrugged. "He's just not that guy. He's too nice for his own good."

"Who on earth would leave Ross for Mike? Ross is perfect."

"I get the sense that he thinks you're perfect, too."

I felt the blood rush into my head as Will smiled at me knowingly. I wanted to change the subject, but couldn't think of how. And finally, Will took mercy on me.

"Shoot straight with me," he said. "The way you are with Lana… That has to go deep. Why do you hate her so much? Does she remind you of someone?"

"Huh?" I said, coming back to reality, and then as his words sank in, I told him she reminded me of Nelle. "I know it's weird, because Nelle's supposed to be my friend, but it's complicated. She's the same as Lana: perfect, tall, pretty, smart, athletic, good at everything, easily gets the hottest guys. I've always felt inferior next to her. And when I started going out with Monty, she acted all happy for me. For years, I'd been daydreaming about Monty. Him going out with me… It just didn't seem real. There were months when I felt like the luckiest girl in the world. And then…"

I took a deep breath. It was hard to admit it out loud without crying. Even now I could remember the pressure in my chest, the cold sweat… *Focus*, I told myself, *Focus*. "And then I found out she and Monty had been sleeping together behind my back for two months straight."

Will hesitantly put a hand on my shoulder.

"When I found out," I told him, "it was a complete slap in the face. I trusted them so much. I'd have put my life on the line for them. And so I had this panic attack. That probably makes it sound like I'm a head case or whatever, but…it was a trust thing, you know? It wasn't just the fact that they had done it. It was that they'd betrayed me when that was the first time in my life I'd ever felt special. Try and imagine… I've got four siblings, right? I'm the youngest, and I was always the last in everything. Monty was the first person who ever chose me because I was me. And Nelle could have had anyone. Anyone! But she had to be with Monty."

I paused, and Will told me, "Whatever you say, the thing about being crazy is just bullshit, Jenna. We all react the way we react. That's how human nature is. And what you went through would have been hard for anybody. Did you forgive them?"

"I felt like if I didn't, I'd be all alone. She was my only friend and he was the only guy who had ever been interested in me."

"Jenna, there would have been others. I mean, you're still a teenager."

"Yeah, but at the time, it felt like the end of the world… So yeah, I forgave them. And I guess they haven't really talked since then. We certainly haven't all hung out together. I think Monty saw the consequences of what he'd done. I don't think he'd make the same mistake again. But at the same time, he's been acting weird. Since I left, you know. He hardly calls me. He just sends me a text once in a while. When we do talk, we fight. As for Nelle, I saw her my last day at home and she was crying and acting all sad. But she's ignored me ever since. I don't want to think it's happened again… And now Lana's here and she reminds me of that whole situation. And I feel terrible. I know I've been taking my frustrations out on Ross and on you and Naya. And I'm sorry. You don't deserve it."

Will was a good listener, and he took his time thinking over what I'd said. Then he responded, "I've never had to deal with anyone cheating on me. And certainty not with my best friend. I can't imagine how I'd feel if Naya and Ross… I mean, it's hard to even picture. They're like brother and sister. But anyway. If I were you, I'd talk to them. Apologize, maybe. They're confused. Neither of them understands what's going on."

"I don't even know what's going on myself," I said.

"Maybe you should go to Lana's party on Saturday and try to make up with them."

"You're right," I replied.

"I always am."

I sighed and said, "OK, to hell with it. I'll go."

9

LANA'S PARTY

"How much longer are you going to be?" Sue asked, banging on the bathroom door.

"Just a minute," I said, touching up my red lipstick.

I looked at myself in the mirror. I was wearing a short black dress Monty had given me a long time ago. That had been weird for him. He wasn't the kind of guy you'd call thoughtful. He had texted and asked me what I was doing that night, and I'd lied and told him I was staying in because I'd have felt weird if he'd asked me to send him a photo from the party and had seen me there wearing the dress. I smoothed out the fabric with my hands, pulled up my favorite black tights, wiped a spot off my midheel leather boots. I couldn't do high heels without putting my life in danger.

As for my makeup… I'd put it on and taken it off three times, and I was only getting less and less secure about it. I had my doubts about this new lipstick, but if I wiped it off and tried another one, I ran the risk of Sue knocking down the door and killing me. So I let my hair down and took a breath.

I was ready. Ready as I'd ever be.

So why did I feel so bad? Even with my low self-esteem, I could see I looked pretty good. I tossed the lipstick in my bag. It was time to go. No more dillydallying.

"Are you…?"

I threw the door open before Sue could finish and found her standing there looking the same as ever. The only difference was that her hair was pulled back. In case she got too drunk and had to puke, I imagined.

"You needed all that time just for that?" she said.

"Thanks for the compliment," I said.

"You deserve it." I could always rely on Sue to make me feel even worse when I was in a bad mood. The two of us walked to the living room, where Ross and Will were sitting on the couch bored, arguing about when Naya would be ready. Will froze when he saw me and said, "Damn, Jenna, you look amazing."

"You, too, Will. Naya's going to be drooling all over herself."

Sue cleared her throat and said, "What about me?"

"I thought you didn't like people to talk to you," Will replied.

"You're right," she said. "Can we go now?"

I could see Ross had been staring, and I had the sense that maybe he and Will had been talking about me. For a moment, his eyes were glassy; then he blinked several times and hopped up, clearly avoiding my gaze. Was he angry about something? The way he looked at Will led me to think so. As did the way he walked past me without a word, grabbed the keys, and just assumed all of us would follow him out.

He rushed into the elevator, and I squeezed in beside him. On the mirrored wall, I caught him checking me out. Every inch of me, it seemed. From head to toe.

Will yelled, "Time to get drunk!"

"How exciting," Ross replied. "Everyone gets to get wasted but me, because I have to drive."

"It's going to be a long night for you," I said.

"Whatever."

He walked to the car and got in the driver's seat, and I hopped in the passenger side while Will called Naya, telling her we were coming to pick her up. When we parked, she wasn't out front, so Will had to go up and get her. The three of us stayed behind listening to music until Sue grunted with frustration and said, "This is enough. It's been more than five minutes. If I catch them fucking, I'll kill both of them."

She jumped out and ran inside, and Ross and I sat there in silent tension. Which was par for the course for us lately. It felt like one of us wanted to say something, but neither of us did. This had been going on for a while. I would look at my shoes. He would look at me. And the sensation wouldn't let up. I was tapping my fingers on my knees and looked up to see Ross watching me. I smiled, then blushed, then looked away, then thought for a fleeting second what it would feel like if it was his hand on my leg instead of mine, the same way he had touched me before. I wondered if we would ever sleep together cuddled up again, if that comfort we'd felt with each other would return.

Was I dreaming, or was it hot in that car?

"Is the heat on or something?" I asked.

"No. I can turn it on if you're cold."

No, I was hot enough already. I closed my eyes and tried to calm myself down as he offered me his jacket. Put on something that smelled like him? Feel the same fabric touch me that had touched him? I wanted to, but I shook my head. That jacket was black leather. I'd never seen him in it before. It was sexy, and the fact that he'd done nothing to his hair, that it was sticking out in all directions, made him even sexier to me, because it was one hundred percent him. Our eyes met, and I forced out a sentence, "They're taking their time."

He grinned and said, "It sure seems like it."

The situation was so uncomfortable, I felt like my jaw was wired shut even though all I wanted was to fill that unbearable silence. Everything I thought of saying would only make the weirdness between us worse. So I was grateful when he finally declared, "I've never seen you in a dress before."

Thank God. A neutral subject.

"Yeah. Fall and winter, you know, they're not really the season. But since it was a party, you know..."

"I'll have to make sure you get invited to more parties," he interrupted me.

As I looked up to see him grinning, I asked myself for the first time how many of those jokes of his were really jokes. Because even if he seemed relaxed, he hadn't stopped staring at me, and that made me feel utterly on edge.

"It's actually the first time I've worn it," I said. "Mon—I mean, Mom gave it to me. I've never seen you in a leather jacket, either."

"I used to wear it in high school."

"So you were a classic bad boy, huh?"

"I wouldn't want you to think that," he said.

"Change my mind, then. Tell me what you were like. Did you talk back to your teachers? Did you go out with all the girls? Did you get in trouble? Were you in lots of fights?"

He smiled like a little angel. "I didn't talk back to my teachers, I'll have you know."

"Oh, so it was only girls, problems, and fights? Funny, you don't really look the type."

"And why not?" he asked.

"I don't know. You're just so..." I cut myself short when I realized I was about to say *wonderful*. Thank goodness I stopped myself just in time. "So calm."

"I wish you could ask my parents what I was like back then," he responded. "I don't think 'calm' is the first word that would come into their minds. I ran my dad's car into a wall one time and totaled it."

"Are you serious? Did you get hurt?"

"Well, let me correct myself. The car ran itself into the wall, technically. I wasn't inside. I had just turned sixteen and I wanted to impress my friends, so I took Dad's fancy, mega-expensive sportscar to pick them up and we parked on a slight hill. I accidentally left it in neutral when we got out, and we didn't notice anything at first. But then it started rolling and we weren't strong enough to stop it. We just had to stand aside and watch the disaster. Dad lost his mind. He sent me to this military camp the whole summer with all these juvenile delinquents. The camp counselors were total psychos who made us exercise out in the sun all day. I did come back with abs, though."

"And to think I got pissed the time my parents took away my phone."

"Wow. That's harsh. What did you do?" he asked.

"Listen: if I tell you, you can never, ever tell anyone else. And you can't make fun of me for it. Jesus, I can't believe I'm even admitting this. Well, whatever. I was fifteen years old, OK? And there was this guy I liked, an older guy. I think he was seventeen. Really, really handsome…"

"Don't make me jealous, now!" he interrupted.

"And the thing was…I wanted to do something to get him to like me. But I was still too scared to really try anything physically. So I was flirting with him and stuff, and uh, one day he sent me a photo of, like, his…"

"His dick?" Ross asked. I felt myself turning bright red as I said yes and then I finished the story. "And so I asked my friend Nelle, who had already lost her virginity, what to do, and she told me I had to send him something back, and so I… Well, I started to, but my brother Spencer caught me before I could."

He was dumbstruck. I had taken for granted that he'd laugh in my face. But he just said, "Wow. So your own brother caught you naked."

"Not quite naked. Just topless. And he tore my phone out of my hands and started shouting at me while I threw my shirt on in a rush. Mom heard us, and of course Spencer told her everything. They took my phone for a month. And my other brothers, the twins, found out, too, and they were in the same class as the poor guy. They're pretty, um, forward, and I think they made it clear to him he was not to have any further contact with me."

Ross laughed and said, "I can't believe it."

"My first romantic failure," I murmured.

"It's better than my camp story."

"You promised you'd never tell, Ross. If Naya comes up to me joking about it, I'll know it was you and there will be hell to pay…" I went to give him a friendly slap, and he caught my wrist.

"I won't tell. I *will* make fun of you for it for the rest of your life. Anyway, you shouldn't complain so much about your love life. I'm sure if you'd sent the damn photo, it would have gotten around your school, and you'd probably have way more guys than that one dude and Mason hot on your heels."

"His name's Monty, not Mason. And there were other guys who were into me. Worse ones, I'm sad to say."

"Worse than Mason? Do tell!"

"I said his name's Monty! Anyway, there was this guy who came a little after my sexting story, when I was sixteen. He was my first kiss. It was gross. He slobbered so much, his tongue felt like a snail. Don't laugh! And to make things worse, he tried to feel me up, and he clearly thought he was a total player, and I couldn't stop laughing. I'm super-ticklish, you know. The worst part was when he tried to take off my bra. I couldn't stop squirming and it made him super mad."

"Poor guy," Ross said, still holding my wrist, which I'd tried and failed to pull away from him. "He was probably traumatized."

"It's not my fault I'm ticklish."

"I'll bet he's never had the courage to try to take off a girl's bra since. I wonder if you're still that ticklish."

In a panic, I shouted, "I am, b-b-but…" I twisted, trying to get away, but I was trapped in the car. His finger dug deep into one of my ribs. "Ross! Stop! Please!"

We were locked in a struggle. I couldn't stop writhing and giggling as I swore at him, trying to get him to stop, but he was having the time of his life. "Stop or I'll hit you!" I shouted. He didn't pay any attention. Finally I managed to trap one of his hands, but the other one was still free. I pulled my legs up and flopped them in his lap, trying to stop his other arm, but it was useless. He kept torturing me.

"Stop! Stop! Please!"

"Wow, you really are ticklish," he said.

"Hell yes I am, asshole!"

"Easy, Jen, you don't have to insult me. I was just checking."

I noticed where his hands had stopped: one on my stomach, the other on my thigh, just where the hem of my dress ended. I got gooseflesh when I realized he was rubbing me softly. I don't think he realized it. And the silence that embraced us then was different from before, with us so close and with the tension finally broken. I had almost forgotten the rest of the world existed when he lurched back and turned around. I didn't know why he was being so stiff all of a sudden until I looked back and saw Will, Sue, and Naya getting in the back. I pulled my legs back, sat up straight, and adjusted my dress.

"I hope we aren't interrupting something," Naya said with a grin.

Ross started the car with a smile and ignored her, instead asking, "What took you so long?"

"She didn't know what to wear," Sue said.

Naya announced that she'd wanted to look cute, and giving her a smug look, Ross asked, "You call that cute?" She leaned in between us and said,

"Jack Ross, I'd like to remind you I know some very embarrassing stories from your childhood. And if you don't want them to come out, you'll change your attitude about my dress right now."

"Don't worry about him," Will said. "He's got no taste. You look gorgeous."

They kissed, and Sue pretended to be vomiting.

When we parked, I looked at the enormous house with my jaw hanging open. "This is a sorority house?" I said. "It looks like a museum." The vestibule was empty when we walked inside, and it wasn't until we'd climbed the marble staircase that we could hear the music. We found people dancing and drinking in the hallway, but Ross walked past them to a door that led into a packed ballroom. It must have been soundproof because we had barely heard any noise coming from it before we opened the door. There was a bar with a bartender, an ice fountain, everything. I would probably have appreciated how impressive it was if it wasn't in Lana's honor.

Will and Ross waved and said hi to people as we ordered our drinks. Sue, well…what would you expect? Even after two years there, she didn't seem to have many friends. I got a beer and looked around, taking a deep breath and feeling worried that everyone could tell I didn't belong there. But I'm not sure why I felt so insecure. They were probably just trying to have fun and hadn't given me a second thought.

Ross joked, "Why are you glancing around so much? Trying to figure out who to send a picture of your boobs to?"

I went to slap him, but before I could, I heard that annoying voice shouting, "Babe!" and there Lana was, interrupting us. *Babe?* Were we really starting with that shit again? He smiled at her faintly and she threw herself—literally threw herself—at him. I limited myself to taking a sip of beer while she squeezed him. Finally, Ross pushed her away, visibly uncomfortable.

"I'm so happy you came! And you wore my favorite jacket! I can still remember the day I gave it to you. You used to look so sexy in it in high school..."

"Yeah," Ross responded shyly, "it's just the first thing I threw on..."

New rule: From now on, leather jackets were out.

"Jenna!" she then shouted, and gave me one of those weird hugs where you don't really touch the person, you just sort of pat them on the back. "I wasn't sure if you'd come."

"I wouldn't miss it for the world," I mumbled.

I'd told myself I'd be nice to her. I'd have to see her if I was going to live with Ross. And she'd never shown the least bit of meanness to me. She didn't deserve to be treated this way. But being nice to her was an uphill struggle.

"This place is huge," I told her, just to say something.

"Once you've lived here for a while, it doesn't feel like it," she said. "But yeah, we've got everything: a library, a common room, two kitchens, a game room, and on the top floor are all the bedrooms. Nobody can go up there though. Maybe to one of the balconies, I don't know, but we tried to lock everything so no one will go in there and break something. Anyway, Ross, you should come with me for a sec. There's a ton of people from high school, and they all said they're dying to see the two of us."

The two of us? OK, I was over this. "I just saw a guy from one of my classes," I said, "I'm going to go say hi." It was a lie, but I needed a break from this. Lana smiled, of course, and dragged Ross off into the crowd. Surprise! There I was alone again. I walked over to the window, looked out, and saw the staircase that led down to the pool. It must have been heated because there were people swimming in it despite the cold. That seemed weird to me, but I guessed it was one of those things rich people did. I felt a hand on my shoulder and saw it was Will. He told me, "Stay here a sec. I'm going to go get a drink." He must have remembered I'd told him I would make up with Naya. She looked happy and asked, "Don't you think this sorority house is amazing!"

"It's bigger than my high school," I said. "But listen, I need to tell you something. I wanted to apologize for…you know…just for being weird with everyone this week. Especially with you."

"Jenna, you don't even need to mention it."

"I'm serious. It's a bad habit of mine. I get upset and I take it out on people, and it's not right. You don't deserve that."

"Listen, you've got your reasons," she said. "I'd have felt pushed aside too if I was you and someone like Lana showed up. And we should have tried to make sure you felt welcome despite her. Anyway, I couldn't be upset with you. I still owe you big time for the night with the necklace. If you and Ross hadn't shown up, I'd probably never have gotten it back."

"What was the story with that, anyway?" I asked. "I mean, this chick invites you over and then treats you like that?"

She tried to protest that it was a long story, but I told her I had time, and she began. "Back in high school, like I said, Will, Ross, Lana, and me were like *the* group. We were always together. But Lana started to feel like kind of a drag to me. She's so perfect, right? Not that I don't like her, but… being her friend is like constantly being in her shadow. And so I got this idea that I wanted to hang out with this other, more popular group of girls. One of them was the chick who invited me to the party. And she basically said if I wanted to be their friend, I'd need to run errands for them, carry their backpacks, do their homework, all that kind of stuff. And I went along with it! And that same girl, one day she threw her food in the trash and told me I had to pick it out and eat it if I wanted to hang out with her. And that was the end of my social climbing. After that, they all started bullying me. Especially about my parents' divorce."

"So you went back to Will, Ross, and Lana?" I asked.

"More or less. Will always stood up for me. For Chris, too. Chris was older, but people picked on him a lot. Ross was there for us, too. Lana, though… She was always just so stuck up her own ass that it's like she didn't even realize we existed, really."

Just then we saw Lana emerge from the crowd, hanging on Ross's arm while they talked to what I assumed were their friends.

"The girl who stole my necklace changed schools, so I didn't even think about her again till the party the other day. I actually thought she'd changed and that she was going to say she was sorry or something. But she made me feel like I was a stupid fifteen-year-old again. You know, I even changed some of my classes here to avoid running into her and her friends. And it was sort of lucky because one of the classes I added was in psychology, and it talked about dysfunctional families, and I think I might actually major in it. That way when I grow up, I can help out people with the same problems I had when I was a kid."

"That's really impressive," I said, and we gave each other a hug.

"Now that I've told you my tragic life story, let's go get drunk till sunup!"

I did drink with her, but not enough to get drunk. It's just not a feeling I like. Two beers were good for me. After that, I went out with her onto the dance floor and hopped and spun and turned like an idiot. But there were so many people there that nobody cared. Naya's friends joined us. They were cool, and it was a perfect night until I started getting overheated. I left Naya dancing with Will and walked off toward an open window, where I took a couple of deep breaths and let the wind blow on my face and down my neckline.

"Are you hot?" Lana asked. She'd come over without my noticing.

"I've been out there for almost two hours," I said, pointing at the crowd. "That's a lot for anyone."

"I try to never go out there. I'm so short, I'm worried people won't see me and I'll get trampled."

I doubted she ever went unnoticed anywhere, but whatever.

"You like the party?" she asked.

"It's great. It must be an amazing feeling, knowing this whole thing is for you."

"It's not, though. Not really. It's just an excuse for people to drink. I don't even know half these people."

"Did you lose Ross?" I said.

"He's off smoking with Will." She rolled her eyes. I was out of things to say, and I stared down at my boots, and then she confessed in the same bubbly tone as always, "You know, I was actually nervous to meet you."

"*You* were nervous to meet *me*?"

That made me feel better. Maybe she was nice. Maybe I had been a little bit of a bitch to her.

"Yeah! I mean, Naya had told me Ross had brought this girl home and everyone was crazy about her. If I'm totally honest with you, whenever something has to do with Ross, I get a little worked up. I remember thinking, 'What will I do if I come over and I find out he's sleeping with a chick that's hotter than me?' But then I met you and…well, I'm not worried about that anymore."

Wait… Did she just insult me? I was almost unsure because her tone of voice hadn't changed one bit. But then she continued. "Like, really, I don't even know what you're doing here. I invited you to be nice or whatever. I didn't actually think you'd show up. I definitely didn't think you'd try to act like you were my friend. But whatever. You're here now. I guess I'll just have to deal with it."

She took a sip of her cocktail with her innocent little smile.

"What the hell?" I asked. "You were nice to me before."

"Yeah, I *was*. It's not like I had a choice. Ross is crazy about you. If I'd been nasty to you, he wouldn't let me in the door. So I keep up the nice girl act when he's around. It's easy, like I said. I've met you; you're nothing to get worked up over."

"To think that I was just beating myself up for not giving you a chance," I said.

"You do whatever you want, but stay away from my boyfriend."

"He's not your boyfriend," I said, starting to get pissed off. "You made that evident when you slept with his brother."

She pursed her lips, then grinned. "Look, I didn't want to be mean, but take a look at yourself. Then take a look at me. If you try to take what's mine, you're only going to humiliate yourself. You don't know anything about Ross. I can promise you that. I mean it. Not a damn thing."

That had hurt. She reminded me of Nelle. I felt a knot in my throat and stepped back, bumping into someone who hugged me from behind. I knew that scent. I didn't even need to turn around.

"Look who it is," Ross said. "What were y'all talking about?"

Even with his lips close to my ear, I couldn't cool down. Lana glared at me before telling him, "I was just letting Jenna know how pretty I thought her dress was."

"I sure like looking at it," he replied.

How could a person be so fake? I wondered. I hated her. I couldn't be in the same room with her. I peeled Ross's arms off of me and he looked at me, surprised.

"I've got to go," I said. "But don't worry, I'll get an Uber."

He turned to Lana for a second and then followed me. I tried to ignore him as I threw open the nearest door and emerged into a hallway. The building was so big that I didn't know where to go. I turned left and walked as quickly as I could, but soon Ross caught up with me.

"Where are you going?" he asked, turning around and walking backward so he could face me.

"Away," I said, on the verge of tears. "I don't even know why the hell I came."

"Jen, wait. Weren't you having fun with Naya? I saw you earlier and you looked fine. What happened? What did she say to you? What did she do?"

I couldn't bring myself to say, so I kept walking until I got frustrated and said, "How the hell do you get out of here?"

"I know the way," Ross said, "but I'm not going to tell you until you're honest with me." I opened a door that led to a balcony, and I gave up, throwing myself down on one of the big white deck chairs. Ross shut the door behind us and joined me.

"Ross," I told him, weeping, "I don't want to sabotage your relationship."

"Are you talking about Lana?" he asked. "Because if so, there is no relationship."

"Oh yeah? Did you tell her that?"

"What did she say to you?"

"Why did you even invite me here, Ross? You must know how she is. Is it fun for you, throwing me to the wolves like that? Because you had to know how she'd treat me."

Great. Now I was crying like a child. How pathetic. I wiped my face. I've always hated crying in public. And doing it in front of Ross was just shameful. Worst of all, it wasn't just him, or just Lana. It was Nelle, and Monty, and just the whole way people treated me. Why did I always have to be number two?

"I don't know, Jen. I thought… I guess I thought she'd changed. She seemed like she had."

"She thinks I'm just a shitty substitute for her. And that's what I feel like. You just missed her. That's why you were so ready to take me in."

"Did she say that to you?"

"She didn't need to. It's obvious. I may not be as hot as her, but I'm not stupid."

He looked almost disappointed as he said, "If you think you're a substitute for her, that's your own issue, something that's in your head. I'm not lying to you, Jen. Maybe you think so, but you're wrong. I invited you in because I knew right away something was special about you. And if you think I missed her after she slept with my brother to get my attention, I'm sorry, but I just don't know what to tell you."

I was shocked. I thought he'd never bring that up. And certainly not that directly.

"I know you know," he continued, "so you don't have to act otherwise. Everybody knows. I'm used to it." He shook his head. "I don't like Lana, OK? I never did like her. She was fine in high school, she was cool she was someone to have fun with. But going out with her was a mistake. It was one of those things I did just because. You know what's funny? I wasn't even upset when she slept with Mike! I mean I was, but I wasn't jealous. I didn't really feel like I'd lost anything."

I looked down into my hands and between my knees, then tried to joke, "If you told her that, maybe you'd knock her off her pedestal a bit."

"Just ignore her," he said.

"It's hard to after what she said to me."

"Then listen to me instead."

I bit my lower lip. What was I doing? I didn't even have the right to ask him for anything. He was just my friend. And there I was acting like a jealous girlfriend.

"You know she still has feelings for you," I remarked. "It's obvious."

"Lana's never had feelings for me. She's just used to everyone fawning over her and she can't stand it if they stop even for five seconds."

"And I take it that's not what you're into."

"Not with her, anyway," he responded. "With you it might be a different story."

I gave him a friendly nudge on the shoulder. "Do you really think Lana is being so nasty just to get what she wants?" I asked. "That it's not about her being in love with you or whatever?"

"I don't think it. I know it."

"How could you go out with someone like that?"

"Jen, it was just something that… It's like I was supposed to be with her. To tell the truth, a lot of it's Naya's fault. She's the one who first got on this kick about how Lana was into me and she was so hot and so cool and I needed to strike while the iron was hot. I ended up convincing myself I liked her in that way. But it was never anything more than a sort of weird friendship. It actually soured me on the idea of having a girlfriend. I've never even gone out with another girl seriously since."

"You're kidding," I said, stupefied.

"Why are you so surprised? You're not suggesting that I'm handsome, are you?"

"You're…nice," I said, laughing.

"Nice? You've just crushed my heart. I don't want to be just nice for you, Jen."

I felt something. The same thing I had felt earlier in the car. Impulsively, I reached up and rubbed his hair. His eyes were looking at me warmly, as always…except for that week after we'd argued. I hadn't realized how much I'd missed that expression until now. I pulled my hand away, and I'm pretty sure he lowered his neck to follow me, to keep touching me a second more.

"There's no way you honestly don't know," he said.

"What?"

"The reason she's mean to you, Jen. It's not just that I ignore her when you're around, even if that's part of it. It's that…when we were together, she used to always tell me I didn't love her enough. She'd say she could tell from how I looked at her that I didn't want to be with her, that I didn't talk to her the way you talk to someone you love. And I know she remembers that when she sees how I talk to you, how I look at you. Because it's exactly the way I never did with her. She doesn't like someone beating her."

I paused, my heart pounding, and he looked for a moment at my lips. My throat dry, I said to him, "Ross, this isn't a race."

He smirked. "If it was, you would have won, though."

Those words made the walls that had been rising up between us crumble in an instant. He reached over, touching my knees, sending an electric shock through every fiber of my body. And then one of us—I don't know who—took the initiative, and the next thing I knew, his lips were on top of mine. They were cold at first from the chilly breeze, then hot like fire, and as we came closer, I could feel the warmth of his skin through his clothing.

I had never felt that. Never. Not with my first kiss. Not with Monty. Never. And that frightened me a little.

But Ross was too close for me to think. All I could do was look at him looking at me as he froze for a second before coming in for more. I was almost dizzy. I didn't know if I could contain myself. I heard him moan, "Jen…"

I put my hands on his neck, felt the burning skin under my cool fingers, watched his lips open as I moved my hands backward and sank them into his hair. All I wanted was to make this moment last. I kissed him again.

And that was when he lost control. He grabbed the armrest and leaned in to me. Our mouths opened wider, and as he gripped my thigh under my skirt, I forgot the rest of the world existed.

I needed to kiss him more than I needed to breathe. My heart was pounding, making my ribs rise and fall. He slid a leg between mine and I moved forward, telling him silently to continue. I had never needed anyone the way I needed him just then. I tugged at his jacket and he tore it off instantly, throwing it to the floor and coming back in. His hands… I felt as if they were holding my entire body suspended over a void.

All I needed then was to touch him, to kiss him, to have him close. Closer than I had ever felt a man's body before.

My dress was open-backed, and he touched my spine, making every hair on my body stand up. I moaned—no man had ever made me make that sound, and I was embarrassed—but it only stoked his desire further. I opened my eyes for a moment as he embraced me and saw the city behind him. I had forgotten where we were. I didn't care if someone came out and found us. All I cared about was that he was there with me. And I needed him, more than I could ever admit.

His fingers were between my thighs now, caressing me, and I opened, I was inviting him into me, inviting him to close every distance. With each millimeter, my nervous system felt a charge like lightning.

Then the door flew open and the magic was gone. Ross was startled and pulled away, and I closed my legs. My panties were exposed. I pulled my dress down clumsily.

A couple had just come out for a smoke. They were laughing, drunk. When they saw us, they said *sorry* and left us alone again. Their giggles bounced off my eardrums as they proceeded back down the hall.

Ross was sitting on the floor now, running his hand through his hair and breathing hard. Only then did I truly realize what had happened. I had kissed Ross. *Yes.* I…had…kissed…Ross.

And you loved it, my brain told me.

Did not, I told myself.

Liar!

I'm not lying!

I'm your brain. I know.

I smoothed down my hair and noticed he was trying his hardest to look at anything that wasn't me. We were equally uncomfortable. I couldn't believe this. And I asked myself why in the hell hadn't I resisted? Or better, why was I upset when we were interrupted?

Because you like Ross, dummy.

Ross stood and tugged at his slacks, trying to waste time before he had to look at me. When he finally did, I wasn't sure what to make of his expression.

"Can, uh…can we go?" I asked, dragging my bag and feeling desperate.

"Yeah, uh…" He grabbed his jacket. "Let's go."

I got up and followed him to the door. I lagged behind him, staring at his muscular back. Why had we done what we'd just done? Would things be weird between us now? Because that was the last thing I wanted.

Halfway down the hall, he stopped and looked at me. I opened my mouth to say something, but I couldn't. He looked at my lips, and I could feel his lips on mine again. And I wanted to repeat the experience. "What?" I asked him.

He came closer, and I almost had a heart attack. He touched my chin, moved it upward, passed a finger beneath my lower lip. My breathing picked up speed, but then I realized he was just cleaning a smudge of lipstick. At least none of it had gotten on him. Because if I'd had to touch his face again, I didn't know where it might lead. When he was done, he left his hand there, and I grabbed his wrist. He must have been able to feel my pulse through my hand.

"Ross, I…"

That was all he needed to lean in close. Close, but not close enough to touch me.

A voice came from behind him, asking, "Are you guys ready to get out of here?" and I saw Naya and Will approaching. They were throwing on their jackets, too. Ross closed his eyes briefly in frustration, then said tensely, "Yeah, let's do that."

Naya and Will looked back and forth at each other. Had they noticed something? Had they seen something in him I hadn't? I didn't know, and they didn't say. Sue ran to catch up with us, but seemed to have no idea anything was out of the ordinary as she tried to finish her beer before we reached the car.

I took the passenger seat, and as we buckled up, Ross tapped his fingers impatiently on the wheel. He was anxious. He looked over at me, but I couldn't interpret his expression. All I could think about was the way he made me feel. And I nearly forgot there was anyone else with us in the car. I could have forgotten everything; he took up so much space in my thoughts. I shivered as I noticed him looking at my throat.

He closed his eyes, shook his head, and looked forward, turning the radio up loud and speeding away.

The others were too drunk or too cranky to know what was happening. Sue and Naya were bickering loudly, Will was trying in vain to make peace. Things were no better when we got home and entered the elevator. *Don't look at him*, I told myself, but I guess I wasn't in the mood to obey. Because he had made me feel…

Something.

I stared at the floor, I felt his eyes on me, I sensed his handsomeness, his warmth. I tried to block everything out, but it was too hard, especially when his hand brushed mine. So I looked up at his neck, his lips, his nose, and finally his eyes. This relieved him, and now he touched my hand on purpose, rubbed his thumb across my wrist. I couldn't speak, but I also couldn't bear the heat, and I drew back gently, wondering what was happening.

I felt throbbing in parts of my body I didn't know existed. I closed my eyes to try to calm myself, and when I opened them, Will was smiling. I saw myself in the mirrors on the walls. My face was fire red.

When the elevator door opened, I ran to the door of the apartment, opened it, and hurried inside. Naya and Will didn't even notice me as I stripped off my jacket. They were kissing, stumbling over each other, giggling on their way to the bedroom. Ross tossed his keys on the bar while Sue set down an empty bottle she'd taken with her.

"Man," she said, "I had more to drink than I thought. I really should hit the sack and try not to puke. Good night, guys, and sweet dreams, and don't do anything I wouldn't."

With her gone, it was just Ross and me. Our silence was oppressive. He walked to his room, and I followed him, unable to control myself. We turned our backs to each other, I on my side of the bed, he on his. I took off my boots and nearly told him my feet hurt, but thought better of it. Once I opened my mouth, I had no idea what I might actually say.

I went to the bathroom to brush my teeth and take off my makeup and try to relax. But that had never been something I was good at. My hair was sticking out in all directions, my eyes were puffy, and there was something in my stare I couldn't identify. I was shaking all over. I wanted to stay longer, but I was afraid he would come check on me, so I forced myself to go back to his room.

He was standing there in his pajamas looking frustrated.

"Are you OK?" I asked.

"Yeah. But listen. I can go sleep on the sofa if you like…"

"No!"

I was surprised by how loudly and quickly I'd said that, and he seemed surprised, too.

"I mean, it *is* your bed."

"Jen, I don't want you to feel uncomfortable with me."

"I've never felt uncomfortable with you, Ross."

And that was the problem. I *should have* felt uncomfortable. Because I barely knew him. Because I had a boyfriend. Because if something happened and it didn't work, I'd be out on the street. And yet…

I told him I could go sleep on the couch, too, and he laughed and said, "There's no way you think I feel uncomfortable." I shook my head, and we both got into bed at the same time. We lay there a few minutes with the lights off before Naya's shouting reached us from the other end of the hall. Could anything happen to make this weirder? Ross and I stared at the ceiling while Will started ramming her so hard that the bed frame was striking the wall.

Great.

I tried to close my eyes. But it only made me remember Ross kissing me. Why had I liked it so much? Was it just because it had been so many weeks since I'd kissed someone? Yeah, that was probably it.

Ross sighed. Was he thinking the same thing as me? Or was he regretting what he'd done? Had he offered to sleep on the sofa because he didn't want to be lying there with me? Was he regretting ever letting me stay at his apartment?

Or was I overanalyzing everything?

It was strange how he was close enough to touch, and yet he felt so far away. And every fiber of my body wanted him. I didn't understand where that longing had come from. I wanted to reach over, grab his hand, pull him on top of me. I wanted to tell him to run his finger along my lip again, to kiss me and squeeze my thigh and press his hand into the small of my back, to…

No. I couldn't do that to Monty.

But you and Monty had a deal, remember?

That was true.

I thought it over.

We had a deal.

A deal that was custom-made for situations like this. He had said that himself. It was fine. Ross and I hadn't even had sex. It was mostly just a kiss. But that kiss—had it been *just* a kiss?

I took a deep breath, turned, and looked at him. "Ross?" I called softly. "Yeah?"

"You remember what I told you about my relationship?"

"Yeah."

I paused. I couldn't believe I was about to say it. I felt as if I were standing on the verge of a cliff. My lips were tingling. My whole body was telling me, *Do it.*

"About how it was OK if I found someone and, you know, did things with them…"

"Yeah."

He turned and stopped me before I could say more, grabbing the back of my neck and turning me toward him. His leg rubbed against mine. He pressed his thumb into my lips. Then he bent over and kissed me, but differently than before. As if it were a secret he hadn't wanted to reveal to me until now. Without me telling them to, my hands climbed his back to his shoulders, hugging him and pulling him in tight. Any distance between us was intolerable. I wanted his chest, his thighs, to touch mine, and now they did. His legs were between my legs, his mouth on my mouth. He must have wanted the same, because he grabbed my hip and pulled me into him.

I'd never felt this before. Never. Not with anyone. My head was spinning. I worried I might faint at any second. But the urge to kiss him was more powerful. I arched my back and he pulled away to take a breath and climbed fully on top of me. I felt his fingers lace through my hair and grip it tight as he sucked at my lips, my chin, my throat. I reached down and pulled up on his T-shirt. He knew what I wanted, grabbed the neck of it, and pulled it off with one hand.

I stroked his shoulders, his chest, his stomach, his ribs, his back. His skin was burning, and my fingers on it were like firebrands. When they passed over his tattoo, I noticed the skin there was a little rougher, and I tried to look, but he guided my hand away. I tried not to groan as he rubbed me down there, over my clothes, careful, taking his time, but making absolutely certain that I knew how much he wanted me. I was a mass of trembling and bated breath. I couldn't take it anymore. And when he gripped the bottom of my sweatshirt, I could see the pleading in his eyes. *I'm dying to do this*, they said. *But I won't unless you tell me it's OK.*

And there was nothing else I wanted in this entire world.

I nodded and he pulled off my sweatshirt and the T-shirt I had underneath, and I felt the cold air on my bare skin. His hand was rubbing my hip now, sending chills up my spine. As he leaned in to kiss my neck, I stroked the back of his head, reaching back with the other hand to hold onto the headboard. I closed my eyes and let myself go.

My memories of that night became a treasure to keep under lock and key. I remember his head between my legs, the way he exhaled through his teeth as I placed my own hand between his, how he was so nervous he tore the condom, then took out another one and stretched me out, his breath on my neck as my hands sank in his hair. I remember him grabbing my hips, turning me around, how I pressed my hands against the wall to push back into him, how he sighed and caressed me as I got on top of him, how he smiled as his forehead pressed into mine and he tensed up, how he held me between my rib cage and my hips as he finished... It was perfect. So perfect that when he fell asleep, I tried to keep my eyes open because I didn't want the night to ever end.

10

___

NOT BAD

The next morning, I wasn't sure what had happened. There was an arm wrapped around me and my face was resting on a shoulder. Then I remembered. All of it. And my pulse started racing.

Ross was still sleeping soundly, arms around me, lips almost touching my forehead. I'd never slept like that with anyone. Certainly not with Monty. And although it was strange, I had never felt so comfortable. I didn't want to leave, but I needed to. I was confused and needed to organize my thoughts. And I knew I couldn't do that with him still in front of me.

He murmured something in his dreams as I rolled aside and stood softly. When he was asleep, he looked like an angel. I walked on tiptoe to the closet and put on some panties, a sports bra, and some shorts. A run—that was what I needed just then. Even if I was exhausted from a very different form of exercise.

I looked once more at Ross and couldn't help but smile. But I tried to stop myself. I needed to slow down. We were just friends, right? Just friends having fun.

Exactly.

Now my brain piped up: *Don't make me laugh.*

OK, I needed to get my mind on other things. I didn't run as far as usual, but I killed some time stopping for coffees for the whole house and a jar of peanut butter for Sue. As I was walking back into the building, I felt my phone buzz. It was Monty.

Don't ask me why, but I decided not to answer.

When I got upstairs, I found Sue digging around in the fridge. Ross was at the bar yawning, shirtless, in a pair of cotton trousers. I couldn't help but look at the eagle tattooed on his back. And when I did, I remembered how I'd caressed and kissed it just a few hours before.

When Will and Naya stumbled in, I announced, "Look what I got you."

Naya responded, "Will, I'm sorry, but you're no longer the person I love most in the world."

"I can deal with it," he said.

And when Sue turned her nose up at the coffee, I announced, "And peanut butter for the lady," getting her to smile despite herself. Her eyes lit up as she grabbed it and turned around to take out a spoon. When I passed Ross his coffee, he gave me a smile meant only for the two of us and touched my fingers, and I wondered if anyone had noticed. He giggled as I drew back, embarrassed.

Taking a seat next to him, Will said, "Hey, guys, I'm sorry about the noise last night. My bed's busted and it makes this noise. I hope it didn't bother you."

"You always bother me," Sue replied, sitting in her favorite armchair.

"I was fine with it," I reassured him.

"Me too," Ross said. "Actually, I slept like a baby. Like, I haven't slept that well in ages. Maybe ever. What about you, Jen?"

I blushed. He knew perfectly well what that question implied. To make time, I took a long swig of coffee, swished it around in my mouth, and swallowed.

"Uh…pretty good," I replied.

He wouldn't let that go. "Pretty good?" he asked, looking almost offended.

"Not bad," I said.

And we went back and forth, with him pressing me each time I gave an answer. *Not bad* wasn't enough for him, so I tried again with *Pretty good*, but he wanted to know exactly how good *Pretty good* was, so I said maybe a seven out of ten, and he asked why I was such a downer, and this continued, with Ross arguing it was a nine out of ten at the least. Everyone was watching us, looking a little lost. Naya asked, "So you guys rate how you sleep? Is that a thing?"

"Yeah, it's one of our hobbies," Ross said.

Sue interrupted us, screaming, "SHIT!" We all turned to see her standing in front of the sink, staring down into the stagnant water. "It's stopped up. And I guess I should go ahead and tell you who's *not* going to plunge it."

Naya nudged Will with her elbow and he said, "Yeah, I'm actually busy."

"With what?" Ross asked.

"With me," Naya responded.

Ross cursed and said he was tired of being everyone's errand boy. Half an hour later, the room had cleared out, the problem still wasn't solved, and he was on the floor with his head under the sink while I sat on the counter eating toast and watching him.

"How's it going down there?" I asked as he emerged briefly to pick up a wrench.

"You think this is hilarious, don't you?" he replied.

"I've done worse things," I said, trying to keep myself from gawking at his nude torso, even though it was the perfect time to do it, since he couldn't see me. OK, I admit it: I wasn't trying that hard. He asked me for a wrench, and I responded, "What's the magic word?" He said, "Pass it to me or I'll do it to you again here and now, and everyone in the apartment will know."

"Those aren't the magic words." I handed him the wrench. "Ross, tell me something. How is it possible that you can take apart a sink but you don't know how to buy your own groceries?"

"Listen, everybody's got their own talents. Though honestly, I'm getting to the point where I'd just as soon call a plumber."

"Oh, Ross, don't disappoint me! You look so manly down there," I joked.

"The things I do for women…"

He looked out at me and, to my surprise and embarrassment, asked me, "Are you enjoying the view?" I said I didn't know what he was talking about, and he laughed. "Sorry, cutie, but I can feel your beautiful brown eyes on me. There's no point in denying it."

Beautiful? Were my eyes beautiful?

He announced he was done, and I tried the faucet. It was fixed. The water flowed down the drain better than before. "I'm impressed," I told him, and he asked, "Who's a seven out of ten now?"

"Don't be silly. It was just a dumb joke. It's not bad, having a handyman around the house."

"I'm getting tired of the phrase 'not bad.'"

"If you want me to call you something better, you're going to have to earn it," I said.

"Well, I aim to please. If you have any notes for me, I'll study them before we meet back up tonight."

That made me clam up—I was still struggling to act normal about what we'd done—and I tried to distract myself by taking another bite of my toast. But he reached up, grabbed my wrist, and took such a huge bite of it that there was barely anything left but the crust.

"Ross, dammit! That was my breakfast!"

"I earned it," he said. And before I could complain more, he grabbed my chin and kissed me, and I would have collapsed on the floor then and there if he hadn't reached down and grabbed my butt at the perfect moment. He separated from me with a mischievous smile while I tried to catch my breath.

"Not bad, right, Jen?" he said before turning and walking off down the hall. I walked into the living room and almost jumped out of my skin as I noticed that Sue was sitting motionless in her chair. She hadn't made a sound the whole time, and I just assumed she was gone. She looked up at me and asked, "So...?"

Oh no.

"How was last night?"

No. Please tell me she didn't hear us. No. No. No.

"Did you and Lana have it out?"

Thank you, God.

"Almost," I replied.

"Turns out she's not such a sweetheart after all, right?"

"Yeah. Anything but, actually. Why do you hate her so much, though?"

"Jen, in case you haven't noticed, I hate everybody."

"Even me?"

"You less than most people. Anyway, listen, if you do come to blows, give me a heads-up. I'm thinking of making a YouTube channel. 'Preppy Bitch Gets What's Coming to Her' could be a good concept for my first video."

I laughed and walked to the bathroom, where I took a long shower. When I emerged, wrapped in a long fluffy towel, Ross was nowhere to be seen. I spent the rest of the morning and most of the afternoon studying for my French exam—which reminded me of Lana and made me wish I'd never taken the class. I'd hoped doing so would get my mind off of Ross, but of course I spent half the time staring at the door and asking myself where the hell he was.

I didn't start worrying until dinnertime came around. I asked Will, who was on the couch toying with his laptop, where Ross had gotten off to, and whether it was normal for him to just up and disappear. He didn't seem worried, and said, "He'll come back when he's tired. Especially now that he's got an incentive."

"Was it that obvious?" I asked.

"Nah," he said, reassuring me. "Naya hasn't mentioned it, anyway. And I won't say anything to her. I'm sure Ross will show soon enough. What do you feel like eating in the meantime?"

"Honestly, whatever."

"You want to cook something?"

"Sounds good. Is Naya coming over?"

"She can't," he said. "She's tired. She's got tests all week. And Sue already said she wasn't coming out of her room tonight and no one should try to bother her."

The two of us went in the kitchen and got to work making lasagna. We didn't have all the ingredients, so we had to improvise, but to my surprise, Will knew what he was doing, and the end result was impressive. We ate on the couch, watching a house reno show and joking about how lame the host was. At eleven, Ross still hadn't shown. Will started yawning and said, "I need to hit the sack."

"Good night," I told him, and I guess he could tell the situation was eating at me because he stopped to say, "Jenna, don't wait up for him. He could be anywhere."

"I won't," I lied.

After he left me alone, I kept watching the TV as long as I could, but soon it started getting on my nerves, so I left for Ross's bedroom. Was it something I'd done? I wondered. Was he hoping I'd be asleep by the time he got back? Had I taken things too far? I felt like an idiot. As I put on my pajamas, I caught sight of myself in the mirror, and I wanted to beat it with my fists. I got in bed. I'd told myself I'd wait up for him and confront the situation like an adult. If I'd made him do something he wasn't ready for, we could work it out. But then I closed my eyes, and when I opened them again, the room was dark, and Ross was sitting on the bed changing pants. I said his name groggily.

"Oops, did I wake you?" he asked. "I'm sorry, I was trying not to make noise."

"Where were you?"

"Well, I see someone's curious. Nowhere interesting, I just had some stuff to take care of."

"Is everything OK?"

"Yeah, don't worry about it. Get some sleep. It's late."

His explanation wasn't satisfactory, but I really was tired. I turned on my side and propped myself up on my elbow, staring again at his tattoo. He grinned.

"You want to tell me what's behind that stare?"

"I'm sorry, Ross, but what do you expect me to do when you're changing clothes right in front of me?"

"You got me. I'm doing it on purpose."

I smiled as he got in bed with me and was surprised at how quickly he grabbed me and pulled me over. We were back in the same position I'd woken up in. He ran his fingers through my hair, and I closed my eyes and sighed, resting my hand on his chest.

"How's my princess?"

For fuck's sake… I'd told Monty a million times not to call me that. He knew I hated it. Honestly, I hated corny nicknames in general. Especially coming from him.

"I don't know, who's your princess?" I replied.

"Jeez, you got up in a bad mood. How's tricks?"

Why was he so chipper? It was a Wednesday, and it felt like an eternity had passed since Lana's party. Things were back to normal with Ross and me. We hadn't said a word to anyone, and the only signs of affection we'd shown each other were the occasional nudge or friendly look. We did still sleep together in each other's arms, though. As for Lana, I hadn't seen her again. And as far as I was concerned, I'd be happy if it stayed that way.

It was late in the day, and I'd gone out to get a sweater to replace the one I'd spilled beer on the day I got high with Mike and Sue. I was back home and was taking the steps (I'd decided it was healthier than the elevator) when the phone rang. I wasn't sure what to tell Monty, especially because I didn't think he cared about my life here. But the party seemed vaguely interesting, so I told him briefly about that.

"Party, huh?" he said. "Is that what you're into now? Drinking? You never used to drink when you were back here. Were there guys there?"

"Of course there were guys. And girls."

"Who'd you go with?"

"My roommates and the girl I was living with at the dorm."

"Your *guy* roommates."

"So what, Monty! Am I supposed to not drink because I didn't used to? Am I supposed to not go to parties because there will be guys there? I'm in college. You can't tell me I should just lock myself up in my room."

"I mean…it's an option."

"You know, a lot of people start a conversation by asking how the other person is," I said.

"OK. How are you?"

"It's too late now. It doesn't count."

"Sorry. I'm being serious now. Tell me about your life, what you've been up to."

I knew it was time. We had an agreement: We could do what we wanted, but we had to talk about it. But it felt so weird!

"Monty, I need to talk to you about something."

"What? What did you do?"

"Nothing bad..." I looked at my shoes, twisting the handle of the bag my sweater was in with my free hand. Why was I so nervous? *Because you liked it,* my brain told me. *You liked it a lot.* Whatever. Shut up, brain. Come back later. I leaned against the wall in the stairwell.

"Jenna...?"

"I slept with a guy." I didn't say it loud, but I had no doubt he'd heard me. He paused for a few seconds that felt like decades.

"But it was just twice! Or three times! In the same night! So it only really counts as once, right...?"

"Who with?" he interrupted me.

"I thought we agreed we wouldn't go into details."

"I asked who you did it with, Jenna."

I bit my lip, nervous. "His name's Ross. I mean it's Jack. I mean, Jack Ross, but everyone calls him Ross..."

"I don't give a shit about his fucking name, Jenna."

So now he was swearing. This was going to get ugly. I closed my eyes and gathered my courage. I needed to prepare myself for whatever was coming.

Monty continued, "So did you like it? Did you like doing it with Jackoff Ross or whatever his name is?"

"Monty, we shouldn't..."

"It's a yes-or-no question."

"No! I mean, yeah. I mean..."

"You've barely had time to settle in, you're supposed to be studying, and you've already spread your legs for the first guy who comes along."

"Monty, you have no right to talk to me this way. I'd like to remind you that this was your idea."

"Yeah, but you must have liked it because you didn't lose any time in testing it out."

"You're being unfair. And don't you dare try to convince me that you haven't done anything. I know you. You would have never come up with this open relationship nonsense if you didn't already have someone in mind."

"Fine, you're right."

"More than once, I'll bet," I told him.

"Yeah, more than once."

"And you've got the balls to complain about me!"

But Monty was so stupid that he legitimately seemed to believe what he had done was OK and what I'd done was wrong. And he was obsessed with how good Ross was in bed. I kept telling him it was none of his business, that I'd never dream of asking him what he had felt with that other girl, but it didn't matter to him. He kept screaming, "Answer me!"

"I didn't like it," I told him finally.

"OK then. Fine."

I was such a bad liar that I couldn't believe I'd somehow gotten away with it. But noticing that made me realize another thing: even after a short period of time, Ross knew me way better than Monty ever would. I guess Monty had gotten a swollen head now, because he started asking me did Ross do this, did Ross do that, did I like it better when Ross did such and such or when he did it. I reminded him: "No details. That was our deal, and we should stick to it. Anyway, I've got to go. It's dinnertime and I think Will's cooking."

"Who the hell is Will?"

"He's Naya's boyfriend, Monty. I'm sure I told you that. Do you want to try and chill the fuck out?"

"I was just checking. What are you guys having?"

"Burgers, I think."

"Burgers again, Jenna? I hope you're not getting fat."

"I go running every morning, thank you. And I'll have you remember, when I gain weight, my boobs are the first things to grow."

"Yeah, I'll bet Jack Ross will love that."

"Give it a rest, Monty. We said we weren't going to be jealous."

"Sure."

"You're still my boyfriend," I told him.

"Cool. Well, since I'm your boyfriend, I want to ask you a favor."

Oh no.

"What?"

"I don't want you fucking that guy again. I know we had a deal. To hell with it."

"I'm sorry, Monty, but you don't get to give me orders. You're not my boss."

"I'm your boyfriend, though."

"Exactly."

"What's with the attitude, Jenna? Is this something you picked up from your new friends? You never used to talk back to me like this. I'm telling you what I want, and you ought to respect it."

I asked him if he'd stopped to consider that what he wanted might not be what I wanted, that what was good for him might not be good for me. He started flipping out about how selfish I was, telling me I only ever thought about myself. He complained that I'd never thanked him for driving me to the dorm. When I reminded him that I had, he screamed that he didn't give a shit. He wanted me to stop talking to Ross, and if I didn't, he would come to where I lived, and he promised I would regret it.

That was scary, and for a moment I fell silent. We'd never had an argument like this before. Jealousy was one thing, but that sounded downright stalkery. I begged him to stop being angry with me. He told me to stop acting like a selfish whore. And then he threatened me: "If I find out you've spoken even one word to him, we're over, understand? You'll be all on your own, and you better think about what that means. And if I decide to come up there, I can promise you that you won't like it."

He hung up. On the verge of panic, I walked the rest of the way up the stairs, where I found Agnes coming out of her apartment to take out the trash. She looked alarmed when she saw me.

"Dear," she said, "Are you OK?"

"Yeah," I said, rushing to get my head together. "Yeah, I just, uh… I think I flunked a test today." I smiled and tried to skirt past her to get to the door, but I was still fiddling with my keys when she cleared her throat and said, "Jenna, may I ask you something?"

"Of course." I turned around and tried to look normal.

"I spent forty years with my husband," she began, walking toward me. Her eyes seemed to tell me she knew exactly what was going on inside me. "It wasn't love; I didn't even have a choice in the matter. It was our parents who decided we should marry. I never complained. I even liked him. He was so attentive at first. He took good care of me. What else can you ask for, right?"

I nodded. My hands were trembling. "He sounds nice," I said, unsure how I was supposed to respond.

"Oh, he was. As long as I didn't do something he didn't like. Or as long as he didn't think I'd done something. When that happened, he wasn't so nice. No siree. I learned, though. I learned to keep my mouth shut, to stay home, never to do anything, because I didn't want to make him angry. I lived that way for so long that I forgot what I even liked to do, where I liked to go, who I liked to do things with. I forgot who I was because I was so busy making him happy. You understand what I'm getting at, don't you, Jenna?"

Of course I did, but I shook my head and tried to play ignorant. She didn't buy it. She was a smart old woman. She took a step closer.

"When my husband died two years ago, I wasn't sad. I just felt lost," she went on, placing a hand on my arm. "I had lost so much of myself with him that I no longer knew who I was. I felt abandoned, vulnerable... But then I remembered some things. I remembered I used to love to go to the beach, so I went there with my two grandsons and my daughter-in-law. I remembered I liked to have a drink now and then, so I started doing that. I started seeing an old friend of mine again. She took me back. She was still close with the same group of women I used to hang out with. We meet every week now, can you believe that? On Wednesdays. My favorite day of the week. Jenna, I let someone steal my identity, and it took me forty years to get it back. Don't you do the same. Don't forget who you are. Not for anyone."

She smiled at me one last time and walked toward the elevator. I had a knot in my throat, and I needed to stand very still for a second to be sure I wouldn't cry. My sister sent me a text just then:

Look at this scary little pirate. We can go ahead and crown
the Halloween king now.

It was a photo of Owen, who was seven years old now, and had the same chestnut hair and brown eyes as the rest of our family. He was wearing a pirate costume and had black makeup around one eye like a patch. I couldn't help but chuckle. I wrote her back and said, Tell him I'll bring him a giant bag of gummies the next time I'm home. She replied:

I'd better not or he'll start bugging me more about when
you're coming home.

Oh, Owen... I sure did miss him. Before he was born, I'd never have guessed I'd enjoy looking after a kid. But I adored him. That one picture had been enough to lift my mood, at least until I opened the door and heard the voice of the last person I wanted to hear: Lana.

As my brother Steve would say, it's never too late for something to ruin your day.

Everyone turned and looked when I entered and dropped my bag on the floor.

"There's little Miss Sunshine," Ross said, grinning when he saw my sour expression and opening his arms for me to flop down in his lap. But I didn't do so, and he clearly didn't like it. "Is something up?"

"Literary criticism," I told him. "That's what I've been studying all day. It would ruin your mood, too."

I wonder if it was evident that my studies hadn't gotten me down, that it was that little blond bitch with her innocent smile who was making me want to scream.

I wondered if I should listen to Monty and try to find somewhere else to stay. Maybe even go back home after all. I didn't want him to feel bad because of something I'd done. But no, that was stupid. What had Agnes just told me? I always did things to fulfill others' expectations. It was time to do something that I liked. And what I liked was being with Ross.

I sat next to him and he passed me a wrapper with a burger in it. I'd thought Will was cooking, but whatever. I was starving after all that drama.

"What were you all talking about?" I asked, licking a blotch of mustard from my lips. When Ross noticed and raised an eyebrow, it was as if I was alone with him for a brief moment, and that made me smile for what felt like the first time that day. Of course, his loser ex had to immediately ruin it.

"You sure left the party early the other day," Lana said. "I was asking everyone why. I missed you."

I rolled my eyes. "I left because I wanted to," I said, trying not to get angry over her girlish games.

"You didn't have fun?" she asked.

"I'm not a big party person."

"Me neither," Ross joined in.

"Too bad," Lana said. "I hope you could afford the Uber back. It must have been expensive at that time."

I wanted to throw my burger at her face, but I stopped myself. That was what she wanted. She was jealous of me, and if I acted out, it would give her the perfect excuse to keep trying to force me out of their little group.

"Don't worry about it," I said, "Ross offered to take me home." I smiled back at her with the same innocent smile she always used, thinking all the time: *Get stuffed.*

That stopped her for a second, but soon she was back on the attack. "Poor Ross, he had to miss the rest of the party just for you?"

"I didn't miss anything," he said, and I nudged him, amused, while Lana scowled at us. We kept eating, and when we were done, Ross and Will went up on the roof to smoke, leaving me alone with Naya and Lana. Lana had tried to ignore me after Ross's comment, but once he was gone, she glared at me before turning to Naya and saying, "Remember that thing I told you the other day? Well, I've got news. It's private, though. Is there somewhere we could talk alone?"

Naya was confused, and responded, "Yeah. I mean, I guess…"

"Don't worry," I told her. "I'll go to my room."

"*Ross's* room," Lana said.

"*Our* room," I replied.

I didn't stick around to see the look on her face; I didn't need to. I was in a rush to shut the door behind me and go back to pretending she didn't exist. When Ross came in later, I was staring at my laptop screen. I could smell the smoke on him even before he got to the bed.

"What are you watching?" he asked.

"*The Avengers*."

"How far into it are you?"

"There are two minutes left."

"Ah, that's too bad," he said. "We can watch it together another day, then."

He put on his pajamas while I watched the end of the movie, waiting through the credits for the final scene as he'd told me to do. Then I closed my laptop and addressed him: "Ross, I don't want to be a pain in your ass, OK, but…"

"I didn't know she was coming."

"What?"

"Lana." He'd known perfectly what I was going to say. "I'm sorry. I didn't want you to get ambushed like that. If it made you uncomfortable…"

"No, not at all," I told him, now feeling embarrassed.

"So…?"

"It's something else," I said, trying to change the subject quickly. "I was wondering… Can I see the tattoo on your back?"

Ross decided to play along and pretend I wasn't jealous. He turned, pulling up his shirt so I could see the eagle in the middle of his back, its wings stretching out across his shoulders. I reached out and touched it and could feel the tiny scars beneath the ink.

"What's it mean?"

"I was drunk and had an extra six hundred dollars."

"It's cool."

"It wasn't the first time. I had some jerkoff do it and it was blurry and slanted. I had to have a professional touch it up afterward."

"An ugly one would have suited you better," I joked.

"I'm going to let that slide because I know deep down you adore me," he said. "What about you? I saw you had one, but you always keep it covered up."

"It's nothing special," I said, turning around and pulling my hair away from the nape of my neck to let him see where I had a small crescent moon. He reached out and touched it, as I'd done with his, and the shiver it gave me made it hard to speak for a moment.

"It's cute," he said, and I explained that my sister had paid for it for my eighteenth birthday.

"When is your birthday?" he asked.

"February sixteenth. We used to always have a party in my backyard. Dad would grill and my brothers would DJ, and sometimes my grandparents and my uncle would come."

"What about your friends?"

"We'd usually go out that night," I said.

"Do you miss them?"

"My friends? Not really."

"Your family," he specified.

"Oh. Yeah. I mean…I do, but at the same time, I'm glad to be here. I don't miss them like *Oh my God, I wish they were here, I feel like I'm gonna die of grief* or whatever, I miss them like I'm where I am and they're where they are and that's cool, but they're good people. Did that sound as bad as I think it did?"

"More or less," he joked. "But if it makes you feel better, when I first moved out, I felt exactly the same way."

"Do you see your parents?"

"More than I'd like," he said. "But my dad especially I try to avoid."

"You don't get along with him?" I don't know why, but that surprised me. I'd just assumed Ross could get along with anyone.

He shrugged. "We just don't have much in common."

"What about your mother?"

"Mom's different." He smiled, and I knew I'd been right to ask about her. "I saw her recently. We spent a whole day organizing an exhibition at one of her galleries that's opening tomorrow night."

"Aren't you going?"

He turned a little shy, which wasn't common for him, as he slid into bed. "Actually, I was going to ask you if you'd want to come with me. I mean, Naya and Will are going. My brother, too, maybe. If he's not fighting with some girl he's hooked up with. Don't feel obligated, of course…"

"Are you kidding? I'd love to go!"

"Really?"

"Of course I would," I said. "I've never been to an art exhibition before. Plus, it's your mom. You know I used to paint, right? Probably I'll be able to see the deeper meaning of all the pictures and then you'll realize how smart I am."

"A lot of it is abstract art. Even she doesn't understand it."

"Still better. I can say what I want, and nobody will be able to tell me I'm wrong."

He laughed.

"Mom's going to love you," he said.

There was only one problem. A little blond problem. "Is Lana going too?" I asked.

"I don't know. I didn't invite her. Why?"

"No reason."

"I'm going to remind you for the fiftieth time, you're not a good liar," he said. I guess getting Monty off my back had convinced me otherwise. Oh well.

"I don't want to talk bad about your friend," I replied.

"She's Naya's friend, not mine. And I'd have to be stupid not to notice that you don't like her, Jen."

"She doesn't like me either."

"Why should you care?"

"Ross, this is the thing. The other day at the party, when you said she

didn't like you, that she was just obsessed with getting what she wanted…
I think you were wrong. I think she really does like you. A lot."

He didn't look happy about it. He didn't look bothered. He just blinked
and said, "I really don't care what she feels." And to change the subject, I
asked him what I should wear to the exhibition. I didn't know how people
dressed at these things, and I didn't want to look out of place. He didn't
help much. He kept saying I'd look good in whatever I wore, and he added
that I'd look even better if I wore nothing. It was pointless trying to get a
straight answer from him, so I grabbed my laptop and went looking for
another movie while he wrapped an arm around me and tickled my ribs
softly. He asked if he could pick, and I said, "Sorry, my laptop."

"Yeah, but it's my bed and my room. And my apartment." He smiled
innocently, and I tried to resist, replying, "You told me I should feel at
home here."

"Maybe I lied," he said, pulling my laptop out of my hands. I felt cold
when he pulled his arm away and immediately started yearning for him
to put it back.

I would never feel anything like that for Monty. I knew that just then.
But I didn't pursue the thought much further. There was a conclusion
there I needed to draw, and I was scared of it. And scared of the consequences of doing so.

Ross read off a list of titles, telling me which ones he was interested
in. In the meantime, I took out my contact lenses. I could barely see the
screen now. I yawned. I knew I'd fall asleep any second.

"Horror?" Ross asked. "Nah, better not. You were traumatized after
the first one. Not comedy, though. I'm not in the mood to cringe at someone else's dumb jokes. I don't want to watch a war flick, either. They're
depressing. I want to be happy, not sit here and cry about what happens
to Private Ryan…"

I leaned my head on his shoulders and said, "What about a rom-com?"

"Screw that, they all suck," he said.

"That's impossible. There's no way every single romantic movie sucks."

"OK, cool, tell me a good one, then."

"I can't," I said. "I've never seen one."

"I keep forgetting that you've come here from another galaxy."

Despite his remarks, he did click on "Romantic." I wrapped my arms around him and kissed him on the cheek. It felt so natural that it surprised me. So I curled up closer and rubbed my nose against his neck. That felt natural, too. He smelled good. He always did.

"If you keep that up, I'm afraid you're going to have to miss your movie," he warned me.

"I like it, though."

"Me too. That's the problem."

I smiled and pointed at the screen. "What about this one?" I asked.

"*Pretty Woman*? I've seen it a million times. Everyone's seen it a million times except you. It's probably *the* most famous romantic comedy there is."

"Come on, Ross."

"No!"

"But I want to...."

He shook his head and said, "I can tell arguing with you is pointless. Why should I think I can choose the entertainment in my own house?"

I kissed his cheek again as he clicked Play. We settled into the bed and I curled up close to him. As we watched, I tugged at his shirt collar. He huffed and puffed through the first scenes, complaining about everything the characters did while I just smiled and tried to understand what they were saying. Halfway through, I told him, "Ross, stop being a spoilsport. It could be so much worse."

"I hate it. It's unrealistic."

"You're just not romantic. Who are you to say there isn't a Julia Roberts out there right now who's just bumped into the millionaire who's going to make her whole life better?"

"Julia Roberts shouldn't need a millionaire to make her life better."

Out of nowhere, a question struck me, and I felt comfortable enough to pause the movie and ask him, "How many girlfriends have you had?"

"Well, that came out of nowhere," he responded. "Two. May I ask why you want to know?"

"Curiosity," I said.

"Yeah, right."

I tried to push him, and he caught my hand, and I leaned in to kiss him. It felt good. And it felt better when he reached under my sweatshirt to caress my back and ran his other hand through my hair. It wasn't like the first time. It wasn't like the kiss he'd given me the other morning in the kitchen. It was…tender. No one had ever kissed me tenderly before. And what do you know? It turned out I liked it.

Or at least I did when he did it.

I cupped his cheek, kissed his upper lip, kissed his lower lip, kissed the corner of his mouth, opened my own mouth and let him kiss me. He was slow as he stroked my back with his fingers, wanting to give me pleasure. He reached up and ran his thumb along my lip, and I began to bend down toward him again, but a knock came at the door and Lana leaned in, not bothering to wait. I jumped back and pretended to look at my laptop, which we'd left sitting in the middle of the bed.

"Can I help you?" Ross asked angrily.

"I need a ride home," she asked with that fake innocence that was starting to get on my nerves.

I tried not to grunt out loud as he stood. Of course, he couldn't say no to anyone. He put on his shoes and looked over at me. It didn't take a genius to know how pissed I was. I could tell he felt bad as he said, "I'll be right back."

"Whatever," I said. "I'm going to sleep."

Very briefly, I saw a look of horror on Lana's face. Just afterward, I knew why. Ross had turned around, was leaning over me, was touching my face, his lips pressed into mine, and the world stopped once again. Pulling away slightly and looking at me close, he said, "Nah, I don't think so. I'm coming home, and I want you to be awake when I get here."

I was as shocked as Lana as he turned around and left the room.

11

UNDENIABLE CHEMISTRY

"What's Ross's mom like?" I asked Will quietly as we got out of the car.

Naya, Sue, and Ross were straggling a few feet in front of us, arguing about who knows what. Well, actually Naya and Ross were the ones arguing. Sue was just moaning and groaning about how she didn't want to talk about whatever it was.

I was nervous. Stupidly nervous.

"Relax," Will said, "she's nice. I've never seen her be rude to anyone. I'm sure she'll love you."

There's always a first. Yeah, thanks for that, brain.

But his words must have cheered me up somewhat, because I realized I was smiling, and not because I was trying.

"It's not like I care, anyway," I said.

"Jenna, of course you care. She's your *friend's* mom." The way he emphasized that word *friend* reminded me that he knew Ross was something more than that.

Naya turned back to us and shouted, "Are you guys coming or what?"

We hurried over. She opened the door for us, and I noticed again how strangely informal she looked. I, who usually threw on whatever, had spent half the day digging through my closet. She, to everyone's surprise, had gotten dressed in no time. Of course, she still looked way better than I did. She just had a gift. She could throw on a potato sack and make it elegant. I was the total opposite.

"How long is this going to last?" Sue asked.

As he hurried past us, Ross said, "It lasts as long as it lasts."

The first thing I saw as I followed him in was two men in suits greeting everyone who entered. I imagined they were assistants or something because Ross just walked past them with a nod. The main gallery was a big white room with four columns. Paintings covered the walls. Some were colorful, some were black and white, some were portraits, some were just strange shapes. People milled about there or walked into the two side galleries with glasses of champagne in their hands, while waiters and waitresses walked around with trays offering appetizers to the guests. When I found the food table, I had the urge to lick my lips, and probably would have if I wasn't worried about having to touch up my makeup.

"You hungry?" Ross asked.

"I'm not going to smear my lipstick that fast," I told him.

A man came over to talk to him about his mother, and I gestured that I was going to go join our friends on the other end of the gallery. I didn't make it over there, though. He grabbed my arm and stopped me. The poor thing didn't want me to leave him alone. Since I had nothing to say, I stood there and smiled politely while Ross talked and talked, as charming as always.

The man eventually left, and I asked who he was.

"No idea," Ross said. As I laughed and shook my head, he said, "Shit, come on," dragging me toward the next room over. "Those are friends of my mom's. They're the most boring people I've ever met, and I don't want them to see me."

His strategy didn't work. No sooner had we set foot in the neighboring gallery than a couple blocked our path. I could tell the conversation would be a long one, and much as I liked him, I wasn't up for it, so I abandoned him in favor of the appetizer table. I needed to calm my nerves, and food seemed like a good distraction.

Once I'd munched on something and gotten a drink, I decided to take a look at the artworks. Ross hadn't spoken of them flatteringly, but I thought they were nice. Some were better than others, of course, but that was to be expected. There was one that consisted of four canvases showing a blue car: in one it drove forward, in two it moved back, in the last one it had nearly disappeared. It didn't take long for me to get bored and look for Ross. He was in the entryway and seemed to be looking for me, too.

We nearly met, but he was intercepted once more, so I decided to browse the last of the galleries. The work featured there was a little sadder, a little more maudlin, with faded colors. I really liked a few pieces, especially one of a girl with her back turned, looking out from a balcony. Everything was black and white except her bright yellow dress. I stared at it for a long time before returning to the entrance, determined to rescue Ross. It was hard not to laugh when I saw how he was struggling to maintain his usual polite exterior with what looked like some of the dullest people on earth. I took a drink.

He shouted, "Babe!" Then he took my hand and gave me a quick kiss. "Why didn't you tell me you were here? I'd have met you at the door."

What was he talking about. I mumbled, "I, uh..."

"Sorry, you guys will have to excuse me," he told the people he'd been talking with. "This is my fiancée and we haven't seen each other in forever. I'm sure you'll understand."

Once we'd walked off, Ross beathed a sigh of relief. "Jesus," he said, "I thought that would never end."

"Fiancée?" I asked. "Is that really the best thing you could come up with?"

"It is," he replied. "And I don't mind saying it worked like a charm. Our chemistry is undeniable." I was about to tell him not to get a big head, but he went on. "Is there anything worse than running into friends of your parents you haven't seen in ages?"

"Do you come to these things a lot?" I asked.

"I try. I'm a good kid. When I don't have anything better to do. I'd probably be a good fiancé, too. Maybe you should consider it."

"Ross, shut up."

We were passing by the snack table again, and I grabbed a canapé and stuffed it into my mouth.

"Where's Mike?" I asked him.

"He could be in Guantánamo for all I care. You'll be surprised to know he's not exactly reliable. He generally limits his appearances to showing up when I don't want him around. Can I ask you a question, though?"

"Sure," I said nervously.

"Is something up with you today?"

"What do you mean?"

"Jen, we've been over this a thousand times. You're not a good liar."

"I'm not lying!" I said.

"Let me guess. You're anxious about meeting my mom."

"I am not!" I shouted.

"Cool. She's right over there. Let me introduce you to her."

"Right now?" I blinked as I tried to get ahold of myself and swallowed my drink in one sip. He was grinning slyly. He knew exactly what he was doing. "Are you sure we won't be bothering her?"

"She's my mom. We're not going to be bothering her, and it's better to catch her early while she's still in a good mood. She'll love you. I've told her all about you."

I hesitated, put my drink down, and grabbed another one to help me through it. He squeezed the back of my neck as I asked him, "What exactly did you say?"

"That's for me and her to know," he answered. "Anyway, she already likes you. That's what matters."

I nodded and prepared for battle.

"She is a little weird, though," he warned me. "Hippie-ish. Easily distracted. You'll see what I mean when you meet her."

Before I could respond, I saw her hurry over, and her hands with their blue-lacquered nails wrapped around his shoulders. She was middle-aged, with long, dark hair and bright eyes that seemed to scan me from head to toe. I stiffened, unable to help myself.

"Hey, Mom," Ross said.

She certainly made an impression. She was wearing flowing gray slacks and a silk blouse, and she had a tattoo of a vine that wove down to her pinky finger. I'd expected someone more formal. But she didn't really look like a hippie, either. She was... I don't know. She was just herself.

"Hello, Jackie dear," she said in a slow, melodious voice. She had a distracted air about her, but she was obviously a woman attuned to her surroundings. I could see why Ross's attitude toward her was complicated.

"Mom, this is Jenna. The girl I told you about."

"Yes, I saw you both when you came in." She smiled at me and asked, "How are you, dear?" She came in for one of those strange hugs where your bodies don't touch. It caught me off guard, but I think I reacted as naturally as I could under the circumstances.

"It's a pleasure, Mrs. Ross."

"Mary," she corrected me. "Mrs. Ross is my mother-in-law's name. I don't like to be all stuffy. And speaking of your grandmother, Ross, I haven't seen her in some time. We need to all have dinner together soon."

Before Ross could say anything, his mother had put an arm around my shoulder and was walking me further into the gallery. I caught sight of his face briefly. He gave me a look as if to say, *This is just how Mom is.*

"So, Jenna," Mary asked, "what do you think of the exhibition? Are you enjoying it?"

"It's great," I said.

"I won't be mad if you say otherwise. My son doesn't like it, and I haven't written him out of my will. Not yet, anyway."

"Mom," Ross said, catching up to us, "I didn't say I didn't like it. I just said it doesn't speak to me. Anyway, if you need someone to suck up to you, there are plenty of people here besides Jen who can do it."

"Hush up, Son. This is a girls' conversation. And you know art isn't a beauty contest. You have to try to understand it, not just say this piece is pretty and that one's ugly."

As Ross rolled his eyes, I mentioned that I had painted a little in high school.

"Oh, really?" Mary responded. "Ross didn't say anything about that."

"I didn't know you needed a full bio of all my roommates before you met them, Mom," Ross interjected.

"Not all of them," she replied. "Just the ones you're kissing in front of all my friends and colleagues."

Once again, I chugged my drink. Ross looked slightly anxious. His mom just smiled. I could tell she was in her element. He tried to explain he'd just wanted to get a couple of boring people off his back, but his mother stopped him, telling him that was his private life, and she didn't need to know the details. We got into a conversation about the paintings. She wanted to know which one I liked best. Seeing I was hanging in the wind, Ross butted in to say everyone's favorite was a picture of a bicycle. "Sure," his mother responded, unconvinced.

I had seen it. It was in the main gallery. A red bicycle with a bright-colored backdrop. It was true that everyone stopped to look at it. I commented that it was fine. Ross's mother prodded me with the question *But...?* And I admitted that I had preferred the one with the girl on the balcony.

From the look on her face, I got the feeling I had passed the test. The pressure in my chest eased a little. She smiled and pulled away to look at me better.

"Funny," she said. "The girl on the balcony. That one's my favorite, too."

She's not even your mother-in-law yet and you're killing it, my brain told me.

"Aren't you supposed to keep those judgments to yourself, Mom?" Ross asked.

"I'm the gallerist, Jackie. Don't tell me how to do my job." She pinched his cheek, and when he told her not to do that, especially not in public, she told me, "He's still embarrassed by me. What do you think about that, Jenna?"

"Ross," I said, "don't be ashamed of your mother."

He scowled as she started to walk off, remarking that she still had many guests to attend to, but that next time, we should try to talk more. *Next time?* I wondered. *Does that mean she assumes there will be a next time?* And my brain shouted at me, *Dummy, even I know there's going to be a next time.* She finished by telling Ross he should come to the house more, and he chided her, "I'm happier at my place. Maybe you should come see me."

Ignoring him, she said, "Why don't you come, too, Jenna? If I can get you on board, perhaps I can get my son to agree to the torture of coming to see his parents once in a while."

"Mom…" Ross groaned.

"I'd be happy to. Thank you for the invite."

"And tell your brother, Jackie," she added. "I haven't seen him in ages. How is he?"

"Same as always," Ross said.

"Of course. Well, thank you for coming, and it was nice to meet you, Jenna. Now I've got to keep meeting and greeting."

"Bye," I said. "A pleasure meeting you, too."

Ross frowned at me once she was gone and imitated my voice, repeating the phrase *Ross, don't be ashamed of your mother.* Then he said, "I'm happy see you two got along. I hoped I'd have an ally, but I guess all's fair in love and war."

"Who said anything about love?" I asked.

He narrowed his eyes and grinned before looking at his phone and remarking that it was getting late. "Have you seen Will, Sue, or Naya?"

"I haven't," I said.

We walked around a bit and soon saw them by the door looking for us. As we approached them, Naya made a bored face, pointed outside, and dragged everyone out there with her, and I tried to hurry Ross out, too. It had been interesting, I guess, but I was ready to go. Just as we were about to leave, Ross's mother reappeared, giving him a kiss on the cheek. He seemed embarrassed, which I found funny, as she added, "Honey, I almost forgot to congratulate you. Now you have fun tonight, OK?"

As Ross tried to rub her lipstick off his cheek, she squeezed my shoulder and took off toward a group of friends. "Congratulations?" I asked Ross. "What's up with that?"

"It's my birthday," he said.

"Excuse me?" I pushed him hard in the chest.

"What the hell is that about?" he protested.

"You deserve it for being a jerk! Were you just not going to tell me?"

"I was! When it was over, at midnight, and you couldn't try to sing me songs or give me a present or bake me a cake."

By then we had caught up with our roommates, who were standing at the car while Will smoked a cigarette. I yelled at him in an accusing tone, "Will, did you know it was Ross's birthday?"

"Of course I did," he replied. "You didn't?"

"I didn't either," Naya said, and Sue, with her typical charm, interrupted us to say, "Birthdays suck."

"I agree," Ross said. "Birthdays suck, and, Jen, I'd prefer you not make a big deal out of it."

"But it's your day. You're turning twenty," I told him, and he corrected me and said he was twenty already. I didn't get it. He was only one year ahead of me at school. But he explained that he'd had a little problem in high school. Strangely, when I asked if he had to repeat a year, he and Will crossed glances, and he told me, "Not exactly." I tried to press him, and he refused to say more, telling me he didn't want me to have a bad impression of him.

We talked about how we should celebrate. He was turning twenty-one; that was a huge deal! Naya swore to me it was a lost cause. Ross said he was tired and wanted to go home; he'd already drunk alcohol a ton of times so it wasn't anything special. Will said he wouldn't do anything till he'd finished his cigarette. I announced there was no way we were going home without getting a few drinks. I got into the car and felt my phone buzz. I hadn't noticed in the gallery, but Monty had called me several times and sent me two messages in a row. One read: Why aren't you picking up? And the other: Who are you with? I want to see a picture.

To hell with him. I wasn't going to baby him because he was throwing a tantrum. Especially not on Ross's birthday. More and more, I was telling myself there was no reason for me to ever deal with that kind of thing. I would need to have a serious talk with Monty about his attitude and about us.

When everyone else got in, Will drove us to the same bar where we had seen Mike's band play before—the only bar where we could reliably drink without getting carded. We grabbed a window table, and all of us ordered beers except for Sue, who stuck with her beloved water, and Will, who got a soft drink since he had to drive. We stuck around an hour or two—long enough for me to have two and a half beers and Ross five. I was tipsy, but he seemed fresh as a daisy, and I asked him, "Don't you ever get drunk?"

"I've got a good tolerance," he responded. "Why? You're not drunk, are you?"

"No," I said, pushing half of my third beer toward him. "But I'm getting there. You can finish this."

He drank it down, looked me in the eye, and said, "What?"

"What, what?"

"I know you want to ask me something."

Damn him. It was like he could read my mind. And my inhibitions were low enough that I didn't feel like holding back. "Fine," I said, "I want to know what happened when you were in high school."

He threw his arm over the back of my seat. I could tell he was uncomfortable, but that didn't stop him. "I had a little problem with a classmate, and, uh, they threw me out. I think I told you, I'm a very different guy now from who I was in high school."

"What did you do?"

"That's a secret I'm keeping to myself. All you need to know is I got kicked out, so I had to repeat a year, and that's why I'm a twenty-one-year-old sophomore."

I wanted to ask more, but I thought I'd have to wait until he was actually drunk to do so, and it didn't seem like that was going to happen that night. And honestly, as the alcohol got deeper into my system, he started looking so good to me that I wanted to do something besides just talk. I tried to suppress my urges since there were people around.

"I still can't believe you didn't tell me it's your birthday," I said. "I didn't even get you a present."

"Here's your present," he responded. "Don't ask me about high school again."

"I won't! I'll just ask about your other girlfriend instead. You did say you'd had two, right?"

"I'm going to go smoke," he said. "You're welcome to come, but you're not getting any details out of me."

Since the other three were engaged in some boring conversation and didn't even seem to know we were there, I followed him out, zipping up my coat and almost cursing the cold. There were benches outside by the parking lot, and as we sat at one of them, I told him he shouldn't smoke so much.

"Here we go again…" He sighed.

"It's bad for your heart, your lungs, your throat. It can give you oral cancer, and it can make you impotent. I saw it on the Net."

"I think we can both agree I don't have any problems in that last department, Dr. Jen. Anyway, I know it's bad for me. I don't need a reminder. We can make a deal, though. I'll quit smoking if you quit watching reality shows."

"I like my reality shows!" I exclaimed.

"Yeah, and I like my cigarettes."

He did stub it out, though, asking me if I was happy and protesting that it must be true love if he was willing to sacrifice half a cigarette for me. Then he grabbed my hand, pulled me close, and reached between my legs with his other hand.

My phone buzzed again in my pocket. Of course it was Monty. Ross had felt it and asked if I wasn't going to answer.

"If it's important, they'll call," I said.

But I was starting to worry about how angry Monty was getting, especially because he'd definitely get angrier if I didn't respond soon. I tried not to think about it. He had told me if I talked with Ross again, he'd leave me. And there I was, obviously talking to Ross. And picking up wouldn't help. If anything, it would just make him act crazier. I was going to lose him. That was a fact. So better to forget about him for now and go on enjoying Ross's company.

"It's kind of funny that your birthday's the day before Halloween, right?" I asked.

"It makes it easy to remember. By the way, did you get a costume yet?"

"No…why would I?"

"Because of the Halloween party tomorrow, obvs."

A Halloween party which, as he soon explained, would be taking place at Lana's sorority house. I was so angry when I heard that, I started to face away from him, but he grabbed my hips and held me. "We don't have to go," he said.

"Ross, I can't keep making you guys avoid your friend because of me. But you can't expect me to just forgive her for how she's acted with me."

"Did I not make it clear to you? She's not my friend. Besides, we probably won't even see her there," Ross said. "And if we do, I'll just tell her to leave you alone."

"I'm not going to put you in that position. Anyway, like I said, I don't have a costume."

"I could take you to get one."

But I didn't have money for one, and I didn't want him to pay, so I tried to convince him they'd all be sold out already. But he had his counterargument ready: I could borrow one from Naya. Or we didn't have to dress up. It was no skin off his back.

"Fine," I conceded, "but if we see Lana…"

"I'll make sure she doesn't bother you. Among other things, because I'll be busy bothering you myself. It's already been hard for me to leave you in peace with that sexy lipstick you've got on tonight."

I smiled and asked, "What are you waiting for, then?"

He bent down and kissed my lips, and I closed my eyes, letting myself be carried away. As soon as I wrapped my arms around him, my phone vibrated again. I reached down and hit the button to silence it. Before Ross could say anything, I tried to kiss him again. I was pretty sure he wouldn't put up much resistance, and I was right. We stayed that way till we heard the door creak and Will and Sue dragged a very drunk Naya out. She had sworn earlier she could keep up with Ross, and now it was obvious where that had led.

"Can we?" Will asked. Everyone helped lift Naya into the front seat. Will drove, and Sue, Ross, and I rode in the back. My legs were touching his. Our arms were touching, too, but it didn't matter; it wasn't enough for me. My fingertips tingled when we took a curve and Ross's body slid into mine. I needed him close. Did he detect it? Because he answered my wishes. He rested his head on my shoulder, kissed me just under the ear, and put his hand in my lap. It was as though we'd been that close our entire lives, but at the same time, I felt he was touching me for the first time.

It was all so innocent, but it made me feel so tense, so different. Was it a good or bad feeling? It was hard to say. It depended on how you looked at it.

It was cold when we parked and got out of the car. Naya was aware enough by then to make it to the elevator on her own with Will's help. As soon as we got into the apartment, they shut themselves in their room. Sue soon did the same, and we decided it was time for bed, too. I walked ahead of Ross. My feet were killing me, and I needed to get my boots off ASAP. When he came in, I said, "Happy birthday, by the way. I don't think I actually said that."

"Thanks," he said with his usual mirthful expression. "But if you want to give me a real present, I've got a couple of ideas..." He jumped into bed next to me and lay back with his hands crossed behind his head.

"I'm exhausted," he continued.

"You shouldn't be," I told him. "I'm the one who went running for an hour and a half earlier. What did you do?"

"It's funny," he said. "You told me you didn't like to do anything when we met. Then I find out you're one of those masochists who likes to go running and you used to paint. What else is there I don't know? Or is any of that even true? I mean, it is weird. I feel like I've seen you hyperventilate walking up the stairs. Do you actually run, or do you just jog for a few minutes and then grab a coffee?"

"You should try me," I said. "I'll bet I'd smoke your ass."

He laughed as I tried to hit him in the face with a pillow. He caught it, we struggled over it, and naturally I ended up kissing him again, grabbing the lapels of his jacket and bringing him in tight as he reached under my shirt. And then, of course, my phone buzzed for the umpteenth time.

Ross watched me take it out and set it on the nightstand as I put it on Silent. Monty's name was on the screen, and since I was pretty sure Ross had seen it, I didn't try to deny it.

"He's a pain in the ass," I said. "Don't worry about him."

"I guess he's the same one who was calling and texting before."

I didn't want to lie, but I didn't want to tell the truth, either, so I said, "Probably," and groaned.

"Are you guys fighting or something?"

"Do you honestly want to talk about Monty right now, Ross?"

He sighed and sat up in the bed, taking off his jacket. Before he could get up to change, I stopped him and said, "What's up?"

"Nothing's up. I'm just getting ready for bed."

"But…"

"I'm sorry, Jen, but it's hard for me to get in the mood with some other dude calling you compulsively."

He shook me off and stood, pulling off his T-shirt and looking through his drawers. Even the eagle on his back seemed tenser than usual. I cursed Monty in my head and walked up behind him.

"Are you mad at me?" I asked.

"No." He sounded honest.

I looked at the clock. It was a quarter after eleven. "It's not going to be your birthday much longer," I reminded him. "Don't you want your present?"

He didn't respond, but I couldn't just go to bed as if nothing had happened, the way Monty and I used to always argue and never make up before sleeping. That had been fine for Monty, but Ross was different. He was so good that you knew there was something wrong if you had a problem with him. And I wanted to solve it. So I hugged him. He stiffened a little. I gave him a kiss in the middle of his tattoo, then leaned my head on his warm skin.

"Please don't be mad at me," I said.

"I told you, I'm not mad at you."

"Well, you're not happy, either. Listen: Things are weird with Monty. We had an argument. I know it's stupid. I know Monty and I have only been together a few months, and now that there's distance between us, honestly, I feel better. It's not that he treats me badly. But I'm starting to realize he's no good for me. And I'm probably no good for him. It's funny, Ross. When he proposed this open-relationship thing, all I was scared of was that he'd meet someone he liked better than me. And now I'm afraid I've met someone I like better than him. I need to talk to him, OK? But I'm scared. That'll probably be the end for us, and I'm putting that conversation off as long as possible. That's why I haven't picked up. And that's why he won't stop calling me. I know it's stupid. But it's also the truth."

He had listened attentively the whole time, and now that I was done, he grinned softly and asked, "You want to watch a movie?"

"Now?"

"You're done talking, right?"

"I guess…"

"Then I'll take that for a yes," he said.

That was different for me. In my world, arguments went from bad to worse, with screaming and who knows what else. Ross and I had disagreed, and now we were watching a movie. I was confused, but I nodded and said, "Yeah."

"Cool. It's my birthday, so I get to pick."

I smiled as I sat next to him in the bed and he scrolled through his enormous library of movies.

"I'm sorry I didn't tell you about Monty," I said.

"Don't worry," he replied, "that's your business. Plus you were honest with me. You *did* tell me you had a boyfriend."

"'Had' is right, I think. Because he told me if I even talked to you again, it was over between us."

"It's for the best," he said after squinting a bit and turning back to his computer. "If you hadn't talked to me, I'm afraid my days would have been pretty boring."

12

ANGELS AND DEMONS

I walked out of class and saw that it was raining. Dammit. Looking out the front window of the building, I realized I didn't have an umbrella, and I'd left my light-rail pass at home. I wondered if I should wait for the rain to let up, and as I was dawdling, I got a message from Naya:

I left a costume on your bed.

I shook my head and wrote back:

Do you think Will would come pick me up?

She responded:

Will's in class. But I know someone who would.

Fine. I rang him after a moment's hesitation and brought the phone to my ear. He responded on the second ring.

"If it isn't my favorite girl," he said.

"Calling her favorite boy."

"So you finally admit it," he said. "Now what can I do for you on this lovely afternoon?"

"Are you busy with anything important?" I asked.

"Not more important than you. Why? Let me guess. You need a chauffeur."

"I mean…I could use one. Like, if you can, you know. I didn't bring my wallet with me, so I can't catch the light rail, and…"

"Jen, you don't need to make excuses. I'll be right there. All I ask for is one kiss of gratitude in return."

"We'll see," I said, giving him directions. "Wait—you're not talking to me on the phone while you're driving, are you?"

"So what? I can do two things at once."

"Ross, no you can't! There've been studies! Distracted drivers cause tons of accidents!"

"Sure, Mom," he said and hung up.

I tucked away my phone, knowing he would be there in no time. Even in bad weather, he drove like a maniac. I'd seen it, and he'd told me he behaved himself when I was with him, so I was terrified to think what it must be like when he was alone.

I glanced over at the announcement board close by and noticed that there were job offers posted all over it. A lot of them looked boring, some of them looked shady, but there was one place that was looking for a waitress, no experience required, and I thought that might work. The hours weren't great, but the place was close to Ross's house, and I still needed money. I reread it, thinking it over, until a pair of hands around my waist frightened me, nearly making me jump out of my skin.

"What are you looking at?" Ross asked.

"Jesus, you got here fast. A job offer," I said.

I grabbed the piece of paper as he frowned and responded, "May I ask why?"

"Uh, because I need a job."

"No you don't. What you need is money. Now it's just a question of how much."

"I don't know," I stammered. "I'm not sure. I mean, I'm OK, sort of, right now. It's just that I need to pay for my dorm fees for next semester. So I can have somewhere to live, you know."

"You could just keep staying with us."

"And let Sue murder me in my sleep?" I joked.

"Surprisingly, Sue seems to like you. And so does Will. Naya you know, and I suppose my opinion's no secret to you, either."

"Whatever. I'm keeping the job posting."

"What's the problem?" he said. "If it's money, all you have to do is ask. I don't mind, and it's better than you working for starvation wages."

"The problem, Ross, is I want to have my own money. I don't want to use you."

He looked almost angry as he said, "Fine, but not this job. This job looks like it sucks. Try and find another one that's better. There are tons out there."

"I'm not sure that there are."

"Don't be silly."

"Whatever. Ross, just take me home."

His face lit up when he heard me refer to his apartment as *home*. I don't know that I'd ever done that before. But I didn't want to dwell on it just then, so I asked him if he had an umbrella. He told me he had something better, and he lifted one side of his coat to cover me up, throwing his hood over his head. I huddled in close to him, almost slipping and falling, and getting water from a puddle all over my shoes and socks. Of course he laughed at me all the way to the car.

"I don't know what's so funny," I said. "You won't be laughing like that when I'm dying of pneumonia."

"Stop being dramatic and take off your shoes and socks."

"And what? Walk barefoot upstairs to your apartment?"

"Jen, if you want me to carry you, just ask."

On the drive, we talked about our Halloween costumes. I didn't know what Naya had chosen for me, but that didn't stop him from taking guesses: sexy nurse, sexy stewardess, sexy fairy… He told me he'd be going as Michael Myers from the Halloween movie. I asked him if he meant sexy Michael Myers, and he said, "Of course. I can't help it. I assumed you knew that by now. Be careful, I might get into character and chase you around all night."

He drove slower with me, just as I'd imagined, and it took us twice as long to get home as it had taken him to get there. When he parked, he said, "Now about that kiss I was supposed to get as a reward…" and I leaned in and gave it to him. I shouted as he grabbed me and pulled me into his lap.

"Hey!"

"Hey, what? I just wanted to make it easier for you."

I shook my head. As I leaned in, I felt his hands moving under my T-shirt, into my pants.

"You know," he said. "We *could* skip the party. If we're going to keep doing this, it might be worth it."

"You were the one who tried to convince me to go!"

"Yeah, that was before this started."

I wove my hands behind his neck and kissed him some more. His stubble pricked my lips. He realized it and said, "Sorry about the beard."

"I kind of like it," I responded.

"You know what I like?" My eyes widened as he grabbed my butt with both hands. "This ass," he said. "This has got to be the best ass I've ever seen in my life. I'm serious. You have to know that's why I always let you walk in front of me."

He opened the car door and hopped out, still holding me in his arms.

When we reached the elevator and he hadn't put me down, I tried to wriggle free.

"Calm down, wild beast!" he said.

"What if somebody sees us?"

He ignored me, getting in the elevator and hitting the button for the fourth floor.

"I can't believe you said that about my ass," I said on the way up. "You're so crude."

"Listen, I like your legs, too. I like lots of things. But a good relationship's based on honesty. So I might as well be honest with you about how much your ass turns me on."

I opened my mouth to reply, but I couldn't before he kissed me.

When the door opened, I heard a familiar voice say, "Hey, you looking for a third?" I nearly had a heart attack. Ross let me down brusquely and asked his brother, "You want to tell me what you're doing here?"

"Hey, don't get all pissed, dude," Mike said. "I wasn't trying to come between you guys. I just thought you might need a pro to step in and show you how it's done." Watching us awkwardly rearrange our clothes and hair as we approached the apartment, he continued. "I just wanted to come say hi to my little bro. Is that a crime? I *am* starving, though, if you want to have me in for dinner."

"We don't have anything," Ross said.

"Jeez. What kind of guy says that to his poor, starving brother."

"Ross," I whispered, "we've got plenty of food," and he grunted, "I don't care."

The whole crew was gathered in the living room, and Mike tried to join them, until Sue nearly attacked him for jumping into one of the armchairs. He must have decided I was a safer bet, so he settled in beside me.

"Mike, to what do we owe the pleasure?" Will asked.

"These two lovebirds invited me in for a slice of that pizza y'all are eating," Mike said. "Just so you know, I caught them in the elevator looking like a couple of wild animals in heat."

I almost choked on my slice of pizza as Ross announced, "We didn't invite him in."

Sue, always the life of the party, asked me where my shoes were.

"Long story," Ross said, saving me from having to give explanations.

When we'd finished eating, Naya dragged me back to Ross's room to show me the costume. I was horrified.

"You didn't say it was so revealing!" I told her.

"It's not! Wait till you see what the other girls at the party are wearing. Anyway, I'll bet Ross will like it."

"Hush," I said, pulling up like a weight lifter to try to get the skirt on. "I think this is a little tight."

"It's not tight, it's formfitting. It shows off that sweet ass of yours."

What was it with people and my ass that day? I looked at myself in the mirror, trying on the top, which Naya was helping me lace up in the back. I wondered if it would be hard to take off later, and as that question made me feel a tingle between my legs, I remembered I had to talk to Monty. Sooner rather than later.

"Oh, I should have told you," Naya said, "but Will found out about you punching that jerk at the party." She seemed to think it was no big deal as she started arranging her hair.

"How?"

"Some guy he had a class with was there and told him. We bumped into him at the bar after Ross's mom's exhibition, and of course he spilled the beans. I was probably lucky I was drunk because he was pretty pissed at me, but he couldn't really show it too much."

"It's still impossible for me to imagine Will mad," I said.

"I can't really complain. I'm the one who usually chews him out. I'm lucky with Will. He's probably the only man on earth who could stand me. And he likes me, even!"

"Don't say that," I told her. "I can stand you. I like you, too. If it wasn't for you, I'd be all alone. You might have noticed I don't have the best social skills in the world. I wish I could be like you in that way. Bubbly, just happy to be with people."

With a shy smile—which was very unusual for her—she asked if I seriously felt that way.

"Of course I do." I threw her top to her. "Now put this on before the conversation gets even cheesier."

We examined each other. She looked stunning in her corset. According to her, all I needed was one final detail—a white plastic halo she put on my head with a giggle. She clapped and said, "Amazing!" and I helped her apply the little red horns to the corners of her forehead.

My angel costume was surprisingly comfortable for how tight it was, and it concealed—just barely—those parts of my body I preferred not to show the entire world. The white, elbow-length gloves and white boots matched the wings perfectly. I had to give it to Naya; she had taste. I just hoped I didn't get makeup on it. But when I told Naya this, she said, "Don't worry, I haven't worn it in years. You can just keep it."

I helped her with her zipper. We were a perfect match. In her red and black body suit, red wings, and high leather boots, she looked like a runway model. We walked to the bathroom together to do our makeup. As we laughed and gossiped, I realized I could be myself with her in a way I hadn't been able to with my friends back home. I hoped that wasn't something I should feel guilty for, but maybe that's what getting older was.

Naya gave my eyeliner a once-over and said, "Perfect. I didn't go too crazy. Remember, you *are* supposed to be innocent."

I saw myself in the mirror: pink blush, dark lashes, red lips. Naya's makeup was darker, more seductive, sexier. But that was just who she was.

When we came out, everyone was there waiting for us, except for Mike, who had disappeared again. When Naya did a turn for Will, he smiled, revealing his fangs. "Mr. Sexy Dracula," she said, "meet Ms. Sexy Devil."

"Not bad," he responded, pulling her over for a kiss.

I walked over to Ross, who said, "An angel, huh? I like it. Take it off now!"

I giggled as he touched the little wings on my back. He wore blue coveralls stained with fake blood and black boots, and carried a plastic knife. He brought it out and pretended to threaten me. I knocked it out of the way and asked, "Didn't Michael Myers wear a mask?"

"Of course. But you think I could deprive you of the pleasure of seeing my pretty face?"

He pulled the mask from his pocket and threw it on. It was terrifying, especially when he tried to lean in and kiss me in it. Fortunately nobody noticed, not even Sue, who walked out in a Wednesday Addams costume that made me nearly split my seams with laughter even though, honestly, it looked good on her, ridiculous as it was.

"Sue," Ross said, "you're supposed to wear a costume. That just looks like the regular you."

"Very funny. Can we go now? I want to get drunk."

Ross drove to the party at what he considered a reasonable speed, and when we arrived, white-knuckled, I was surprised by the quantity of people there. Maybe it seemed like more because they were all wearing costumes? Naya had been right about one thing, though. I looked like a nun compared to some of the girls there.

Ross grabbed my hand and guided me through the crowd into the kitchen. We saw a girl who looked like a kitten and meowed at us. She was eyeing up Ross, and I got pissed until I turned around and saw he was completely hypnotized by me. Or, more concretely, by my skirt.

"For the love of God, Jen, please dress like an angel for the rest of my life."

I laughed and pulled two beers out of the giant ice bucket on the floor, handing him one. He opened it with his bare hands, then offered to do the same to mine. I'd never understand how he did that without hurting himself.

I wasn't usually in the mood for dancing, but that night was different. I dragged him out on the dance floor and we soon found Naya and Will. We stayed out there almost two hours. Even Sue joined us, making weird movements with her neck and arms. Once I was three beers in, I started to feel hot and walked out to the balcony. Ross soon joined me.

He pointed at what was left of my beer and said, "You're doing better than the other day, but if you need me to finish that for you, just say the word."

"I'm OK. I've realized four is my limit. Four and I'm drunk. I'm at three and a half right now. No, you know what? I've changed my mind. You take it."

He laughed and accepted, and I said, "Can I ask you something?"

"You're already asking me something."

"Jerk. I'm serious. What I wanted to know was...do you ever bring girls home?"

"I brought you home."

"Don't be stupid. You know what I mean. I've seen the way girls look at you. Tell me the truth."

"Fine," he said. "Yes, I've brought girls home."

I'd been the one to ask, but that admission felt like a kick in the ribs. Instantly, I could see him doing with other girls the things he'd done with me. I resented it, and I knew it wasn't fair. He was talking about stuff that happened before we'd even met, before we'd had...whatever it was we had with each other.

"Jen, don't look at me like that."

"I'm not looking like anything."

I had no right. Even if I were his girlfriend, I wouldn't have a right. I looked down until I felt his hand on my halo. He turned me to face him, leaning one hand on the parapet, and said softly, "That was a long time ago."

"I shouldn't have asked. You don't owe me an explanation."

"It doesn't matter. You're asking me, and I'm telling you. Of course I was with girls before you. But I'm not now. And I don't want to be."

"You know you can't lie to an angel, right? You'll go headfirst to hell."

"I told you before, I've never lied to you. And I've got no intention of starting now."

His lips were damp with beer. I wanted to taste them. But I still had more questions.

"You don't ever feel like doing it again?" I asked.

"Not a bit. Why? Do you?"

"Of course not!" I said.

"Me neither, then. For the same reasons as you, I'd bet."

Why was I asking this? Was I trying to sabotage myself? Could I not just enjoy what we had? Couldn't I try to be more like Naya? Fuck. I really needed to talk to Monty. I was worried even breaking up with him wouldn't get rid of him, but I needed to try. For me as much as for him.

I wrapped my arms around Ross and sank my face into his chest. I was surprised by how familiar he felt to me. As if he were my boyfriend. That confused me so much, I wanted to cry. But just for a moment, because his embrace was too warm to be sad for too long. I closed my eyes and barely heard him as he asked me, "Are you OK?"

I nodded and said, "Can we go back home? Just you and me?"

He hesitated briefly. Then he took out his phone, called Will, exchanged a few words with him, and hung up. He grabbed my hand and walked me out. I could tell he was nervous, but I needed something from him, too, and as he began to ask me, "Jen, are you…" I stopped him and said, "Ross, I need you to promise me something. I don't want you to worry about Monty."

He almost laughed and said, "Sorry, Jen, but I don't give a damn about your—"

"He's not my boyfriend. Or not anymore. Not really. But that's not what I'm saying. I... OK, when you and I did what we did that first night, I tried to convince myself that it was just because Monty and I had a deal, and I was having fun, exploring or whatever. But it's not true. I like you. I already liked you then. I've liked you since I first met you. And I need you to promise me that you know that. That you know you were never just a fling for me."

"OK, I promise. Sure. But I don't understand..."

I kissed him. I didn't need him to understand more. I just needed him to take me home. He started the car, a little tense, and I reached over and rubbed his shoulder as he drove. I felt better, less confused, when we reached the parking lot.

"I think this is the first time I've been here alone with you," I said.

"You know your moods are difficult as hell to read, Jen."

"My brothers say the same thing. They call me hysterical. I think they mean it in a nice way. I hope so."

When we got in the elevator, it was déjà vu. I remembered us kissing in there earlier. I think he did, too, because he grinned as I turned my back to the wall and pulled him into me. All that tenderness we'd shown on the balcony and in the car vanished into animal hunger as we held each other tight. We stumbled out when the door opened, and I couldn't help but laugh as he stuck the key in quickly and threw the door open.

"You in a rush?" I asked.

"You aren't?"

"I don't mind taking it slow," I said.

"Liar."

He pulled me into the apartment and dragged me back to his room. As soon as he closed the door, we were kissing again. I sighed against his mouth, unzipping his coverall and pulling it off of his shoulders to caress his skin, leaving him exposed to the hips. He stood back to pull it the rest of the way off, struggling with his work boots, and I took off my halo, tossing it aside and lowering my skirt. Everything was fine except for the stupid wings, which I couldn't figure out how to remove. I was jumping up and down, hoping they'd just fall off, in vain. I shouted at Ross, who found the whole thing hilarious, "Stop laughing and help me!"

As he came in and embraced me, his arms wrapped around my back. He unfastened the wings and they fell to the floor. I kicked them away and stroked his back as he caressed me over my corset. I realized he was trying to untie it and couldn't. He'd managed the top knot, and the eyelets just below it, but there were twelve more. "Screw this," he said. "I'll buy Naya a new one." And he grabbed it under my armpits and tore it off of me.

My phone rang.

I reached over to silence it as Ross unfastened my bra and threw it aside. As he bent down to kiss my nipples, it rang again.

"Goddammit!" I said, silencing it again.

"I've hardly ever heard you curse," he said.

"I don't do it unless the occasion demands."

He pushed me toward the bed and…my phone rang a third time.

"Wouldn't it be easier to just answer?" he asked.

"Or put it on Do Not Disturb."

"That would work, too."

I rolled onto my stomach, feeling something like ecstasy as he rubbed my shoulders and pressed his warm chest into my back. But when I saw my screen, my smile vanished. I had twelve messages from Monty and twenty-two missed calls. I froze. I glanced at a couple of the messages. It was just the same paranoid ranting as before. He called again, and I nearly hung up. Nearly. But, without knowing how to say it or why I was saying it, I told Ross, "Listen...I'm going to pick up, OK? Just so he'll leave me alone."

"Sure," Ross said, understanding.

Feeling grateful, I threw on my pajama shirt and walked to the living room, picking up just in time before he hung up.

"Monty," I began, "the last time we talked, we said..."

"Jenna, I'm so sorry," he interrupted me.

"Monty, are you crying?"

"I'm sorry, Jenna. I'm sorry for everything I said. I shouldn't have talked to you that way."

I had been ready to give him a piece of my mind, but now I wasn't sure. Something might really be wrong, I thought. I'd never heard that tone in his voice before.

"I'm an idiot," he continued. "It's just that I love you, Jenna. Every time you don't pick up the phone, I feel like I'm going crazy. I shouldn't have said all the stuff I said. I'm sorry. I was jealous. I thought you'd leave me for that other guy. I'm sorry. I was a jerk. I don't deserve you."

I rubbed my eyes, feeling guilty because of course, he was right. I had even told Ross he was right, that Monty and I were likely done.

"Don't be so hard on yourself, Monty. You're not a bad guy. It's just..."

"I know what you're going to say. We had a deal. You're right. And you can keep seeing that guy as much as you like. Just know that I love you, Jenna. And I trust you. Completely. And I know you'd never betray me. I take back what I said about breaking up with you. My feelings are too strong for that. And I know you wouldn't actually betray me. Please forgive me. I'll make it up to you. I promise."

I closed my eyes and tried to gather my thoughts. It was breaking my heart, hearing him hurting so much over something I'd done. I fell down on the sofa and murmured, "Why should I believe you?"

"Because I'm telling the truth. And you know it. You know no one could love you the way I do. And I'm doing what I'm supposed to do, right—asking for forgiveness? I'm tired of the paranoia and the bad attitude. I just want us to keep going. You tell me under what conditions. And I'll agree. And I won't blow up again. I swear. Just give me one more chance. That's all I'm asking for."

I could have cried from frustration. In our hearts, we must have both known how this was going to end, but still I found myself unable to hurt him. And it all felt so much worse when I looked up and saw Ross in the hallway, leaning against the wall, fully conscious of all that was going on. I wanted to say no, I should have, but I couldn't bring myself to break Monty's heart, and I found myself whispering, "Fine. One more chance."

I knew Ross was watching me, and I forced myself to look away. I knew what I saw would sting. And I knew I deserved it.

"Thank you, Jenna," Monty said, relieved. "I love you. You can't imagine how much I love you. I mean, for a second, I thought… Never mind. It doesn't matter."

"I've got to go, Monty."

"I love you," he repeated.

"Good night."

I hung up and stood, unable to confront the situation. I was drowning, and I knew Ross was watching me. He didn't even seem angry. Just disappointed. Hurt. I told him I was sorry, and he told me I shouldn't be. "He *is* your boyfriend, right?" he said.

"It's not that easy, Ross. He…"

"You don't owe me any explanations." After a moment's pause, he ran his hand through his hair and said, "I think I'm going to go back to the party, though. I'm not sure I feel like sleeping yet."

"Ross, you don't have to go. I can sleep on the couch. If it'll make you more comfortable."

"Why should I feel uncomfortable. We're friends, right?"

I didn't know what to say. That remark cut deep, but I'd deserved it. He shook his head and walked away. And I lay down on the couch and asked myself if what I'd done was wrong.

13

THE LASAGNA

Ross and I didn't talk much the next day. I didn't call Monty, either, and surprisingly, he didn't bother me. Or not at first. It was better that way. At least for a day, I needed to be alone to work things out. Even if that was selfish.

But late in the evening, I learned I wouldn't be getting off that easy. I was still on campus when the call came through. I answered. I didn't want to make matters worse.

"Hello?"

A pause. Then, "Jenna, you want to tell me why you haven't talked to me all day?" There was that tone again: angry, insecure. It usually meant bad things were coming. So I told him to relax.

"Relax? Relax when my girlfriend has been ignoring me for an entire day?"

"Yes, relax," I said.

"That's easy for you to say. If you ever called me, I'd pick up immediately. But when I call you, you always leave me hanging."

"I'm busy, Monty."

"Busy doing what? Busy with Jack Ross's dick in your mouth?"

"Don't you dare talk to me like that! I get that you're angry, but that doesn't give you the right to…"

"Either you tell me exactly what you've been up to or I'm going to assume you've been putting me off on purpose."

I tried not to let him get to me. Telling him off wouldn't do any good. So I pinched the bridge of my nose, took a deep breath, and tried to be rational, glad, at least, that he wasn't here and the worst thing he could do was punch his pillow.

"Monty, you're angry, OK? And you're about to make me angry. And you shouldn't talk about things when you're angry."

"You've done something. I can tell. You've done something and you feel guilty, and that's why you won't give me a straight answer about what you've been up to."

"Monty, I need to go."

"You listen to me right now, Jenna. From this moment forward, you better answer all of my messages."

"You're acting like a psycho," I said.

"Oh, really? You want to know what you're acting like?"

"No," I replied submissively.

He could tell I was backing down, and he seemed to like that. In a cloying voice, he continued, "Now be a good girl and promise me you're going to respond to me when I write or call."

"Monty…"

"Jenna, are you fucking hearing me?"

"Fine, I promise," I said.

"Now tell me what you're wearing."

I did so, and then he asked what I was doing that night, and I told him it was none of his business. Of course he wanted to know if I was going to see Ross. I told him he was taking things too far, and he went back to calling me a whore, and I said our conversation was over. I could still hear him screaming when I hung up.

Arguing with him was exhausting. And it was always the same. I was sick of it. Why couldn't he be the same charming guy I used to know? Why did he have to turn into a jealous weirdo who kept cursing at me? He had promised he wouldn't get nasty with me again, and he hadn't even made it a day. My phone rang again. This time it was Ross. He'd hardly spoken a word to me this morning, and now he was calling? Why?

"Hey," I murmured when I picked up.

"You busy tonight?" he asked, cheerful as ever.

"Why?"

"Mom wants us to come to dinner. All of us, Will and Naya, too. May I confirm your presence at the banquet?"

"I, uh…" I was so confused. Things were so weird the night before and now he was inviting me to his parents' place? I didn't get it. I was on the verge of tears.

"Jen, are you OK? Do you need me to come pick you up?"

"Sorry," I said. "It's just Monty. We had an argument. I don't want to talk about it. Seriously. It's not anything you should worry about."

"Of course I should worry about it. Anything that makes you stop smiling concerns me. And listen: no pressure, but you should know the moment you're tired of fighting with him, I'm here."

How could he be so sweet? And the strange thing was, I don't even think he was aware of it. And I liked him even more for that. I told him, "You know, you'd be right to be mad at me."

"I don't know if I could be mad at you."

I smiled. "You might regret inviting me. I don't know if you can tell from my tone, but I'm a disaster right now. You'll realize it when you see me."

"I was kidding about it being a banquet, Jen. It's just a normal dinner. And I should warn you, my mother's a pain when she wants something. She even makes Naya look chill. If you don't go, you'll never hear the end of it the next time she sees you."

"Fine, I'll go. What time should I…"

"I'll pick you up now. Same place as last time."

He hung up before I could answer, leaving me there to struggle with my feelings about him, about Monty, about my own lack of nerve. Five minutes later, he was pulling up. He eyed me up quickly as I got in and said, "Disaster's not the word I'd use for you." He must have realized flirting with me would make me uncomfortable, because he turned up the music then so I wouldn't have to respond. Naya and Will were already waiting for us outside when we pulled up. They were chatty when they got in—something about Naya's classes. I had my own things to deal with and didn't really listen. I don't think Ross did, either.

I asked how far away his parents lived, and Ross said ten minutes. By then I'd cheered up enough to make a joke. "What you mean is, they live twenty minutes away, but ten minutes with you driving."

When I watched him laugh, when I saw how easy it was to make peace with him, I couldn't help but think how hard things were with Monty. *Duh, Ross is better,* my brain said. Thanks again, Brain.

"You actually don't drive bad for someone who goes so fast," I said.

"I've got good reflexes."

"Tell that to the traffic cops when they pull you over."

"*If* they pull me over," he responded.

His prediction was right: ten minutes on the dot and we were in a residential area with big houses with big yards and expensive cars. Almost like my own neighborhood, but nice. Because it was nighttime, I couldn't see too much, just that the house was handsome, white in color, with doors made of dark wood. He stopped in front of the garage, which opened soon afterward, and he parked next to what I assume were his parents' cars. It was so big and neat, so different from my parents' sorry garage, which was now where Steve and Sonny ran their so-called business.

Ross once again had read my mind and lingered behind to ask me if I was nervous as we were on our way in. I nodded.

"A bit. Who all is going to be here? Just your mother and us?"

"Mike, too, probably," he said.

"And your dad?"

"Nah. He's not coming." I noticed the tension in his face as he said this, but I didn't press him. As we caught up with Naya and Will, they both remarked on how hungry they were. As soon as Ross opened the door, it smelled like food. "Lasagna," Naya said. "It's got to be."

I walked in first. The house inside was simple, formal, austere, but attractive, just as it was outside. Orderly. Very clean. It looked perfect and it smelled like money, if that's possible. Ross guided us through the entryway to a giant living room with a fireplace and a TV that took up half the wall. From there, we walked on to the dining room, where there was a long glass table already set. Over it hung an enormous, beautiful chandelier that I couldn't help staring at.

"Hello? Mom?" Ross called, peeking into the neighboring kitchen.

"Ask her if she made lasagna," Naya said.

"You've got a good nose," Ross's mother said as she came out. "Now go on, give me some space. Your father and your nightmare of a brother are going to be here soon."

"Dad's coming?" Ross asked.

His mother responded with an almost apologetic look and said, "Yes, honey, he called me an hour ago. I didn't know he was coming or I would have told you."

I could tell Ross wasn't happy with the surprise. He seemed frozen for a moment, unsure what to do. Then he remembered I was there and guided me back to the living room, where Naya and Will had taken their places on one of the couches. I took my time looking at the shelves full of books, the paintings, and the photos, all of which I supposed were Mary's work. There was a huge piano by the window. It was all so sophisticated. So luxurious. And it made me jealous.

"Can I ask you something obvious, Ross?" I said.

Arching an eyebrow, he said, "Shoot."

"Why the hell do you live in your apartment when your parents have this mansion?"

"I like my apartment."

"But you have everything here!"

"Not everything," he said. "At the apartment, I have you."

It was a sweet comment—Naya apparently thought so, too, I could tell from her expression—but this wasn't right. I couldn't play with Ross's feelings. He took my hand, but I pulled it away quickly. Before Ross could ask why, the front door opened, I heard someone whistling, and Mike appeared, saying hello to everyone and taking a turn that reminded me of Michael Jackson. "The party can start now," he said.

Naya remarked, "I guess nothing good can last."

Ross and I had taken a seat on the couch. Mike jumped on it and landed between us. I thought Ross would kill him as he said, "Did you not notice there are plenty of other places for you to sit?"

Mike ignored him and asked, "Hey, Jenna, what's up?"

"Same old, same old," I said. "I thought you weren't coming."

"I'm always up for a free meal," he responded. "Especially with good company."

Ross objected, saying, "The company doesn't care about you."

Mike went on pretending he hadn't heard him, telling me he had new *stuff* and that I should call him when I got bored. "Tell the bitchy one, too," he added. "The three of us make a pretty good team."

Mike and Ross started bickering at each other as a middle-aged man appeared at the top of a winding staircase twenty or so feet away. His hair was combed back perfectly, he had a salt-and-pepper beard, and he was wearing black-framed glasses. Right away, you could see the resemblance. He had almost the same face as his two boys, with a sharp jawline, high cheekbones, and light-brown eyes. Ross was a bit taller and a bit leaner, like his mother, while Mike was shorter and stockier, like his dad.

"Boys," Ross's father said in a stiff, formal tone.

"Dad," Mike said.

The man walked past us and into the kitchen. It was weird that Ross hadn't said hello to him, I thought, but I was the only one who seemed to have noticed. We went in soon to sit down, and I was given the not-exactly-enviable place between Ross and Mike. At least I wouldn't be bored, I thought. Will and Naya were across from us. When the lasagna arrived, they looked like they were going to take off running with it. Will's parents sat each at one end of the table and didn't look at each other, and when we were served, everyone focused on their food without talking. Ross looked angry, his father looked serious, and Mike kept refilling his wineglass. The rest of us waited for someone to say something. It was so uncomfortable that I imagined the lights going out and coming back on with someone murdered, as in a game of Clue.

"Well," Ross's father finally said, breaking the silence. "You must be Jenna. You're the only one I'm unacquainted with here."

"Yeah," I said, feeling put on the spot. "Nice to meet you."

"I'm not sure if it's thanks to you, but if so, I'm very grateful you managed to convince Jack to come. It's been months since I've had dinner with him."

"Why do you say that?" Jack asked with a surly expression. "Did you miss me?"

Sensing the tension, Mary tried to change the subject, saying, "Jenna, I told my husband you have quite an eye for art. That you and I have the same tastes. And trust me, I—"

"What are you studying?" her husband asked, interrupting us.

I had the feeling he was inquiring as to my value, the way he might with a fancy watch or car. I doubted I'd make the grade, but I responded, "English."

"English? Oh no, you should drop that. That won't take you anyplace. If it's true you have an eye for art, you should…"

"Honey," Mary said sweetly, "don't start. We're trying to have dinner."

"I'm just making a suggestion," he responded without looking at them. "And I'm sure Jenna appreciates it, don't you, dear?"

"Uh, sure," I said, feeling like an idiot.

His mouth full of lasagna, Mike interjected, "I was supposed to play a concert today. I skipped it to come to this lovely feast. I hope everyone's happy."

"We're very happy to have you here, Michael," his mother responded with a smile.

"I hope none of your fans kill themselves," Ross replied.

"I don't know about that," Mike said, "but I'm sure there's a number of girls at home crying. You've seen them. Remember how they were all over me at my last show? It just does something to you when you see a girl in a tight T-shirt with your name on it and a pair of shorts so short you can see her…"

"Michael, I believe we get the idea," his father said.

To try to inject a note of happiness into the evening, I told Mike I'd really enjoyed his concert the other day. It wasn't true, but I didn't think sincerity was the most important thing just then. He thanked me, saying, "You'll make a hell of a sister-in-law."

Naya burst out, "Jenna, I think you might need to get your ears checked," but Will stopped her, serving her more lasagna and telling Mary the exhibition had been interesting.

"Thank you, honey," she said. "Too bad Michael missed it."

"I had a thing," Mike told her.

His father said arrogantly, "So, you're still with your little band." His expression was condescending, and Mike's face showed how little he cared. When he told his father it wasn't just any band, it was *his* band,

and they were good, and he should check them out some time, his father stopped him with the question, "And has it ever crossed your mind to get an actual job? One that would, for instance, pay you and bring some stability to your life?"

"No can do, Pops," Mike responded. "That's just not who I am."

The look on Jack Sr.'s face was like the look on my father's face when Shannon told him she was pregnant. By now, Ross seemed to have given up on interacting and had been staring into his lap for the past five minutes. Instinctively, I reached out and took his hand under the table. When he looked up, surprised, I smiled at him. That relaxed him, and I stroked his fingers until it was time to break the silence again, which I did by telling Mary how good her lasagna was. Will agreed, and she seemed grateful and started telling us what her trick was, but her husband interrupted her, asking me what my parents did.

I didn't like telling him. What did it matter to him? Probably he would just look down on them. But I had no choice, so I replied, "My mom's a nurse and my dad was a truck driver."

"Was?"

"He hurt his back and he had to give it up."

"Brothers or sisters?" he asked.

"Four. Three brothers, one sister. All older."

Trying to be positive, Mary remarked that we must be very close, since my face lit up when I talked all of them him, but her husband seemed to ignore her completely, needling me further, "And is a nurse's salary enough to take care of such a large family?" He stared at me as he took a sip of his wine.

I squinted as I tried to find the right words, and struggled to understand why I felt ashamed. Ross's hand tensed in my lap. I don't know if he was squeezing to help calm me down or himself.

"Dad gets a disability payment. And my older sister's out on her own. She's got a kid. She had him when he was seventeen…"

"He must have been an accident. Why didn't she get an abortion or give him up for adoption?"

"She just didn't. And I'm glad, and everyone else is, too. We love Owen. And it was good for my sister. She matured overnight, and I'm sure she'd never regret her decision."

I sounded angry now, and I didn't care. Ross's father gave me a snobbish smile as he said, "I see." I knew that look. I'd seen it before. The last time was when Nelle had asked me to go to some fancy perfume shop and I'd shown up in jeans and a T-shirt. I remember she looked at me and the cashier and rolled her eyes, and the cashier had giggled. I felt as insulted then as I did now, and Ross could tell. He tried to pull his hand away, probably to bang it on the table. But I stopped him.

When his father asked what my brothers did for a living, Ross stopped him, saying, "This is a dinner, Dad, not a job application. I don't know why you always have to interrogate everybody."

It was at that point that the conversation turned ugly. Ross's father asked if I had a job, and I said no, but that I was looking for one. The next thing he wanted to know was whether I paid rent. Ross tried to stop him, but he said he was just curious, and when Ross protested that it was his apartment and he could do as he liked with it, his father asserted that he had a right to know what was going on with his son's life. I had to admit that I didn't pay anything, at which point Ross's father asked Will whether he paid rent. Will looked at me almost apologetically as he admitted that he did. Ross was furious. I tried to interject, saying I was just staying there temporarily, and Ross's father said, "Yes, roommate situations usually are temporary. And they usually involve paying rent. Tell me now, Ross, is Jenna your girlfriend?"

"Why do you care?" Ross responded. Naya tried to defend me by saying I had a boyfriend, but I don't know if that helped. Ross's father simply said, "Oh, so you have a boyfriend, but you're sharing a bed with my son. Very interesting. What is it exactly that you do, then, Jenna, to live with my son for free?"

My mouth fell open as Ross stood and kicked his chair back, knocking it over. "We're done here," he shouted. "Come on, Jen." Confused, Will and Naya stood up, too. Ross's father shouted, "Oh, don't be childish," but we were already on our way out. Mary buried her face in her hands. Even Mike, who was usually impervious to everything, looked upset. Ross turned back around and shouted something, but Naya took my hand and led me away, through the living room and out to Ross's car.

I didn't know what to say. I felt humiliated. And guilty. Because it was my fault Ross was arguing with his dad. Will told me not to take it personally, and Naya said the old man wasn't supposed to be here. He was usually away traveling, she added, and reminded me not to blame myself. "He doesn't get along with either of his sons. There's always something."

"He doesn't get along with anyone," Will asserted.

Five minutes passed, and I was starting to worry about Ross when the garage door opened and he walked in. He looked like hell. He got in and slammed the door. I was almost scared at how angry he was. He turned the key, and Mike rapped on his window. Since Ross seemed paralyzed, I lowered my window and he came around to my side of the car and asked, "Hey, little bro. Can I stay at your place tonight? You can imagine I don't really feel like sticking around here."

Will nodded to him, Mike hopped in, and Ross jetted out of the garage. The drive home was terrifying—I was white-knuckling it the whole way. Speeding was one thing, but I don't know how we even stayed on the road. I reached over and touched Ross's hand, and he slowed down a little. Then he grabbed my fingers and his hand dropped into his lap. We dropped Naya off at the dorm, and I went back with the three guys. When we got inside, Mike flopped down and said, "I guess I'll take the sofa." His brother didn't react; he just dropped his keys on the bar and walked wordlessly to his room.

Mike grinned a little sadly and said, "He's never been able to take Dad's nonsense. Some things never change. They could argue about anything. This time, though, Ross was in the right. That was too much."

My nerves were raw, and I didn't think talking about it would help, so I said good night to Mike and Will and headed to Ross's room while Mike turned on the TV. I closed the door behind me. Ross was changing clothes and didn't seem to have cooled off one bit. I didn't know whether I should speak to him or respect his silence. I'd never seen him like this, and I didn't know what he needed. So I just put on my pajamas and got in bed. Eventually he sat with his back turned to me.

I was about to say something, but he beat me to it. "I'm not sure if I should let him stay here."

"Who, Mike? Doesn't he have his own place?"

"He did. They kicked him out. I don't know why, but it isn't the first time. He used to always bounce back and forth between his different apartments and Mom and Dad's place. Now he doesn't want to stay with them, and I get that, but…"

"Ross, you did the right thing. If you hadn't let him come over, he'd be sleeping on the street."

"Maybe he should sleep on the street, Jen," he murmured. "Maybe that way, he'd finally wake up to reality for once."

I took off my glasses and laid them on the nightstand. I looked at my hands. They were shaking.

"My fucking father," he continued. "How dare he tell me what to do with my apartment. It's mine, not his. He's never even set foot in here."

"I don't know, Ross," I said, my heart in my throat. "I mean, I've been here two months already. Maybe I've overstayed my welcome. I can't just live here for free forever. I feel like I'm taking advantage of you. I don't contribute anything. I just get in the way. My mom said maybe she'd be in better shape soon financially. I should probably check on that and get a job if it doesn't pan out."

"Why do you want to go?" Ross asked.

"I don't."

"It sure seems like it, the way you can't stop talking about it when I told you I don't care about the money and I want you here! You know what, though? Whatever. If you want to go, go. I don't care. I need some fresh air and a cigarette. And I need to be by myself."

He got up to go to the balcony, and I tried to stop him, but that just made him explode again. "I told you I don't want your money. I want you. I want you to live here with me and Will and Sue, like now, and I know you want that, too, but for some stupid reason, you're trying to convince yourself otherwise. And I can't understand why. Because if that's not it, I'm completely baffled, and you're going to have to tell me what you do want."

"I don't know!" I admitted.

He attacked again. "Is this what you plan on doing? Going through your life letting the things people like my father say matter to you? He's always been a jerk. He's always loved making other people feel bad. That's why I didn't want you to come to my house when he was there. I knew he'd try to ruin everything. And it looks like he did."

"Ross," I told him, "don't talk about your father that way."

"He hasn't been my father for a long time."

I stood and walked toward him. "Can't you understand how hopeless I might feel being here and not paying for anything? Do you not get that I need to feel useful? That I don't want people to take pity on me, that I want to do something for myself?"

"I don't feel sorry for you, Jen."

"Not now, maybe, but you will if I just stay here scrounging off of you."

He seemed calmer for a moment and asked, "Wait, is that it?" His voice was softer then. "Are you scared I'm going to get tired of you? Like Monty when he told you he wanted an open relationship?"

"You don't know anything about what happens between us," I said, feeling so exposed I wanted to run away.

"I do. I know how you act with us, and I know what happens to you every time he calls or texts. You're scared of him, Jen."

"I am not!"

"You are. Just admit it for once. You're scared of being with him, and you're scared of leaving him. Any fool can see it. That's why you agreed not to break up with him the other day. You might feel like shit with him, but you're more comfortable than you would be actually trying with me. You're scared because you think I'd hurt you. And it's easier for you to just accept someone you don't like mistreating you than to let in someone who really likes you. Tell me I'm wrong, Jen."

"Shut up!"

"No! I'm tired of shutting up! I'm tired of seeing you getting upset over that dickhead. Can you not just love yourself for once?"

Love myself. Those two words lit a wick inside me, and all the frustration I'd been accumulating without realizing it exploded. And Ross was the victim. I pushed him so hard it surprised him.

"You want me to love myself? Well, what about you, Ross? I told you I had a boyfriend, I told you we had a deal that I could have sex with other people, and you just accepted that. I left you high and dry the other night because of my boyfriend, and you were nice about it. You tried to hold my hand and I pulled it away, and what? Where was your reaction? Do something for once. Get mad at me. Throw me out of your bed, dammit. Throw me out of your apartment."

I nearly pushed him again, and he stepped away, shouting, "This is a fucking joke, right? You're actually mad at me because I'm not mad at you?"

"Ross, I'm treating you like shit and you're just taking it. Why the hell won't you get mad at me?"

"I don't know… OK, Jen!"

"Fine. But don't tell me to love myself, because I don't see you doing that," I said.

"You're mixing up two very different things," he responded. "Maybe I'm being irrational sometimes, but it's because I know what I want. I want you, and if I have to make some sacrifices, so be it. You, though… You don't know what the hell you want. Your family tells you to come home and you're like, *Maybe I should just go home.* Some loser you don't even care about tells you he needs you and you're like, *Poor Monty, he needs me.* A man you've never met in your life makes insinuations about you living at my apartment, and you listen to his opinion and don't give a damn about mine when I'm the one who actually cares about you! And I'm sorry, but I know you care about me. If you didn't, you wouldn't be here. You wouldn't look at me the way you do. You wouldn't act the way you act when I'm around. Lie to yourself if you need to, but don't lie to me. If you need time, I get that, but I can't do it like this. Not with you just staying in a rut because it's the easiest thing to do."

I couldn't stop myself from crying. He didn't try to console me, and I was grateful for it because it would only have made me feel worse. I covered my face with my hands and tried to calm down. Even after I'd wiped away my tears, I couldn't bring myself to look at him.

"I don't want to be like that," I said. "I don't like it when I'm like that. I do want to be my own person. But I don't know how," I admitted. I don't even think I realized I was speaking aloud. Now Ross did come over and put his hands on my shoulders.

"Jen, you are your own person. It's just a matter of recognizing it and letting yourself be free."

He sounded so sure of himself that I almost believed him. "I don't want to play with your feelings," I said. "But I also don't want to hurt Monty."

"Dammit, Jen, can you not forget that idiot for a moment? Just for a moment, to ask yourself what *you* want? What would make *you* feel good?"

I thought for a moment. I felt like I was standing before an ocean of uncertainties. But of course, in my heart, I knew what was right for me.

"I don't want to be with him," I murmured.

"Then I guess it's time to take care of some things, isn't it?"

"I guess." I smiled through my sorrow and looked up at him. "I still feel like you must be mad at me, though."

"Of course I am. And I'm mad at myself that I'm not madder at you. It's frustrating, but what's a guy to do?"

"I don't know what to tell you, Jack Ross." It seemed funny, using his full name, and we both looked at each other a little awkwardly before I continued. "Look, I don't want to go. I like being here, I like you, I like Will and Sue. But I still feel like I owe you something."

"You don't owe me anything. But I wouldn't say no if you wanted to get back in bed with me."

It was strange how natural that sounded. And I felt relaxed as I nodded, walking inside as he dropped his jacket into the chair. I lay down and waited for him. When he was next to me, he sighed and turned out the light, saying, "Good night, Jen."

I wanted to cuddle up with him, but I couldn't. I shouldn't. Not till I had settled things with Monty. Take care of that first, and then I could have Ross all to myself. Before I fell asleep, I just said one thing.

"You know, I like the sound of Jack. I think I'm going to call you Jack from now on."

"Great," he said.

"So good night, Jack."

On my way out of class the next day, I saw dozens of messages and missed calls from Monty. The loser. I'd written him that morning and told him it was over between us. That was cowardly, I know. But I was a coward. And Ross was right about one thing: I was scared of Monty. He was acting crazier and crazier.

I wouldn't answer him, but I did want to call my sister. She put Owen on for a little bit. He always put me in a better mood. You're not supposed to pick favorites in your family, but I had. Him and Shannon. They were the ones who always made me feel better. I waved at a couple of classmates on my way out the door, ready to go home and take a shower. I was exhausted.

"Jenna!" It was Mike. He was wearing a pink stocking cap. "Are you going to Ross's?"

"As always."

"Cool, I'll come with you."

"Nice hat," I said.

"Yeah, I got it out of lost and found. By the way, did you piss someone off? Because there's a huge dude over there walking toward us and he doesn't look happy."

I grinned, thinking this was just another of Mike's dumb comments, but then I turned and what I saw made me freeze. There he was, big, blond, tall, and furious. "Hello, Jenna," he said coldly as he stopped in front of us. My eyes opened wide as I tried to take him in and make sure he was real and not a dream.

"Monty?"

14

A LITTLE FAVOR

I could feel all the blood draining from my head. I don't think a ghost could have frightened me worse.

Monty was tense, with pursed lips and clenched fists. He looked over at Mike, who seemed to have no idea what was going on. "Who's this?" he asked.

Mike replied with his usual smile, "My name's Mike. Pleased to meet you, whatever your name is."

"What are you doing here?" I asked.

"You know perfectly well what I'm doing here," he replied. Then he turned to Mike and said, "And you—why don't you fuck off?"

I didn't want a scene, and I could tell Mike was about to say something smart-assed back to him, so I stopped him and said, "Mike, please go. I'll see you around, OK? I'm fine, I promise."

He nodded, but he didn't seem sure. Monty almost shouted, "Did you hear her, dickhead? She told you to beat it."

I put a hand on Monty's arm to try to calm him down and let Mike know we could talk later.

"Sure," he said. "I'll see you at Ross's."

No. No, no, no, no, no.

Monty tensed up like a live wire and I closed my eyes. As soon as Mike was gone, he shook me by the shoulders. He was furious.

"Ross, huh? That's the guy, right? The guy you've been fucking?"

"Monty, you need to calm down." People were already starting to stare.

"I need to calm down? Why don't you tell me what the fuck you meant with that message you sent me?"

I was embarrassed and afraid in equal parts as I looked around. He grabbed my arm, pulled me close, and shoved his phone in my face, so quickly I thought he was going to hit me. My text message from that morning was on his screen.

"What the fuck?" he asked, squeezing my arm so tight it started to hurt. "Who the hell are you to decide to dump me, you whore?"

"Let me go," I said.

"Let you go? What I ought to do is…"

"Are you OK?"

We both turned and saw two girls who had approached, looking worried. One was looking straight at me and the other had her phone out and aimed at Monty, ready to record whatever he did.

"Listen," one of the girls continued. "We can call the cops right now if he's bothering you."

"I'm fine," I said.

Monty told the girls rudely to mind their business and dragged me across campus to the parking lot as I struggled to break his grip. Only once his car was in sight did he let me go. I walked back a couple of steps.

"Monty, I don't know what you think you're doing here, but I'm not getting in that car with you. You need to go back and read that message you shoved in my face, because I made myself perfectly clear. We're done."

"Screw your message. You're not done with me. I'm your boyfriend, goddammit! You can't just break up with me!"

"Monty, you need to calm down." There was a threat in his eyes.

"Calm down! You selfish bitch. Who are you to tell me to calm down after what you've done? I had a million things to do today, but instead I had to drive seven fucking hours just to get you to recognize that I exist."

Was he right? Should I have answered his calls? He was in pain—that much I couldn't deny. I reached out cautiously and touched his shoulder, and when I did, he clutched the back of my neck and pulled me close, trying to kiss me. Impulsively, I jerked away. That only reignited his fury.

"Are you serious?" he screamed.

"Monty, we're broken up. So I don't want you to kiss me. Do you not understand?"

"Oh, yeah, I understand perfectly. I understand that I love you and instead of loving me back, you come up here and the first thing you do is spread your legs for some jerk-off named Ross. And the very day I come visit, you're supposed to be going to his apartment. What were you going to do over there, Jenna?"

Fuck. He didn't know I was living there. I needed to make an excuse, fast.

"They're having me over for dinner. What's wrong with that?" I asked.

"Sure, with your tits hanging out of that V-neck. Bullshit. Give me your phone. I don't need to listen to you lying to me. I'll judge for myself."

"I'm not giving you my phone."

"Give it to me right now, Jenna!"

When he pushed me and started pawing me all over, I didn't even try to resist. There was no point. He was too strong, and it would only make things worse. He pulled my phone from my pocket and scrolled compulsively, breathing hard through his nose. I realized then he wouldn't find Ross's name because I'd saved him under *Errand Boy*. I had never imagined I'd be so happy about it.

"Are you happy now?" I said.

"Fuck no, I'm not happy. I know something's going on. I just don't know exactly what. I'm going to figure it out, though. Now get in the car."

"No. Monty, you're being ridiculous."

"Get in the goddamn car or I'll pick you up and put you in it. Jenna…"

"No."

He grabbed my biceps hard, opened his car door, and shoved me into the passenger seat. I tried to climb out and he grabbed me around the neck and pushed me back inside before shutting the door so hard I could see the side mirror shaking in its frame. He got in on his side and said, "Don't you dare try to get out." I bowed my head, humiliated, as he sped off toward my old dorm. I was trying frantically to think of an excuse when I saw Chris at the door. Monty parked and said, "Get out and go get your shit."

"What?"

"You heard me. We're going home. Do it now. It's not a suggestion."

"This is my home now. You're the one who needs to go back home."

I stared straight ahead and he cut the motor.

"Monty," I said as calmly as I could, "I'm going to repeat this very slowly so you understand. I don't want to be with you. This thing that's happening right now is a perfect example of why I don't want to be with you. You act crazy. And I can't deal with that. I'm at school, I have a life now, I have other things I need to think about."

"Yeah, like Jack fucking Ross."

"First of all, Monty, Jack Ross isn't my boyfriend either. And second, you told me you wanted us to be in an open relationship. If you can't deal with that, it's on you."

"Fine, I take it back. I'll be faithful to you. I want to. I want us to go back to how we were. We'll pretend this Jack Ross thing never happened. It'll be just the two of us. You'd like that, right? What do you say?"

Was he about to cry? It was so strange how he could move so easily between rage and sorrow. A little voice inside my head told me he was trying to manipulate me, but I didn't know how I was supposed to react to that.

He continued, "We were good together. You know we were. We might have had a fight or two, but we've always gotten through it, right? And I love you, Jenna. You know I do. You can't blame me for reacting like this. You'd do the same. Remember how upset you were when you found out about me and Nelle? It's the same thing, right?"

"I can't, Monty. I like it here. I have friends here. I'm not going anywhere."

"I thought I mattered to you. You don't even love me, do you? I tell you I love you every time we talk, in every message. And you never say it back. It's three simple words. They're easy to say. But you can't even bring yourself to do it."

"Monty, I can't. I can't just say something I don't feel."

"Just say it, Jenna!"

"No! Those words mean something to me. I've never said them to anyone except my family, and I'm not going to until I absolutely know the feeling's true. I'm sorry you're hurting, and I'm sorry you're angry, but you can't force me to stand here and lie to you."

"Listen," Monty said. "I get it. I surprised you, just coming here like this. And we're not going to solve this problem in the car. Why don't we go up to your room where we can talk it over in peace."

"I'd rather not," I said.

"I'd rather we did."

Now I was scared. But I couldn't think of a way out of it. Being with him had made me so tense I couldn't think straight anymore. I got out and we walked into the building. I entered quickly so he wouldn't try to hold my hand. When Chris looked up from his desk, I said, "Hey, this is my ex-boyfriend. He wants to see my room."

I hoped Monty didn't notice the confusion on Chris's face as he looked at me for a second in silence. With my eyes, I tried to tell him, *Please just go along with it*, and I guess my psychic abilities were working that day, because he smiled awkwardly and replied, "It's your room. Go for it."

I said, "Chris, I can't find my key. Can I use your copy?" He handed it to me.

Able to breathe slightly better, I guided Monty up the stairs. It was strange even being there now. Especially when I opened the door and saw Naya was gone. I guess she was at the apartment with everyone else. *My* apartment. *Ross's* apartment. Monty walked in and looked around. He saw a photo of me on Naya's nightstand. "Aw," he said, "how cute."

"Can we go now?" I asked, hoping I could get him out of there before he started asking questions. But he just stood there, slowly examining every detail.

Then the questions began. *Where's your laptop? Where's your contact case? Where are all your shoes?* I tried to make excuses: *I let Naya use it. I left them in the library.* He opened my old closet to look through it. I yelled, "Hey, that's private!" But he didn't care. My heart almost froze when he found it empty.

"Let me guess," he said. "You loaned out all your clothes, too. Do you think I'm a moron, Jenna? It's obvious you don't even fucking live here. I can't believe this! You sleeping with another guy is one thing! Are you fucking living with him, too!"

"Monty! Just stop!" I shouted.

But he was out of control now. He started kicking things, overturned one of the mattresses, grabbed one of Naya's dresses and tore it in half.

"Stop it!" I shouted again. "You have no right…"

He pushed me, and I was so angry I pushed him back. I couldn't believe what I was doing. I'd never fought back against him before. His features stiffened, and I stepped back. He knocked my glasses off my face. He knew how expensive they were, and he knew my parents couldn't afford to buy me new ones. And now I could barely see.

"You fucker!" I said. "I can't believe you!"

"Whatever. Tell your new boyfriend to buy you another pair."

He went on destroying everything he could lay his hands on: clothing, framed photos, a calculator. There was nothing I could do to stop him. And yet, it was almost as if my failure to react made everything worse, as if he wanted me to scream or break down in tears. He stomped on my glasses and then grabbed a book and threw it at my face. I barely managed to dodge it.

"You asshole!" I shouted. "You nearly broke my nose!"

"Like I care! You broke my fucking heart!"

I was frightened that his rampage would begin again, but luckily just as Monty clenched his firsts, the door opened and Chris peeked in. "Hey, guys," he said. "I'm sorry, but I've been getting noise complaints, and… what the…?"

Monty picked up his jacket, which he'd slung on the bed, and pushed brusquely past Chris on his way into the hall. I stayed there looking at the wreckage with tears in my eyes.

"Are you OK?" Chris asked.

"Yeah," I responded, surprised at how self-assured I sounded.

"Should I call someone? The cops?"

"No. I just need some time to clean all this up and then I'll go."

"Sure. Do you want me to help you?"

"No, Chris. Don't worry about it. Thanks. And sorry. Tell whoever complained that I apologize for the noise."

He nodded, turned away, and closed the door. I looked around at the wreckage. It was like a hurricane had struck. A favorite T-shirt I had left behind, one I'd held onto for years, was torn down the middle. And my glasses… I had wanted those frames so bad, and I remembered how my parents had tried to convince me to get a generic pair and I had begged and pleaded. It had been such a sacrifice for them, but they'd bought them to make me happy. And now they were crushed, shattered, because of one jealous idiot. I sat on the floor and cried hot tears and buried my face in my hands. Then the door opened again.

It was Ross. He looked confused and deeply worried.

"Dammit," I cried. I had hoped Chris wouldn't tell anyone. It was stupid—I was grateful Ross was there—but I had to get out my frustration some way. Ross must have known this wasn't the time to get angry, to plan revenge, to say *I told you so*, because he held very still for a moment, then knelt and asked in a soft voice, "What happened?"

"Monty," was all I could manage to say.

"Did he hurt you?"

"No," I said, shaking my head.

"OK," Ross said, kissing me on top of the head and beginning to patiently push everything torn or broken into a pile. I joined him. For the fifteen minutes it took, he said nothing. I picked Naya's photo of me out of the pile and smoothed it out. At least that was one thing I could save. I wanted to say something, to thank him, but I was afraid I'd start crying again. Finally, I turned to him and said, "I'm an idiot."

"This isn't your fault," he responded. "There's only one person who did this, and it's him."

"It is my fault." I reached under the bed, where I had left a small rolling bag, and stuffed everything that was on the floor inside of it. "It's my fault for not handling this sooner. If I had, we could have avoided this. I am a fucking idiot."

Ross came closer and said, "There's no way you could have known that this would happen."

"I could have, though." My voice cracked. "It's always like this with him. I tell people we don't fight, but it's not true. We'll be happy for a while, he'll buy me presents and stuff, and then he'll get pissed about something that's not even my fault and fly into these rages where he destroys things. I mean, never like this, and he usually says he's sorry right afterward, but…I could have known."

I closed the suitcase and put it on the bed, pulling back my bangs, which had fallen into my face.

"Thanks for helping me, though," I added. "Can we take this to the trash?"

It wasn't just the aftershock of our fight that had upset me, or all those broken things I'd have to explain to Naya. It's that I was ashamed. Ross pulled me in for a hug. I didn't have the strength to resist him, and anyway, I was grateful for contact from another person that wasn't being screamed at or being shoved.

"Naya will understand, Jen. She loves you. And I can pay her back for whatever."

"That's the thing, though. She shouldn't have to be paid back. This should just never have happened." I put my hands on my knees, looked down, and took a deep breath. I didn't want to cry anymore. I just wanted to get out of there and forget what had happened.

When I stood back up, I pointed at the suitcase and asked, "Can you grab that? It's a little heavy for me, and honestly, I just don't want to touch it."

He nodded and picked it up, and we walked downstairs. There was a group of girls there talking. They must have heard the commotion. Chris looked at me warily, probably worried I was angry with him for calling Ross, but he didn't say anything and I wordlessly handed him back the key. Anyway, I realized now I owed him. When we reached the car, my phone buzzed, and I almost startled thinking it would be Monty. But it was my sister. I asked Ross if he minded, then picked up.

"Hey there," she said, bubbly as ever. "Guess who just found a fifty-dollar bill on the street? Should I have tried to find out who dropped it? Maybe. Did I go buy myself a new pair of shoes? Yes…"

"Shannon," I interrupted her. "Monty came to see me."

"What? At your friend's apartment?"

"No. On campus. He did the jealous boyfriend thing right in front of everybody. And it was way, way worse than it's ever been. He tore up the clothes I'd left with my old roommate, he broke a bunch of her stuff, he stomped on my glasses…"

I knew Ross was listening, even though he pretended to be distracted. But he deserved to hear it. I should have been more honest with him before.

"Please tell me you kicked him in the balls," she said.

"Honestly, I didn't really know how to react."

"Are you OK? He didn't hurt you, did he?"

"I'm fine," I responded. "I'm with Ross."

"That son of a bitch," she said. "I'll take a shotgun to his house right now. I'll be damned if someone's going to do that to my sister."

"Shannon, it's over."

"It better be, because I swear to God, if I found out you've called him again…"

Frustrated, I said, "Thanks for being so understanding."

"Let me talk to Ross."

That was the last thing I wanted to do, but she wouldn't stop insisting. I had no idea what she was going to tell him. But Shannon wasn't someone you could say no to. So I sighed, turned to Ross, and said, "She wants to talk to you."

He took my earbuds without hesitation, said a polite hello, and listened to her for a few seconds. I leaned in to try to hear what she was saying, but the noise of the traffic was too loud. For a few moments, Ross's expression was neutral; then he grinned at something, clearly amused.

"Yeah, good," he said. "Not that I know. Sure, of course. Yeah, don't worry about it."

After a few more of those vague comments, he handed my earbuds back. Shannon had hung up. I asked Ross what they talked about.

"A gentleman never tells," he said.

I grimaced and stuck my phone back in my pocket.

When we came across a dumpster, I tossed the suitcase in it. I was happy never to see it again. Monty had bought me that suitcase. I remembered that day, how he'd pretended to be so proud of me because I was going off to college. I only hoped I would never see him or it again.

Anxiously, I asked Ross, "I know this is weird, but do we have to go back to the apartment right now? I honestly just don't want to deal with other people."

"Not if you don't want to. Did you have something else in mind?"

"Maybe we could catch a movie?" I asked shyly.

"Now you're speaking my language."

"I'm sad, though, that means this time I get to pick."

"I can't wait till I'm rich one day," he said, "and I'm going to buy my own movie theater. It'll be all superhero movies and comic movies, and I'll never have to care what anyone else thinks. I'll be able to sit there by myself—or with you, if you behave—there won't be anyone talking or making noise, and I'll have unlimited popcorn and soft drinks."

I smiled, looking out the window. Ross had managed to make me forget Monty for a moment. He had a talent for transporting me away, and I appreciated it just then. He put on some music, which was just what I needed. Because it was a weekday, the lot was almost empty, and Ross parked right by the door. We argued over what to see—there was a poster with blood splatters on it, which was like catnip for him, and I said I wanted to see a comedy. Finally we settled on a mystery that was starting so soon, we didn't even have time to go to the concession stand.

The film was passable. We were almost alone in the theater. There were a few tense moments where I grabbed Ross's arm. Apart from that, nothing special.

At least, not until we got to the sex scene.

When I saw the main characters kissing, I wanted to turn to Ross and do the same, but his eyes were fixed to the screen. Soon, the scene got hot. I started feeling nervous. Ross and I looked at each other. Embarrassed, I stared back at the screen. He didn't, though. I started clearing my throat, fidgeting, all the things that gave away how nervous I was, but I couldn't help it. And trying to stop doing it only made it that much worse. At least I managed to keep my mouth shut. Who knew what kind of ridiculous thing I would have blurted out if I'd talked. The worst part of the day was over, so why the hell was I so on edge?

As we left, Ross said we should grab a bite out, and I agreed. I was a little worried he'd pick somewhere fancy and try to get all romantic, but no, he stopped at a diner that looked like something out of the nineteen-fifties. It started raining on the way, so we ran inside as soon as we got out. The place smelled of coffee, old furniture, and fryer oil. It was a funny combination. Everything in there looked dated: the tables, the chairs, the pictures on the wall, even the people. It was clearly not a destination spot. There was just one couple there besides us, at the other end of the room.

Ross grabbed a table near the door and we sat across from each other.

"Call me crazy," I said, "but I get the feeling you didn't choose this place because it's where your parents brought you when you were little."

"How'd you guess?" He laughed. "Nah, this was Agnes's favorite. Still is. She's crazy about the burgers. The grill guy, I think his name's Johnny, he's been here for ages. He's a weirdo; he listens to the Spice Girls and Britney Spears while he cooks. They must inspire him, because he can cook his ass off."

"Well, I'm glad to hear that," I said, "because I'm starving."

Our waitress came over soon—a tired woman in her thirties—and we each gave her our order. Even in that, Ross was different from Monty, who always ordered for both of us, pretending to be a gentleman. But whatever. I needed to stop thinking about him. He didn't deserve it. And I could finally, honestly say he wasn't my boyfriend anymore.

Our burgers came out in no time along with our beers. To my surprise, the waitress hadn't carded me when I'd ordered one. She barely said a word as she dropped them off. After my first bite, I knew Ross had made a good choice. I should have told him, but I couldn't stop myself from chewing. Only when I was halfway through did I put my burger down, eat a fry, and say to him, "You know something? I get the impression sometimes that you'll talk about anything but yourself."

"Really? You live with me, though, Jen. I feel like you know me pretty well at this point."

"Maybe. I mean, I know how you *are*. But your life, the things that made you who you are? I hardly know anything about all that."

"Cool," he said. "What do you want to know?"

I thought it over for a moment. I knew my real question was why he got along so badly with his father. But I couldn't just come out and ask that. So I tried to come at it from a different angle, asking him to tell me about his childhood. "Was it happy? Sad? Were you a loner or an extrovert?"

"Probably more of a loner."

"Were you weird?"

"It's not that," he said. "It's just my brother was the fun, outgoing one. I didn't have so many friends. I didn't care, though. I was happy doing things by myself."

"Sounds sad."

"It wasn't. Trust me. Plus, as I got older, people thought it was cool that I did my own thing. It made them curious, and I wound up with more friends than I would have had otherwise."

"And girlfriends, I assume."

"Yeah, I had a girlfriend. I don't see why you need to interrogate me about that, though."

"Ross, you literally know what kind of panties I wear when I get my period."

"Fine. I had a girlfriend. Her name was Alanna. She was kind of like the first version of the Lana, you know."

"Right down to the name," I said. I remembered Will saying something about her. "How long did the two of you go out?"

"Not even three months. We broke up because—you'll never believe this—Mike slept with her."

I had been told that, too, but I didn't want to let him know. So I acted surprised and sympathetic, but he didn't seem to need it. He continued, "I wasn't what you'd call in love, so it wasn't a very painful breakup."

He'd said the same thing about Lana. To think that Mike could be so funny and lighthearted and then treat his brother that way…

Ross said, "What about you? You've told me about the tickler, the guy you sexted, and Monty—he's clearly a real catch—but have there been any other guys in your life?"

"I mean, I kissed this guy at a party one time. It was gross. He tasted like he'd been drinking battery acid. How old were you when you had your first kiss?"

"You mean like a real kiss, not a little peck? When I was fourteen. It was in front of my house. I had no idea what I was doing. I have the proof, which is that the girl never talked to me again. What about you?"

"I was sixteen. The guy in question was older, and he had braces, and every time I kissed him, it cut my lips. We tried going out for a month, in which time I got three pretty serious gashes, and at that point I said to hell with it."

Ross laughed and shook his head. Now I'd pop the real question, "How old were you when you lost your virginity?" He smiled enigmatically, trying to wriggle out of it, asking me to tell him first, but I stood my ground. Finally, he admitted, "I was fifteen."

"Is that even legal?" I asked.

"You'll have to check with a judge. Now it's your turn."

"Uh…" I thought for a moment. "When did the school year start again?"

"I don't know. Like two months ago?"

"OK. So let's say two months and a week?"

"You can't be serious," he said.

"I am. I mean, I don't know. I was nervous about the first time. And he was kind of a brute, so I didn't really trust him to be gentle. But when I was already starting to pack to go, he convinced me that I needed to do it before I left, that I'd regret going off to school a virgin. So we did it. And honestly, my first reaction was like: sex is so overrated. It was fine, you know, but it wasn't earth-shattering the way I'd imagined. Then I met you, of course."

"And I changed your mind."

"I didn't say that, Ross."

"I don't need you to." He took another sip of his beer. "I'm surprised. You didn't seem like a virgin."

"Come on now!"

"I'm serious." I started turning red, and he laughed at me. After that, we left off with the Q&A, paid the bill, and walked back to the car. The whole drive back, I couldn't stop looking at him. Thankfully, he didn't notice. There was a band playing on the radio, I think called Brainstorm. I'd never heard of them but he knew everything about them, and his eyes gleamed as he told me their story. I thought of Monty again, briefly, and I was almost thankful that his insane behavior had brought me closer to Ross than I'd managed to become on my own. Ross realized at some point that I'd stopped responding to his little music history lesson, and he turned to me and asked, "Is something up?"

"Not a thing," I said, smiling and looking out the windshield.

Yes, in the end, Monty had been a step in the right direction.

15

ONE MORE

I was sitting by myself in the living room, drinking a beer and rereading my linguistics notes, concentrating so hard that I didn't hear Ross coming down the hall.

"You should relax," he said. "You've got a giant wrinkle in your forehead. You don't want it to stay that way."

I rubbed it out and he laughed, continuing, "I'm sorry, but it was worth it to see you grimace like that. What are you working on?"

"Linguistics. I've got an exam in two days and I barely know anything."

"Yeah. That's why some people try studying throughout the semester instead of waiting…"

He knew how much that pissed me off.

"Thanks for the advice, Dad," I said.

"Your phone's ringing," he told me.

I sighed and turned my phone upside down so I wouldn't have to see Monty's stupid face on the screen. He'd been calling me constantly since our fight a week before. It goes without saying that I hadn't responded. Ross had been sweet enough not to bring up the subject, but he was human, and I was sure his patience was close to running out. He confirmed that when he said to me, "Look, you can't just leave things hanging like this."

"What am I supposed to do then?"

"Block his number, for starters."

"If he can't call or message me, he might freak out and come up here again," I said, closing my laptop and setting it aside.

"Let him come. I'll defend you."

"I'd prefer it not have to come to that," I replied.

"Jen, are you sure he never did anything to you? Physically, you know? Because I can't get the thought out of my head, and it really bothers me."

Uncomfortable, I said, "Ross, we already talked about this. No, he didn't. And you can stop worrying about it." I could tell my answer didn't satisfy him, but I couldn't go into that right now, and I tried to change the subject, saying, "God, I hate fucking linguistics!"

"Why do you keep studying this shit when it's obvious you don't like it?" he asked.

"Well, one, because it's paid for, and even if I want to change majors, I can't just fail all of my classes and start over. And even if English is stupid, who's to say what I picked afterward wouldn't be even worse?"

"English isn't stupid."

"Whatever. Complicated, then."

"Maybe you need a distraction," he said, lifting his eyebrows.

I tried not to smile back at him and asked, "Why do you have to make everything sound sexual?"

"Easy now. You said it, not me. But of course, if that is what you need right now, I'm more than happy to comply…"

I chuckled—I couldn't help it—and he did, too. But then he leaned in and started tickling me. No, not again! I struggled to try to escape, but he trapped my ankle and pulled me toward him, then lay down on top of me to hold me there. Let's be honest, though. I didn't really want to escape. Especially not when I felt his lips against my neck. We were very close, and I tried to ask him what he was doing, but his lips soon covered my mouth.

I was propped up on my elbows as his hands traced their way down my back. Shamelessly, he squeezed my butt before moving aside and pulling me on top of him.

"Jeez. I thought you guys were trying to pretend you weren't into each other."

That was Will's voice. He was in the kitchen. Who knew how the hell he'd ended up there. Ross scowled at him and Will went on. "Hey, sorry to interrupt your exchange of body fluids or whatever. I just wanted to let you know Naya's on her way over."

With whatever we were about to do interrupted, we pulled apart from each other and relaxed with Will in the living room, talking about school and other nonsense until Naya knocked at the door. When Will let her in, she came over and gave me a big hug. I don't know how or why, but she hadn't even blinked when I'd had to tell her about Monty destroying her room. She'd said it was just stuff, and the only thing that mattered was I was OK.

Will said he was hungry and asked if we should order out, and if so, what we wanted.

Naya responded, "You guys get something if you like, but Jenna and I are on a diet."

I looked over at her, confused. The word *diet* wasn't part of my vocabulary.

"I'm on a diet?" I asked.

"You are now. I've decided I want to lose a little weight and really, teamwork's the only way to do these things."

I looked down at my belly. I guess I was getting a little chubby. It was hard to eat with Ross every day and not put on a few pounds. Not everyone held onto their adolescent metabolism forever. I could still fit into my clothes, but lately I was having to squeeze more than normal.

"Cool," I said. "We're on a diet, then. It's official."

The guys just stared at us as if we were out of our minds.

"If you want my humble opinion," Ross said, "you both look good just the way you are."

Naya rolled her eyes and said, "You're a grown-up man who reads comic books. Your opinion doesn't count. Now, Jenna, maybe you can come help me out in the kitchen. I'm making grilled chicken and salad."

Seeing the expression on my face, Ross laughed at me, as did Sue, who had just walked in. I don't know if she knew what was going on or was just taking advantage of the moment to make me feel stupid. I have to admit, I wasn't exactly looking forward to such a bland meal. It was one thing to have it at Agnes's place—she was old, and she probably needed something easy on her stomach. But here I wasn't so sure, especially because Naya wasn't what you'd call a gourmet chef.

"Jenna, you've still got time to back out," Will said.

"No." I crossed my arms. "I'm on a diet. For the next week, at least."

"Yeah, well, I'm going to get some Mexican. My body can't sustain itself on salad and grilled chicken. Sorry about that."

A half hour later, I was salivating as I stared at the tacos, sour cream, guacamole, and queso dip while I waited for Naya to finish our so-called healthy dinner. I was sitting on the floor while Will, Ross, and Sue occupied the sofas and chairs. "Why are you sitting there?" Ross asked, adding, "Get over here," and when I walked over, he pulled me into his lap. Then he remarked, "Maybe I was wrong about that diet. I feel like a boulder just fell on me."

"Very funny," I said, elbowing him.

"I'm kidding. Anyway, don't worry, even if you gained a bunch of weight, it wouldn't change how I feel about you."

"Very romantic, Ross," Sue commented. "Is that from *Romeo and Juliet*?"

I tried to ignore the salad I was forking up as we watched another home reno show. Every time Ross grabbed a taco and started chewing it next to me, I wanted to jump out the window. I'd been on a diet for exactly one hour, and I wanted to end it all. To make matters worse, Ross kept offering me a bite and waving his dinner in front of my nose. "It's really good," he said, tempting me.

"I hate you," I replied.

When the torture was over and Sue had left us again, I heard my phone buzzing on the coffee table. I picked it up despite myself, because seeing Monty had called again was the last thing I cared about. But it wasn't him. It was someone much, much worse.

My mother.

"Hey, my future mother-in-law's calling!" Ross joked.

"Oh no," I said. "This is going to be bad."

Everyone asked if I was OK. I didn't know what to answer. I took a deep breath and brought the phone to my ear, trembling in terror.

"Jennifer Michelle Brown!"

"Hey, Mom," I responded, trying to sound enthusiastic. But I was so scared I almost dropped my phone. Will and Naya seemed worried about me. Ross, of course, was just laughing at my perfectly normal middle name.

"Are you listening to me?" Mom yelled. "What is this I hear about you living with a boy and not telling me anything!"

I got up to leave so everyone wouldn't listen in on our entire conversation, but Naya stopped me, reminding me that there was only decent coverage in the living room. She looked way more amused by that than she should have been.

"Mom, I was going to tell you," I said. "I've just been so busy with class and all that I forgot, and..."

"You forgot! You never tell me anything! You've completely abandoned me, and here I am with these loafers..." She turned away from the phone to tell my brothers to shut up, then continued. "Your poor mother has to find out what's happening to you from other people, like you were a stranger."

"Mom, if you'll let me explain…" I couldn't believe Will, Ross, and Naya were just staring at me as if I were a character in a soap opera.

"There's nothing to explain! And let me tell you, it's not just me. Your father is very angry, too…"

"Dad never gets mad…"

"Well he did this time. Or if he isn't mad, he ought to be."

"Mom, I was actually going to call you tonight…"

"I gave birth to you," my mother said. "Don't think I don't know when you're lying to me Now tell me who this young man is."

I tried to put her mind at ease without going into details, but Ross made it hard on me, because he wanted to comment on the entire conversation. When she asked if he was a good guy, he whispered to me to say nice things about him. When I said he could be a pain sometimes, he chided me for not being grateful to him. He called me Michelle, and I told him I'd throw out all his cigarettes if he did it again. I hesitated when Mom asked me if he was a friend, and then she lost it, asking, "Is he your boyfriend? Don't tell me you broke up with Monty!"

"Mom, no he's…"

"Because if so, thank the lord." She sighed. "I know you liked him, sweetie, but I never could stand him. He's good for nothing. I've told you that before. With his basketball practice and all that, he never could focus on you. Please tell me this new one's not a basketball player, because I don't want to see you fall into the same trap. And remember how he used to fly off the handle? That was a little bit much. But I'm just talking on and on, and it's your turn. Tell me about this boy. How long have you been together? Why am I just hearing about him now?"

"Mom, I literally can't tell you because you won't be quiet."

"Pass me the phone and I can introduce myself," Ross said. I grabbed a cushion and hit him in the face with it.

"Listen!" I said. "Yes, Monty and I broke up. I sent him a message, I told him I was done with him, he showed up here acting totally crazy, but he's gone now, and I'm not getting back with him…"

I guess that was as long as she could go without hearing her own voice, because she interrupted my story to ask, "What about you coming home? Have you got a ticket yet?"

"Mom…"

"I knew it! I knew you'd leave and forget about me. It's always the same! You've grown up and you don't need me more, and now you're abandoning me like a broken toy or an old shoe. It happened with Shannon."

"Mom, two things. One, I want to come see you. I really do. But I can't pay for the trip myself. And I know how you guys' finances are. You may have forgotten, but the whole reason I'm living at this apartment is because you couldn't make the payments on my dorm room. If I can figure out a way to make a few bucks, I promise a trip home is the first thing on my list, but…"

"What about driving?"

"It's seven hours each way, and I don't even have my license."

"Yeah. If only your brother Spencer weren't so lazy, he could come get you. But we both know that will never fly."

I heard her breathing harder, and I knew she was about to cry. In part because she was sad, but in part because she wanted to twist my arm.

"I can't believe I'm turning sixty years old and the one thing I want is to see my daughter for my birthday, and I can't do it," she moaned.

"I'll get a job, Mom, and I'll get you a present to make it up to you."

"I don't want a present, Jenna. I want to see you."

I was trying to figure out how to console her when I felt my phone getting torn out of my hand. Before I could look up, I heard Ross say, in his most charming voice, "Hello, Mrs. Brown."

"What are you doing?" I shouted, jumping on top of him and trying to grab my phone back. But his fingers were like vise grips and I couldn't pry them away. "Ross, give it back now!"

"No," he said, responding to my mom's questions, "it's my place. I own it… Jack, actually, it's Jack Ross… Yes… Friends? Yes, I think so, but it's hard to say. Your daughter doesn't seem to want to decide… No, no, don't worry… I understand completely… If my mother were turning sixty and I didn't go to her party, of course she'd be sad. I could never let that happen to her."

Will, who had been watching all this with evident amusement, grinned and said, "He's such an ass-kisser."

I kept yelling at Ross and he kept batting me away, reminding my mother she needn't worry and he would be happy to take care of something, and I could hear my mother's nasal *Thank you, thank you, thank you*, and he told her the pleasure was his. At last, he told her he was going to put me back on and passed me the phone.

"Thank God you left that Monty. I mean, with this Jack Ross, how could you possibly stay with Monty? This one's a catch. You better hold on to him tight."

"Mom, it's the twenty-first century. Eighteen-year-old women aren't out looking for husbands."

"I don't care," she said, "and listen, everything's settled so don't you dare tell him no. I'm paying him back, and that's the end of the story. I'm so happy we'll all be together again. Your new boyfriend's wonderful. Now I've got to go. One of your brothers needs something. Love you. 'Bye!"

She hung up before I could say anything, and I couldn't help but stare at my phone in disbelief. Naya announced she was going to bed, and Will agreed emphatically, and a few seconds later, I was alone with Ross, who was grinning at me ridiculously.

"What?" he asked.

"What was my mother talking about when she said she would pay you back?"

"We agreed that I'd get you a ticket to go see her."

"Ross! You can't do that! I can't just be dependent on you! You can't pay for everything!"

"It's not for you. It's a sixtieth birthday present for your mom."

"A present is a bottle of perfume, Ross, not a plane ticket!"

"Nice try, Jen. I know how picky women are about perfumes, you're not going to get me to step into that minefield."

"Can you please take me seriously for once!" He smiled and said he did, and I told him he didn't. Seeming surprised by my outburst, he asked whether the problem was that I didn't want him to meet my family. But it wasn't that. It was the money. I already felt like I owed him, I certainly didn't want my parents paying him back, and I had no idea how I ever could. He swore he would never ask me for it, but that wasn't the point. He wanted to know why I worried so much about money; I wanted to know why he never did. I thought how nice it must be to just never think about where my next meal was coming from. He told me there were many things more important than money, like happiness, and I replied, "To be honest with you, I think I'd rather cry on a yacht than be happy on a park bench."

"Look," Ross said, "here's the real story. I've got my own money. I had a YouTube channel that was a pretty big deal for a while. The money's just sitting in the bank earning interest, and I don't use it for anything apart from paying the mortgage on this place. I really don't have anything to spend it on. The last thing I bought was a forty-dollar sweatshirt. Now I have something I can spend it on, and I want to. So what's the big deal?"

When he put it like that, I could see why he didn't fret over money. But I didn't want to take advantage of him. I mentioned that, and he cracked a joke as usual. "You can take advantage of me as much as you like. Nothing would make me happier." But then he turned more serious and told me to think about my mother and how happy she'd be when she saw me.

He picked up the remote and started scrolling through the channels looking for something decent to watch. Finally he settled on a film and I asked about his YouTube channel.

"It was just goofy short movies," he said. "Stuff I wanted to go viral. But I had a knack for it. It got to be pretty well known, and that was how I started taking movies more seriously and decided to go to school for film. It even got me some kind of important contacts."

"Why'd you never mention it?"

He reached into my salad, pulled out a piece of lettuce, and tossed it in his mouth. "I don't know. You didn't ask."

"How would I have known to ask?"

Instead of responding, he stared at the screen with a self-satisfied grin. I think it was only then that it hit me that I'd be seeing my family in a couple of weeks: my brothers, Shannon and Owen, my mother, my father. Maybe even my grandparents. Hopefully not Monty and Nelle, although anything was possible...

"I can't believe I'm actually going home," I said. "I'm going to see my family!"

"I'm glad you're happy about it," Ross replied.

I hugged him and gave him a sloppy kiss on the cheek. "You're the best!" I screamed.

"Now that's more like it."

"Promise me, though," I said, "that this is the last time you pay for something for me."

"Sorry, no deal there."

"Ross, I'm serious. At least, not until I pay you back for the trip."

"Anything you pay me back is getting invested in our dream home," he responded.

I shook my head. I was holding on to him like a koala. I wasn't the most touchy-feely person, but with him, I couldn't help it. And he didn't seem to mind. As he murmured proudly that he thought my mother might like him better than me now (she certainly liked him better than Monty), I pulled away to look at him until he finally said, "What?" I realized I'd fallen in a trance and said, "Nothing," but of course, I was thinking something, and I knew very well what.

"You wouldn't be tired by any chance?" I asked him.

"You're not trying to get me into the bedroom, are you?" he replied.

I looked up as he leaned in to me and closed my eyes for the kiss that I saw coming. Then, when it didn't arrive, I reopened them. Ross was rolling his eyes as he looked toward the hallway, where Sue was staring at us with disgust on her face.

"No," she said, "please no. Not another couple in this house."

"Can we help you?" Ross asked.

"I was going to wash off my plate. But I don't think I can keep from vomiting if you two are there cheesing it up."

She crossed her arms, waiting for us to go. I didn't need any encouragement to go to the bedroom, and apparently Ross didn't, either. We hurried off, hearing Sue exhaling with frustration behind us.

It was late, but I still hadn't fallen asleep. I was lying there with Ross's head on my chest. His eyes were closed; his breathing was regular and soft. He'd been like that for a while. I stroked his face, toyed with his hair. He liked sleeping like that; he'd done it a lot lately. And I certainly didn't mind.

I ran a finger down his jawline, circled his chin, traced it up to his kissable lips. I wondered if that was a word: *kissable*? His upper lip was shaped like a heart. His lower lip was thick and juicy.

I passed my thumb over his nose, his dark brows, his eyelids. Ross's eyes were pretty: chestnut-brown, with green and yellow flecks in the iris. I wondered if anyone had told him how pretty they were. Except for me that night I was high, of course. He sighed as I massaged his neck and his shoulders, and my eyes started to close. But as I drifted off, something brought me back suddenly. A noise? Was it someone at the door?

I had to be imagining things.

I closed my eyes again, but the noise returned. And now there was no doubt it was real. I tried to sit up, and Ross squeezed me, still dreaming and murmuring incomprehensible words.

"Ross," I whispered, shaking him. "Ross, wake up."

"Mmmm," he mumbled.

"Ross, get up!"

"Jen, if you want to go at it again, I'm going to need a little more sleep."

"Idiot! There's someone at the door!"

He sighed and curled up, his cheek lying over my heart. "Whatever," he said. "It's probably just Sue or Will. Or the neighbor. What are they going to do, steal the salad Naya bought? Go back to touching me."

"I'm serious. We need to get up!" Finally I convinced him, and he got up and stretched, looking unworried as he threw on a pair of cotton trousers. I slipped on some panties and asked him to pass me a shirt, and he told me I should stay behind. "What are you going to do?" he asked. "Stare at the thief until he dies?"

"Maybe I'll use you as a human shield and take off running," I said.

That time the sound came again—loud, undeniable. Ross turned serious as I said, "See?" and told me not to move.

"But…"

"Jen, stay here."

I did for a minute, but as soon as he'd walked out, my anxiety got the better of me. I threw on the T-shirt he'd passed me and walked out. "Could you not listen to me for once?" he asked as he noticed me behind him.

When we reached the door, it was obvious someone was trying to open it. I stayed in the living room while Ross threw the door open, ready to strike. Then he shouted, "You want to let me know what the fuck you're doing here?"

"Well, hello to you, too," Mike said. He stumbled in and looked at me, and I realized the state I was in, half-dressed, hair sticking out in all directions.

"I hope I'm not interrupting something," Mike continued, and Ross grunted. "Nice to see you, Jen."

"Yeah, always a pleasure, Mike," I said, shaking my head.

"I asked you a question," Ross repeated. "What the fuck are you doing here?"

Mike walked into the living room and dropped his bag on the floor. "I had an argument with my girlfriend—sorry, ex-girlfriend now—and I was wondering if I could stay here a few days. I know what you're going to say: Why should you care. But seriously, Ross, I'm your brother. Throw me a line."

Ross was furious, and Mike's excuses were only making it worse. If he didn't shut up, I thought Ross might explode.

"You need to go," Ross said, but Mike ignored him, making jokes about how he guessed he *was* interrupting something, and congratulations, Ross, and it was too bad Mike and I could never be a thing, and Ross got angrier and angrier and finally started shoving him out the door.

"Come on, Bro," Mike protested. "You can't just shove me out on the street."

"You can't stay here," Ross replied. "There's no room for you."

"You really don't have space for your own brother?"

"I mean, the couch *is* open," I told Ross.

Mike responded, "Look, even she wants me here."

When I saw Ross's face, I regretted opening my mouth and rushed to add, "I never said I wanted anything."

"Tonight," Ross almost shouted. "You can stay tonight. And you're leaving in the morning. I don't care where you have to go."

"Sure, man, sure," Mike said, sitting down and taking off his shoes. As Ross and I headed toward the hallway, he went on. "Yo, what's the rush? Don't you guys want to stay and hang out for a little while? Jenna?"

"We don't," Ross said, "and leave Jenna out of this. Every time you come over, you start your bullshit with her. Another comment and I *will* throw you out on the street."

Mike raised his hands in surrender. But you could tell he wasn't really listening.

When we were back in Ross's room, I apologized for saying anything.

"It's fine," Ross said. "It's just…even having him one room away puts me in a bad mood. Mike is trouble. He always has been."

He sat down on the bed, looking stressed. I felt bad for him. I curled up in his lap and wrapped my arms around his neck, saying, "What does it matter? It's just a day. Not even that. One night. He'll leave in the morning."

With a bitter smile, Ross replied, "It's obvious you don't know him. We won't get rid of him that easily."

"Maybe he and his girlfriend will make up?"

"Jen, when my brother says the word *girlfriend*, he doesn't mean the same thing you or I do. This could be someone he's been sleeping with and fighting with for years or someone he just ran into at a bar last night."

Maybe he was right—but I had to do something to make him feel better. I straddled him and kissed the tip of his nose.

"Well, if we can't get rid of him, maybe we can do something so you won't think about the fact that he's here," I said.

He seemed to like that and replied, "That's pretty persuasive."

I kissed him on the lips and pushed him backward until we were both holding each other, our hands gliding hungrily over each other's bodies. And yet he didn't seem to want to go further. He didn't even try to take off my clothes. I think sometimes he just needed someone to hold him and caress him and tell him how special he was. It sounds cheesy, but that's just how Ross was. And I certainly didn't mind being the person who did it.

When I opened my eyes the next morning, he was still asleep, so I dressed in my running clothes and tiptoed out of the room. Mike was still lying on the sofa. It entertained me to have him there, despite everything. Maybe they didn't get along, but they had more in common than either of them would admit.

I ran a long time, called my brother Spencer, bought a coffee, and walked back home. In the elevator, I said hi to a neighbor who sometimes went out running at the same time I did. When I walked back into the apartment, I heard a whistle coming from the kitchen. I'd just assumed it would be Ross, but no, it was his brother.

"You're active this morning," he said, looking me up and down.

"Have you always been this big a pain in the ass?" I replied. He started in on me with one of his corny lines about us hooking up, but I ignored him, turning my attention to Will, who was yawning as he stomped out of the hall. When he noticed Mike, he turned to me with a curious expression. "Ask Jack," I said.

"Jack?" Mike asked with a laugh. "We're calling him Jack now?"

I ignored him. Will opened the fridge to take out the milk and asked him, "When are you leaving?"

"No idea. When I get bored."

I reminded him that he had told his brother he'd be leaving that morning. And he told me he had a hunch Ross had already told me how easily he changed his mind.

Frowning, I announced I was going to take a shower and walked off, shutting the bathroom door behind me. When I was naked, with the shower door closed, rubbing shampoo into my hair, I heard the door fling open, screamed, and covered my mouth. When I peeked out, I saw Mike standing there peeing without a care in the world.

"What the hell are you doing?" I shouted. "I'm showering!"

"Relax, I'm leaving right now. Anyway, it's not like I can see anything."

He was right. The shower door was almost opaque. But I didn't care. I didn't want him in there.

"Mike, get the fuck out!"

"OK, I'm going, damn." He zipped his fly slowly. I could feel myself turning red from embarrassment and anger. As he washed his hands, he said, "You know, you shouldn't worry about me being here. Just keep doing what you were doing."

"GO!"

I must have said that loud enough for Ross to hear me, because soon he was peeking through the door looking ready to kill his brother. "What in the hell are you doing?" he asked.

Before Mike could make an excuse, Ross had grabbed him by the collar and dragged him out, slamming the door. When he came back in a second later, he said, "Sorry, he's an idiot."

"It's fine, but if he does it again, I'm gonna squirt body wash in his eyes."

"Honestly," Ross responded, "I'd pay to see that." Then he looked at me for a moment and continued. "So…is there room for anyone else in there?"

Advantages of showering with Ross: someone to soap your back, someone to massage you while doing so, someone to make you laugh, someone to wash you slowly all over with the showerhead, and someone to put a hand over your mouth so the others wouldn't hear what you're doing in there.

Disadvantages of showering with Ross: making it to class thirty minutes late and getting chewed out by my professor.

16

THE LEGENDARY DAISY

Naya and Will had gone away for a few days and Sue was gone, too. I guess everyone was antsy and needed to get away. I was leaving that weekend to go home myself. I hoped everyone would be back the next day, so I could see them before I left. But I can't say I was upset about having an entire night alone with Ross ahead of me.

Sorry I said *alone*. I should have mentioned Mike was still in the apartment. And that was a problem.

He was pacing back and forth in the living room, looking frantic, as I stepped out into the hallway, confused. I watched him pick up his jacket, turn out the pockets, and throw it on the floor.

"Is something up?" I asked.

He looked pale, nervous. He didn't smile. That wasn't the Mike I knew.

"I can't find my fucking wallet," he said.

"Here, let me help you," I said.

"Do you have any cash on you? It's urgent…"

My instincts told me not to, but what if he was really in trouble? I felt myself starting to reach for my wallet, but I stopped. "Sorry," I lied. "I don't have anything on me. I could call Ross…"

"No! Just leave it."

He opened the drawer of the end table, didn't find what he was looking for, and slammed it shut, sitting down and scratching his temple.

"Listen," I told him. "I don't have time right now, but if you don't find your wallet, text me and I'll try to come back and help you find it. I'm sure Ross will give you money if you need. Or maybe I can take some out of the ATM."

Mike didn't respond. He seemed to want to be by himself, so I gathered my things and left. In the elevator, I set Ross a message:

Mike's acting weird. I think he needs money. Maybe you should call him.

I didn't wait for a response because I was running late. I just tossed my phone in my purse and took off running for the train.

I was tired when class was over. I hadn't slept well the night before. It was getting late, and I was also starving. On my way down the stairs, I thought I heard someone say my name. I looked around, and my eyes settled on a woman standing in front of me. It was Ross's mother.

"Mary?" I said, surprised.

"Hello, dear." She was smiling the way she usually did, but something in her face seemed worried. I continued down the stairs, feeling my pulse speed up, and asked her if everything was OK.

"Of course," she hurried to reassure me, although I wasn't sure if I believed her. "We're having a dinner at my place, and Jackie didn't have time to come pick you up."

"How come?" I asked, following her to the parking lot. Ross hadn't mentioned anything to me about being busy.

"He had to get Mike," she said simply.

She drove an Audi, gleaming gunmetal blue, that probably cost as much as Ross's apartment. It smelled sexy inside, of leather and polish, and I almost felt bad about resting my damp old boots on its immaculate carpet. Mary smiled as she started the engine.

Did she know about my relationship with Ross? What it really was? For that matter, did I? I wasn't sure, but I asked her how Ross was.

"He's fine, why?"

"Because this is the first time he's ever sent someone else to pick me up."

"Well, he's been a bit busy these days. You know he's working on his short film…"

I did know that, but he hadn't said much about it. Just that he wouldn't be home much for a while. Ross didn't like to talk about his work or studies—I just assumed that was an artist thing, and I tried to give him his space.

"Yeah," I responded. "We miss him back at home."

"You know he's also worried about whether he'll get into the program abroad."

"What program?"

"Well, you know, honey, Ross wants to do the film program in Cannes. He probably hasn't mentioned it to you because he's so anxious about it. That boy really is a handful."

Trying to conceal my anxiety, I asked, "It's for film?"

"Yes. It's a wonderful program, in Cannes. Jackie's had his eye on it since he was a teenager, but I don't know. He's completely unpredictable. He didn't apply until the last minute, and now I wouldn't be surprised if they accepted him and he decided not to go."

The mention of Ross's teenage years must have gotten her to reminiscing, and she started telling me stories about Mike and Ross when they were boys. She was finishing a story as she pulled into her garage. I saw that Mike and Ross hadn't arrived yet, and once we entered the house, there was no sign of their father, which also put my mind at ease.

She must have read my thoughts because she said, "I try to be sure my children and my husband don't run into each other." She opened her fridge and checked the temperature of a gazpacho that made my mouth water. "As you already saw, they don't get along very well."

"I kind of got that impression," I replied. I looked up at her to be sure the remark hadn't angered her. To the contrary, she seemed amused.

"Are you in the mood for a glass of wine while we wait for those two disasters I call my boys to arrive?"

"I'm not a big fan of wine."

She took a beer out of the fridge and handed it to me instead. "You should drink up now," she said. "Once Mike's here, they usually disappear."

We walked together to the living room. I felt like a little girl around her, unsure what to say or do. I wanted to make a good impression on her, but...who was I to impress someone? Especially someone like that? I was much better at embarrassing myself, in all honesty.

"You know you can have a seat," she said, patting the couch cushion next to her.

Oh no, I thought. *She's going to interrogate me.*

Maybe Ross and I weren't technically going out, but it still felt like it had when I'd met Monty's mom. And she hadn't been happy at all that I was stealing away the love of her pampered only son.

"How are things with your boyfriend?" she asked.

Brilliant. What a way to begin. I'd forgotten the subject had come up at our dinner with Ross's dad.

"I ask," Mary continued, "because Agnes told me your story."

"Oh," I said. "We're done."

"I'm so sorry."

"Don't be. I mean, we broke up a few weeks ago, but for me, it was like we'd already done it a long time before. Things really changed when I met R—You know, when I moved here."

I could feel myself blushing. Brilliant. Mary took a drink of her wine and looked closely at me. She was so kind, but I couldn't stop feeling she was inspecting me. "Well," she said, "tell me a little something about what you're studying. English, right?"

"Yeah. I can't really say I'm that crazy about it."

"You know, you could change majors. You should think it over. College is a time to learn about yourself. What do you do in your free time?"

"Nothing much. I run. I did track in high school, mainly because one of my brothers kind of forced me into it. But I did like it. My nephew's in Little League and I helped them train before I left. They did pretty well; they made it to the county championship. I feel like that's sort of it. There's another thing, but I'm embarrassed to say it around you. I did used to paint. I think I told you at the gallery. But it was nothing compared to what you do."

"What kinds of things did you paint?"

"Just stupid stuff," I said. "My friends used to like me to make portraits of them. They weren't very good, but..."

"They couldn't have been that bad if your friends wanted them."

"Maybe they weren't horrible, but trust me, I'm no Picasso."

"I got my start doing portraits, too," Mary said with a smile. Just then, the door opened, and we could hear Mike and Ross bickering long before they made it to the living room.

"Boys, do we have to start with this already?" their mother asked. Ross was the first to come in, and he looked so angry that I'm not sure he saw us as he tore off his jacket and threw it onto the sofa. Mike followed him with his usual slightly smug smile. "Hey, Jenna," he greeted me.

Ross turned and realized we were there.

"Everything OK?" I asked.

"Yeah," Ross responded, "everything except I had to go pick this idiot up from the police station. For another fight. You know, Mike, you might at least try to change things up now and then. This must be the fifth time I've had to bail you out for the same thing."

"I didn't start it," Mike said. "I was minding my business, this guy got in my way, so I gave him a little shove."

"You broke his nose," Ross corrected him, sitting down next to me. "Couldn't you at least have taken off running instead of sticking around for the police to come?"

"I'm a good citizen," Mike told him. "I'm prepared to face the consequences of my actions."

"The least you could do is say you're sorry," Ross said.

"I'm sorry," Mike replied.

"Not to me, to them," Ross instructed him.

Mike sighed. I was starting to feel uncomfortable. "Mom, future sister-in-law," he said, "I'm sorry."

Mary seemed as entertained by what Mike had called me as he was. I, of course, wished I could vanish on the spot.

Mike asked what was for dinner, and when Mary said there was gazpacho in the fridge, he shouted, "Gazpacho!" And took off running. Ross followed him. Not wanting to be alone with Mary after that uncomfortable exchange, I asked where the restrooms were and she pointed me to Ross's room, the last one upstairs on the right, which had its own en suite.

"You don't think he'll mind me going in his room?" I asked. When she rolled her eyes, I said, "OK, OK…"

The stairs were made of metal and glass, and my boots echoed on them on my way up. I felt self-conscious about even walking in the hallway. The carpet was flawless and looked very expensive. The doors were all of glowing hardwood, and everything smelled fresh and clean. It was so different from where I lived. With my brothers around, there was never any point in picking up. Five minutes later, they'd trash it all again.

There was a radioactive sticker on Ross's door. That made me grin. It was so him. I opened it and flipped on the lights. It was so much bigger than our—than his—room, with plush carpeting, a California king bed with blue sheets, cushions all over, matching furniture. There was a full-length mirror covered in stickers, what looked like a walk-in closet, and a huge shelf full of records, though I didn't see a record player anywhere. He had an even bigger shelf full of DVDs, graphic novels, and books. Every inch of the place exuded Ross's energy.

I wanted to look around more, but I was on the verge of peeing myself. So I walked into the bathroom, which was big and luxurious. It was still hard for me to imagine he could prefer his apartment to that room. This was the first time I'd ever been in a real mansion!

When I finished up and came out, I was surprised to find Ross lying on his bed with his arms crossed behind his head.

"Did you lose your phone?" he asked.

"Huh?"

"I tried to call you like a million times to tell you my mother was going to pick you up, and you never responded."

"Oh, sorry. I tossed it in my bag and I didn't look at it for most of the day."

It felt weird not to have an argument about that. Monty would have lost his mind over it.

"Are things OK with Mike?" I asked.

"If you want my opinion, he'd be better off in jail, but sure, he's fine as far as I can tell."

"I meant because of the message I sent you. About his wallet. He really seemed like he was bugging out."

"Oh, that… I guess now's as good a time as any to tell you Mike's had his problems with drugs. It's been a year since he's done anything serious. I know he smokes weed, and I'm not crazy about that, but it's nothing compared to what he used to be into. And I think today he nearly had a relapse. I've seen him steal to get money when he's in a bad place; he's capable of anything. But I guess getting in that fight pulled him out of it. So whatever. It could have been worse."

"Yeah," I said, "he asked me for money, and I didn't give it to him. It just didn't feel right. I could tell something weird was going on."

"You did the right thing, Jen," he said.

I nodded, then decided to change the subject, hoping to lighten his mood. "So this is the lion's den," I said.

"Yeah. I miss it. As you can see, it's still got all my stuff the way I liked it when I was younger."

"Younger? Ross, you're twenty-one years old."

"It doesn't feel like it some days."

He opened a drawer in his nightstand. I saw a strip of condoms. I can't exactly say that made me feel comfortable. He noticed that I had noticed, but thankfully we didn't have to talk about it. Then he pulled something out. It looked like a glass tube with a little metal piece sticking out. "Here it is!" he announced. "The legendary Daisy!"

"What is it?"

"She is called Daisy, and please don't tell me you've never seen one of these before. It's a bong. A water pipe. Call it what you want, but she'll always be Daisy to me."

"So first I tell you to quit smoking cigarettes, then you get mad at me for smoking weed one time, and now it turns out you have a favorite pipe?" I asked, sitting down and taking it from him carefully. It weighed more than I thought.

"Listen, there were more sad, lonely afternoons than I can count when she was the only one to keep me company."

Deciding to continue with the joke, I asked him, "Are you two still together?"

"No. I've changed."

"You were an outlaw before."

"Let's just put it this way, Jen: If I'd met you when I was in high school, things would probably have been different between us."

"It wouldn't matter. You'd never have noticed me anyway," I said, slipping Daisy back into the drawer. "I like those stories as much as anyone: the school bad boy notices the silent girl in the back of the room, they fall in love, she melts his cold heart, whatever. I'm pretty sure that never happens in real life."

"I'd have had a hard time ignoring that ass," he said.

"Jack!"

"I'm serious. The me from back then would have wanted to get down to business. I kept my feelings under wraps then. It's kind of sad in a way that I turned out so boring. But you know..."

"What?"

"I was just thinking." He narrowed his eyes. I could tell he had something naughty on his mind. "Will and Naya are gone. Sue's not home, either. It's the first time we'll have the apartment to ourselves. Maybe this is the perfect moment for the bad Jack Ross from high school to make an encore appearance."

He grabbed my hand and started pulling me toward the door. "Jack!" I said. "Don't be rude! We're supposed to have dinner with your family tonight!"

"Change of plans. We're going back to the apartment. I'll order in or something. It'll give Mom and Mike a chance to catch up."

He rushed me downstairs, and as Mike saw him approaching, he threw on his jacket, only for Ross to tell him, "NO!"

"But, Bro..."

"You can sleep here," Ross said.

"Dad's coming tomorrow! I don't want to have to run into him."

"Life sucks."

But of course, Mike ended up getting his way. In the car on the way home, he couldn't shut his mouth. I almost wanted to laugh, seeing the irritable look on Ross's face. When we got back, we put on a movie and had a quick bite to eat. At a certain point, Ross threw his arm over my shoulders, and I curled up next to him, and neither of us could concentrate because Mike was making so much noise trying to open a bag of candy. That sound, and the noise he made chewing it afterward, drove home how annoying he could be, and I remembered that this was my last night there before I left to see my parents—my last night with Ross until Monday.

And that made the approaching weekend look eternal.

Mike reached back and offered us some candy. I said no and impulsively grabbed Ross's hand. I was usually shy about public displays of affection. Ross tensed up, but soon he relaxed again. Even his brother's smacking and grunts seemed to stop bothering him as I traced little circles on his skin with my thumb.

I felt good with him. So good I could hardly pay attention to the film. I don't think Ross could, either. I cleared my throat just before the movie was over and announced I was going to go to bed. Mike didn't seem to care. Ross lingered behind a moment, then followed me.

When he entered our room, he shut the door, and we spent a moment just looking at each other. I had always felt attracted to him, but in that moment, it was different. It was another kind of attraction. Sexual, but something more… I just needed to feel him as close to me as possible. It was a strange feeling, one I'd never been familiar with before. But that was to be expected. I'd never known anyone like Ross before, either.

Ross pulled me out of my thoughts, asking, "Do you need to get ready for tomorrow?"

"Yeah," I murmured. "I mean, I packed my backpack. I don't really need much stuff. It's just two days. Two and a half."

"Two and a half days sounds like a long time to me."

"I've got clothes at home, too." *Home*—I think it was only in that moment that I realized that was where I was going. "I can't believe I'm actually going to see my family. I've missed them so much."

"What about your friends?"

"I don't know. I mean, if I see Nelle, I'll definitely give her a piece of my mind. Like ask her why in the hell she's never answered any of my calls and messages."

"Sounds like it'll be an interesting weekend," he said.

"There'll probably be some hiccups and then everything will be normal."

Hs stood there, still, and I knew in that instant he wouldn't come close to me and wouldn't touch me. He turned around to change T-shirts, and I stared at the tattoo on his back. I didn't understand the sudden change in attitude, and once again, I wished I could know what was going on in that head of his.

Since that was how it was, though, I decided to put on my pajamas. As I took out my contacts, and he sat on the bed. I slid into the sheets and looked at him for a moment before asking, "Are you OK?"

He said he was, but I knew him better than that. "Come on, what's up?"

"Nothing, Jen. Nothing I feel like bothering you with right now."

"I want you to bother me with it. I don't care what it is."

"It's not a big deal. It's just that…I'm going to miss you. I know it's not a long time, but I'm going to miss you."

I knew as soon as he said it that there was something else, but I didn't say anything. Not even when he came close and hugged me.

"My mom will be asking about you the whole time, so at least you'll know you're always going to be on my mind."

"I hope she gets a good impression of me," he said. I was going to respond, but he leaned in close and kissed me. The way he did it was different from before. It was too slow. Almost sad. I squinted at him as he turned and said, "Let's get some sleep," pulling me in. I felt confused as we lay there, his arms wrapped around me the way they had been the first time we slept together. Even as I drifted off, I knew he was still awake and tense, staring up at the ceiling.

17

MEATBALL BOMBER

There we were at the airport, all looking almost unbelievably sad. Naya had come prepared with a box of tissues. Just before security, I turned and looked at everyone and reminded them, "It's only two days."

"Two and a half days!" Naya shouted, bear-hugging me. I felt amused, but also a little perplexed. I don't think anyone had ever been so open with me about how much they'd miss me. Apart from my mom, I mean.

"Have fun," Will said, clapping me on the back.

Sue was…well, Sue. Uncomfortable, weird, probably sweet deep down. She nodded to me. That was a lot for her.

I hesitated when I looked at Ross. He seemed to be waiting to see what I would do. A little voice inside me told me he wasn't willing to take the first step because he wasn't sure how I'd react. I'd never kissed him in public before. But maybe now was the time. I stepped forward, but then I stopped—I chickened out—and gave him a hug around the waist. If he was disappointed, he didn't show it. He just smiled and wished me a pleasant trip.

Oh, Ross. You're too good, I thought.

I had a knot in my stomach as I descended from the airplane. When I made it to arrivals, my heart froze as I saw my parents and Spencer, who was holding a sign that said *Welcome Home*. I smiled and teared up.

Dad looked same as ever: short, white goatee, golf shirt. Mom had pulled her brown hair back in a bun and was wiping her eyes with her kerchief, which reminded me of Naya. My brother towered over me. I noticed he'd gotten a tattoo of a lady pirate, but before I could mention it, my mother shouted so loudly that half the airport turned to look at us.

"Oh, honey!" She planted kisses on every inch of my cheeks. "You can't imagine how much I missed you! You're here! Did you miss me? You better have!"

"Mom, you know I did."

I couldn't help but start giggling as she squeezed and cuddled me. Dad just smiled. He wasn't one for physical contact. He asked if I'd lost some weight, and that was enough to throw Mom into a panic: "Are you not eating enough?" she shrieked, and when I told her I was just running a lot, Spencer said, "I'll bet you're still slow as a turtle," hugging me and lifting me off the ground. "Man," he continued, "you look like an actual grown-up."

"Don't you dare touch my hair!" I shouted as he reached toward it malevolently, getting ready to give me a noogie.

"I swear you're getting shorter," he said.

"I swear you're getting older," I replied.

As we shoved each other, Mom told us not to start, and Dad, getting uncomfortable with the scene we were making, recommended we head home.

It was much colder at home than at school. I held Mom as we walked behind the two men. Spencer put my suitcase in the trunk of his car, and I got into the back seat with Mom. She couldn't stop asking me the whole drive about college, my new friends, and of course, Ross.

"Don't stress her out," Dad said.

"I'm her mother. I'm not stressing her out; I'm showing her that I care."

When we reached our street, I looked out the window, noticing our house in the cul-de-sac, facing the ocean. I shivered as I thought how cold it must be now. Where we lived, the beach was always littered with bottles from the teenagers who went down there to get drunk at night. The nicer area was to the north, where all the hotels were.

Spencer parked by the garage and helped me with my backpack. Inside, the scent of home invaded my nostrils. I had forgotten that home had a smell, but now I realized it and I loved it. I walked into the kitchen and crouched down as a huge ball of fur barreled toward me.

"Biscuit!" I shouted, letting my dog lick my face.

I patted his head and back for a long time, then walked to the living room, where Steve and Sonny were arguing about a game they were watching. "Hey!" I shouted. They looked at me and frowned.

"She's back," Steve murmured.

"Didn't take her long," Sonny said, nodding. "How long did we bet?"

"I said a month, you said two weeks, Spencer said three months, and Shannon said she was gone forever."

"I guess everyone loses, then," I said, crossing my arms. "You know, you guys could at least pretend you missed me a little."

"We've got our own bathroom now," Sonny said. "You can't really compare with that."

"Yeah," Steve said, scowling at me as if I were the source of all their problems. "This house is going to become a war zone."

"I love you, too, idiots!" I replied, jumping in the twins' laps and laughing as I listened to them grumble. Why was it always so much fun to bother them? Biscuit joined in, and the two of us slumped on top of them like a couple of sacks of potatoes. But they deserved it. The two of them had decided to open a garage, which meant it was their fault I had to move out of the dorms. Maybe I should thank them for it, though? After all, if it weren't for them, I wouldn't be living with Will, Sue, and Ross.

My father walked in and ordered them to give me a hug while they struggled to shove me off of them. Sonny protested, "We're busy!" With that whiny tone in their voices, you could tell they were the youngest in the family, except for me, who got to be the butt of all their jokes.

I turned Sonny's ball cap backward. That used to always drive him crazy.

Mom came out of the kitchen and said, "Look at you three, just like in the old days. Honey, are you sure you can't just stay?"

"Mom, don't start again," Spencer said. When I asked about my room, Mom said it hadn't been touched, and Steve groaned, "Yeah, I tried to move in, but she wouldn't let me."

Sonny asked, "Why do you care? I heard you were living with your new boyfriend."

"He's not my boyfriend!" I said. But I was already blushing. That had been a bad mistake. Now the real torture would begin. All three of my brothers pounced, repeating, "Jenna's got a boyfriend" in a dumb, sing-song voice, asking me what I did to make him not want to come with me, speculating on what was wrong with him that would make him go out with me, and so on, chasing all the way up to the third door on the left, which I opened with a smile on my face, my whole body a bundle of nerves, entering a place it felt like I hadn't been in for a thousand years.

It was true: everything was exactly as it had been when I was last there. My little bed between the two windows, the desk I had made Steve paint an ugly shade of pink that I now hated, my closet almost empty, the white carpet where I used to stretch out and study with Nelle.

I looked at my record collection, a gift from my aunt when I was young. She must have thought those albums would mean so much to me, but I'd never listened to them. If only Ross could look through them. He'd probably know each and every single band.

That afternoon, I hung out at home, helping my father—the house chef—prepare a birthday cake for Mom for the next day: chocolate with sugar cookies frosted to the outside. Perfect for my so-called diet. I tossed one of the cookies to Biscuit thinking of the panic Naya would fly into if she found herself surrounded by all these calories. I had told myself I'd go out when night came, but there wasn't really time, and I didn't care, I didn't want to see anyone else anyway. We watched a football game together, and I cheered for the team everyone hated just to piss them off. Mom joined me. I could see she'd missed me really bad. And I got it. It couldn't have been easy being the only woman in the house with those four guys.

After dinner, my brothers said I had to do the dishes because they'd shouldered the burden ever since I left. I shrugged and set to work, and soon Spencer returned to the kitchen to pour himself a bowl of chocolate cereal. Just what a gym teacher should be eating.

"I thought gym teachers were supposed to have a healthy diet," I said, blowing my hair out of my face.

"Do as I say, not as I do, that's what I always tell the kids." He scarfed his cereal down and dropped the bowl and spoon in the sink among the other dirty dishes before sitting on the counter to talk.

"So," he began, "I heard you dropped the basketball player guy..."

"Did Mom tell you?"

"No, Shannon. She told me to pretend I didn't know if you brought it up."

"Well, I guess you get an F there."

"I didn't feel like faking," he said.

"I can't believe you two are the oldest and you're so gossipy."

"Is that a yes?"

I thought it over a moment. "It's a yes," I said. I wondered whether I should tell Spencer what had happened between me and Monty. If I said too much, he'd probably go over there and knock Monty's lights out. Or worse. And all I wanted was never to think about him again. So when he asked again, I said, "Nothing, it was just stupid stuff. The usual. It's over now."

"Jenna, be careful. You know what he's like. I wouldn't be surprised if he showed up at your apartment one day."

"That's why I've been running so much, so I can get away," I joked.

When Spencer stared at me, I tried to reassure him that Monty wouldn't dare, and if he did, Ross, Will, Sue, and Naya would show him the door.

"Is Ross your boyfriend?"

He caught me by surprise, and I dropped a plate in the soapy water, splashing my shirt. Spencer laughed and said, "Never mind, that's the only answer I need."

"I didn't say yes!"

"You don't need to."

I thought he was going to say something more, but the twins started yelling and cursing, and he turned and left to see what was going on with the game. When I finished, I went upstairs to my bed—*my* bed, not Ross's, strange as that seemed, and closed my eyes. It felt so big, like I was drowning in it without him next to me. *Stop thinking about school*, I told myself. *Stop thinking about Ross*. But then Naya sent me a message telling me everyone wanted to know how I was. It was like witchcraft. I sent her a photo of my pajamas with little sheep on them and she responded with a laughing emoji.

I'd only just left, and already I missed them. I rested my phone on my belly and covered my face with my hands. I wanted to call Ross. Badly. Twice, I even picked up the phone, looked for his number, put it back down. What was I doing? I didn't know. But finally I did dial.

He picked up on the first ring, and I was so nervous I started toying with the edge of my pajamas. Why was I so nervous to talk to a guy I saw literally every day?

"Shouldn't you be in bed?" he asked.

"Hello to you, too," I said. "My flight was fine, everything's good, thanks for asking."

"It's after midnight."

"I'm not tired."

"Jen, you got up at six in the morning."

"I'm energetic. You know that. And you certainly don't complain when I want to stay up till 4:00 a.m. with you."

He paused, and I wondered if I was being a little too smart with him. Then he chuckled and said, "It's too bad you're not with me, then."

Was it just me, or did his voice sound sexier over the phone?

"How's your family?" he asked.

"My mom is whiny, my dad's a complainer, my brothers are trying to pretend they're too cool to give me a hug. Everyone makes fun of me. In other words, order has been restored. What are you up to?" As I asked, I couldn't help but look over with longing at the empty side of the bed.

"I'm just in my room watching a movie."

"Without me?"

"Look, I admit it's better with you, but I've got to do something to pass the time while you're gone."

Smiling, I said, "I still feel betrayed."

"I'll make it up to you."

"How is everyone?" I tried to sound normal, however much that last comment of his had turned me on.

"Jen, you've been gone for ten hours. Everyone's exactly the same. Naya's frantic and pacing back and forth, Will's trying to keep a cool head while he's dealing with her, Sue's sitting there like a potato, and then there's me, just trying to survive for the next forty-eight hours. What about you? Have you seen any of your friends?"

"No. You know, I wish you could see what I was looking at right now. I have a huge collection of music in front of me."

"I thought you didn't listen to music!" he said.

"Well, it's not exactly mine. It was a gift from my aunt. I've never even heard of most of the groups. I'll snap some photos, and you can tell me if you want me to bring you back anything."

"Maybe you should surprise me. Usually, when a guy's girlfriend comes back from out of town, she brings a surprise for him."

"Hush!" I said.

"Wow, that was cold."

We talked awhile longer about his favorite bands. I say awhile, but it was two in the morning when I looked at the clock. I couldn't believe how quickly time passed when I spoke with him. And I still didn't want to hang up! And we were going to see each other in two days. Seriously, what was going on with me?

I clenched my teeth and said, "Sorry, Ross, I've got to go to sleep. I'm supposed to help my dad cook tomorrow. And somehow I need to keep a smile on my face while my family tries to drive me insane."

"Sure, Jen. Get some rest. Good luck. And sleep well."

"Good night," I told him and hung up, holding the phone tight to my chest for a moment, and feeling there had been something I still needed to say. But I didn't know what it was. I looked at the screen a minute, biting my lip, thinking of sending him a message.

But no. I needed to calm down. It was just two days.

I laid my phone on the nightstand and turned over, closing my eyes to try to sleep.

I spent the whole next morning in the kitchen with my dad, and as soon as we were done, our guests started arriving: my grandparents, my aunts and uncles, and Shannon with Owen, who jumped into my arms and shouted, "Aunt Jenna!" Plus Spencer's stuck-up girlfriend, whom no one could stand, and my little cousin, who spent the whole time staring at her phone as if the rest of us didn't exist.

It was fun. For me and for my mother, too. And that was what mattered, since it was her birthday. I took advantage of it to eat all the things I'd been avoiding because of Naya and her diet. I could almost feel her calling me a traitor from a distance.

My father waved me into the kitchen, and we lit the candles on the chocolate cake and sang "Happy Birthday" as we set it down in front of my mother and my grandmother snapped photos. Only one of them came out good, because she had her finger in front of the lens in all the rest of them.

I should say, the woman I call my grandmother is actually her sister, my great-aunt. My grandmother died before I was born, and so did her husband, but my great-aunt always treated me and my siblings—especially me—like her grandchildren. She hadn't had an easy life. She'd worked her knuckles to the bone since she was little. And yet it hadn't made her bitter. She had a hard exterior—she'd had to, to make it through life—but inside she was one of the sweetest women I'd ever met.

As she was cutting the cake, my brothers started cracking jokes about me, and she lifted the knife and warned them, "Be careful, I've got pretty good aim." She was saucy like that and had been the only one who always defended me against them. When they piped down, she laid the biggest slice of cake on my plate.

That afternoon, Shannon came up with the ridiculous idea of us going to the mall with Spencer. I don't know if it was supposed to be a bonding thing or what. Obviously, we left the twins out of it. They never did anything separately, and if they came along, they'd just made fun of me the whole time.

Spencer bought me a shake, which I slurped while he carried on about his gym class. Sometimes, when he and Shannon were together, I felt like I was ten years old again. With them, it was always their jobs, the people they were going out with, adult stuff. And since they couldn't help seeing me as their kid sister, they never opened up to me about those things. Spencer walked off to say hi to some friends, and Shannon used the opportunity to grab my shake and throw it in the trash.

"Hey!" I shouted.

"You shouldn't be drinking that trash. Now come here." She pulled me into a lingerie shop where she pretended to browse, but what she really wanted was for me to tell her about Ross.

"I've been waiting all day," she said. "Now spit it out."

Looking at a bra and playing innocent, I said, "I have no idea what you're talking about."

"You're going out with some hot guy who's your age and who treats you well *and* has money…"

"Shannon, his money doesn't matter."

"And, he likes you!"

"Try not to sound so surprised."

"I'm not surprised, Jenna. It's just that it's a relief after Monty. Or let's say a pleasant surprise. So when do I get to meet him?"

"We're not actually going out," I said.

I meant that when I said it. Because the night before I left, something had been up with Ross—I was sure of it. And it definitely had to do with whether or not we were actually a couple.

"For now, you're not," she responded. "I think Spencer sees us. Here, give me that." She grabbed the slinky bra-and-panties combo I'd been looking at without much interest. "It's your size, I think. Go try it on. If you like it, I'll get it for you. I'm sure it'll turn your new boyfriend on."

"Shannon, I've never worn anything like this in my life!"

A half hour later, I was walking out of the shop with a bag in my hand with a set of pale pink underclothes inside. They were the second thing

I'd tried on. Shannon liked them better than the first. I did, too, though I'd never admit it.

Spencer was waiting for us by the fountain, looking at his phone. He put his arm around me as we walked toward the car. Mom was already bugging us all, telling us we should be at home spending time with her. Everything was nice until Spencer said suddenly, surprised, "Hey, Jenna, isn't that your ex?"

Oh no.

I looked over at a coffee shop where I used to hang out with friends when I still lived there. And I saw him. Monty. Sitting with…Nelle.

I can't say I was surprised, but at the same time, everything seemed to freeze for a moment. They looked relaxed as they talked, but I could tell something was up. I knew Nelle. I knew her well, and I knew how she dressed when she had her eye on someone. I knew her expressions, the way she talked. And I could tell they weren't just friends. It felt like a slap in the face.

"I can't believe it," Shannon said, shaking her head.

Maybe I wasn't with Monty anymore, but did he have to go out with Nelle? Did she have to go out with him? Was this why she hadn't responded to me all those months? How long had they been together? Had she betrayed me again? Had Nelle been who Monty was referring to when he dropped me off at school and brought up the whole idea of the open relationship?

I'd trusted her. I could feel my eyes starting to sting. The idiots. But I mean, I was an idiot, too.

"I'm going to kill them," Shannon said. Spencer put a hand on her shoulder and said, "Easy, Tiger," then asked me, "Jenna, are you OK?"

I shook my head. No, I wasn't OK. I felt so stupid. So betrayed. So naive.

"Come on, guys," Spencer said, managing to guide us toward the car despite my sister's grumbling. He hugged me, trying to support me, while I kept thinking to myself how stupid I had been all those months. In the car, the atmosphere was tense, with Shannon complaining and telling Spencer to turn around so she could give them both a piece of her mind. Finally Spencer shouted, "Shannon, will you shut up, please! You're acting hysterical."

In the back, I stopped trying to struggle against the tears, and when my brother and sister heard me sobbing, they turned back toward me. Shannon, sensitive as ever, said, "Don't cry over those two dumbasses," but I couldn't stop myself. My family couldn't help me just then. I knew who could, though. I pulled out my phone and called Naya. She picked up right away.

"Hello, stranger!" she said. Then I heard her tell everyone it was me. "Sorry, Ross," she continued, "she wants to talk to me right now. She'll call you when she wants to talk to you. Now don't be a pain. How are things, Jenna?"

"Bad. And I really need to talk to you. Do you have time?"

I didn't want to worry Ross. I knew he was perfectly capable of driving here to make sure everything was OK. And I didn't need that craziness. I heard Naya go back to telling everyone, especially Ross, to leave her alone, that it was private, and finally I heard a door shut and she told me, "OK, I'm in Will's room. Spit it all out before Ross comes in and takes my phone."

"I thought you couldn't get service in Will's room."

"There's one little corner. I figured it out recently. But who cares about that? Tell me what happened now."

"Naya, you remember Nelle and Monty, right? Well, I just saw the two of them together at a café."

There was a moment of silence as she digested what she'd just heard. "Unbelievable," she said. "He's obviously a dickhead, and you're better off without him. As for her, she can burn in hell."

I think she wanted to say more, but Ross burst in. I heard them arguing, and then he wrenched the phone from her hand.

"What's up?" I heard him say.

"Ross, I called Naya. I want to talk to Naya right now. This isn't anything I need you to worry about."

"Sorry, Jen. You've got me on the line now. And I am worried. So get to explaining. I'm not going to give Naya her phone back otherwise."

As Shannon looked back at me coyly—I can't believe she was enjoying listening to me talk to him when she knew how upset I was at what had just happened—I told him, "I just saw Monty."

"Did he do something to you?" Ross immediately fired back.

"No! He didn't even see me. He was with Nelle. They were together."

"Well," he said, "at least you know the truth now."

"I know, but..." I couldn't help it; I started crying again. "I thought... I don't know. I guess I still believed she was my friend. Or I tried to convince myself she was... Maybe I was hoping everything could go back to being the way it had been before. I tried so hard to forgive them when this happened the first time... And now..."

"Jen, don't cry, please."

"I can't help it. I feel so dumb."

"If you don't stop crying, I'm getting in my car and driving there right now."

"Would you really do that?"

"Of course I would. I can't just sit here with my arms crossed knowing you're hurting inside."

I sat there thinking, trying to get some sense of what I was feeling, while Shannon kept staring back at me and I ignored her. I had managed to stop crying, but I still felt I could start again at any time. Ross kept asking me if I was OK. I didn't know the answer, but finally I said, "I've got two bodyguards, so nobody's going to hurt me, but they're listening to my every word, so this isn't the best time to talk. Stop worrying. I'm fine! I really do want to talk to Naya, though, and she probably wants to kill you since you took away her phone. Let's see if I can keep her from doing something drastic."

He laughed. "Yeah, that's probably not a bad idea. She's got murder in her eyes."

"Isn't that so sweet?" Naya said cheerfully when she picked up. "The way he worries about you, he really is a true gentleman." Then she shifted gears and started ranting against Monty and Nelle before giving me a quick update on her life. By then, we had arrived home and it was time to let her go. I was grateful that no one brought up what had happened. My mother was overjoyed to have us all eating together as a family. When we were done, we watched my dad's favorite show—about fishing—he was literally the only person who liked it—and when he nodded off, we changed the channel.

Shannon and Owen left, and I lay down with my head in Spencer's lap while Steve channel-surfed, bored. My phone buzzed. I just took for granted it would be Ross, and my heart sank when it turned out to be Monty. I tried to ignore the message, but my curiosity got the better of me. It read:

I'm outside. Come talk to me.

I hesitated. How did he even know I was home? Had he caught sight of me at the mall and just not reacted?

I didn't want to see him. But I figured I'd have to at some point. I told my brothers I'd be right back, grabbed my coat, and walked down the stairs. There he was, looking a little thinner than before. We stared at each other and I realized that now, for me, he was like a complete stranger. And when I remembered how he'd acted before, I realized I didn't know who he was, that I'd never really known him at all.

"Hey," he murmured.

"How'd you know I was here."

"I saw you."

"When you were with Nelle."

"It's not what it looks like, Jenna. I'm not with her. I haven't been with her for months. Not since you found out about us the first time. But she wouldn't leave me alone. She kept insisting, so I finally decided to meet with her."

"Monty, I'm not an idiot, and I don't care. It's your life."

"I'm telling the truth, though. I haven't been with her. I haven't been with anyone since you left, except for that one time, and I told you about that. I don't even like Nelle. I didn't even like her back then, but she wouldn't leave me alone, and finally I just gave in."

"Why didn't you tell me that before?" I asked.

"I don't know. Because she was your friend, I guess? Like I thought it was better for you to just blame me than take it out on her."

I wasn't sure what to say. I had hated Monty so much since he came to my school that it was hard to believe he'd done something nice for me. Spontaneously, I gave him a hug. It felt strange, though. He wasn't my friend, I wasn't his girlfriend, so what exactly were we doing?

He brushed my hair out of my face and said, "Come back with me."

I sighed and tried to pull away from him, but he held me tight around the waist.

"Monty, let me go," I said.

"Please, Jenna. I love you."

"No. I can't."

"Why not?" he asked. "We were good together."

"We weren't."

"We were! I've never felt for anybody the things I feel for you."

He bent down to try to kiss me, but I turned away and his lips struck my cheek. I could hear him grunt with frustration.

"Why are you doing this to me?" he said.

"Monty, you went on a rampage and destroyed my old dorm room. I'd have never done anything like that to you. Maybe I should have told you I was living with Ross, but that didn't give you the right to lose your mind and go there threatening me."

"Jenna, just come back to me," he said, grabbing my hand just as I'd managed to break away.

"I said no."

"I promise I won't hurt you again."

"I can't."

"Why? Is it because of that Ross guy?"

"It is," I told him, and as I did so, I realized that was it. I liked Jack Ross. I liked him a lot, and I had liked him ever since I'd met him. If I'd been hesitant to admit it, it was only because I was scared, because I knew once I did so, it would only feel that much more real. And it was real. So real it scared me.

"So this is how you treat me after all the time we've known each other? You go off to school meet some jerk, and now you're with him?"

"He's not a jerk. But yeah, I am with him."

"What's he got that I don't have?"

"Monty, we don't have to do things this way, but since you won't let it go, it's very simple: I like him. I like him more than I like you! I like him more than I ever could like you!"

I don't know what I expected. That he'd accept it? That he'd just understand, finally, that we weren't right for each other? How stupid. Obviously he turned into his same old insane self, pushing me against the handrail on the porch and grabbing the collar of my sweater. Before I could even think about how to react, I'd slapped him across the face.

He stepped back, and I froze. I'd never slapped anyone in my life. The kid at the party who was being mean to Naya didn't count; that was a punch, not a slap. The most I'd ever done to Monty was push him to try to keep him away from me. He raised his hand to his cheek. I knew I hadn't hurt him, but I'd wounded his pride. My heart was pounding, waiting to see what he would do. I knew he'd try to pay me back. I'd seen that look before. Adrenaline and terror flooded my veins.

Trying to escape him, I tripped and fell on the stairs. He grabbed the collar of my sweater again and I could hear the fabric tearing in his grip. I jerked and tugged, but he was too strong. I felt the collar tighten around my throat and shouted, "Let me go!" But he was in a rage, and I don't even think he heard me.

When I finally broke free of him, I was hyperventilating. He came after me again. My only hope was to get inside and shout for Spencer. I couldn't face Monty alone, no matter how many boxing lessons I'd gotten at home. But before I got away, he punched me in the ribs. He'd never done that before. I fell back on the stairs, struggling to breathe, terrified that more violence was coming. But when I looked up, he was gone.

My ribs ached. I grimaced as I stood, wondering if something was broken. When I lifted my shirt, I could see a huge red spot where he'd struck me that spread almost to my belly button. I only hoped it wouldn't bruise.

At least I could forget Monty now, I thought. He'd never dare come near me again after that. I wondered if I should tell Spencer. If I did, my whole family would go after him to make him pay. But what if they took it too far? I thought of the shotgun in the closet and decided it was better to keep this story to myself. Anyway, I just wanted not to think about it.

Besides, I couldn't just run to my family every time something bad happened to me. I needed to learn to fight my own battles. And I'd stuck up for myself, right? I wasn't sure, but I decided to go inside, say nothing, rush to my room, and change my sweater. I hoped that was the right choice. When my brothers asked what I'd been doing, I just told them I had to make a call. They believed it. I flopped back on the sofa and petted Biscuit when he came over, grateful that he seemed to want to console me.

The next day, when I got up, the first thing I did was look at my ribs. I saw a small purple circle surrounded by a much larger red one. It didn't hurt too bad, but the sight of it made me want to faint. Then I tried to get dressed. Immediately, a sharp pain extended from my side all the way down my arm, and when I stretched out, it hurt every time my heart beat. If getting hit once hurt this bad, what did boxers feel after a fight?

My sweater was torn, ruined. What else could happen? I was starting to be thankful I only had another day there. My plane was at eight, which meant my time with them was short, and I should try to take advantage of it. I spent the morning with Mom and Dad, going to the mall—thank God, I didn't see anyone this time—and then helped my brothers out in the workshop, or tried to. Since I didn't know the first thing about cars, all I could really do was change the radio station for them and wash my hands every time I touched something, because there was nothing in there that didn't have grease, oil, and dirt on it. Naturally, my brothers just complained that I was in their way.

Spencer went out for lunch with his girlfriend, and Steve and Sonny went off who knows where, so I hung out with my parents, washing up after we'd eaten. Looking out the window, I saw the back wall of the old tree house, and Mom told me no one had gone up there since I'd left.

"No one?"

"We didn't want you to come back and have a freak-out over it," Dad said.

I knew where he was coming from. My grandparents had built that tree house for my brothers and me, but I was the only one who ever used it. They said it was kids' stuff, and after that, I declared it mine. The only person I'd ever allow inside was Nelle, and that was just one time because she spilled a soda on the rug up there and I decided she wasn't responsible.

Oh, Nelle... It still hurt when I thought of what had happened. I'd tried to reach her the whole time I'd been away. Now I didn't want to. I knew we'd have to talk again sometime about what had happened. But not now. Just dealing with Monty had been enough for me. I walked outside, with Biscuit circling me at my feet. As I started climbing the ladder, he looked up at me curiously. My head popped up through the trapdoor and I saw the dusty interior of my little cabin.

I hadn't been up there since I started going out with Monty. It was weird, almost like I'd forgotten the real me once our relationship started. Why hadn't I realized that?

I wasn't sure, but I needed it back. I needed to recover the old essence of myself. And since I didn't have much to do, I opened the little windows that looked out onto the ocean, and for an hour, I wiped up all the dust and dirt.

There were my old board games, my favorite dolls, a set of toy cars, my red backpack, the aforementioned rug—it was so soft, I just loved to curl up on it—and a table with the magazines I liked to read when I was a little girl, full of the guys from TV I used to think was so hot back then before...

Before you met Jack Ross.

Brain, I think you need a cold shower.

By the time I went back inside, Shannon and Owen had arrived for a visit. Owen hugged me tight, and I played video games with him. I was terrible, but it entertained me to log in with my brothers' accounts and ruin their stats.

"When are you coming back?" Owen asked.

"I don't know," I said. "But I'll be back soon. And you're getting so big! Soon you'll be bored with me and you'll tell me you don't have time for me anymore." I wished I could tell him I'd see him anytime he wanted, but I had no idea what my future held.

Owen didn't seem convinced, but he didn't argue with me, either.

Eventually, it was time for me to go to the airport. Obviously that was Mom's cue to burst into tears. Shannon rolled her eyes at her, and Dad told me he would drive me. Spencer had already complained that he'd been the one supposed to take me, and Steve and Sonny... Well, they were Steve and Sonny.

As Dad grabbed his keys, Mom came over and hugged me so tight, I had to tell her I couldn't breathe. She sighed, blew her nose, and cupped my face in her hands.

"You'd better eat right," she said. "And keep warm. I watch TV. I see those college kids walking around in shorts and flip-flops in the middle of winter. I'd better not find out you're doing that."

"Don't worry," Sonny said, "Jack Ross will keep her warm." He and Steve started laughing. Spencer, who was standing next to them, gave them each a smack on the back of the neck.

Mom ignored them, telling me she'd put some food in my backpack and that she'd gotten paid the day before and had given me a check to pay *my boyfriend* back.

"OK," I told her. I'd given up on telling them he wasn't my boyfriend. They wouldn't let it go. Uncertain, I asked, "Can I take food through security?"

"What, you think they're going to single you out as a terrorist?" Steve asked.

"Yeah, watch out, TSA, the Meatball Bomber's on the loose," Sonny added, and they both started giggling again. The rest of us looked at each other in despair. They were idiots—they always had been—and there was nothing we could do about it.

"Don't worry," Dad said. "I'll warn them I'll sic your mother on them. That should do the trick."

Shannon managed to shove Mom aside to give me a quick hug of her own. Too quick for my taste. She was the one I always missed the most.

My best friend, if I was honest with myself. She made me promise I'd call and keep her up to date, and she smiled sadly. Owen grabbed onto my leg. I had to peel him away, the poor thing.

Spencer hugged me, too, Biscuit licked me all over, and Mom forced Steve and Sonny to look up from their PlayStation and say goodbye, and I stuck my tongue out at them on my way out the door. Once in the car, I put on my seat belt and let out a long breath of air. I was nervous. Anxious. And I wanted to go back home.

To Ross's home, I guess I should say—but it felt like my home now.

Dad didn't say much on the way. I'd always liked that about him. At the same time, I had the feeling we should be talking about something, so the silence wasn't as pleasant as usual. And on the short ride to the airport, I got sad watching my neighborhood thin out and fade into the background. I thought about the beach, which was one of my favorite places, and how the seniors at my high school used to all start the winter season by jumping into the ocean fully dressed. I had skipped it. Unlike my brothers, I didn't want to ruin my clothes, and they still threw it in my face to this day, calling me chicken.

Dad spoke up, "Who were you talking to last night?"

Shit. I hated this. And I knew him. He wasn't just asking. He knew exactly what had happened.

"It's fine, Dad. It doesn't hurt."

"Where did he hit you?"

"In the ribs."

He pursed his lips. It surprised and sometimes scared me how well he could keep his cool. "Does your mother know?"

"No. Of course not. She'd have lost her mind. The same way Shannon and the guys would have."

Dad was different from them in that way. He didn't see it as his role to solve my problems. Instead, he tried to make me see what I needed to do on my own. And that was probably the right thing to do, even if I was afraid I'd made a mistake by letting Monty get away with it. Since he didn't respond, I added, "I'm fine, Dad, OK?"

"Sure."

I knew he was thinking something, and I was feeling defensive, so I asked, "What?"

"Nothing. Is there something you want to tell me?"

"Dad, I hate it when you do this to me. And don't tell me you're not doing anything, because I know you are. It wasn't my fault he hit me, OK?"

"I never said it was."

"What, then?" I asked.

"Jenny, neither of us is surprised that he hurt you. You have to recognize that. We've both known for a long time that this wasn't going to end well."

"Well, what was I supposed to do, Dad? Come in and tell you guys, *Hey, my ex-boyfriend just punched me in the ribs. Do you feel like going to grab some tacos?*"

"This isn't something to make light of." I could see he was getting mad. And while that happened rarely, when it did, hell could rain down from above. He continued, "For God's sake, I'm not blind. Maybe your mother doesn't notice these things, but I know it's not the first time. I saw you with a bruise on your arm where he'd grabbed you last summer. I saw the bruise on your shoulder."

I was ashamed to respond because I knew he was right. When Monty got mad, he'd grab me and shove me, and more than once it had left a mark. Until the night before, he'd never punched me, it was true, but in a sense, that didn't matter because I always felt like shit after those fights.

"Is that what we taught you? To go out with guys who abuse you? That a loser like that is the best you can do?"

I don't know why I was defending him, but I replied, "Monty's not a bad guy."

"Of course he's not. He sleeps with your best friend and hits you, but apart from that, he's the life of the party."

"He only hit me once."

"I'm going to warn you: Don't lie to me."

"So what? So he slapped me that other time. It was just a slap, and I was the one who provoked it."

"Do you not realize you have a serious problem when someone's hitting you and you're trying to say it's your fault? Seriously. Stop defending him. If he's really out of your life, make sure it stays that way. And have a long, hard think about who you are and what you're accepting for yourself."

"I do think about that stuff."

"If you did, you would have given him a kick in the balls that would have dropped him to the ground. We taught you to defend yourself from worse things than some loser who's too free with his hands."

I clenched my teeth and said, "Violence isn't always the answer."

"Maybe not, but when somebody forces you and the situation does turn violent, you better make sure you're the one who comes out on top."

I almost wanted to laugh, but the situation was too tense for that. Why was he making me feel so ashamed of myself? I asked him if he really wanted me to go through life ready to strike out at anyone who pissed me off.

"No. What I want is for you to be who you really are. My daughter. A girl I taught not to go out with guys who don't love her, guys who hit her. A girl I didn't teach to just take it when someone mistreats her and then blame herself."

I stared out the window, trying to think of some sharp reply, but nothing occurred to me, and he went on. "At least, with you being away from home, you've started to open your eyes a little bit. I'm glad for that. When you were here, you treated him like an angel fallen from heaven."

I had to admit that he was right there. Monty had never been a catch, but I sure had tried to act like he was.

"And on that subject, you've got, what, another month before your break? Have you thought about what you're going to do? I know your mother's hammering on about how she wants you to come home, and look, I'd love to have you around more, but I've got to be honest, you look a lot happier now than when you were here. I realize it's not just the months away, that there's a certain person involved, but…well, from what little I know, this Jack Ross sounds like a good guy."

Now I knew what he was getting at. We had always understood each other in that way. It was incredible; sometimes all it took was a glance. "Don't tell me you want to meet him. You've never cared about anyone any of us have gone out with."

"None of my kids have ever gone out with anyone who seemed worth a damn, pardon my French. And this Jack boy, he's done a lot for you. I'd like to thank him. So yes, bring him to meet us sometime. And there's one more thing: if you hear another word from Monty, promise me you'll notify the police. Men like him are not to be toyed with, Jenny."

Those words echoed in my head two hours later when I got into the plane. And all I wanted to do was to see Ross again. As I looked out the window, I was nervous, anxious, tired.

But I was going back home.

18

ORIGINAL

I felt almost lightheaded as I reached arrivals. I wasn't sure why I was so nervous, but I was. My legs were trembling, I was gnawing at my lower lip and I felt claustrophobic as I emerged among a wave of travelers. Past the barrier I saw families reuniting, and I felt a pang that I'd left my own family behind. But then I saw Naya. She pushed through the crowd, stepping on toes and shoving aside little kids to get to me. She didn't care, and I loved that about her.

I saw Sue looking half-asleep and munching on a bag of chips. But honestly, the simple fact that she was there melted my heart. Maybe she really did like me after all?

Jack was there, of course, looking calm on the surface, but I could tell he was tense. Naya shrieked loudly enough to make the whole room turn to face her. I guess making a scene in airports was starting to be my thing.

She jumped into my arms, almost knocking me over, shouting, "Finally! It feels like you've been gone forever! Imagine how hard it was for me without you, all alone with those three!"

"Sorry…" I mumbled.

"Are you done yet?" Ross said, bringing me back to reality. "You're not the only one who wants to say hi to her, Naya."

"She's done," Will remarked, grabbing her by the shoulders and pulling her gently away.

When I looked at Ross, I realized exactly how much I had missed him. It was as though I were seeing him again after an eternity. Not that I *needed* him, but I had felt his absence physically as I slept alone, as I walked around the house feeling cold because his eyes weren't on me, as I sat on the sofa without him there, watched TV without hearing his commentary...

Knowing this both excited me and made me feel afraid.

I was afraid because I'd never felt like that, so emotionally open to someone, as if I were exposing more of myself than I was used to and in that way, perhaps, making myself a target. I thought he was going to say something, but there was no need to. And why bother? It was evident what we felt when I grabbed the cords of his hooded sweatshirt and pulled him toward me. His body tensed with surprise as my lips touched his. When I'd finished kissing him, I didn't dare look at him. I just hugged him tight, hid my face in his shoulder, and sniffed. I had even missed his scent.

What was happening to me? I smiled at Will over his shoulder, and Will reached up and mussed my hair. Naya was shocked. Will less so. He grinned and nodded. He reminded me of Spencer. Like a better version of Spencer, one who didn't throw his chocolate cereal in my hair when he got mad.

"How are your parents?" Ross said.

"Good. Actually they've never been as nice to me as they were those two days."

"That's how it is when you miss someone," Sue said. I took advantage of the moment to thank her for coming, and she gave me a confused look. I don't think she was used to being thanked for things.

"Shall we?" Ross said.

"Can we please?" I asked. "My contacts feel like they're burning through my irises."

They had come in Ross's car. I smiled when I saw the stickers on the back of it. I sat in the passenger seat and took off my coat. He smiled as he turned the key and took off.

"So what have you guys been up to?" I asked.

"I hung out with my dad," Naya said. "Will and Chris and I had dinner with him."

"We also went to another one of Ross's mom's exhibitions," Will said. "His mom obviously asked about you right away. I think it made Ross a little jealous."

"If it makes him feel any better," I responded, "my family asked more about him than they did about me. How was the exhibit? I wish I hadn't missed it."

"Don't worry, you can go to any of the next fifty. They get more and more boring every time."

I told them what I had done with my time at home—about my parents, my siblings, my nephew. I didn't mention Monty, of course. Thankfully no one noticed—except Ross, I think. He kept looking at me expectantly. When we parked and went inside, we ran into Agnes, and she asked about my visit. She was sweet, as she always was. Before going inside, she told us Mike had just shown up. And when we opened the door, we saw him sitting on the couch yawning. He stood and hurried over to hug me, picking me up off the ground. I was taken off guard and didn't know how to react.

"Finally, the peacemaker's back," he said as his brother scowled.

"Excuse me?" I asked.

"I've come to realize your boyfriend's mood is entirely dependent on whether or not you're around. Now at least he won't want to bite everyone's head off all the time."

Ross sighed and pushed him back toward the sofa, telling him to stop being an idiot. I walked back to our room and changed clothes, putting on my pajamas—a.k.a. Jack's sweatshirt and sweatpants. And it felt like heaven. My bliss lasted just a few seconds though, because when I walked out of the bedroom, there was Lana.

I didn't say anything to her, even when I saw she was looking at me. I didn't want a spat. Not tonight, anyway. I just wanted to get along. And I definitely didn't want to cause problems for Jack now that I knew she was going to be around. When everyone turned to me, I said, "I've got a surprise for you all."

I took out the two Tupperware containers my dad had left in my suit-case and told them, "My father's cookies. His special recipe. And he went all out…"

Before I could even finish talking, Jack had taken them from my hands. Everyone jumped at them like seagulls. Will was the only one who even remotely tried to get anyone to behave. He wrestled the con-tainers away from Ross and set them down on the table as I said, "Will, you're the only true gentleman here. Now, those are for everyone, so please share."

The only person who didn't try one was Lana, who just observed everyone with a frown on her face. When the cookies were half-gone, I asked her, "What's wrong? Aren't you hungry?"

"I just don't want to gain a hundred pounds," she said.

"They're whole wheat," I responded. "My mom's on a diet. Or she pre-tends to be. So she forces my father to cook healthy."

I don't know why I was trying to be nice to her. She certainly hadn't been with me. But I knew it was stupid for us not to get along, and I wasn't going to act like a child with her. She hesitated, but she must have sensed there was going to be a peace treaty between us—for now, at least—so she grabbed one, and I think it was the first time I ever legitimately saw her smile.

"Shit!" Naya called out. "I just remembered you and I are supposed to be on a diet, Jenna. Don't tell me you broke it while you were home."

"You're literally eating a cookie right now, Naya," Ross told her.

"It was my mother's birthday. I didn't have a choice!" I protested.

"Traitor!" Naya said.

I apologized for my weakness, but said my diet was officially over. Jack welcomed me back to the normal world, and Sue asked whether they could throw out all the bags of salad in the fridge. Will reminded Naya that she'd just had a hamburger the day before for dinner, and she finally gave in, saying, "You know what? I guess the diet's over for me, too." I threw a cookie at her, but when it landed in her lap, Mike snatched it up and ate it.

We hung out and talked and ate for an hour—especially Ross and Will, who, despite their thin frames, were like two bottomless pits. Lana didn't hold back either. When it was close to bedtime, Naya decided she wanted to go back to the dorm. Lana announced she would leave with her and gave a goodbye hug to everyone except Sue and Mike, and that included me. It was weird—she'd never even touched me before. Confused, I clapped her on the back. I didn't know if she was just in a good mood, if she had some wicked trick up her sleeve, or if my father's cookies worked miracles.

Once they were gone, Will announced he was going to bed and Mike encouraged Ross and me to leave, too. "I've got a lady friend I need to call, and I don't need you all here pestering me," he said. Jack warned him against bringing her over, and Mike shot back at him, "Bro, I just said I needed to call her. It *is* kind of fucked up, though, when you think about it, that you can do whatever you want back in your bedroom with Jenna and I have to stay out here on the couch all by myself." Ross scowled at him one last time as we walked back to the bedroom.

Once I lay on the bed—so soft, so comfortable—all my stress and all my worries disappeared. I asked, "Would you think I was crazy if

I told you I'm so used to sleeping here that my own bed at home felt weird to me?"

Ross smiled, but didn't say anything, and I added, "Oh, I forgot. I've got your check for the cost of the plane ticket."

"Keep it," he said.

"It's yours, though, Ross."

"Think of it as an early Christmas gift, Michelle."

"If you call me Michelle, I'm going to start calling you Jack."

"OK, Michelle," he said, and I threw my phone at him. "Wow," he said, "you must hate it if you were willing to sacrifice your beloved cell phone to get me to stop. Is there any particular reason why it bothers you so much?"

The look of curiosity on his face was so intense that I didn't feel I could leave him hanging. "Look, it's dumb," I said, "but as a kid, literally anything could get under my skin. And I guess around that time everybody was into Disney movies and whatever. And so in *Mulan*, there's this character Mushu. That's what I've been told, I really don't know anything about it. But this kid found out my middle name was Michelle and thought it would be funny to call me Mushu, and it caught on and the whole school started doing it."

From the look in his eyes, I could tell he was about to crack up laughing, and I warned him, "It's not funny!"

"You shouldn't get mad, Michelle. Mushu is a wonderful character..."

"Listen here, Jack. Call me Michelle one more time, and I'm going out there to sleep on the couch with your brother."

"Sorry, Michelle."

"Idiot," I said. "By the way, I got you a present."

He sat up on the edge of the bed. "Is it sexy underwear?"

"No, Jack. Good lord. Here." I handed him a thin package wrapped in silvery paper. "I've felt bad about your birthday ever since it happened. I didn't get you a present, and I left you hanging because of the Monty thing, and I don't know... I wanted to make it up to you somehow. So here. Open it."

He tore open the paper, excited as a little boy—after all my struggles to wrap it well. Then he held his gift up. He looked confused for a moment. His lips parted. "It this...?" He was so excited, he didn't finish the phrase.

"I hope this is a good one, I kind of grabbed it at random," I said. "Because you told me you liked Thor and all. I guess it's the first of that series."

As he sat there, frozen, I nudged him. "You do like it, don't you?"

"W-w-where did you get this?"

Was he stuttering?

"I told you my brothers are into comics. I found it in my brother Spencer's room. I don't think he ever looks at them anymore. I just asked him for one of the rare ones, and that was one of the ones he showed me. He made me clean his car in exchange."

Ross's mouth hung open as he carefully turned the pages.

I added, "If it's not the right one, I can try and get a different one from him." I hoped it was all right, though. I'd hated cleaning that car, and I didn't want to have to do any more favors.

"Of course I like it. This thing's worth money, Jen. But that's not the main thing. The main thing is you did that for me. It's probably the most romantic thing anyone's ever done for me."

"Clean their brother's car? I'm assuming no one's ever done anything romantic for you before, then?"

"Honestly, I don't usually get many presents. From my parents, maybe, but that's different. Like they gave me the car, obviously that was generous, and I use it a lot, but it's not the same as when a person really knows you and picks out something small but perfect for you. For them, it's just money, you know."

"Jack! You should try to appreciate what life's given you. I'd kill for a car. I got socks last Christmas. And they were ugly!"

"Yeah, but your family probably meant it. They wanted to do something sweet for you. My parents are just doing what they think is their duty, or else trying to keep up appearances, which is even worse."

I hadn't really thought about that—for me, a present was just a present—but I could see what he meant. He reached out and grabbed my hand and asked, "So, on another subject…are we kissing in public now? Because I have to admit, you caught me off guard."

"Yes," I said. "That's our new thing. We kiss in public now, and I call you Jack. Get used to it."

"Oh, I will." He reached up and wrapped his arms around me and sat me on his lap. "Especially as I'm assuming this means I won't have to hold back anymore when everyone's around."

I didn't answer him. I didn't feel like talking anymore. What I felt like was… Let's just say something else.

I held his face in my hands and kissed him, and he kissed me back. I liked his kisses—so different, so much deeper, than any I'd ever known. And I knew then that despite all his joking around, he really had missed me. His lips moved from the corner of my mouth to my throat and his hands climbed my back. As they reached my bra, I felt a sharp pain—the same one as that morning. He hadn't even reached the bruise, but my body was protecting itself, remembering the pain. I had wanted to hide it from him, but he could tell, obviously.

"What's up?" he asked.

I didn't know what to tell him. I hadn't come up with an explanation for when he saw it.

"Sorry," I lied. "I'm…on my period."

He could tell I wasn't being truthful with him. He always could. He was even worse than my sister in that way. I needed to practice, because

I couldn't have someone seeing straight through me twenty-four hours a day.

"Jen, what is it really?"

"Nothing. It's stupid." I tried to kiss him again, but he jerked backward, stopping me.

"Lift up your shirt. Let me see," he said, narrowing his eyes. I made a joke: I said I'd gotten his face tattooed on me as a surprise, but it was still healing. He didn't laugh, and when he tried to lift my hem and get a look himself, I stopped him. He stood up angrily.

Was I wrong for trying to hide it? I just didn't want him to see. I didn't want him to think of me as a victim, and I didn't want to think about Monty or Nelle or any of that nonsense back home. Jack was too sweet to have to worry about all of that, too.

"It's not your problem, all right," I told him.

"Jen, you are my problem."

How did he do it? How could he be so tender, even at a moment like this? And how could I keep acting so stupid when he was so kind and gentle with me? He asked me softly to show it to him, and though I hesitated, I had to admit to myself I couldn't hide it forever. I raised my shirt up to the level of my bra. Just under my ribs was a blue and red spot. It looked bigger and darker than it had before.

"Are you happy now?" I asked, angry and ashamed.

"Do I look happy?" he replied.

"It's not such a big deal, Jack." But the look he gave me back showed me how stupid I had been to say that. It hurt, that look. I'd never seen him with that expression on his face before. I wanted him to smile at me the way he always did. Even if I knew that couldn't happen now.

"Someone hitting you isn't that big a deal? And don't try to tell me you just fell down or whatever. I saw your ex when he was here, and I saw the way you tried to hide this from me. I understand what's going on."

"I hit him, too."

"What happened?"

"He tried to kiss me."

Why did I feel I was always being interrogated? I had a knot in my throat again. I could see Jack was about to lose patience with me. He looked down and pursed his lips, and when he turned his face to me again, it was red with rage.

"How the hell can you go on defending him like that? He came here and destroyed Naya's room, he hit you, God knows what else he's done. There's something wrong with him, Jen."

I felt scared, but it wasn't the fear I'd felt with Monty. I knew Jack's anger wasn't directed toward me, or not in the same way. That his anger was a form of care.

"Jack, we all screw up sometimes," I said.

"Dammit, Jen, this is not you screwing up! This is abuse! There is no justification for it, period! It's not right, and you sitting here trying to minimize it is like giving him a pass to do it again. Were you alone with him? Why didn't you ask for help?"

"I can take care of myself!"

"No, you can't. Not with him, at least. I know you act tough, I saw you hit that guy, but with Monty you turn into a submissive little girl."

"Don't call me submissive."

"Don't act like it, then. Your relationship with Monty was toxic. That's the only word for it, and until you admit that, you're never going to be able to move on."

"Just let me live my own life, Jack."

"I can't. Not when you living your own life means letting some weirdo hurt you."

"Maybe you're just jealous!" I said. I should have stopped myself, but the words came out too fast. I felt my mouth go dry as I uttered them.

When I saw the disappointment in his eyes, the anger, it hurt worse than any blow Monty could have given me.

"I'm sorry," I said, "I didn't mean that."

But Jack interrupted me and said, "Yeah, I'm jealous, OK? I am. I like you, you know? And that's why I can't stand this. If it was different, if you had been with a guy who had made you happy, then maybe I could try to find a way to deal with this. But you expecting me to just stand by and watch you let someone you don't even like treat you this way...it's too much to ask. You don't deserve to be treated that way. Nobody does, but especially you. You deserve better."

"I know, Jack. That's why I broke up with him. I'm not with him anymore. You and I agree, so there's nothing to argue about."

"What would you do if he came and knocked on the door right now crying and begged you to get back with him? Are you telling me you wouldn't forgive him?"

"I wouldn't, Jack."

"Be honest, Jen. Imagine if instead of coming here on a rampage, he'd been all sweet and corny and asked you to get back with him. Are you telling me you wouldn't?"

"I can't say what I would have done a month ago. But I can tell you what I'd do now. And I know it, because he asked to get back with me, and I said no. I said no because I like you, not him."

I had to look down as I said this. I was too shy to get it out otherwise. And I'd never liked any guy the way I liked Jack. I knew now: If this turns out bad, it's going to hurt. But it was worth it. I saw something strange in his eyes, something frantic, as if he were calculating, trying to see exactly *where* we were right now, *what* we were. Something strange was happening inside him, and he looked like he was on the verge of tears as he asked, "Is that why he hit you? Because you told him you liked me?"

Poor Jack. He felt guilty. My heart was melting. It wasn't his fault. It had nothing to do with him.

"Does it hurt?" he continued.

I shook my head. It did, but I could take it. "It's fine, Jack. I don't need help. I don't need you to do anything. All I want to do is forget about it. I promised my dad if Monty shows back up, I'll go to the police. You're right. Monty's toxic. I guess I just couldn't bring myself to admit it because I felt like that meant I was at fault, because I was so stupid for ever going out with him. I shouldn't have defended him. I'm sorry."

"It's fine. I'm sorry for pressuring you, but I just needed you to open your eyes. Now tell me about where he hit you. Can I get you something? Some ice?"

"I told you it doesn't hurt," I said.

"And I've told you a million times now, you're not good at lying. Stay here, I'll be right back."

When he returned, he had a damp rag wrapped around some ice. He waited for me to take off my sweatshirt and held it to my side. I wasn't embarrassed anymore—wasn't afraid to let him see me, not my body and not who I was inside.

"Fuck, that's cold!" I said.

"Yeah, Mushu. It's ice."

"That's the first and last time you ever get to call me that, Jack."

And just like that, everything returned to normal. I lay back, he lay beside me, and we looked up at the ceiling. Then he stretched out his arm and I curled up under it. He kissed my scalp. I thought about the first time we'd ever slept together in each other's arms.

"You know," he said, "the kids in your class must not have been very original. Mushu's a pretty stupid nickname."

"Have you got a better one?" I asked.

"Yeah. Girlfriend."

What? Had he said it? Had he really said it? I could feel my brain yelling at me, *Answer him*! But I couldn't, and he continued, "I'm not sure what I expected, but I suppose it was something better than horrified silence."

"Jack..."

"It's OK! I don't want to rush you, and I don't want you to feel uncomfortable. There's time; we see each other every day. I know you just got out of a relationship, maybe it's too soon, I think I just had this thought that I would say it and you'd..."

"Jack!" I interrupted him. I had been trying to for a few seconds, but he was so nervous he just kept talking. "Don't be stupid," I said. "Yes, you can call me your girlfriend."

I climbed on top of him and kissed him, letting the rag fall onto the mattress. He held the back of my head, stroked my face, smiled.

"This is the third best thing that's happened to me today," he said.

"The third?!"

"Easy, Mushu. I aced my exam, I drank a beer earlier. Some things are hard to beat."

"Jerk. I told you, don't ever call me Mushu again."

"I won't."

"You promise?" I asked him.

"Of course not."

19

THE JUJITSU CHAMPION

"Sooo… Does this mean it's official?" Naya asked.

I bit into my toast to try to make time as she, Sue, Mike, and Will stared at me. "Ahem," I said, clearing my throat. "I guess so?"

Naya shrieked so loudly that Sue fell out of her chair and shouted back, "Can you stop doing that?"

"Finally!" Naya continued, ignoring her. Looking at Will, she said, "Remember when I introduced them and I told you they'd wind up together? I was right!"

"I was right," Will said. "I'm the one who said that. You thought Ross would scare her away."

"So," Mike interrupted, "I guess we really are brother- and sister-in-law now. That's too bad. Our romance can never be."

Rounding the corner from the hallway, Jack said, "You never had a shot, Brother."

"That's what you think," Mike responded. "But there was chemistry there."

Coming up behind me, Jack hugged me and kissed me just under my ear. It made me nervous, showing our affection in public—it was still new to me—and I struggled to get down the piece of toast in my mouth.

Everyone was watching us. The two guys were more or less indifferent, Naya was smiling ear to ear, and Sue was sticking her tongue out with disgust.

"Our sweet little Ross is finally getting his act together," Naya said. "I never thought I'd see the day. We should celebrate! Dinner, a movie maybe?"

"We're not going to the movies again!" Sue grunted. "It's not the nineteen-eighties. Why can't we do like normal people and get drunk?" Mike agreed, and Will reminded us that there was always a party at Lana's sorority. Everyone discussed whether we should go, and when, and who should drive, and Mike was enthusiastic, saying he could find someone to hook up with there. I don't think anyone was in the dark about my feelings about Lana, but I tried to be nice. Jack asked, "Are you sure you want to go?"

I said, "Of course, why not? The only thing is, I wonder if Lana will be comfortable with the fact that…"

"That we're going out?" he replied. "Honestly, I couldn't care less. But I think she's over it. Normally when you two are together, you stare daggers into each other the whole time, but when she was over last night, everything seemed fine."

"It was Dad's cookies that did the trick," I said.

"Sure," he responded, giving me a quick kiss. "Now go get showered and I'll drive you to class."

School was getting dull, but at least I'd managed to make a few friends I got along with, especially Curtis, the guy I'd pretended to be hanging out with when I was talking to Agnes. He was cool. He was in my rhetoric class, and we always talked shit about the professor together. We were walking out of the department building complaining when we noticed it was raining. I tried to decide how I should get home, but then I saw Jack across the street. I smiled, ran over, and hopped into his car. The heat was on. It felt wonderful.

So this was it. This was what it was to be part of a real couple. What now? I was supposed to kiss him, right? That was what boyfriends and girlfriends did. I leaned in and got it over with, and he grinned and said, "Nice to see you, too, Jen. How was your day?"

"Boring. What about you? Didn't you have a test today?"

"Do you really need to ask?"

"I'm not sure if your constant self-assurance is your most attractive trait," I said.

"Whatever. You'll learn to deal with it."

As he took off, I looked at my phone. Shannon had sent me a message asking for updates about what was going on in my life. I gave her a quick summary of what had happened the night before—omitting the steamy details, obviously. She was my sister; I wasn't going to tell her *everything*.

"Listen," Jack interrupted me, "I want you to know you don't have to go to the party tonight."

"Why? Are you not in the mood?"

"I'm kind of whatever, to tell the truth. Also, Will told me to grab something for dinner. Are you in the mood for anything in particular? Please don't say pizza."

"Barbecue pizza."

"Or do say pizza, I guess. I'll cut you some slack since you've been out of town. I guess I'll grab some wings or something for the rest of us."

He parked and walked into a take-out place, telling me to wait for him in the car. As soon as he was gone, I called Shannon.

"I'm assuming you're alone and have time for me now?" she said.

"That I do."

"So…you've got a boyfriend again?"

"Yes. It's official."

"Moooooom!" she shouted. I shuddered. I hadn't realized she was with my parents. I heard her announce it loud enough for the whole family to hear. "Your daughter and Jack Ross are officially boyfriend and girlfriend!"

"Shannon, dammit!"

"Sorry, but I promised I'd keep Mom informed."

"You could have at least waited for me to hang up," I said.

"Jenna, you know what a bundle of nerves Mom is! She needed this. And Spencer and Dad told me not to leave them in the dark, either."

"Don't you think they should ask me?"

"Sis, don't get all offended, but you know how hard it is to get a straight answer out of you. Now, let's not argue. I want to hear details. I gave you twenty-four hours to get everything sorted out, and I can't wait anymore. So spill it."

I felt myself start sweating—I wasn't the type to kiss and tell—and it only got worse when Jack returned to the car, leaving our food in the back seat. He looked at me, narrowed his eyes, and said, "Let me guess: your sister."

I nodded as I told her, "Sorry, I'm not getting into all that."

"Oh, Jenna, don't be so boring!" she said. "Or wait… He's with you, that's it, right?"

I looked over. Jack had started the car and was pulling out and pretending to pay attention to the road, but I could tell he was listening to every word we were saying.

"Yeah."

"OK, fine, I'll deal with it. But just so you know, Mom and Dad want to give him an inspection. They won't shut up about it. So you should probably go ahead and start making plans to bring him home one day."

"We've just been together a day! Can I not enjoy myself for a while before we start doing introductions?" I asked.

Jack butted in to tell me, "Call it a day if you want, but you know what's going on with us didn't just start yesterday."

"Don't you pipe up!" I snapped at him before turning back to Shannon. "I'm tired of this conversation, so I'm going to hang up now."

"Fine. Be that way. And have fun with your new boyfriend!"

I shook my head and ended the call.

"Did you get my barbecue pizza?" I asked.

"Can you not smell it?"

"You're the best, Jack."

"Yeah, but you already knew that."

When we got back, I had to eat fast because Naya needed my help picking out her outfit. As usual, she tried on fifty thousand things before settling on the first one. I didn't bother trying to look fancy. I already had the guy I wanted, so there was no need to impress anyone. I was sitting on the bed tying my boots when Jack came in and announced that Sue was having a panic attack because we were taking too long to get ready. "I hope she never has kids," he added, "because she'll be the most neurotic mother in history."

"What the hell?" I said. "It's Naya's fault. I would have been dressed forever ago if it wasn't for her."

As I bent back over, he ran a finger up my spine and said, "What if we make her wait a little longer, Michelle? Because you're looking really good today."

"One: I swear if you call me Michelle again, you're getting hit with this boot. And two: Sue will kill you if she finds out you're making me take any longer."

"It might be worth it," he said, raising and lowering his eyebrows.

He grabbed me, and less than a second later, we were lying on the bed kissing. I laughed and tried to push him away, saying, "Seriously, Jack. I don't want her to murder you already. Let me at least have a couple of months with you first."

"Damn you, Sue!" he shouted, shaking his fist. "Fine, let's go to the stupid party."

Will drove that night. Naya rode with him up front, and Jack, Sue, and I were in the back. We were more or less silent. Naya chatted away the whole time. Will nodded and responded as though he were listening, but I had the impression his thoughts were elsewhere.

The party was similar to the ones before. The only difference was that there were more people than normal. We all went to the kitchen where Naya poured us drinks while Will and Jack opened a couple of beers and walked off to talk about guy stuff.

Lana soon came over to us, radiant as ever. I tried not to get anxious.

"Fancy seeing you guys here," she said. "Hello, Sue."

"Very not happy to see you, Lana," Sue growled.

"How nice. By the way, Jenna, I heard you guys are official," Lana said to me.

"They are," Naya responded for me.

I took a sip of my drink—actually, a gulp of it. I needed some time, and maybe the relaxation alcohol could give me, to keep from saying something stupid.

"Well, I'm glad," Lana replied. Her smile was so sincere that I didn't know how to react. "Ross is clearly very happy with you."

She offered us another drink. I was so stunned by her change in attitude that Sue had to nudge me to bring me back to reality. We spent most of the night together while Jack and Will were off with their friends. And we had fun—more fun than I'd expected. I did overdo it on the drinks, enough that I somehow wound up on the dance floor with Sue. She played along until she couldn't stand it anymore, then dragged me to the kitchen for another drink.

"Jesus, it's fucking gross out there," she said. "All those sweaty bodies. I feel like I'm being rubbed on by a bunch of animals in heat."

I laughed, but she was kind of right. There were couples all out on the dance floor, some of them looking like they were about to strip their clothes off then and there.

"I guess you're not into dancing?" I asked.

"Do I look like I'm into dancing?"

"I don't know…" I said. "I guess not. Me neither, really."

"I'm not surprised," Sue said. "Let's be honest, you're a little bit of a priss, Jenna."

"Am not!"

"Are so!"

She made me think about my sister earlier. As we went on arguing about which of us was more of a prude, which of us was more boring, some guy came up next to me. I flinched when I saw him. I hadn't even realized he was there.

"Do you need something?" I asked, looking around to make sure I wasn't blocking his access to the keg.

"Yeah. How about your name?"

It wasn't until then that I realized he wasn't trying to get past me on his way somewhere. He was trying to hook up. Amazing. The first time since I'd been to college that a dude had hit on me, and it had to be the day after I started going out with Jack. I looked over at Sue, hoping she'd help me, but she remained tight-lipped, clearly amused at the situation, before finally telling him, "Her name's Jenna."

I shot daggers out of my eyes at her as the guy repeated, "Jenna, it's a pleasure."

"Yeah, uh, same," I murmured.

He took that as permission to go on the attack, asking if we were alone and why. Sue's nasty side came out, and she told him we had come by ourselves and were bored. I think she wanted to string him along just to embarrass me. He mentioned that he had a friend for Sue, and that the four of us could hang out if we liked, and Sue told him brusquely, "Yeah, you can leave me out of it."

"Look," I told him, "I'm sure you're a nice guy, but I'm here with my boyfriend. He's over that way with his friend."

"He must not be that interested in you if he's off hanging out with some guy instead of dancing with you."

Finally, Sue stepped in and said, "Listen, dude, I was trying to have some fun making fun of you. But this is getting boring. She's taken. Go find someone else."

The guy ignored her, and as he kept flirting, I looked around, trying to find Jack. The guy got angry and shouted, "Hey, what the fuck is your problem?"

"Problem?" I asked.

"Yeah. I'm here trying to talk to you. And let's be honest, you're like an eight at best. You should be happy a guy like me wants to show you attention. Instead, you're fucking ignoring me, and…"

"Why don't you piss off, you little brat," Sue said.

"Stupid bitches," he responded. Maybe I wouldn't have laughed so much if I hadn't been so drunk. Sue was almost turning purple trying to keep herself from giggling and that only pissed the guy off worse. As he started screaming at us in his ridiculous, high-pitched voice, I heard Will, who had appeared from out of nowhere, asking what was going on.

"Will! Finally! This guy just called us stupid bitches," I said. Then I told the other one, "Bad news for you, dude. This is my friend Will. He's a jujitsu champion. Watch out, he'll grab you in one of those armlocks or whatever…"

By now Sue was cracking up, Will looked completely baffled, and the kid was narrowing his eyes, trying to figure out if what I'd said was true. As he walked off, Will buried his face in his hands before asking me how much I had drunk.

"Less than you, probably."

"Did you at least eat something," he said.

"A little, but Mike stole half my part of the pizza."

Will shook his head. I realized then that he was totally sober. Will said we should find Jack, and I protested that I was fine, and furthermore, I was a grown-up and didn't need a babysitter. "Come on, Sue," I said, "let's hang out here and piss off more guys who want to hook up." But I think even she realized I'd passed my limit.

Will told me I could come with him on my own or he could find Jack to carry me out of there, and when Sue announced that it was five in the morning, I sighed and let them each put an arm around me so I could walk out without falling and breaking my nose. We had to walk through the people on the dance floor, and all that heat and the stuffy air made me a little sick at my stomach as I heard a familiar voice say, "Hey, is everything OK?"

"I'm afraid your girlfriend's had a bit too much to drink," Will told him.

I felt Jack step in and relieve him, holding me up. How warm he felt, how familiar. I looked up as he grabbed my chin, forcing me to look at him, and I had to blink to see him clearly. "Jackie!" I shouted. "What's up?"

"How much did you drink?" he asked.

"I don't know. It's Naya's fault. She started it." Grunting, he crouched, and the next thing I knew, the world was turning upside down as he threw me effortlessly over his shoulder. People watched us as he walked down the hall and the stairwell. I was giggling as my hair danced in my face, and then I shouted for him to let me down. "I'm wearing a skirt!" I said. "I don't want anyone to see my panties."

Ross reached up, felt my butt, and replied, "Don't worry, no one can see anything."

I was yawning by the time he deposited me in Will's car. After buckling me in, Jack settled down next to me. I turned and laid my head in his lap and stretched my legs across Sue, who said, "You better get your legs off of me or we're going to have a problem."

"Oh, Sue," I told her, "stop being such a bitch all the time."

"Jackie," I said, as he shook his head in disappointment, "I didn't tell you, a guy tried to hook up with me. But I scared him off. I told him Will knew jujitsu."

This provided entertainment for much of the ride home, with Naya proud that the guy had believed me and Jack telling Will he had to start wearing a black belt every time they went out. Sue kept pushing my legs off of her, and finally I had to sit up.

When we got home, Jack dragged me to the bathroom and took off my makeup as best he could. Fortunately I wasn't too drunk to take out my contact lenses on my own. Everything looked like a blur as he carried me back to the bedroom in his arms and dropped me on the bed. I couldn't help but laugh as I bounced up and down.

"What now?" I asked.

"I'm going to help you put on your pajamas."

I frowned as he started untying my boots. "Boooooring!" I shouted. "Did you forget it's our first night as a real couple?"

"Do you even realize how drunk you are, Jen?"

"I'm not that drunk!"

"Says you," he replied. "At any rate, there's not going to be any action tonight."

"So it's our first official day as a couple, and you're already neglecting my needs? What kind of boyfriend does that?"

By now, I was stripped down to my underwear and waiting as he dug around in the closet for something for me to wear to bed.

"The kind of boyfriend who's not going to take advantage of you when you're not all there," he said.

"Lame."

He smiled and pulled my arms up in the air so he could slide a sweatshirt over my head. Then he walked around to my feet and put the leg holes of his shorts over my ankles.

"You know, it's nice to be wearing something that smells like you again," I said, lying back and closing my eyes. I felt him lift my head to place a pillow beneath it. I yawned and curled up, looking for his arm to wrap around me, and when I didn't find it, I opened my eyes and looked over at him. His back was turned to me as he changed, and I could see his tattoo.

"Jack, what's the deal with that tattoo?"

He tensed up. "Go to sleep, Jen."

"I've touched it before, Jack. It feels weird. Is there something under it? Is it covering something?"

"I'm not going to tell you. And why bother asking? You probably won't even remember tomorrow."

He pulled on a T-shirt and got into bed next to me, pulling me close until my head was on his chest. I tried to move back to look at him, but he held me there.

"Are you really not going to tell me?" I asked.

"No."

I sighed, and he brushed my hair out of my face. I closed my eyes. I was exhausted.

"OK, I'll tell you," he said. "It's a scar."

"A scar from what?"

"That's enough secrets for today, Jen."

My mind was moving in slow motion, floating out toward my dreams. I yawned, and he moved a little to let me get more comfortable. "Good night, Jen," he murmured just as I drifted off to sleep.

20

THE INNER SHARK

When I woke, I felt something like hammer blows inside my head.

Jack was still in a deep sleep. No surprise there. My morning run was the last thing I was interested in doing that day. But I should be responsible, I thought, and it would probably help to sweat out the poison. So I stood, put on my tights and my sports bra, and walked out to the living room.

When I made it back an hour and a half later, sick to my stomach but feeling more awake, I found Mike up and talking on the phone. He seemed angry, which was weird for him, and he was almost whispering, so I guess he didn't want anyone to hear him. It must not have been working, though, because Will, Sue, and Jack were standing at the bar staring at him.

Jack grabbed me around the waist as I came past and kissed me on the lips, almost leaving me breathless. I'd need to learn to get used to that, because I knew a lot more kisses were coming, but every time still felt like the first. Sue snorted, and when I asked her, "What?" she replied, "I just realized I'm the only single person in this apartment."

Mike hung up and told her, "I'm single, too," and she sneered at him before saying, "I'm sorry, I was speaking of the human beings that inhabit this apartment, not lower life-forms like yourself."

Mike remarked that it was too bad I wasn't still single—again, he called me *sister-in-law*—and Jack told him to get used to it and to keep his trap shut. It was strange to me that no one asked about that phone call, which they'd all seemed so attentive to, so I decided to ask myself. "Is everything OK."

"There's no easy way to answer that question," Mike said. "Maybe you should ask your boyfriend."

"Don't tell me…" Jack said.

"I'm afraid so," Mike murmured, trying to grab a piece of toast off his brother's plate. "You know how he is. He loves his traditions. And of course, he's crazy about the two of us."

Detecting the sarcasm in his voice, I said, "Sorry, guys, I know you two are brothers and you have some kind of ESP with each other, but the rest of us have no idea what you're talking about. Can you explain?"

Jack pursed his lips and sighed. "Every year, my father celebrates his birthday at the lake house, and every year, he tries to get the whole family to join him. And since it's just three days away, I thought we were in the clear this year. But apparently I was wrong."

"You don't want to go?" I asked.

"You know, you should switch your major to psychology," Mike said, "because you have an incredible knack for telling what other people are feeling."

I slapped him on the shoulder. But before they could tell me more, someone knocked at the door. Jack muttered a curse under his breath as Mike answered, walking back inside a few seconds later with their mother, Mary. Jack's expression darkened further, while Mike, for some reason, found the whole thing entertaining.

"Hello, everyone," she said.

She was always so well dressed that she made me feel like a monster. Especially in my running clothes. But her genuine smile told me I had nothing to worry about. She reached up and grabbed Jack's cheeks, trying to turn his frown upside down, and when he stubbornly resisted, she asked me, "I guess the cat is out of the bag about the lake house?"

I nodded a little cautiously.

"Well," she continued, "my husband wants everyone to come. You, too, Jenna. He says he's looking forward to seeing you again."

"That's a no," Jack said coarsely. "Does he really think he can treat her the way he did last time and have her come to his birthday? Screw that. He can leave her in peace."

"Son, please. Watch your language. And I'm sorry to tell you, but I'm asking Jenna, not you."

"And I'm speaking for both of us when I say no."

"Ross," Mike said, "don't you think it's time for you guys' big coming-out?"

"Shut up, Mike," Jack and I both replied in unison.

"Jackie, your brother told us you two have made it official," Mary told him. "So your father wants to see you as a couple. It will hurt his feelings if Jenna can't come. I'm sure he'll behave better than last time now that he understands."

"Would it kill you to try and keep your mouth shut once in a while?" Jack asked Mike.

My first question was if their whole family would be there. I wasn't sure I could face meeting a bunch of strangers. But Mike reassured me that it would just be the four of us, their father, and Agnes. "She hit him with her cane last time," he said. "It was amazing. Maybe we'll see a rematch this year."

"Mike, don't forget that time you brought a girl and ruined everything," Jack said.

"That won't happen this year," Mary rushed to add. "Jenna's a wonderful girl and she'll be a perfect addition to the party. If you can make it, we're heading out tomorrow morning. The house is an hour away by car, or probably half an hour if one of my sons is driving. Now don't forget a bathing suit."

"It's winter, though," I said.

"It's for the hot tub," Mike informed me. I couldn't believe it. I'd never met anyone who had their own hot tub. Jack started complaining that his mother had played a dirty trick on him, just showing up at their house like that. He told me not to let her guilt me into going, and she responded by doubling down, reminding me that Agnes would be disappointed if she didn't see me there. I felt everyone's eyes on me, almost as if I were shrinking on the spot. And of course, my brain kept telling me, *Hot tub, Jenna. They just told you there's a hot tub there.*

"I'll go," I announced.

"Perfect," Mary said, her smile radiant, as her younger son tried to stutter a response. When she asked if she should pick me up, Mike interjected, "Ross will take us both."

"Perfect. Try and make it before lunchtime," she told them, adjusting her jacket and saying she had to go. "I've got tons of work. You all have a lovely day now."

And she left, as though the ensuing chaos were no concern of hers. For a moment, Jack stared at me so intensely I think it frightened everyone else. Even Mike was uncomfortable and announced he was going to take a shower. Sue put the ice cream she'd been spooning up back in the freezer and made an excuse to leave, as did Will. Thanks, guys. Just leave me hanging over here.

"Jack," I said, "you're looking at me like I just killed your puppy."

"Why'd you say yes?"

"It seemed rude not to."

"After the way that asshole treated you, he doesn't deserve any better."

"Jack, he's your father. Don't call him an asshole. Maybe he wants to apologize. He deserves a second chance."

"Trust me, he doesn't," Jack said, picking his plate up and dropping it in the sink. I reached up and grabbed his hand. Instantly, I felt him soften as I pulled him toward me.

"It'll be fun," I said. "I want to see your lake house. We can just spend the whole time in your hot tub."

"It's overrated."

"And your bedroom."

He smiled. "Now you're speaking my language."

I giggled and pushed him away, and he came back in for a kiss.

"So then, the killer grabs her by the foot, and bam! She's dead. And when the police show up, they've got no idea what's going on, so he gets away with it! Amazing! Right, Jenna! Right?"

Mike spent the entire drive to the house recounting every detail of some stupid movie that apparently was filled with blood, guts, and murder, and the whole time he kept getting louder and louder, until toward the end, he was basically screaming at us. Jackie had on his sunglasses and was looking straight at the road, but I could tell he was fantasizing about doing the same thing to Mike that the movie killer had done to all his victims. Since I could tell he had no intention of answering Mike and that made me feel bad, I said, "Yeah, incredible."

"At least one person's listening to me," Mike replied. "What's wrong, Jack? Your girlfriend didn't give you any this morning?"

"What's wrong is, I can feel my IQ dropping the longer this story goes on," Jack said.

"He didn't sleep well," I told Mike, but Jack instantly corrected me, "I slept like a baby."

Jack had been in a good mood, despite everything, but that changed the moment we got in the car. Admittedly, Mike was being more annoying than usual, but the real problem had to be his parents. Hoping to distract him after a long, uncomfortable silence, I asked Jack if he'd gotten his father a present. When both brothers looked at me strangely, I continued, "That is what people do for someone's birthday, isn't it?"

They still didn't answer. It was bizarre how similar their expressions were. I didn't know if they were trying to make me feel nervous, but I went on, "Hello, are you guys listening to me? You know, birthdays, presents, that is a thing? You guys like getting presents, don't you?"

After still more incredulous silence, I said, "Fine," crossing my arms. "I guess we'll just be silent for the rest of the trip."

Jack had spent much of the trip with his elbow resting on the edge of the window, his cheek propped on his arm, but when I finished talking, he sat up and cleared his throat with a grin and asked, "Hey, Mike, that movie you were talking about…Isn't there a part two? It sounds familiar."

In that way, the conversation started again, and for a moment they seemed to be getting along well, but then Mike said he thought Tarantino sucked and Jack threatened to pull over and kick him out of the car. That made me realize I'd been mistaken to try to break the silence. Jack put on some music, which was a better option than listening to them bicker.

We had left the city heading east, where it was warmer. The houses thinned out as we kept going until at last the highway was empty, with nothing but farmed fields and livestock for miles. At a crossroads, Jack turned onto a smaller road that passed through forest, and after five minutes, he started to slow down. We stopped in front of a gray fence, newly painted, that opened automatically onto a gravel road that forked, leading toward the main house and another house, equally big but a little further off.

There was a carport off to the side with one car already parked in it. Jack stopped there, and Mike and I got out. It wasn't until I was in front of the house that I realized how big the place was. It dwarfed their home in the city. Everything was hardwood, marble, and stone, with an immaculate lawn and a pea gravel path.

Jack and Mike hadn't bothered packing; they already had everything they needed there. But Jack was a gentleman and took my things for me without asking.

"Is it me, or is it almost hot here?" I asked.

"Listen, I'm open-minded. If you want to take it all off and turn this into a nudist retreat, go for it," Jack joked.

"I'm serious, Jack."

"Just wait. It'll get cold tonight. The daytime here's a different story, though. That's why I told you to pack something besides just sweatshirts."

He gave me his hand. It was still warm from gripping the steering wheel. He guided me toward the wooden porch with its elegant stairs. There were cushioned seats all around, and the double oak doors had small windows near the top. Mike rang the doorbell.

A middle-aged woman I'd never seen answered. I thought it was supposed to just be the family and me. She greeted them and Jack said, "Hello, Lorna," with a smile.

I could be wrong, but I think her eyebrow rose slightly when she saw we were holding hands. It was so fast, so subtle, that I couldn't tell. Then she stood aside and let us through.

Inside it smelled like cooking, and my appetite awoke with a bang. The vestibule was huge, with armchairs and shelves all around. In front of us, a doorway led to a huge living room. The dominant tones were brown and red, and everything looked very expensive. Windows lined the walls, some looking out onto the forest and some giving a view of the lake. It was stunning.

Jack must have realized how impressed I was. I won't say he smiled proudly—he was too down-to-earth for that—but he looked happy that I was happy. It was clearly nothing special for Mike, who just walked into the living room and jumped onto one of the sofas as he always did, before groaning, "Shit, I forgot there's no TV here."

"There's internet, though. You can stream something on your phone."

I was dying with curiosity as I looked into the kitchen. It was as big as the bottom floor of my home. And the smell...

"Jen," Jack called to me. "Let's go put up your things."

I nodded and followed him through the living room, past a dining room with sophisticated wooden furniture, and up a staircase to the second floor. There were more rooms above us, but here he crossed a hall through a round room with armchairs and a piano and stopped at the second-to-last door on the right.

"If this room doesn't work for you, feel free to pick another," he said. "We have plenty."

He opened the door to a room with an exposed brick wall and wooden shelves full of books and keepsakes I didn't have time to look at. The windows were immense, with cream curtains that were pulled back at that moment. A gray rug lay under the huge bed with its gray sheets. Walking over to the window, I saw the small dock leading out into the lake and a furnished back deck with a bar and grill.

"Why don't you live here all the time?" I asked. "I feel pretty sure I could die happy here."

"I think you're exaggerating a bit. But the thing is, Dad doesn't really like it out here. He says it's too far from everything. Which some might see as a good thing, but I don't know. Hey, are you stealing my glasses?"

I had just picked up a pair of sunglasses from his shelf and tried them on. "They look better on me," I said.

"You've got me there." He pulled me on top of him and onto the bed and kissed me in that special spot just under my ear that made all my hairs stand on end. I loved it. I wasn't used to a man being so sweet.

"Who was that woman downstairs?" I asked, sitting up a bit.

"Lorna," she said. "She and her husband, Ray, take care of the house when we're not around. They live nearby. They look after the neighbors' place as well. You know, mowing the lawn, dusting, raking leaves, that kind of thing. I don't think we'll see them again."

"Jackie?"

Agnes's voice reached us from downstairs. When we went down to see her, we found her with Mary and with Jack's father, who must have just arrived. Agnes looked happy to see me—she always did—but Jack's presence was clearly a joy to her, and she immediately started pinching his cheeks the same way his mother did. And he complained the same way he did with his mother.

"How are you, Jenna?" Mary asked, coming over and hugging me. "I'm really so, so happy you came."

"Yes, it really is a pleasure having a few new faces around here," Jack's father added. "I hope everything's to your liking."

I wasn't sure how to react—I'd only seen him once, and he'd been cruel and stuck-up then—but I wanted everything to go well, so I just smiled and said, "You've got a beautiful home. I was just telling Jack."

"Speaking of Jack," his father said, "what kind of host are you, Son? It looks like you haven't even offered your guest something to drink."

"He did," I lied, "but I'm fine."

Mr. Ross left to arrange things in his room while Jack went to find Mike. I stayed with Agnes and Mary in the salon.

"Well," Mary said, "they seem to be getting along. At least, I haven't heard them screaming at each other yet."

"Give them time." Agnes sighed.

"Why do they get along so badly?" I asked.

Maybe I shouldn't have. I noticed the two women looking at each other a little nervously before Mary replied, "They have very different personalities."

There had to be more to it, I thought, but I wasn't going to insist. My job while there was to make a good impression. Jack walked in just afterward with his brother. Mr. Ross remained upstairs, which I found strange. We talked and laughed for close to an hour before Mary and Agnes went to the kitchen to see what Lorna had left for them to eat. I got the sense that they were making excuses and they really wanted to talk by themselves. Looking a little bored, the brothers brought out a deck of cards and started throwing money on the table. I felt a little nervous betting the one twenty-dollar bill I had in my billfold, but if I lost, I figured I could work it out somehow later. Jack encouraged me, telling me he'd distract his brother so I could beat him.

"Shut up, Ross," Mike said. "You should try and focus on actually learning to play instead of trying to drag me down."

"Sorry, Bro. There's twenty dollars at stake. This is no time to fight fair."

Silence overtook the room as Mike laid down his two aces. Too bad for him, I had a three of a kind. "Yes!" I shouted, and Mike said, "Wait a minute... Was my brother sharing his cards with you?"

"It's called teamwork," Jack said, hugging me to his side and kissing me on the lips. "I was coaching her. And I'm as proud as if she just won the Olympics. Plus, I need a protégé. I've been beating your ass at cards since I could crawl." He gathered up the bills on the table and pulled them toward us.

Mike was grouchy, then tense, and I turned to find his father on the stairs, observing us. I felt Jack stiffen as well as his father said, "Please, don't interrupt anything on my account. It's so rare to see you two boys having fun together. I suppose you have something to do with that, Jenna."

I smiled, a little embarrassed, but also grateful. On the surface, the comment was friendly, but something about his expression—an expression that said *I'm rich and I know it, and I don't need you*—made it feel almost like an insult. Especially when Jack gripped my shoulder tighter, consciously or unconsciously. I wasn't sure. Mike gathered the cards without a word. I wondered if Mr. Ross was aware he'd ruined our amusement, and if that had been the point.

"Jack," he said with a cold smile, "when you have a moment, I'd like to speak to you in private. Now, preferably. I'm assuming you'd like to keep this issue between you and me."

I wondered if *this issue*, whatever it was, was bad, because I could hear Jack's teeth grinding. After a glance at me, Jack stood, and he and his father walked out on the back porch. When the sliding glass door closed, Mike exhaled audibly, and I asked him if they were fighting about something.

"Maybe?" He shrugged. "I'm trying to stay out of it."

"Can I ask what it's about?"

"Trust me, you don't want to know." He stood, changing the subject. "Is that mashed potatoes I smell?"

Thankfully, our dinner was less tense than the last one. Mr. Ross barely spoke, and Agnes and Mary were the life of the party. Not to mention, the food was delicious. At one point, Mary asked me how my parents were.

"Great," I said, swallowing what I had in my mouth. "They miss me, obviously. But it's kind of nice because they treat me special now that I don't live there. I've never experienced that before."

"Yes, I remember how I started to truly treasure these two disasters when they left home," she responded.

"Wow, Mom, thanks for the unconditional love," Jack said.

"Yeah," Mike added.

"See," I said, "isn't this nice how family brings people together? You two never agree about anything." I thought my comment was funny, but my smile vanished when they both glared at me. It was almost frightening how similar they looked in those moments.

Mr. Ross's silence was weird, and when he left the table, long before anyone else, I almost thought Jack would say something, the way he stared at him. Then Agnes stood, left the room, and returned with a sneaky smile and a bottle of liqueur.

"Uh-oh," Jack said.

"Now the fun can start," Mary announced, rubbing her hands together.

"Jenna, hand me your glass please," Agnes asked. I tried to comply, but Jack put his hand on top of mine, telling both women, "Sorry, I didn't bring my girlfriend out here so you two could get her drunk."

My girlfriend. It still sounded so strange. And yet so right.

"Come on!" I said. "I want to try."

"Do you even know what absinthe is?" Jack asked.

"No…"

"Then trust me."

But I told him he was being a party pooper and pushed his hand aside. Agnes agreed with me, chided him, and poured me a small glass. All of us drank our first glasses in one gulp—all of us except Jack, who abstained. He murmured, "Everybody take it easy."

The taste was… I wouldn't know how to describe it, but it brought the biggest frown imaginable to my face. How it burned! All the way down. Unable to control myself, I started coughing, to the amusement of everyone but Jack, who said, "OK, that was fun now, but nobody give her any more."

"I'm fine," I argued, but I couldn't help adding, "God, it tastes awful!"

"It'll get you drunk, though," Mike said.

Jack tried to stop his grandmother from refilling my glass, but she told him cheekily to respect his elders. Soon enough, I was feeling… Let's just say tipsy, even if the truth was I could barely stand. Agnes was perfectly in control, even if she had a chronic case of the giggles, and it was nice to hear her like that, laughing from her stomach, from her soul. Mary did the same. Mike was sitting next to me guarding the bottle as I caught Jack staring at me.

"Why are you staring at me, stalker?" I asked.

"I like seeing you have fun," he said.

I nestled close to him. "Funny enough," I told him softly, while everyone else had their attention focused on Agnes, "you seem to be the person I have the most fun with. Good, clean, innocent fun, you know."

"Is that all?" he asked.

"I don't know. The night is young. We'll have to see where it takes us, won't we?"

I gave him a quick peck on the corner of his lips, and when I turned around, I saw that everybody had fallen silent and was watching us. The two women looked happy. Mike was refilling his glass.

"Don't hold back on my behalf," Agnes said. "It's so rare to see Jackie actually being sweet with someone."

"I'll have you know I'm very sweet," he said, sounding like a little kid.

Mary butted in. "Well, I've known you for twenty years, and this is the first I've heard it. To tell the truth, I thought you'd never end up with a nice girl…"

"Yeah," Mike added, "there wasn't much in his past to suggest it would ever happen."

"It's true," Agnes said, "Jackie doesn't usually have very good taste. But that finally seems to have changed."

I tried to keep from grinning as Jack turned back and forth, scowling at everyone, including me, and saying we were getting on his nerves and he was going to go to his room. I stood to follow him while everyone else hooted and made fun of us. But instead of going up, he walked out onto the back porch. With his long legs, he had nearly made it to the dock before I reached him. The people inside couldn't see us anymore, but we could still hear their laughter.

"Jack, don't get mad at me," I said, reaching out to him.

"Great, they got you drunk," he hissed, but he did take my hand and squeeze it.

"I'm not drunk. I'm just happy. Aren't you?"

It occurred to me then that I'd never seen him drinking anything stronger than beer. As I wrapped my hands around him, I asked why, but he pretended he hadn't heard me and said, "We should go for a jacket. You're going to freeze out here otherwise."

"Jack, I'm fine. Just stay here and have fun with me." Feeling the cool breeze from the lake, I told him, "You know, my parents live by the ocean. And on the first day of winter, all the seniors go out there and jump in with all their clothes on. I didn't do it, and my brothers still throw it in my face. They say I'm chicken."

He seemed to be wondering what I was thinking, and that only worsened when I let his hand go and walked to the end of the dock.

"What are you doing?" he asked, his brow furrowed.

"Mushu's not going to be a chicken anymore," I joked. "Mushu's a dragon!" I stumbled as I took off my shoes. He tried to catch me, but I sidestepped him, saying, "Uh, uh, uh."

"Jen, don't be stupid," he called out, but I just smiled at him, walking backward. He cursed, and I laughed and turned around, running toward the edge of the dock, hearing his footsteps slam behind me on the wood. Of course he reached me quickly, when I still had four feet to go. Given our difference in size, I'd actually made it pretty far, I thought. He went on telling me to chill out, and I called him boring. We went back and forth for a few seconds, and finally, I tried a different tactic. "All right, then," I said, "take me to your room. I'm dying to see it."

"What are we going to do there?"

I brushed against him hard, awakening his perverted little smile, and said, "Come with me, and you'll see."

He started following me, and I turned around. "Psych!" I shouted, proud that for once, I'd managed to fool him, and as his expression turned to horror and he shouted, "Jen, no!" I threw myself into the water, screaming, "Woo-hoo!"

Splash!

It was freezing, and all my senses awakened at once. I stayed under the surface for a moment, feeling my hair and clothing hovering. Then I emerged. Up on the dock, Jack looked like he was going to kill me.

"Relax, dude," I said, smiling ear to ear as I treaded water. "You're acting like a frightened grandmother. Get in! It's not that bad!"

"You get out before you get hypothermia."

I repeated what he'd said in an exaggerated, high voice, and he said, "Don't make me call you Michelle."

I stuck out my tongue and said, "Come on, Jackie!"

"Yeah, no, thanks."

"But Jaaaaaack....I'm all alone out here in the dark. What if a shark comes?"

"In a lake?" he asked sarcastically.

"I don't know," I said, "anything's possible. Maybe you're the shark and I should be watching out for you." I tried to give him an innocent look, hoping it wouldn't work, and soon I saw a face I was more used to and liked better: the face I often saw when we were together in bed. My tricks were working... I didn't let up, reminding him that it was dark, that no one would see us, and finally he said, "Fuck it," taking off his shoes, and I shouted, "Yesss!"

He ran, jumped, and landed a few inches away from me, and I had to close my eyes to keep the splashing water out of my eyes. When I opened them, I didn't see him anywhere. I didn't have time to ask where he was before he grabbed my legs and pulled me under. We struggled for a few moments before he let me go, and when we both came up, I saw how sexy he looked with the water dripping from his hair. I'd never thought water droplets could be sexy before, but I was learning new things every day.

"You're right," he said, "it's not so bad."

"You jerk, you made me swallow a bunch of water. I'm probably going to get a disease or something."

"It wasn't me. It was my inner shark."

"You could have killed me!" I said.

"Don't be so dramatic."

I splashed his face. I realized then that his feet touched the bottom and mine didn't. I had to tread water the whole time. So I decided to grab onto him like a koala. He didn't seem to mind.

"You know," I whispered, "we probably don't need a bed." I kissed him, following a line from his lips to his cheek to his jaw, feeling the short, sharp hairs on it, then moving up to his ear, wishing I could kiss him all over his body.

"I was complaining," he said, "but if this is what being drunk does to you, maybe I could get used to it."

Thank you, alcohol. I told him I was in the mood to do something crazy, something that was a complete break with the person I had been before.

"You want to have sex in the lake?" he asked.

I kept kissing him, both lips, his neck, his chest. But when he came in for more, I pushed him back.

"I want to get a tattoo," I said. "I was hoping you'd go with me."

Jack's smile froze on his face as his excitement drained away, and finally he managed to get out the words: "Are you fucking serious? I thought you wanted to…"

I climbed the ladder attached to the dock. The cold water had sobered me up completely, and I didn't even sway or stumble on my way out. Jack followed me, still looking shocked.

"I'm not trying to be selfish, Jen, but most tattoo artists don't work the night shift, and they usually turn away drunk eighteen-year-olds in soaking-wet clothes."

"I can put on something dry. Plus, you probably know someone who can do it, right? There might be a reward in it for you afterward…"

I had been half-joking, but his eyes lit up. I think the idea of me doing something bad turned him on. He tossed me a towel and we walked over to the deck chairs and lay down.

"OK, maybe—let me repeat, maybe—the guy who did my back piece can help. He's been my friend for a long time. But he might also tell me to go piss up a rope."

"Can you try, Jack? Please, please, please, please, please?"

He frowned, dried himself off, and went inside to look for his phone. I could hear his family laughing when they saw his wet clothes. When he came back out, he was already talking on the phone. He hung up, looking resigned to my little adventure, but he warned me, "This little lark of yours is going to cost you double the normal price."

"No worries," I said.

"Let me get this straight: You've complained about how you're broke ever since I met you, and now all of a sudden you want to waste a pile of money on a tattoo?"

I responded, "I never told you I wasn't a hypocrite."

He smiled, shook his head, and asked, "Where the hell did this idea come from, anyway?"

"I don't know, I'm just in the mood to do something ridiculous."

I dried my hair as best I could and tiptoed up to my room to change clothes. I asked to borrow one of his T-shirts. I don't know what it was, but I just needed to wear something that smelled like him. Without telling the others where we were going, we walked outside and got into his car. He kept asking me if I was sure, if I knew what I was doing. He told me he was worried I'd regret it the next day.

"Trust me, I'm never going to regret anything that happens tonight," I told him.

An hour later, I found myself lying on what looked like a massage table with my T-shirt pulled up over my belly. The tattoo artist gave me a surprised look when he saw the bruise on my ribs, which was just starting to fade away.

"That must have hurt," he said.

"It's nothing compared to what the guy who did it has in store for him," Jack assured him, grabbing my hand as the needle approached my flesh.

"I'll tell you," the artist continued, "I've been asked to do some strange things, but getting up at one in the morning to give a drunk chick a tattoo is pretty high on the list."

"I'm not drunk," I protested, and both guys looked at me as if to say, *Yeah, right.*

"Maybe I should get a new one, too," Jack said. "I could get your name on my butt."

"How romantic," I replied, trying not to grimace as the tattoo gun moved across my flesh. By the time we returned to the lake house, everyone was asleep. We tried to walk silently up the stairs to his room. As soon as I entered, I stopped in front of the mirror and lifted my shirt to look at my waist.

"You sure that was a good idea?" Jack asked.

"I like it," I said.

"Copycat."

"Loser."

I'd gotten the same eagle he had on his back, but just above my hipbone.

"I guess if it gives me an excuse to get you to take your shirt off, I'll deal with it," he said.

I smiled and turned to wrap my arms around him.

21

PROTECTION, FOR GOD'S SAKE

When I got up in the morning, Jack had disappeared. I sat up in bed, my head aching slightly, and blinked, trying to make out the note on the nightstand: *Dumbass Mike left his phone charger and none of ours work with his phone. I took him to pick it up. I'll be back in a while.*

I shook my head and walked off toward the bathroom. As I brushed my teeth, I had to look at my tattoo again. It still had plastic wrap over it and it stung, but I liked it, and I liked the way I looked with it.

Walking downstairs in presentable clothes, I noticed the smell of paint immediately. I followed it out to the back porch, where I found Mary sitting on a stool in front of a canvas. She was blocking out a sketch, but I couldn't really tell of what. She must have just begun.

"Good morning," I said, rubbing my eyes as I approached.

"Good morning, dear. Did you have breakfast?"

"Nah. I'm not hungry anyway."

My mouth was cottony, though. Damn alcohol. As Mary mixed her paints, she said, "I woke up feeling inspired."

"I can see that. What is it?"

"You know, if there's one thing my years of painting have taught me, it's never to say what it is. It's best for every person to just give their opinion when the picture's done. You want to join me?"

"Me?" I asked, confused.

"Not with this one, obviously. But I have ten blank canvases stretched and ready to go. You did say you liked to paint, right?"

"Well, uh…" I was in a panic. "It's been a long time since…"

"What did you usually paint with?"

"I really was more into drawing. With charcoal, you know."

"Oh," she said. "Charcoal was never my strong point. I could never master the wrist movements, and my work was always too stiff. I like oils. But I'm sure I have some charcoal and paper you can use."

Before I had time to say no, I found myself sittingin front of a blank sheet of paper with charcoal, a kneaded eraser, and a blending stump. Mary grinned as she asked me, "What are you going to draw? You said you used to do portraits, right? Maybe you can do one of those for me."

Instantly, Jack's face came into my head. But I was too ashamed to draw him in front of his mother, so I decided on someone else.

"When it comes out terrible, don't say I didn't warn you," I told her.

"It won't be terrible. And if it is, we just won't tell anyone."

As I traced out the first line, I had the sense that I was utterly clueless, but I just kept going, trying to relax. It's not as if I had anything else to do, anyway.

"Did you ever study art?" Mary asked.

"Just one class. The only thing I remember about it was the teacher freaking out because someone had put on rubber gloves. He said if you wanted to be an artist, you had to get your hands dirty."

She told me she'd had a teacher who was similar, and then she talked about all the crazy professors she'd had when she was studying in college. We spent more than an hour together. It had been so long since I'd touched any art materials that I was nervous, and I progressed slowly. But I did better than I'd thought. There was one eye I had to erase and redraw three or four times, but I was proud of myself. At least until I turned and saw Mary's picture, which was perfect, harmonious. I put down my charcoal and watched her work until I heard two very familiar voices emerging from the living room. Mike was the first of them to appear. "Mom," he shouted, "can you please tell your younger son to leave me in peace?"

"What is it now?" she asked.

Jack appeared and said, "This moron told me he'd left his charger behind. Great. I agree to take him back, since he can't use our chargers because he's the last person in America who doesn't have an iPhone, so I take him to some chick's place, and he breaks into her house."

"So what?" Mike said. "I needed it. Besides, it was just a moment, and nobody saw us."

Jack said, "I'm going to tell you this slowly so your tiny brain can process it. Breaking...into...a...house...is...a...crime. C-R-I-M-E."

"Only if you get caught," Mike responded.

"Well, enjoy your phone, because that's the last favor I ever do for you," Jack hissed, before noticing the two easels and continuing, "What's this? I didn't know you worked with charcoal, too, Mom."

"That isn't mine," she said.

"Did you draw that?" Jack asked me. As his mother walked inside, he and Mike stared at me with surprise.

"Is it really that astonishing?" I replied.

"I didn't know you were an artist," Mike said. "Is there anything you don't do well?"

As I shrugged, Jack asked who it was, and I told him it was my nephew, Owen. Jack asked if he could pose for me some time, too. Distracted, Mike lit a cigarette, and that reminded me that it had been a long time since I'd seen Jack smoke. He didn't say anything, but I could tell that his brother doing it was getting on his nerves a little. So I tried to take his mind off of it by asking, "What's the plan for today?"

"I don't know about in the afternoon," he said. "At night, we all have to pretend we're just crazy about Dad while we wish him a happy birthday."

"It's amazing how much love there is in this household," I said.

"Trust me," Mike responded. "You don't know him." Jack nodded in agreement. Looking through the window, I saw Agnes wander into the kitchen looking like she hadn't slept a wink. The hangover, I guess. My phone rang. Jack grabbed it off the table and handed it to me. It was Spencer. I was always happy to talk to him.

"Hey, little sister, how are things?" he asked.

"Good. How about with you? Is something up?"

"Well, I don't know if I'd say anything was *up* exactly, it's just…Mom's here with me, and she's a little nervous, or excited, or whatever you want to call it. Because Shannon told us you're not with that loser Monty anymore and that you really are with Jack what's-his-name, and you're supposedly spending the a few days with his family…"

"The traitor."

"And Mom's freaking out because you didn't tell us. She wants to know why you told Shannon and not her. She says hanging out with his family is serious, and…"

I guess my mother was getting bored with his attempts to be diplomatic, because I could hear a scuffle through the receiver before she yelled, "Jennifer Michelle!"

"Mom!" I felt myself turning red as Jack heard her and mouthed the word *Mushu*. Damn him and damn that stupid name.

"I can't believe you would go to your boyfriend's parents' house and not even tell me. I *hope* you're using protection, for the love of God! I know you and I never had *the talk*, and it's probably too late now, but…"

"MOM!"

"You really need to know that proper birth control can save you all sorts of headaches. I'm not trying to say anything bad about you children, but it hasn't been easy… Now this week, I want a phone call and I want to know each and every detail of this new relationship of yours. I certainly hope they're taking good care of you."

"With Jack's mom here, I feel right at home," I said.

"Of course you do. There are things all mothers understand. Now I've got to go. But you'd better call me or I'm going to get mad. Love you! Kisses, honey."

"Kisses to you, too, Mom," I said. When I hung up, I saw both brothers looking at me. Mike said, "Kisses to you, too, Mom," and I threw a cushion at his face. He blocked it with the hand that wasn't holding his cigarette. When Jack copied him, I told them they were both a couple of children, and hearing their laughter behind me, I got up and walked to the kitchen.

Agnes was sitting at the island looking on the verge of death.

"Good morning?" I said. "Or maybe not so good?"

"Every time I hear one of my grandsons laughing, I tell myself I should never have reproduced," she said. "So that tells you about the morning I'm having."

I filled a glass with orange juice and took it over to her. She muttered a thanks and took a tiny sip.

"When I was your age," she told me, "I could drink the contents of an entire liquor store and be fresh as a daisy the next day."

"Time comes for all of us," I responded.

Mr. Ross walked in just then, polishing his expensive glasses with his shirttail. He actually looked nice, and it was hard to believe he was the same man who had basically thrown me out of his house a few weeks before.

"Good morning, Mr. Ross. Happy birthday," I said.

"Thank you, Jenna." He squeezed my shoulder. "Mother, did you drink last night? You know at your age you shouldn't…"

"At my age, I don't need anyone telling me what to do. Just leave me here to suffer with my orange juice in peace."

I chuckled, but stopped as soon as I saw Mr. Ross looking at me.

"Jenna," he suggested, "how about you and I have a little talk." I could tell from his tone that saying no wasn't an option.

"Of course," I said.

As I followed him out, I saw Jack arguing with his brother through the window. They didn't notice us passing by. My nerves frayed even further when I saw Mr. Ross start to walk up the stairs, but I had to follow him, I thought. He walked all the way to the room with the piano, where he pointed to one of the black leather chairs with a kindly expression that still weirded me out, saying, "Please."

He walked over to the piano, leaned against it, and tipped his head to one side. "What do you think of the house?" he said.

"It's beautiful. And very homey. I don't know if that's funny to say."

"Not at all. I feel the same way as you. I was thirty when I bought this place. I always wanted some place on the lake to get away to. The city's nice and all, but it can start to weigh on you. But that's beside the point. What I wanted to say was…I don't think I behaved as I should have when you and I met, Jenna."

Oh. So that was it.

He went on, "I didn't know what your intentions with my son were. When you have money, you have to be careful. I hope you understand."

Translation: you don't understand, because you don't have money, but just trust me.

"Now, though, I see that the two of you do get along. And you get along with Mike, too, which is… Well, I probably shouldn't say this, but Mike's complicated. I don't think that's any great secret. Nothing is serious for him. Yes… Anyway, I just wanted to say I was sorry, and I hope we can start over from zero."

"Of course," I said. "I understand. He's your son. You want to protect him."

He smiled, and I thought he was going to say something else, but then Mary appeared in the hallway. Her expression was cautious, and she looked back and forth between us. Something didn't feel right, and I could tell her gaze was trying to communicate something to him. When he ignored her, she said to me, "Jenna, dear, would you mind waiting for us downstairs? I have something I need to discuss with my husband."

I told her I understood and walked off down the hall. Instantly, I could hear them arguing, but I didn't want to be nosy, so I hurried down the stairs to find Agnes and Jack talking and Mike sitting on the floor playing with his phone, which was plugged into the wall.

When Jack asked where I had been, I told him his father had wanted to talk to me, and he looked furious, wanting to know what he'd said to me, what he'd wanted, what he'd done.

"Everything's fine, Jack," I said. "He just wanted to apologize for the other day. He said we should start over from zero."

For a second, I thought everything was OK, but then Jack stood, and he looked far angrier than before. I tried to follow him, but Mike caught my eye and shook his head.

"That goddamn manipulator," Jack said, taking the stairs two at a time. I looked at Agnes, hoping for an explanation, but she still seemed paralyzed by her hangover, and when I tried to listen, I could only hear vague sounds and footsteps. At some point, the word *Mike* was audible, and Mike went upstairs, too. I had no idea what was going on.

Agnes fell asleep with her chin resting on her hand. I said her name to make sure she wasn't just resting, and when she didn't respond, I climbed the stairs. The voices grew more intense; then Mike flew past me in a rage, making me stumble. I could barely process what was going on when Jack appeared with my backpack in his hands. "We're going," he said, making it clear no discussion was possible.

Mary passed by in turn, trying not to cry. Looking down the hall, I could see her husband sitting in one of the leather chairs, apparently indifferent to whatever was going on.

"Jen, come on," Jack called out from the steps.

I followed him. Mercifully, Agnes was still out of it. When we were outside, Jack threw my things in the back and the three of us got in. Mike stared out the door with a serious expression. Jack slammed the door and sped off.

I was too scared to ask anything. But I couldn't understand how things could have spoiled so fast. Maybe I shouldn't have agreed to talk to him? Maybe I shouldn't have repeated what their dad had said? I reached over, grabbed Jack's hand, and brought it to my lap.

"Everything OK?" I asked.

"No," he replied.

Neither he nor Mike gave me the least indication that talking was a good idea. So I remained silent until we got home, thinking that this was the strangest vacation I'd ever taken. In the apartment, we found Sue and Will in the living room studying their notes. "Well, you guys look like you had fun," she said.

Jack dropped my backpack beside me and said, "I'm going to go shower." Mike walked back out the door. When I heard the window in the hall sliding in its frame, I figured he must be going on the roof to smoke.

"What happened?" Will asked.

"No idea. Everything was fine and then Jack's dad apologized to me for last time, and all of a sudden, everyone was pissed and they argued and we had to leave."

Will shook his head. "That's pretty much what happens any time Ross and his father spend more than an hour together."

"I just don't understand what the big problem with them is," I murmured.

"If it makes you feel better, I don't, either," Will replied.

If Will didn't know, that meant Jack hadn't told anybody. I flinched as my phone rang. It was Monty. Great. Just what I needed. I didn't answer.

When I saw Jack was done with his shower, I followed him into the bedroom and shut the door. As he put on a pair of pants, he tried to stop me from talking to him, saying in an acid voice, "I'm fine."

"Jack, I hope I didn't say anything wrong."

"Jen, I told you before, I don't want to talk about my dad."

I hesitated, then nodded and told him, "OK, but I just want to tell you, if you ever do need to talk to anyone, I'm here."

He tried to laugh the situation off, saying, "Trust me, Jen, I know. I know how nosy you are. I caught you sneaking up the stairs to try to eavesdrop on us."

"I'm not nosy!" I shouted. "Anyway, you would have done the exact same thing."

He smiled and walked past me to the bed.

"How about you sit down here and we watch a movie and just forget any of this ever happened."

22

THE TEST

It was weird for Mike not to joke around. But that morning, he'd hardly said a word. Even Jack was starting to worry about him.

We assumed it would pass, but the next day was no different. All he did was watch TV and stare at his phone. I figured it had to do with his dad, but since I kept being told that they didn't want to talk about it, I stopped asking.

My classes that day seemed like they would never end… What else was new? Naya and I were supposed to meet for lunch. But when I saw her, she had Lana in tow. My first reaction was to turn and run, but I tried to remind myself I had made a resolution to get along with her. Even if it was just for Jack and Naya's sake. So I smiled and acted cordial and the three of us walked to the cafeteria.

I don't think I had ever heard Lana talk about anything except for the guys she'd hooked up with and her dozens of trips to Europe. She never said anything about her homework or her classes. Maybe she was one of those people who didn't need to study? Chris had said she got excellent grades. Remembering Chris, I asked Naya, "Hey, how's your brother? It's been forever since I talked to him."

"Same as always. *The Enforcer*, they call him. He never met a rule he didn't like. But oh well. I still love him."

"I still remember when I was in the dorms," Lana said, smiling. "I almost had a heart attack one time when I came back and Ross had climbed in through my window and had been hiding in my room all night…"

She stopped herself, remembering that I was there. I think it was the first time she felt bad for mentioning something about her and Jack. When her cheeks reddened, I said, "It's OK, Lana. I know he had other girlfriends before me. You're not going to kill me."

She looked at me with uncertainty, then the tension eased. I guess we were getting along now? I hoped so. My phone vibrated. Ugh…Monty again. He had called me a million times by then. I was starting to hate seeing his name on my screen. I silenced the phone as both girls looked at me and Naya asked, "Is it him again?"

"Who?" Lana asked. "Your ex?"

For some reason, I felt like telling her the whole story. Well, not the whole story, but everything Naya knew. I kept the worst details for Jack, who was the only one who had seen my bruise. A bruise which, thankfully, was finally almost gone.

I had actually taken out a restraining order against Monty, with Jack's urging. He drove me to the courthouse. I had to fill out a form, explain the situation, and show the judge my bruises. It was only temporary—to get a permanent one, there was a hearing, and Monty could be present to defend himself—but at least for now, I felt safer. It was ugly, and I wasn't happy about it, but it had to be done.

Lana was shocked when I told her the details and asked me why I didn't block his number. He actually wasn't allowed to call me according to the terms of the order, but of course that didn't stop him.

"Listen," I murmured, "if I block him, he's the type who would just show up here. He's unbelievably stubborn and he just doesn't want to accept the truth."

We talked a while about how Monty had treated me in the past, his jealousy, and men in general, the way three friends would who had known each other their entire lives. And that sudden feeling of comfort gave me an idea. I needed to take advantage of this opportunity because I didn't know when a similar one would arise again. And so I did something… something I'm not very proud of.

Looking at Naya innocently, picking at my food with my fork, I said, "Can I ask you a question?"

"Of course," she replied.

"Do you know why Jack and his father don't get along?"

I turned to her because it was obvious Jack wasn't going to tell me, and Mike wasn't the type to talk about his emotions. Will would never betray his friend. Naya and Lana, though… I felt I could overcome their resistance. I had imagined they'd look back and forth at each other, wondering whether it was all right to tell me, but they both just shrugged. Did they really not know? That was the last thing I had expected.

"I don't think even Will knows," Naya murmured.

"It's just always been that way," Lana added. "Even back in high school. Ross used to sleep at Will's house a lot of the time because he couldn't stand being under the same roof as his dad."

I tried again. "He told me before he went through a phase in high school…that he was a little less chill then than he is now. That he used to get in trouble, that he hooked up with random girls, stuff like that."

"'Less chill' is the euphemism of the century," Lana said, almost laughing.

"For real," Naya seconded her. "Jenna, when Ross was in high school, he was…"

"A total fucking disaster," Lana interrupted her.

"How so?" I asked.

"He skipped class," Naya began. "He talked back to his teachers, he got in fights, he was nasty to everyone, he would do weird random shit like get that tattoo of that giant eagle…"

"And he drank," Lana added. "A lot."

"But that's not the worst of it," Naya said. "Because… Well, you've seen his family. He had more money than sense. So he got into drugs, too."

What? Jack? My Jack? Impossible!

"Nothing too strong," Lana objected. "Well, let me correct myself. He didn't get too deep into the hard stuff. But…"

"I thought Mike was the one who was into drugs," I interrupted her.

"Mike's issues came later," Naya corrected me. "Back in those days, Mike used to actually take care of Ross."

Was I in a parallel universe? Everything I thought I knew was being turned upside down. I asked them to tell me more about the drugs, and they said he used to throw lots of parties and started hanging out with a rough crowd. And it happened suddenly, in a matter of weeks, his transition from a nice, sweet, responsible guy to a gruff rule breaker, and that was what made them think something bad had happened to him. Naya told me he changed a little when he moved in with Will. He left the drugs alone, at least, because he'd wanted to help Mike, who was now starting to lose his head. But personality-wise, he was still thorny and hard to be around.

"I think it was his dad," Lana said.

"So what, then?" I asked. "You both think he just needed time away from his family to start settling down?"

Naya and Lana looked at each other and then at me, as if each of them were daring the other to say something they were both thinking. The responsibility fell on Naya, who told me the real change hadn't happened until I had come along.

"That can't be," I said. "He's been the same guy the whole time we've been hanging out."

"Exactly," Lana replied. "You didn't know him before. Between the time I left and now, there's been a hundred-and-eighty-degree turn. It was like the guy I'd known before he fell apart in high school was back."

"I don't know if you remember this," Naya said, "but the day we were moving into the dorms and I told him not to scare you away, I wasn't joking. He was one of those guys who would just hook up with a chick and then throw her aside like an old pair of shoes. Then I introduced you all and everything was suddenly different. Ask Will. Even he was surprised. I remember that first night the two of you went to his room. I just took it for granted that you were finished, that he'd do what he wanted with you and leave you hanging like the others…"

I remembered then how Naya had burst in on us and asked if we were doing something inappropriate. I had thought it was just a joke, but now that I thought about it, she did seem to be wanting to rush me back to the dorm.

"Yeah," I responded. "He was an absolute gentleman, though. Always has been."

"That's surprising," Lana said.

"Do you think that's one of the reasons Sue was so pissy when I showed up?"

"It could be," Naya responded. "She must have been tired of seeing all those girls coming and going. Remember that day Ross cooked and she made that nasty remark about how he wanted to fuck you and we all just froze? Now you understand."

"Why wouldn't Ross tell me all this?" I asked.

"Jenna," Naya said, "Ross is terrified that you'll think he's not the person he tries to be with you. He's in love with you. I don't know if you haven't realized that yet, but it's obvious to all the rest of us."

Lana hung her head a bit. It must have stung, hearing that her ex-boyfriend loved someone more than her. I felt bad for her, but I didn't know what to say.

"Just him stopping drinking was a major change," Naya continued. "I don't think I ever saw anyone who could put it away like him."

"I noticed he stopped smoking, too," I said.

"Yeah, Will told me that," Naya responded. "Oh, your idiot ex is calling again."

I looked down at my phone, which I'd left on the table. Monty's name was on the screen. I wondered if I should tell the police as I sent the call to voicemail.

"If Ross finds out, he'll solve that problem permanently," Lana said. I responded that I didn't want them to ever cross each other's path. I had seen how violent Monty could get. I was surprised by how they laughed nervously then. They reminded me that I'd only met Ross in his good-boy phase and informed me that he knew how to handle himself in a fight. After that, we moved on to other subjects, and eventually I went back to class. But I was bored and distracted, and the hours seemed to drag on as I turned those two girls' words over and over in my head.

So Jack had changed. For me. Maybe. Or maybe I had just been the catalyst and there were lots of other factors. But what did it matter? The important thing was that he'd tried to change. And I had dillydallied for so long, unable to decide between him and Monty. I felt like a fool. Of course, he was the one I wanted to be with. I needed to make it up to him somehow.

When I got home, I felt a timid smile on my face as I found Mike, looking a little less depressed, sitting in the armchair and watching TV with Sue. Naya and Will were curled up together, and Jack was alone on the other couch.

"Back after a long, hard day at the grindstone?" Jack asked.

I dropped my bag, and even though Jack had scooted over to make room beside him, I sat down in his lap. He raised his eyebrows, and I surprised him even more when I touched his cheek and kissed him on the lips. I wasn't used to showing my feelings in public, but that was going to change, I told myself. Because I knew he liked it. And I think I did, too; it was just that it embarrassed me. I would get used to it, I told myself. I would do it for him.

"I guess you missed me?" he asked.

"Something like that," I responded.

Everyone around us pretended they weren't paying attention except for Sue, who made a throwing-up gesture, and Mike, who was laughing. Jack was obviously happy with all the attention, but after a third peck, he looked confused and asked me, "Jen, are you all right?"

I nodded and said, "Yeah. I was wondering if you could come help me pick out some pajamas, though."

"I'll give it a try," he responded with a grin. "But who knows if I'll be able to find them."

Looking him in the eye, I reached out a hand and he grabbed it, seeming to finally understand. He smiled and sprang off the couch. And once we were in the hallway, he rested a hand on the small of my back as he guided me back to his room.

When we returned an hour later to have dinner with the rest of the group, Will asked mockingly whether I'd found my pajamas. I blushed. Obviously everyone was perfectly aware of what we'd just been doing. They had ordered delivery, and as I sank my teeth into my burger, I realized how hungry I'd been. Naya's home renovation show was on and I watched, engrossed. I'm sad to say I'd gotten addicted to it. My phone buzzed now and then as my sister sent me photos of Owen and asked how I was doing. I wrote her back, curled up under Jack's arm. I felt an electric charge as he casually caressed my shoulder.

Monty's face reappeared on my phone screen, I sent it to voicemail, and he called again. Jack's hand stopped moving, and when I looked up, I saw he'd noticed.

"Is he still bothering you?" he asked.

Fortunately no one else seemed to have heard him. I was grateful that he could be so respectful in these moments.

"A little," I admitted. "But don't worry. I can handle it."

"Honestly, I'm not sure you can," he said. "There are some people who can't be handled. I know you're a tough girl, but this isn't your responsibility. You should get in touch with the police."

"I don't want him to be arrested, though."

"Then let me do something," he said.

"I didn't realize you were a bodyguard for hire," I joked. But since he didn't think it was funny, I tried to reassure him, "He'll get over it. He'll find some other girl to bother and he'll leave me in peace."

Almost offended, Ross shook his head and said, "Jen, you're not the kind of girl someone can just forget."

I was surprised by how frankly he'd come out with that. He went on. "If you ever, ever feel unsafe, promise me you'll let me know. And call the police."

"I will."

"Promise me, Jen."

"I promise."

"Good. OK. Good."

The next morning, I was studying like crazy for a test. I even skipped my usual run. I felt bad about it because it was part of my routine now, and I missed it. How proud Spencer would have been if he'd known.

Jack and Will had said they were going to get me a cake to celebrate my good grade. I wasn't so confident. I read and reread my underlines in my book and seemed immediately to forget them. But when I sat down for the exam, it all came back to me, and I aced it! When I walked out the door of the department, I found them there waiting for me. I had intentionally pretended to be upset to get Jack to come over and console me. When they saw me, Will nudged him and he came over and wrapped me in a bear hug, saying, "If you want, we'll go up there and threaten your professor until he changes your grade."

"No need," I said, laughing. "I aced it! I just wanted to see how you'd act. Congratulations, you passed the test!"

On the way home, I told them to drop me off at the supermarket so I could buy some beers. I was in such a good mood as I walked there that I didn't notice a car I knew very well in the lot in front of the store. At least not until Monty grabbed my arm, stopping me in my tracks.

"Surprise, surprise," he said in a nasty tone. "I see you're still alive."

Oh no. Not again. Please, no.

I tried to tell myself this was a nightmare. That I could blink and open my eyes and he'd be gone. But he was real. He was back, with no warning. And I was scared. My ribs stung, as if remembering the time he'd battered them.

"I'm going to call the police," I warned him, but when I felt my pocket, my phone wasn't there. It must have slipped out in the car. Looking over at the door to the supermarket, I told myself I couldn't run there in time. I'd have to hold him off until somebody walked past and I could ask for help. The streets were empty, though. *Please, God, someone come help me!*

Monty grabbed my shoulder, digging his finger into my collarbone. "What are you going to tell the police?" he asked. "That I came to see my girlfriend because I was worried about her, because she wouldn't answer my calls or messages? That's not a crime, Jenna."

"I've got a restraining order, Monty. You're breaking the law right now. This isn't a game anymore."

"You think I give a shit about a restraining order? Besides, it doesn't matter. If you'll just listen to me and see how I feel about you, I know you'll come back with me."

"I'm never getting back with you, Monty, and there's nothing to talk about. And if you don't let me go, I'm calling the cops."

He started tugging me off toward his car, and as I shouted for him to let me go, he told me, "Screw that. You're going to get in my car, you and I are going to finally fuck again, like we should have when all the trouble first started, and you're going to forget all this bullshit."

"Monty, I wouldn't fuck you if you were the last man on earth. You're not my boyfriend. You're nobody to me. Let me go right now!"

"No! You listen, bitch! I told you to get in the damn car!"

"I'm not getting in the car, I don't want to talk to you, and I don't want you to ever come near me again!" I shouted. Trying to get hold of myself, I went on. "How many times do I have to tell you to leave me the hell alone? Is a restraining order not enough for you to get it through that thick head of yours? What else do you want?"

My heart was racing from the fear. I prayed for someone, anyone, to come rescue me. I looked at him and wondered what I would do if he tried to get me in his car. Punch him in the throat? Kick him in the balls? But I didn't want it to come to that. And what would I do if I missed?

He wrapped both his arms around me and lifted me up, carrying me toward his car. I thought that would be enough for someone to jump in, but the one or two people who walked by just pretended we weren't there. A switch flipped in me, and I stomped on his foot as hard as I could. When he stumbled, I broke away. He yelped and leaned back against his car.

"Who in the hell do you think you…?"

"You listen here, you moron. You will not touch me again. You will not hit me again. And if you even try, there'll be hell to pay." I spoke so angrily I surprised even myself. Monty needed a few seconds to recover from the shock.

"I barely hit you, you bitch. And trust me, that was nothing compared to the emotional damage you've done to me."

Almost crying, I shouted, "How in the hell could I have wasted four months of my life with you?"

"I was the best thing that ever happened to you," he said. "And you're going to learn to appreciate me. I'll be damned if I'm going to let you keep treating me like trash after all I've done for you."

I stumbled backward and felt a pair of arms holding me. Jack. He'd appeared from out of nowhere. He pushed past me and grabbed Monty by the neck, slamming him against his car like he'd done it a thousand times. He didn't even break a sweat. Monty's aggression had turned into panic. "Let me go," he shouted, "or I'll…"

"Get her out of here and call the cops," Jack said. I didn't understand what he meant until I realized Will was there, too. He put a hand on my shoulder gently and told me to go with him.

But I was reluctant to turn away. I was still scared of what Monty might do. Ignoring me, Jack said, "Will, please," and Will threw me over his shoulder and took off toward the apartment. I couldn't see a thing, and I kicked and screamed trying to get down. He didn't stop till we'd reached the elevator in the lobby.

"Dammit, Will, go back there now!" I shouted. "You just left your best friend with a maniac! Are you not scared?"

"Not in the least," he said calmly. "Ross knows exactly what he's doing."

Sue and Mike looked surprised when we entered. Will shoved me into the apartment, then shut the door behind me. I was trembling from head to toe.

"Will, did you forget which one was your girlfriend?" Sue asked.

I turned around and tried to get back out, but Will backed into the door and held it shut. "Let me go, Will!" I shouted. "I'm serious."

"Ross told me to keep you here. Now call the police. Your phone's over there on the bar. You left it in the car." I did as he said, fingers shaking. The woman who answered told me they'd be there in no time. That made me feel a little better. But only a little.

"They're on their way," I said. "But that doesn't make up for you leaving my boyfriend with Monty. What if he gets hurt while you and I are just standing around up here?"

"Trust me," Will said, "Ross doesn't need our help. Now stop trying to get past me. I'm not moving, and I'm not letting you go downstairs. Whatever's happening right now, Ross doesn't want you to see it."

I tried once more, but it was obvious I could never get through him. So I sat on the edge of the sofa, running my hand through my hair. An eternity seemed to pass, and I felt like I was going crazy. I'd seen what Monty could do before. I remembered a time a guy had hit on me and Monty had broken his nose. Just the thought of him doing that to Jack made me want to cry.

A knock came at the door, and I jumped up. Jack was there, looking utterly calm, without a scratch on him. There was a police officer with him. The way Will and Jack looked at each other, I could tell they were communicating something, and I was angry that I couldn't understand what.

"Miss Brown?" the policeman said. "We need you to come with us down to the station."

I nodded as if in a trance, almost feeling as if it were another person acting for me. Jack and Will accompanied me, and I told them everything that had happened. I didn't see Monty, thankfully, but I did hear him screaming from a nearby cell. The police said if I chose to file charges, he could be looking at prison time, most likely six months to a year.

"If the prosecutor goes along with it," the policeman said, "I would encourage you to testify. You're not guilty of anything. He knew what he was doing, and he knew the consequences. Jack here told us he's been calling and messaging you constantly, in violation of the restraining order.

Most likely he's been watching you at school and at home. We've seen these cases before. Lots of times, unfortunately. And if the law doesn't intervene, they usually won't stop."

I told the officer how grateful I was, and that I was there if he needed a statement or any other information, and I walked out of the police station with Will and Jack, in a state of shock. I didn't utter a word the whole way back. I couldn't find the words.

When we got home, Mike was pacing anxiously and Sue was sitting there with her arms crossed and worrying. "Are you OK?" she asked as soon as I walked in. "What happened? Please tell me you're all right."

I was so shaken that Will told me and Jack to go relax in our bedroom. "I'll explain the situation," he said.

I don't know if I'd ever felt so grateful to someone. I thanked him for being such a good friend, and he said it was the least he could do. Jack walked to our room ahead of me and sat on the bed. I wasn't sure what to say to him. I approached him with caution, and we both asked each other at the same time, "Are you all right?"

An uncomfortable silence followed. Then I warned him, "Jack Ross, I want you to promise me right now this is the first and last time you try to take on an idiot like Monty on your own."

"It wasn't such a big deal, Jen," he said.

"Wasn't such a big deal? Jack, he's dangerous! I've seen him when he's angry! I don't care if you can fight, I don't care whether or not you're scared. I'm telling you, I don't want you to ever do a thing like that again."

"Jen, it's over. I'm fine."

I guess that was true. I looked him over, and there wasn't a mark on him.

"Forget him," Jack continued. "I don't think he's going to bother you anymore."

"I'm not worried about me, Jack, I'm worried about you!"

"And I was worried about you, Jen. Don't you get it? I don't care if something bad happens to me, I don't care if someone hurts me. In that moment, all I knew was I had to get you out of danger."

Hearing him say that, I couldn't feel angry any longer. It almost irritated me how easy it was for him to make my anxieties disappear. He was so gentle… I adored him, and I tried to forget how scared and upset I was, touching his cheek and hoping I wouldn't cry.

"You're right," I said. "You defended me. Even if you had to act like a dumb meathead and show how tough you were. For your information, though, I was handling it. I was just about to give him a kick so hard between the legs that we wouldn't have to worry about him reproducing."

"Wow," Jack responded. "Lucky for him I got there in time."

I smiled, and we curled up closer to each other, with him letting me rest my head on his shoulders.

"I'm sorry you have to deal with all my stupid problems, Jack."

"The truth is, it keeps me entertained," he said.

"Entertained?" I asked. "You sure have a weird idea about what entertainment is."

23

PRODUCTIVE MORNINGS

Jack was half asleep with his head resting on my chest, and I was unconsciously toying with his hair as I looked out the sliding glass door at the night sky. Sounding like a groggy animal, he murmured, "I like it when you do that," without opening his eyes. "It's relaxing."

I kept doing it, happy I could do something for him. A few days had passed since the dustup with Monty, and we hadn't spoken of it again. He had been right about one thing, though. Whatever it was he'd done, Monty hadn't bothered me again. Not a text, not a call, nothing.

"Jack," I said, "I don't think I thanked you enough for what you did for me with Monty."

"You don't have to thank me. I enjoyed every second of it."

"What…what did you do, exactly?"

"I just held him down until the cops came," he said, moving closer to me.

"Did you hit him?"

"Do we have to talk about this? You wanted him to leave you alone, right? Now he's leaving you alone. Problem solved."

"You know, Jack, you don't have to be scared that I'll take off running if I find out something bad about you. I get the feeling sometimes that I barely know you."

"What do you want to know? My favorite color? My favorite brand of sneakers?"

"I want to know how many fights you've been in," I said.

He tensed up and opened his eyes. I guess he wasn't groggy anymore. He looked anxiously as he asked, "Let me guess: You talked to Naya and she told you something."

"Naya and Lana," I admitted.

He sighed and turned on his side, and my body felt suddenly cold. I probably shouldn't have brought the subject up, but now it was too late. I could see he was angry. "What did they tell you?" he asked.

"All I want to know is why you never talk about your past, Jack."

"Because I'm not proud of it."

"I wasn't proud of my failed attempt at sexting, but I told you about that." He chuckled at that remark. At least I'd managed to lighten the mood somewhat. That was one minor victory.

"I've seen your hands, Jack. My brother Sonny was a boxer. He used to hit the heavy bag with no gloves. And his hands look like yours. I'm not going to judge you, but we can't pretend you don't have a past. So just tell me. How many fights?"

"I lost count," he said with a shy smile.

"How many girls have you been with?" I blurted out.

"Don't make me, Jen…"

"How many?"

"I lost count of that, too."

"How many since you started college, then?" I asked.

"More than I'd like to admit. Mostly girls from off campus. I didn't want to ever run into anyone in class. But it doesn't matter. That's not who I am anymore."

"Lana told me you were a different guy in high school. What made you be that way?"

He analyzed me for a few seconds. I knew then that when he acted so calm and indifferent, there was much more happening inside him. That there was a tension, a dissatisfaction that was always bubbling up within him.

"I don't know," he admitted. "It's complicated. I just... Fighting and sex were the only things that made me feel alive? But I'm not proud of it. There are times when I try to forget that whole period of my life. Even then, I knew what I was doing was wrong, but it's just how it was. I realize that may not make sense to you."

"It does, Jack. It does make sense. And thanks for telling me." I kissed the corner of his lips. "I still may not know all the facts, but I think I can understand the situation. Do me a favor, though. Don't be mad at Naya and Lana for talking to me."

"Wait a second," Jack said. "You're telling me not to get mad at *Lana*? Who are you, and what have you done to my girlfriend?"

"I don't know," I responded. "Maybe she's not so bad after all. Imagine, we might even become best friends. Then I could get her to tell me all your dirty secrets."

"I don't have any dirty secrets."

"We all have dirty secrets, Jack. But I won't tell you mine until you tell me yours."

"Whatever," he said. "I need to get up early tomorrow and you're interrupting my sleep."

"Good night, Sleeping Beauty," I told him.

"Good night, Maleficent." He smiled and I went back to stroking his hair. A few minutes later, his breath had evened out. He was asleep.

I was in a good mood the next morning when I went for my run. At last, it wasn't drizzling. I stopped once to call my dad and Shannon and tell them what had happened with Monty. Dad grunted approvingly when he learned what Jack had done and what the police had said. Shannon couldn't help going on a rant about how horrible Monty was and what an idiot I'd ever been to even give him the time of day.

When I was back home, I found Agnes opening her apartment door. "Hello, darling," she said with a smile.

"Hey there!" I said. "You look better than you did last time!"

"I guess I'll learn to drink responsibly one day." She shrugged. "But you know what they say: 'Practice makes perfect.'"

I laughed as I took out my keys. And out of nowhere, I asked her, "You wouldn't want to come in for a minute?"

She smiled and entered without a word. What I hadn't counted on was finding Mike sleeping on the couch with his mouth open. But Agnes was used to it. She just shook her head and took a seat with me at the bar. I offered her a coffee, which she accepted gratefully. As I set it down, she asked, softly enough so she wouldn't wake Mike, "How's Jackie?"

"Good," I said, remembering how we'd escaped from the lake house. "I'm more worried about Mike, to be honest."

"He's such a sensitive boy. He's always struggled to fit in. That's true of his friends and his family. He did tell me you took good care of him, though. And I thank you for it. But that's not what I wanted to talk about. Christmas is coming in a few weeks…"

"I know. My final exams are already coming up."

"You'll do fine. You're a smart girl. And so I wanted to ask you… well… Jack's father has asked me to try and get him to come for Christmas dinner. And I'd like that, too. But you know how he'll react if I bring it up. So I thought maybe I could convince you to ask him."

"I don't know," I said. "He's very hardheaded. He won't even talk to me about his father. Especially since that day at the lake. I've tried…"

"Maybe we could sweeten the deal somehow?" she asked slyly.

"What are you thinking, Agnes?"

"Well, you two have been together for some time now. Three months by my count. Oh, I know you'll tell me it wasn't *official*, but that doesn't mean a thing in my book. I could tell as soon as you came around that there was a spark there. And so I was thinking, maybe it wouldn't be such a bad idea for our families to get to know each other."

I was taking a sip of water just then, and I nearly choked on it. She smiled innocently while I pounded on my chest, trying not to lose consciousness.

"Easy, honey," she said. "It's not that crazy an idea, is it?"

"Uh, my family doesn't live close to here. And they definitely couldn't come up here."

"Oh, no, honey, we would never just expect them to do that. Our thought was that we could go down there and meet them. It was actually the boys' parents' idea. They thought it might be a good way to make peace with them."

I literally couldn't imagine the situation. I told her I wasn't sure, and that I'd need to talk it over with everyone, Jack and Mike included.

"Oh, I know," she said. "And I know you'll find a way to convince them." She stood and finished her coffee. "Keep me informed. The sooner the better. I need to go now, sweetie."

As she was almost at the door, I cleared my throat and called her name.

"Yes?" she asked.

"You remember that conversation we had about your husband? I just wanted to tell you I took it to heart. And I've taken the steps I needed to. I'm staying away from my ex. Forever, this time."

"Now, I'm very happy about that, dear," she said.

"I wanted to tell you because…what you said really helped. It was crucial, in fact. I really don't know what would have happened if we hadn't had that conversation. And so I wanted to thank you. From the bottom of my heart."

She smiled, then shook her head, then started to tear up and asked me to forgive her. "I'm just a sensitive old woman," she said. "Still, though. I'm proud of you, Jenna. From now on, whatever you do will be your decision, not someone else's. And that means something."

She walked out before I could respond. I leaned on the bar a minute, thinking, until I heard Sue stomp in, half-asleep, her hair looking like a bird's nest.

"I hate mornings," she said, taking her ice cream from the freezer.

"Good morning to you, too, Sue."

"Look at this guy over here," she replied, staring at Mike. "My life's goal is to have so few cares that I can just lie around like him. He looks like he's hibernating."

As Will emerged, Mike stirred and opened his eyes, complaining that we had woken him up.

"Here's an idea," Sue said. "You could rent your own apartment."

"That's not a viable option in my present financial situation," he said, walking over and sitting at the bar. He told me good morning, called me his sister-in-law again, and started up with his usual flirting. Will cut him off, asking where Jack was.

"I think he's still asleep," I said.

"You should go wake him up," Will replied. "He's got class in an hour. I'm surprised he didn't set an alarm."

"You shouldn't be," Sue said. "Did you hear the two of them last night?"

I felt instantly guilty. Jack had had his phone in his hand the night before when I started...er...distracting him. He'd probably been setting his alarm just then, and by the time we finished, he must have forgotten.

Embarrassed, I said I'd get him up and rushed back to the bedroom, where he was sleeping on his back, mouth open, head resting on my pillow. I tiptoed over and shook his shoulder.

"Jack?" I said. "Jack? Get up, you're going to be late for class."

"Oh well," he said, turning over.

I walked over to the window and pulled the curtains, letting in the sun. He frowned. "Jesus, Jen. You remind me of my mom."

"Come on, you're going to be late."

"Yeah, but if I don't go at all, I can't be late. Look at it that way."

I leaned down and nuzzled with him, then kissed his ear and bit his earlobe, tugging at it slightly.

"I'll tell you one thing, Jen. That is not the way to get me to go to class. Now you've got me thinking of much more productive ways to spend my morning."

"I *will* go get a jug of cold water and dump it on you," I said.

He groaned and I got up once I felt him finally moving. I tossed him a pair of pants when he sat up, and he put them on lazily, standing up as if it were the greatest challenge a human being had ever faced on his own. I couldn't help but laugh as I told him, "Jack, you're twenty-one years old, not ninety."

"Leave me alone," he grunted, walking toward the living room. Jack yawned and sat next to his brother, and I stood there between them, grabbing one of the chocolate doughnuts Will had brought us.

Mike complained that we'd startled him awake while his brother had gotten the soft treatment. Jack told him to find a girlfriend of his own, and Sue seconded him, saying preferably one with an apartment so he could leave the rest of us in peace. Everyone laughed and Mike frowned, but I rested a hand on his shoulder, telling him he didn't bother me. I felt he needed it, and this was the first day in a long time he had seemed like his normal self.

"Thanks, future sister-in-law," he said. "You're the only person I actually like in this house. You think about me, you save me stuff to eat, you ask me how I am, and you don't stomp in the hall like an elephant when you get up to pee in the middle of the night. The rest of these jerks act like I'm not even here."

He was partly joking, but there was truth in what he said as well, and I felt bad for him until he wrapped me in his arms and hugged me tight, burying his face in my cleavage. I could hear Jack slamming his orange juice down as Mike said, "You're too good for my brother. But it's all right. I'll be here waiting patiently for you when you get tired of him."

"Do that again and you'll be sleeping on the street," Jack threatened him.

"It was just an innocent hug!" Mike protested.

"You were stuffing your face into her boobs," Sue remarked.

"Yeah, but they're just so… Ow!"

Mike blinked and rubbed his eyes as Jack threw a doughnut at his face.

That was a declaration of war, and soon a piece of buttered toast flew in the other direction, followed by a jar of jelly, a box of cereal, and who knew what else. A half hour later, the two of them were grouching and cleaning up as Sue walked around telling them which spots they had missed. When Jack finished, he flopped down next to me, looking exhausted.

"I guess you won," I told him. "You didn't go to class, and you did spend your morning doing something productive."

He glared at me, clearly not amused.

When I finished class that day, a call came in from Shannon.

"Are you busy?" she asked.

"No, I just wrapped up. What's going on?"

"I've got to talk to you about something. I know you said you were thinking about getting a job. Well, I guess the track coach at Owen's school quit, and I remembered you were a good runner, and I was thinking maybe you could apply for that."

"Shannon, I don't think you just drop off a résumé that says *I run in the morning* and they hire you. I'm pretty sure there's more to it. And also, in case you forgot, I'm going to school."

"Well, Spencer's on the hiring committee, if you change your mind.

But I guess you've got more than one thing keeping you there. Speaking of, how is your Romeo?"

"He's fine. He's lovely."

"Yes, I can only imagine you two must spend every night staring into the stars together. I'm asking for details, Jenna."

At first I was offended, but then I decided I might as well play along, and said, "No, we do more than that. And FYI, not just at night."

"Excuse me?" she shouted. "Is this the same Jenna I know? Have you been replaced by an evil twin?"

"Nope, it's still me."

"Amazing. I thought you'd actually die the last time I talked to you about something sexual. While we're on the subject, I may as well tell you my part-time boyfriend is now a non-boyfriend. It's no great loss, though, so don't bother shedding tears for me."

As I punched my ticket on the light rail, I remembered what Agnes had said and told her, "Since I've got you here, there's actually something I need to talk to you about. Jack's parents want both our families to get together for Christmas and…I don't know, I'm nervous. It feels a little rushed."

"I hear you," she said. "But there's something to keep in mind, Jenna. How serious a relationship is doesn't just depend on how much time you've spent together. You and Monty were together for a while, and in my book he hardly counts as a boyfriend. I've heard you talking about Jack Ross. I know he's special to you. So I don't think it's that crazy. How many times have you seen his parents?"

"His dad, just twice, but his mom at least five or six, I think."

"Are you worried about what they'll think of our family? We can lock Sonny and Steve in the basement. I'm one hundred percent on board with that."

"I mean, I guess it would be nice if everyone met," I responded.

"Well, Mom and Dad would be over the moon. He's already captured Mom's heart and you know Dad. He's so traditional, I think he wants to pull your boyfriend aside and talk to him man-to-man. And I don't need to tell you I'm going to have to give him my approval before you guys can take it much further. The only one who worries me is Spencer. You know how he can get. He's so protective... Anyway, look, I'll mention it like it's a distant possibility, just to see how everyone reacts."

"I owe you one," I told her.

"By the way, I didn't get the whole story about the fight. Did Monty do a number on Jack?"

"Not even close. Jack didn't have a scratch on him. Speaking of Jack, he doesn't even know about this Christmas plan yet. So take the temperature there, but don't get everyone all excited, because it may come to nothing."

"That's fine, Jenna, but if I were you, I'd get a move on. The holidays are only two weeks away."

"I'll try and convince him. Thanks for calling, Shannon."

I shook my head and hung up. When I got home, Jack wasn't there, but everyone else was scattered around on the couches and armchairs, doing the usual.

"Where's your brother?" I asked Mike.

"'*Oh, hello, Mike. Nice to see you...*'" he began sarcastically. Then he added, "You do know that I'm a person, too."

"Here he goes again..." Naya said.

"Actually, it's good that he's out," I told him. "I want to talk to you about something. Don't get too excited, though."

Mike jumped out of his chair, and Will warned me, "Are you sure you know what you're doing?"

"I'll be OK. I think I can handle him. But yeah, it's something personal. I'll see you guys back in a minute."

Will looked unconvinced as Mike and I walked out into the hallway and climbed up to the roof. Mike went first and was waiting for me with his hands in his pockets as I came up.

"Spit it out, Jenna," he said. "What was it you wanted to talk to me about?" He walked forward into my personal space as he asked.

"First," I said, "stay in your place. Second: How are you getting along? I know things have been a little rough for you lately."

Looking a little shy, he said, "Yeah, I'm better." I couldn't believe it. Mike, who could blurt out the most embarrassing things at the drop of a hat, Mike, who flirted with me every chance he got, and not very subtly, either… Mike was being timid with me!

"Good," I told him. "Because I know this might be weird, but I need your help with something, and that means I need to talk to you about your father, and I know that can be very tough for both of you. But I need to know why he and Jack don't get along."

Mike opened his mouth as if to say something, but then stopped himself, shaking his head, and replied, "I don't want to talk about that. It's complicated. And anyway, why do you care?"

"Because your father wants to come to my house for Christmas dinner and I need to try and convince you and Jack to accept, but I can't if I don't even know why you all are mad at each other."

He grimaced. He was so clearly uncomfortable that I was starting to feel uncomfortable too. Was it really so hard just to talk about it?

"It's not just that they don't get along. Not exactly. It's that…something happened. But I shouldn't tell you, Jenna."

"Please, Mike. Jack won't tell me, and I've tried…" I grabbed his hand.

Mike began to bite his thumbnail, looking as if he were really considering it. Then he began, "OK, there were always problems between them, right? And so when Dad caught him… Well, let me back up a minute. We were in school, OK, and Ross and Dad…"

Just then, Jack's voice interrupted us. I let Mike's hand go, and he turned around quickly. Jack hadn't heard him; he was too focused on the physical contact between us. His lips were pursed, his eyes furious.

"We were just talking," I told him, but Jack knew me too well to believe it was just a casual chat. His stare was terrifying, and Mike started walking backward.

"Talking about what?" he asked.

"Bro," Mike interjected, "we were…"

"Don't *bro* me. I didn't ask you, Mike."

I walked over to Jack and grabbed his hand, feeling him relax a bit, but Mike wisely kept his distance. I needed to do something. So I told him I'd brought Mike up there myself because I wanted to ask him something about them.

"Why didn't you ask me?" Jack half shouted.

I stared at Mike out of the corner of my eye, and he must have gotten the message, because he hurried off. Jack scowled as he watched him depart. As we heard his footsteps making the fire escape clang, Jack said, "I don't want you to be alone with him."

"Mike's not so bad, Jack."

"I don't want you to be alone with him, Jen. I'm serious. Anyone but him."

I sighed. I knew he didn't trust Mike because he had a habit of sleeping with Jack's girlfriends. I nodded and kissed him on the lips. Sounding less angry now, he asked, "What were you two talking about?"

"My parents want you to come to Christmas dinner."

He looked surprised, then elated, and said, "So what's the big deal? That sounds amazing! I'd love that!"

"There's a small problem, though…" I told him. "They want to meet your family."

His smile vanished, but I kept squeezing his hand, peering into his eyes, praying he'd say yes anyway.

"My mother can go," he responded. "But that's it. Not Dad. You don't know him, and I can't run the risk of your parents thinking I'm as big an asshole as him."

"Jack, I get that you and your dad have problems, but he tried, he apologized to me, he tried to make me feel comfortable in your house."

"That's what you think. There's more to the situation you don't know about. And now Mom says he's expecting me to apologize to him. Well, to hell with that. I'm not apologizing."

"What if I got him to apologize to you?" I asked, feeling the slightest bit of hope that maybe I could salvage the situation.

"Jen, forget it. You're so sweet. I know you're trying to make this happen, I know you've got everybody's best interests in mind, but I don't want you talking to my dad, and least of all just the two of you. Do you hear me? I don't want you to be alone with him. And if it happens, I will cut him out of my life. I'm serious, OK?"

"Why? If you're going to tell me something like that, it's only fair that…"

"I'm done!" Jack exclaimed. "I'm tired of talking about this shit!"

"All right," I said, defeated. "I only wanted to understand…"

"Why do you need to understand?" He was losing patience. "I've never hidden anything from you. You know you can ask me anything and I'll answer. But not that. I told you I don't want to talk about that and you know it and you keep asking. Now, please God, don't tell me that's what you were talking with Mike about."

He let go of my hand. I was speechless, so he continued. "What did he tell you?"

"Nothing."

"Good."

"But now I want to know," I said. "You wouldn't get pissed off over nothing. There's something there and you need to tell me."

But he refused. At first he tried to tell me I was seeing things, inventing problems that weren't there. Then he asked why I couldn't respect him when he said he didn't want to discuss something. Finally he admitted that he wasn't ready, that he still needed time, that he wanted to open up to me but couldn't bring himself to do it.

I asked him if it was something that I'd done. Because I noticed the way he got angry with me sometimes was different from the way he got angry with other people. He denied it, but when I stood my ground, he told me he was sorry. I said I didn't need an apology; I needed to know what was going on. But still, he wouldn't talk. He went back to his old tactic of changing the subject and said, "Let's go eat dinner."

It wasn't fair. He never gave a second thought to pressuring me into saying something if he felt like it; he even pretended he was doing it for my own good. But then when I tried, he shut down completely. I told him that, and then I thought to myself I'd wasted enough time up there, and I turned around and walked down the fire escape in a rage. I was tired of begging—of begging just to get to know him better. Once I was inside, I went to the bedroom to put on my pajamas. He entered behind me, but stood at a cautious distance.

"I don't want you to be angry," he said.

"No problem," I replied. "If you don't want me to be angry, you can talk."

But I knew he wouldn't. I'd never complained when he'd wanted to know my secrets, but there he was, trying to stage-manage our relationship.

"Don't be like that," he said. "Come to dinner."

"No. You can give my food to someone else, or throw it in the trash for all I care."

"Jen, can you not drop it? At least for now?"

I'm sure he could tell I wouldn't, though. And why should I have? I told him to leave me alone. That upset him, but he did as I asked. I finished changing, took out my contacts, and got in bed. I was tired of all the secrets. I had opened up to him completely. And the way he was acting made me feel like he didn't trust me. I hated that. And I hated being made to feel that way. I could hear Shannon's voice in my head telling me to stop acting like a baby, but I couldn't, and I didn't want to.

The lights were off, and I was turned away from the door when I heard him come in and stand at the foot of the bed.

"Are you mad at me?" he asked.

I didn't respond.

"Do you want me to go sleep somewhere else?"

"Do whatever you feel like," I responded.

"What I feel like is sleeping here with you."

I didn't say anything back. I heard him changing his clothes, and a few seconds later, I felt the bed sinking under his weight. He tried to stroke my arm, but I pulled it away.

"Jen, please. I just want to hold you," he said.

I imagined his hand coming over, rubbing my head, squeezing my shoulder, and I wanted to tell him, *Yes, do it please*, but I held back. He pulled at me softly, rolling me over on my back, and I saw him leaning on his elbow and staring at me.

"I don't want you to be mad at me," he murmured, tracing a finger along my jawline.

No. Not this time. I wasn't going to let him distract me with caresses. That was what he always did, and I was tired of falling for it.

I pushed his hand away and told him to stop.

I knew he was looking for an excuse to disobey me, something that would let him off the hook without him having to tell me what I wanted to know. But I had made my choice. And when he leaned over and asked if he could kiss me, instead of responding, I turned away. He rested his forehead on my cheek, frustrated, and begged, "Jen, dammit, don't do this to me."

"If you're so uncomfortable, I'll find somewhere else to sleep," I said, pushing him off and turning my back to him again.

"I'm not uncomfortable. I want to sleep with you. But not like this."

I knew he was still staring at me, but he didn't try to approach me again. I was thankful for it. And eventually I fell asleep, without a single part of our bodies touching.

24

THE COLD-SHOULDER APPROACH

That morning, I ran harder than usual. I didn't feel good about how I'd treated Jack. I even wanted to say I was sorry for not being more mature or giving him his space. But I was also tired of the secrets, I was tired of him putting himself before me, and that kept me feeling angry.

I took the stairs back up and found Agnes in the hallway. Saying hello, I opened our door and noticed someone was cooking. Pancakes! I'd know that smell anywhere. My stomach was growling.

Sue, Will, and Mike were sitting at the counter staring hungrily into the kitchen, where Jack was deep in concentration, brows knit, cooking. He looked like he'd never held a frying pan in his life. I couldn't help but chuckle.

"How much longer?" Mike asked, "I'm starving."

"Shut up," Jack murmured.

"I am, too," Sue said.

"You can shut up along with him."

Taking off my headphones, I asked what was going on. When Jack turned, he almost dropped the pan on the floor before smiling and saying, "Good morning. You hungry?"

I shrugged as he opened the oven, pulling out a plate that had been warming, and dumped the last of the pancakes on top of the pile. It was evident he'd never made them before, but they looked amazing.

"Excuse me," Mike said loudly. "Our agreement was that you'd be making breakfast for us, not her." But Jack just told him to pipe down again, and when he and Sue insisted, he said the pancakes were all for me. Knowing, I guess, that insulting me wouldn't get them anywhere, and that they weren't going to change Jack's mind, they started sucking up to me, talking about which one of them was really my friend, and then Sue insulted Mike, telling him he was just a parasite, that he didn't even really live there. Jack interrupted, calling them a pair of hyenas, and reminding them that the pancakes were mine and there was nothing they could do about it. They crossed their arms as I sat down and ate the first bite, feeling everyone's eyes on me. I felt like I was taking a test, and, mouth full, I asked "What?"

No one said anything until I asked them to stop staring at me. Then Jack inquired, tapping his fingers on the bar, "Are they...good?"

I swallowed and nodded. "Amazing. It's hard to believe you've never made them before," I said.

"Thank God." He sighed and gathered his mixing bowl, spatula, and pan, dropping them into the sink.

Looking angry, Mike and Sue slunk off to their usual places in the living room, sitting as far from each other as possible, while Jack lingered, looking on edge, still fidgeting.

"Did you sleep well?" he asked.

"I've slept better. You?"

"Same. Are we...are we good?"

Again, I wanted to tell him I was sorry for being so stubborn, but I stopped myself, taking another bite of pancake. When I was done chewing, I said, "I don't know. Did you have something you wanted to tell me?"

Instead of answering, he tried to distract me with his usual nice-guy approach. He offered to take me to class; I said I'd catch the light rail. He mentioned we could do something afterward; I told him I had plans. Huffy, he walked back to his room.

Will had gotten up and gone to his room for a moment, but returned for much of the pancake argument, which he eavesdropped on while digging through the fridge and the cabinet looking for something to eat. I could tell he was amused.

"I didn't peg you as someone who liked drama, Will," I told him.

"In this house, you can't avoid it. Let me give you some advice, though, Jen. The cold-shoulder approach isn't going to work with Jack, and if you want my opinion, he doesn't deserve it."

"Did he tell you something?" I asked.

"He didn't need to. When he woke me up out of nowhere to ask me if I knew how to make pancakes, that was all I needed to know something was up. I never thought I'd see the day Ross voluntarily cooked breakfast. All he's ever cooked is his famous chili. It was clear there was some kind of crisis going on. So let me guess: You want him to tell you something, and he doesn't want to."

"You know what, Will? There are times when I hate how well you guys understand each other. You're like twins or something. Do you think I'm being too hard on him?"

I needed someone's objective opinion. I already knew what everyone else would say: Naya would want me to forgive him, Sue would tell me he could suffer, Mike wouldn't care, or else he'd talk trash about Jack and tell me for the umpteenth time that I'd be better off with him. So that made Will my best option.

"I don't know, to tell you the truth," Will admitted. "I'll let you know one thing, though: I've never seen Ross show the kind of commitment for another person he shows with you. And one of the things that means is he's never been in a position of really caring whether somebody forgave him for something."

I didn't want my heart to melt when I heard that. My heart didn't care, though. *Damn you, Jack Ross. Did you have to be so charming?*

"So what does this mean, then?" I asked. "If you're saying he is trying to get me to forgive him...does that mean I have to say I'm sorry, too? Because he genuinely cares and I'm holding back from him?"

"That's not what I'm telling you," Will said. "Hell, maybe he needs this. Feeling like he's chasing someone for the first time in his life, and not the other way around. If I were you, I'd leave it for now. Get through your day, see how he acts tonight. It'll all work out."

He grinned and walked back to his room after saying that.

I'd told Jack I had plans that day. I hadn't told him what they were, and to say I wasn't excited about them was an understatement. I needed to get Jack's father to say he was sorry. It wasn't going to be easy. And it sure as hell wasn't going to be fun.

I'd sent a message to Mary asking if her husband would be home. And now I was standing there at their door. She opened it with a smile on her face. I'd never entered through the front door. I'd only gone with Jack, and we'd come in through the garage. I was stunned for a minute as I stared around the enormous vestibule.

"Hello, dear," Mary said.

"Hey."

It was pleasantly warm inside, and I was freezing. Mary rested a hand on my lower back and guided me in after I hung my coat on the coat rack.

"So you said Mr. Ross is here?" I asked. I didn't see any reason not to get to the point, especially because I still had classes to get back to.

"He is," Mary replied. "There's one thing, though. I know I told you he was willing to talk to you, but now that I've thought it over, I believe it's best if you two aren't alone together. So I'll be going upstairs with you."

"That's not necessary," I said.

What was going on with these people? Why were they all so concerned about my being alone with Mr. Ross? He couldn't be that bad.

"Honey, if Jackie found out I'd let you go up by yourself, he'd…"

"He won't find out," I assured her.

He will, my brain told me, but as usual, I told my brain to shut up, and after thinking things over for a moment, Mary said, "Well, er… I'll just be down here. On the sofa. So if you need anything, you can just call down to me."

It was strange to hear a person sound so wary of her own husband. I took a breath and hurried up the stairs. Soon, I could hear the notes of a piano. His delicate, skillful playing was amazing. I stopped in front of the room Jack had called *The Ogre's Lair* the first time we'd been there.

The door was open, but Mr. Ross's back was turned, and he didn't notice me coming in. And the sounds were so beautiful, I stopped a moment to enjoy them. Only a few seconds later, I knocked at the door.

The music stopped. Jack's father turned and adjusted his glasses.

"Oh, hello, Jenna. Come in."

I smiled and started walking toward him, but then he stopped me, telling me to shut the door. That was strange, but I didn't see why it should make me nervous. So I obeyed. He walked over to a love seat and motioned for me to sit beside him.

"I suppose you're here to talk about the Christmas dinner. Am I right?"

"Yeah."

"And I suppose Jack prefers that I not go."

It made me sad that he was aware of that, and I tried to persuade him it wasn't true, but he stopped me. "Jenna, I've known my boy since he was born. I know how he is, and I don't need you to lie to me to make me feel better."

He was almost as good a mind reader as his son. Or maybe I was just terrible at hiding what I was thinking. I tried to be honest. "The truth of the matter is, we were talking about this last night. And you're right. He told me he wanted to come have dinner at my parents' house, but he didn't want you to come."

He didn't look sad. He didn't look offended. He simply looked a little confused.

"You can't have come here just to tell me that," he said.

"No," I admitted, grinning.

"What is it, then, Jenna?"

"Well," I began, looking for the right words. "I don't know what happened between you and Jack, but…"

"He didn't tell you? How interesting. I would assume, if there was anyone in the entire world he would have spoken of it to, it would have been you, Jenna. It's interesting that he never did, don't you think?"

I didn't. Not really. In fact, I thought it sucked. I thought it sucked that he was supposed to be my boyfriend and he didn't even trust me. But that didn't matter right now, and I sure as hell wasn't going to admit that to Mr. Ross.

"I can't say, sir. But that's not why I'm here. I have the impression that there's a chance—maybe just a small chance, but still—that Jack's willing to make peace with you. If only for a night. And I'm trying to make that happen. But that's going to take something from you. You're going to have to tell him you're sorry."

I was worried he'd laugh at me, tell me no, and send me on my way, but he just observed me in uncomfortable silence for what felt like an eternity. Behind his glasses, his eyes glistened and he asked, "Does my son know you're here?"

"No."

"You do know he'll be very angry when he finds out?"

"He won't find out unless I leave here with good news. And if that happens, it's my problem, not yours."

He laughed. I had never seen him laugh before, and it felt strange.

"I like you, Jenna," he said.

"Uh…thanks."

"I like you a lot. I'll do as you say. I'll apologize when I see him."

He leaned forward, resting his elbows on his knees. I was surprised by how quick and easy that conversation had been. I wasn't used to things going well for me. And I was happy to see that Jack's stubbornness didn't seem to run in the family.

"Thanks, Mr. Ross," I said, standing.

"Leaving so soon?"

"I've got class," I said, standing up and throwing my purse over my shoulder. I had a sudden, strong urge to leave that I didn't really understand. As my hand touched the doorknob, he pronounced my name, stopping me, and said, "Can I ask you a question?"

"Sure."

"Has Jack been acting strangely these days?"

I wasn't sure how to respond. Of course he'd been acting strangely… but did I need to share that with his father? Apparently it didn't matter. My expression must have been answer enough.

"I'll tell you why," he said. "A few weeks ago, he was accepted to a very important film program in France."

Those words hung there in the air as he tried to gauge my reaction. I remembered Mary saying something about that, and about how this had been Jack's dream since he was little. But it had faded from my mind, and since it never came up again, I assumed it wasn't so important. Mr. Ross went on, "Classes start over there in February, and as you can guess, that means he'll need to move overseas."

"How…how long does the program last?"

"It's a year and a half."

He seemed to be enjoying my perplexity. He had a malicious grin on his face. But at that moment, I hardly cared. I wanted to know why Jack hadn't told me, why he'd chosen acting weird and jealous, hot and cold, to just opening up to me. I felt terrible. I hated having to find out things like this from other people. Why in the hell couldn't he trust me?

Mr. Ross interrupted me, "You needn't worry about that, though, apparently. Because he doesn't want to go. We haven't told the school yet, but Jack is insistent about it. I'm sure you can imagine why."

I nodded, and he nodded, too, and his once-warm smile vanished instantly. In the silence that followed, he grinned again, but with bitterness or calculating malice or something else—I couldn't really tell. Then he pointed at the door, telling me, "If you'll forgive me, I have a bit more practice to get through before my day is over."

I found Mary looking nervous as she sat on the sofa. When I stepped out, she stood, looking terrified, as though she'd seen a ghost. She asked me what had happened, and if I was all right.

"Yeah, I'm fine," I said. "But I should go. I'm worried I'll be late."

I didn't know if I could tell even her what I'd just heard. Did she know? I wasn't sure. I needed to talk to Jack. Immediately.

She nodded and told me, "I'll drive you to school."

I won't lie, I couldn't stop thinking about what I'd heard all day. And it didn't get better when I went downstairs from class and the first thing I saw as I opened the door was Jack's car. There he was, leaning against it with his hands in his pockets, waiting to pick me up. I guess he wanted us to get along again. I was tempted to smile, but I tried to keep a cool head.

"Hey," he said nervously.

"Jack, you didn't have to come here."

I could tell he sensed something strange in my tone of voice, and that put him on alert. It was unbelievable how well he could read me.

"I wanted to," he said.

We got into his car, and he turned up the heat, but he didn't touch the radio dial the way he usually did. There was a tense silence as he drove me home, and when he parked in the lot, we froze, looking straight ahead and not knowing what to say.

"There's something…" he began. "Something I've been meaning to talk to you about for a few weeks. I, um, I got accepted…"

"I know, Jack."

"How?" He turned to me.

"You're talking about France, right? Your father told me this morning."

His face, briefly perplexed, now turned dead serious. "How?"

"I went to talk to him."

"You were alone with him?"

"He agreed to apologize to you, Jack."

That seemed to throw him off, but his anger faded away slightly. He looked out the window, frustrated. I could almost hear the gears turning in his head before he turned back to me, asking, "And he didn't want anything from me in return?"

"He said he wanted you to get along."

That wasn't a total fabrication. Was it? I mean…Mr. Ross must have been thinking that, even if it's not exactly what he said. Jack's surprise probably helped me get away with this white lie.

"When were you going to tell me about France?" I asked.

"Just now."

"Why not before?"

"Because I don't know if I want to go. Everyone else thinks it's such a big deal, but I…"

"Your mother told me you've been dreaming about it since you were little."

"Sure. Since I was little. I'm not little anymore. And I don't think I want to give up everything I have here to go to some program on the other side of the globe when I don't even know whether or not I'll like it there."

"But it's an opportunity…"

"Do you get now why I didn't want to say anything?" he interrupted me. "I knew you'd do this. I knew you'd try to get me to go. Just like everyone else. But it's my decision, OK?"

I nodded. "Of course it is. And I won't bring it up again. As long as you agree to accept your father's apology."

"I feel like you're twisting my arm, but fine, we have a deal. It better be a damn good apology, though."

As I felt all my muscles relax—one less problem, I thought—he asked me, "So, are you still mad at me?"

I shrugged. "A little."

"What if I told you there's a barbecue pizza waiting for you upstairs—even though I hate it and it's the worst flavor known to man—just because I know it's your favorite?"

"You're slowly crawling out of the doghouse," I said.

"I'll take that. Let's go upstairs. I'm dying of hunger."

I got out, and when I saw the cheerful look on his face, I felt bad about being angry at him all day. But maybe it was worth it to clear the air between us. In the elevator, he stared at me, and I could tell he was asking himself if he could approach me or no. I didn't bother waiting. I stepped forward, clutched the back of his neck, and pulled him in. He didn't resist, instead grabbing my waist and squeezing me tight.

25

NEVER HAVE I EVER

I admit, I was nervous when Mike, Jack, and I went down to the car to go to his father's house. Supposedly that was the day that the two of them were going to apologize to each other, but with them, nothing was ever that simple.

"So it's happening," Mike said, leaning forward from the back seat, "we're actually going to get to know your family. I hope you've prepared them for us so they won't think we're total weirdos."

I'd called my father that morning and gone over our plans with him. He went quickly from overjoyed to stressed at the impression he might make. He sure wanted to meet Jack, though—that much was obvious.

"I said nice things," I assured him.

"About me," Jack told his brother. "They don't know you exist."

"Well, they're in for a surprise," Mike announced. "They may well find themselves wanting me for their son-in-law instead of you."

Jack rolled his eyes.

When we reached his house, he held the door for me like a gentleman, though Mike had to rush in ahead of me, telling his brother in a joking tone, *Why, thank you, sweetie.* We found Mary and Mr. Ross in the kitchen. They fell silent when we walked in. Mike immediately started snooping in the oven. He asked what was for dinner. Mary said chicken salad, and he wrinkled his nose, unconvinced. I remembered my diet attempt with Naya and couldn't help but giggle.

I had wanted to say hello to Mary and give her a hug, but Jack was gripping my hand like a vise. I soon saw why: His father was observing him inexpressively, and Jack seemed to want to show him where his sympathies lay. I felt uncomfortable, and I think Mary noticed, because she soon hurried over to interrupt their silent battle, saving me by stretching her arms out and saying, "Oh, honey, I'm happy to see you as always."

Jack finally let me go so I could hug her. When we were done, I turned to his father and said, "Mr. Ross," and he smiled and nodded, saying simply, "Jenna, Jack."

I can't say it was the best start, but that was nothing compared to what came afterward. I ended up sitting between Jack and his father, and despite Mary's attempts at conversation, everyone seemed to prefer not uttering a word. I helped her as much as I could, but everything I said sounded idiotic. For a moment, things eased up as Mike started talking about his band, but his father soon cut him off, telling him he couldn't care less what he did with his fans. As we were finishing our plates, Mr. Ross said, "Jenna came to speak with me yesterday."

I looked at Jack and saw that he was staring at his father with complete indifference. Mary seemed nervous as I was. Mr. Ross continued. "I think she was right about everything she said."

Jack asked suspiciously, "Are you serious?"

"Yes, Son," his father replied. "It's stupid for us to continue fighting about something that happened five years ago."

So I still had no idea what was going on...

"I know what I did was wrong," Mr. Ross said. "And I understand you being upset with me for so long. I do. And I'm sorry."

Jack's mouth opened, stupefied. Mary seemed surprised, too. Even Mike had stopped playing with his scraps and looked up.

"You are?" Jack asked, perplexed.

"I am. I don't think it's healthy for our relationship to be like this. Not for me or you, or for your mother and brother, or even for your girlfriend. We should be able to go to her home acting like a normal family, don't you think? I would like that, and I'm sure her parents would like that, too. We should forget what happened. That's best for all of us. Or if we can't forget, we should try to deal with it like adults and turn the page. What do you say? Can you forgive me?"

Jack was stunned, and I reached under the table without anyone noticing and touched his knee. He blinked and came back to reality. He looked back and forth between his father and me as though his brain was short-circuiting. Then he cleared his throat and nodded slowly. His mother's face, especially, showed surprise as he said, "I can try."

"Good," his father said, exhaling. "I'm happy to hear that, Jack. I feel as if a burden's been lifted from my shoulders."

Mary had tears in her eyes. When she acted that way, she reminded me of my mother and of Naya. She wiped them away and tried to pretend nothing was happening.

"Would any of you like dessert?" she asked.

For the little time we stayed there afterward, it was clear that the tension had declined. Jack even talked with everyone. His father seemed happier, too, and I was glad. I didn't know what had happened between them in the past, but it had to be something they could get through, I thought.

Once it was time to go, Mary walked us out to the garage. She hugged both her sons, and when it was my turn, I felt a more intense emotion from her than I had before. "Thank you, honey," she said. I didn't know how to reply. Jack motioned for me to get in the car, and when I did, it was as if I could breathe easier than I had in days. I reached up and touched Jack's cheek.

"Feeling better?" I asked him.

"I don't know," he confessed.

I leaned over and kissed him, our lips continuing to touch until Mike cleared his throat from the back seat. "Either we all get a kiss or none of us gets a kiss, all right?" he said.

Jack started the car, and when we got home, I was surprised to find not just Naya, Will, and Sue, but also Lana and Chris in the living room drinking beers, and something told me they'd been at it for a while, because they were having too much fun to be sober.

Obviously Sue was excluded from that description. She looked pissed to even be there, pissed that there were all these people ruining her peace and quiet.

"Jenna!" Naya jumped up and ran over to hug me. "Finally we have female reinforcements!"

"What about me?" Lana asked.

"Leave me out of it," Sue butted in.

Naya told me they were celebrating passing their exams and encouraged us to drink with them. Mike, certainly, needed no invitation: he plopped in the open armchair, while I sat down with Chris. Jack went to the kitchen for beers as Chris remarked that he hadn't seen me in ages. "Not much has changed," I told him, and he replied, "Yeah, except for you and Ross…"

"Did that girl ever kill her roommate with the corkscrew?" I asked, hoping to change the subject.

"I hope not, because no one told me, if so," he said. "I miss seeing you in the dorm, by the way. It was nice to have someone there who actually talked to me instead of just ignoring me. Of course, if I had to deal with your current boyfriend, I'd probably just as soon skip."

"You don't miss me, Chrissy?" Jack shouted.

"Don't call me Chrissy!" Chris replied.

Naya announced it was time to play Never Have I Ever, which Chris hadn't heard of. Instead of making fun of him like everyone else, who jeered that Chris had never done anything cool in his life, Will explained that someone begins with the phrase *Never have I ever*, and whoever has done the thing they say had to take a drink. After some arguments and trash talk, Naya announced that it was time to begin, saying, "Never have I ever blamed another person when I've farted in public."

No one moved in the ensuing silence. Naya was angry. "Are you guys serious?" Mike said he was up. He asked if the person had to actually say something they'd never done, or if they could lie and then take a drink with everyone else after. When it was agreed he could, he said, "Never have I ever slept with someone under eighteen when I was over eighteen."

To my surprise, Will, Lana, Jack, and Mike took a drink. I stared over at Jack, my eyes bulging.

"We were seniors!" he said. "I was eighteen and she was seventeen. I'm twenty-one years old, not forty."

"And Naya's a couple of months younger than me," Will added. As for Lana and Mike, they both seemed to think the less they said, the better. Which, honestly, was fine with me.

Sue leaned in with a sinister expression when her turn came and suggested we liven the game up a bit. I told her she was scaring me, and she continued, "I'll take that for a yes. So: Never have I ever cheated on my boyfriend."

Silence. Mike and Lana took a drink. No surprises there. I looked at Jack out of the corner of my eye, but I'm not even sure he heard the question. How I wanted to know what he was thinking sometimes...

"If it's going to be like that," Will said, thinking for a moment, "Never have I ever had a sex dream."

Shit.

Damn you, Will.

Lana, Naya, Mike, and Chris drank, and I did, too, reluctantly. I felt everyone's eyes on me. Especially Jack's.

"About who?" Naya shouted.

"Why are you asking me?" I responded. "I'm not the only one who took a drink!" I was dying of embarrassment. Especially given who was sitting next to me. Of course, Naya was too smart or too stubborn to give up that easily, so she called out, "Never have I ever had a sex dream about someone I know."

I sighed and drank, as did the same people as before, and once again, everyone was staring at me. It was supposed to be someone else's turn now, but Naya spoke again, "Never have I ever had a sex dream with someone I've only known for…three months?"

"Hey! That's against the rules!"

"Drink!" Sue shouted, shutting me up.

Goddammit. My face must have been the color of a plum. As I drank again, Mike cracked up laughing. "Now we're getting somewhere," Will said.

"I can't believe you never told me, you bitch!" Naya screeched. "Now I'll never tell you about my sex dreams."

"About…?" Will asked.

"You, of course, dear," she said.

Sue looked at me cruelly and said, "Never have I ever had a sex dream in the last three months with the person sitting to my left."

All eyes were on Jack now, and he seemed amused and expectant, waiting to see if I would drink. I looked down into my glass, gathered my courage, and took a drink. Jack looked more surprised than anyone.

"Can we ask what happened in the dream?" Mike asked.

"No!" I was trying to calm down. My face was on fire. "I don't even remember."

"I'll bet you do," Jack said, laughing.

"Can we drop it?" I shouted.

The jokes and laughter rose up and subsided, and finally Lana said, "You're up, Ross."

He thought about it for a moment and said, "Never have I ever had a sex dream with Jack Ross while I was going out with someone else. And never did I love it."

"Dammit! We said we were going to drop it!"

"Come on, now, Jenna, you have to respond," Will said, looking at Jack and grinning.

"I hate you guys," I announced. As I took another drink, Jack pulled me toward him and kissed me on the cheeks. I nearly choked and shouted, "Careful."

"So you wanted me as bad as I wanted you, huh?" he asked.

"Jack, dammit," I protested again. I wriggled away from him and asked Chris, "Can you save me, please?"

"Sure," he said, and seemed to be thinking before calling out: "Never have I ever sent a naked or half-naked photo to someone."

Oh for heaven's sake. Jack naturally was splitting his sides by this point. We kept the game going for a while, until all of us were good and drunk. I had tried to restrain myself, but even I'd drunk two whole beers, which was more than enough for me, and I was getting drowsy, leaning my head on the sofa. The only one who was sober was Jack. He had been drinking water the whole time, much to the irritation of his brother, who wouldn't stop making fun of him for it. But with every joke and jibe, Jack just smiled. I tried not to think about what Lana and Naya had told me about Jack's former problems as we decided to have one more go-round before we fell asleep on the spot.

"I'll start," Naya said. "Never have I ever had sex in a public place."

I don't know about the others, but I certainly saw Jack take a drink. I raised an eyebrow and he smiled at me like a perfect little angel.

Lana: "Never have I ever had sex with someone without knowing their name."

Jack drank.

Sue: "I've never had a three-way."

Jack drank.

Sue: "Four-way?"

Jack drank.

Mike: "Five-way?"

Now he didn't drink. But as he refilled his glass, he tried his best not to look at me.

"Never have I ever filmed myself having sex," Mike said. It was clear at this point that no one cared what anyone else had done. They all just wanted to see how far Jack had gone. Me, I wasn't sure. I didn't want to picture those things in my mind, but I didn't want to get left in the dark, either. Jack grinned, embarrassed, and drank.

Sue: "Never have I ever had sex with two people in the same day."

Everyone watched Jack take a drink as Sue continued, "Three? Four?" Thankfully, Jack left his glass on the table for that.

Chris: "Never have I ever had sex with someone and then thrown them out."

Jack drank.

Sue told me it was my turn, and I replied that I wasn't sure if I wanted to keep playing. Jack remarked that it was getting late, but Naya told him to stay where he was. I tried to pretend I didn't care about all I'd just heard, but I'm sure he could read my feelings on my face, and he sighed with frustration.

Now they started in on how many people he'd slept with. The number rose from five to ten to fifteen. Jack kept drinking, reluctantly, and asked if we really had to keep playing. Could this really be happening? Could my boyfriend really have slept with more than fifteen people? Wasn't I supposed to know these things? I remembered how we'd argued about his refusal to tell me about his past. How he was upset when he learned that Lana and Naya had spoken of it to me. Was he ever planning on being honest with me? A part of me knew the answer. And I didn't like it at all. And I especially didn't like that he didn't trust me.

And on and on it went. *Never have I ever slept with someone I knew had a partner. Never have I ever gotten in a fight. Never have I ever gotten in five fights. Never have I ever broken someone's bones.* And Jack drank and drank. He drank so much I couldn't imagine how he kept from peeing himself, and every time he lifted his glass, it was like a dagger was being stuck in me. *Not this time, not this time,* I kept praying, and with every question, my prayers were frustrated. Who was Jack? How could I have gone out with him all that time without having any idea who he was? And where was he? Where was the gentle, tender guy who liked comic books and movies? The one who wouldn't hurt a fly?

"Never have I ever provoked someone just to have an excuse for a fight," I said.

"Jen…" Jack began.

"We're still playing," Sue reminded him. Angrily, he took a sip.

"Honestly, I can't believe…" he began, but I cut him off. "Never have I ever beaten someone so bad they had to go to the hospital."

He closed his eyes. Then he looked at Will, who was obviously deeply uncomfortable, and took a drink.

"Two people?" I asked. He didn't drink. I was watching him like a hawk. Reality had slapped me in the face. He stared back at me, looking like he was being tortured. And I wanted to tell him everything was OK, that all that was in the past and didn't matter to me. But it wasn't true. I had a knot in my throat.

"Jen…" he began, asking me with his eyes to forget everything.

Will made me turn back as he uttered the words, "Never have I ever been in love."

Naya and he drank. We all knew their answer, but I also knew he had asked that question for us, for Jack and me. I turned to him, feeling a throbbing in my temples, squeezing the beer in my hand, staring into his pupils. I was frozen—I could barely even think. He brought his glass to his lips and took a bigger sip than he had all night. And then everyone's attention focused on me.

I understood then why Jack hadn't wanted to tell me about his past. He hadn't wanted to frighten me. And he had, but it wasn't because of all that he'd done... It was because I thought I knew him better. And I deserved to, because he knew everything about me.

I felt a dryness in my throat as I saw sadness overtake his stare, darkening it with every second that passed. He wanted me to drink. Everyone did, everyone expected it, but there was something else happening inside me. This wasn't a game anymore, this was something that was happening between Jack and me. The entire world was moving in slow motion.

Was saying I'd been in love the same as saying *I love you*? It wasn't, right? Because I wasn't ready to say *I love you*. Just the thought of it was terrifying. It was stifling. It would take things to a place I wasn't ready for. And I didn't know if I'd ever be there.

And yet...my own arm started moving against my will, my body telling my mind what it needed. Jack's eyes opened wide as I brought the beer to my lips and took a sip.

Silence.

The silence was horrible.

He watched me drink. I swallowed. It was done. And even if I wasn't ready to admit it, I knew this was the truth: I did love him, even if I wasn't ready to admit it. Even if this wasn't the moment.

What felt like ages passed, and Jack blinked and looked away. I didn't understand. Was that it? Had all that tension, all that inner struggle happened just so he could stare down into his glass?

I passed the time that followed in a trance, and I hardly realized what was happening when Chris asked if he could sleep here because he was a little drunk. Lana hugged me goodbye. I couldn't really focus on her, though. All I could think of was Jack, who had escaped to his bedroom when the game was over. I caught Will glancing back in that direction. When he looked up at me, he smiled gently.

My heart was pounding as I went back there to find Jack sitting on the bed, his head in his hands. I closed the door and approached cautiously. He ignored me completely.

I didn't understand. Hadn't he taken a drink, too? Didn't that mean he loved me? Did he regret it? I was shaking all over. *No, please, no. Don't let him regret it.* The mere thought made the world collapse around me.

"I'm not going," he announced.

I had been thinking he might tell me to leave, that it was pointless, that what we had was over. So what was this?

"I'm not going to France," he said, looking me straight in the eyes. "I don't want to be so far away from you."

"Why?" I asked.

"Because I love you."

My pulse began racing as I tried to process those words. But I still hadn't as he stood and held my face to kiss me intensely.

So intensely that I forgot I hadn't said *I love you* back.

26

CHRISTMAS DINNER

"I can't believe we're actually going to see my parents," I said as the plane began to descend.

"It's going to be fun," Jack replied, looking radiant.

It was just the two of us. Jack's parents, Agnes, and Mike would spend Christmas Eve at home and arrive the next day for Christmas before we all returned together. I had been a bundle of nerves all day, but when we approached the arrivals gate, it almost became too much to handle. Of course, Jack couldn't sympathize; he looked like he was having the time of his life.

"What's with you?" he asked. "I'm supposed to be the worried one."

"I need to tell you something," I said before we crossed the doorway.

"What's up? Are you OK?"

"Yeah, of course. It's not that, it's…"

I let my voice trail off as I thought how to phrase it.

"Jen, are you about to tell me your family's in a satanic cult or something?"

I took a deep breath. "No, it's not that, thank God. It's my big brother. He thinks it's his job to scare the shit out of any guy I go out with. He's not going to try to fight you, or I don't think he will, but he's going to be a pain in the ass. A big one. And if he sees you getting too familiar with me, he won't be shy about telling you to keep your hands to yourself."

"Got it."

"The twins are a headache in their own way, too. They're like two gorillas constantly fighting over a banana. They make fun of me constantly, when they're not playing video games or pretending to work in their garage. If they try to start anything with you, just give them a piece of your mind. It won't hurt their feelings… I'm not sure they even have any feelings. Or a brain, for that matter. At least, I've never seen anything that would prove it."

"Jen…"

"As for my sister, she's going to interrogate you the whole time. You won't have time to think, and that's on purpose. She's an expert at getting the truth out of people, no matter how hard they try to hide it. So be careful with her. And don't compare me to them. I'm different. Not like I'm saying there's anything wrong with them; it's just we're different, OK?"

"Sure, Jen. I'll keep all that in mind."

"My mom is very touchy-feely, like almost to a creepy degree. It can get old fast. She's not trying to pester you. It's just how she is, you know? So don't get weirded out when she starts hugging you all the time and calling you 'honey.'"

"I can learn to live with it," Jack said.

"She'll ask you lots of questions, too. It can be a little intense. She's not as nosy as Shannon; she just can't help herself. It's like a nervous tic. And my dad…"

"Jen!" He gripped my hand. "It's going to be fine. Just relax."

"I can't!"

He smiled and kissed me. "I don't care what they're like," he said. "They're your family I'm sure I'm going to love them."

He waved me ahead of him and said, "Let's get to it."

The double doors opened, and I thanked the stars that the entire gang hadn't come, just Spencer, Mom, and Shannon. So Jack had time before he'd need to face Dad and the two idiots. Thank heavens.

We walked right up to them without them noticing. I don't think they were used to being in an airport, and they were staring at all the strangers, the TVs on the walls, the bars and restaurants. *You can still run away*, I told myself, but I knew I couldn't abandon Jack, so I cleared my throat and said, "Hey, Mom."

She turned around and her mouth fell open. "Jenna! Honey!" But her excitement didn't last long before she turned to my boyfriend, inspecting him. "And you must be Jack! I'm so happy to finally meet you. Come here, dears." She hugged us both tight. Jack looked amused. I was dying of embarrassment.

"Mom, please..." I muttered.

"Stop being embarrassed about your mother," she said. "That's not right, is it, Jack?"

"It sure isn't," Jack said, amused.

OK, I deserved that. I had told his mother the same thing, more or less.

Shannon was polite—I'd asked her to try to act normal—and limited herself to saying, "I'm Shannon. We talked on the phone before. I've heard a lot about you, Jack. Like a lot. I guess you know Jenna's not the best at keeping her trap shut when she's excited about something."

"She's said a lot of wonderful things about you, too," Jack said, smiling and hugging her in turn.

So for now, everything was OK. The worst, of course, was still to come. Spencer's eyes were narrowed. *Please, no*, I thought. Please don't let my brother's nasty character emerge from hibernation right here at the airport, before we've even made it home.

"Spencer," he said, extending a hand.

Jack took it in stride, shaking hands with him and saying, "Jack Ross. You can call me Jack or Ross. It doesn't really matter."

"I hope you're taking good care of Jenna," Spencer told him. Knowing Spencer, he was probably squeezing Jack's hand to the point of breaking to see if he'd react. I kicked his foot, starting to blush, and said, "Spencer, let him go."

"Are you taking good care of her?" he repeated.

"I do what I can," Jack said.

I nudged Spencer again, and he wrapped an arm around me. "He takes great care of me, Spencer," I said. Finally Shannon salvaged the situation with a quick change of subject. "Spencer, you know about Jack. He's the one who kicked Monty's ass."

My brother blinked, surprised, the hardness in his expression vanishing.

"I didn't like the way he was treating your sister," Jack said.

Friendly now, Spencer grinned and said, "You should have started with that!" He clapped Jack on the back. "Come on, I'll help you with your things."

They helped us with our luggage, and when we got to the car, Mom made me sit in the front with Spencer while she and Shannon made Jack take the spot between them so they could pester him with questions. Even Spencer joined in. Poor Jackie. He was a good guy, though, and he responded patiently to all of them.

"Leave him alone already," I finally said.

"We're just excited to meet him!" Shannon shouted.

"Yeah, shut up," Spencer added, reaching over and turning my face back toward the road with his giant hand.

Jack laughed, and the flood of questions started up again.

When we turned onto my street, I felt so tense I was worried I'd explode. Mom started telling dumb stories about me, Jack listened closely, I begged her to stop. No one had listened to me. It was like I'd ceased to exist and I was the only one who still hadn't figured that out.

Spencer parked in the garage. A little ball of fuzz barreled toward me and I shouted, "Biscuit!" as he jumped all around me and started licking my hands. Jack stood and watched. I'd told him about my dog a million times. Biscuit sniffed him briefly, decided he was OK, and started licking him, too.

"Hey!" Jack said. "I'm fitting in. Even your dog likes me. That's an achievement."

I rolled my eyes and he laughed. Now came the big challenge: Sonny and Steve. I was sure they'd do something horrible.

And then there was Dad, too... There was no telling what he'd do. But when we walked inside, he was nowhere to be found: in the living room were just Sonny and Steve, so absorbed in whatever video game they were playing that they didn't even notice we were there. That was for the best. One problem at a time, I thought.

"Here are my other two brothers," I said. No reaction.

"Hello, idiots," I repeated.

Sonny shouted at Steve to stay out of his lane. Steve shouted at Sonny to stop blaming him and learn how to drive.

"I said hello!" I shouted. Sonny jerked, and on the screen his car crashed and burst into flames. "Noooo!" he shouted, dropping his controller. "No fair, she distracted me."

"Yeah, I really care," Steve said, laughing in his face.

Spencer asked, "Don't you guys want to meet Jenna's boyfriend?"

They turned and looked at him, and Sonny nodded, and said, "So you put up with our sister, huh?"

"And she doesn't even pay you?" Steve added.

"I get a little something in return," Jack said, making all three of my brothers chuckle while I turned red as a tomato. Traitor.

"You know how to play?" Sonny asked, pointing at the screen.

"You know how to lose?" Jack replied.

"I like your attitude," Spencer announced, then told the twins, "It's us against you. Prepare to get your asses beaten."

I was the only one left standing there doing nothing while the four guys hooted and poked fun at each other, all more or less hypnotized by the TV. I bent over and told Jack if he got bored, he could come join me in the kitchen. But there didn't seem to be much danger of that. "I need to put my future brothers-in-law in their place," he said with a wink.

I felt a bit like I was throwing him to the wolves, but he'd shown he could handle them, so I walked out and took a seat at the kitchen table, where Mom and Shannon were sitting. They instantly fell silent.

"Am I interrupting something?" I asked, grabbing a cookie from the dish. "You look like you were in the middle of a serious conversation."

"We were just talking about our first impressions," Shannon said. "I'm assuming Jack's fitting in OK with the guys?"

"They're playing video games. So…what do you think?"

"He seems like a good guy," Shannon said, trying to act nonchalant.

"But…?" I asked.

"But…" Shannon replied, "he's with you, so clearly something's wrong with his brain."

"Screw you," I said.

"Language!" my mother interjected.

I flipped my sister the bird and asked where Dad was. Shannon told me he was on his way, then remarked that I looked a little nervous. I reminded her that *she* had been nervous when she'd introduced *us* to *her* boyfriend, but she reminded me that I wasn't pregnant, so the two situations weren't comparable. "But then…" she continued, "you always were Dad's favorite, being the little one and all that, so I can imagine it might be worse for you. Who knows how he's going to react when he's face-to-face with a guy who's been smashing his daughter."

"Smashing?" Mom said. "What is smashing?"

"Just, like, going out," Shannon said with an innocent smile. "Anyway, I'm on the edge of my seat. Hopefully nobody will make a scene, right?"

"Shannon, could you shut up?" I said. "I'm edgy enough already."

I returned to the living room, where Spencer and Jack were crushing the twins, and asked whether I could have some time with my boyfriend. They protested he was having more fun with them, and that Mom and Shannon must have already gotten all their questions out of the way in the car. I had to threaten to cut the cables to get Spencer to finally agree to save the game and get back to it later, though he was clearly disappointed.

Jack stood and followed me up the stairs. When we were alone, he asked mischievously, "Are you going to show me your bedroom already?"

"Get too frisky and I might show you the door," I said.

He laughed and shook his head. Actually, I was nervous to show him my room, but I opened the door and let him in first. I couldn't quite read his expression as he looked around. "Interesting," he said sarcastically.

"I know, it's very pink."

"It's very you, Jen." He turned away from the bed to the shelf and said, "Is this the famous record collection?"

When I nodded, he crouched down, and for five minutes he flipped through the albums. Then he snooped through my photos, my closet... everything! I just sat on the bed, too weirded out by the whole situation to react. I'd never even let Monty come up there. When we did...*things*, it was usually on the sofa when everyone was out. Showing him my room would have meant revealing a private part of myself. But Jack was different.

I crossed my legs and said, "I hope you're enjoying yourself."

"I am," he responded. "Your family's nice, too. They're not the monsters you made them out to be. And they seem to like me, so that's something."

"Mom adores you. Almost as much as yours adores me."

"I will tell you one thing," he said. "It hurt me to do this, but I let your brothers win a couple of times so I could get in their good graces."

"I've got to be honest," I told him. "It's literally impossible for me to imagine your parents sitting downstairs hanging out with all of them. I feel like we're so…average compared to them. I don't know if that's the right word."

"Jen, I understand being nervous, OK? The whole flight down I was asking myself what I needed to do to make a good impression. But I'm having a blast, and everyone's behaving, and I think it's time for you to relax."

"All right," I said, and leaned in to kiss him, but then I heard the front door open and close with a bang and I froze in midair.

"What is it?" Jack asked. "Did a serial killer just come through the door?"

"Worse. My dad. Get ready," I told him, and held his hand, guiding him back down the stairs. Dad heard our steps and turned toward us. Jack was calm, polite, and reached out to shake hands as he walked over and said, "Mr. Brown."

"Jack," Dad said in a neutral tone, eyeing him. "I've heard a lot about you."

"Only good things," I threw in.

"Very good things," Dad corrected me. He shook hands with Jack, then laid an arm over his shoulder and asked if he'd seen the garage yet. It was easy as that. Sonny and Steve hopped up to join the two men. Jack looked back at me and winked.

Our first activity as a family—minus Mom and Shannon, who hated that kind of thing—was going to the annual Christmas fair. I rode the Tunnel of Love, tried to avoid the mini roller coaster, played Whac-A-Mole, ate funnel cake and cotton candy. It was fun, especially because it was nighttime when we got there, and most of the kids were gone.

Jack, with a bemused expression, described the whole thing as *interesting*.

My three brothers ran off toward the bumper cars, ready to kill each other, leaving Jack and me alone. I don't know where Dad had gotten to. I asked Jack what he wanted to do, and he recommended the mini roller coaster, which I hoped he hadn't seen. I didn't want to tell him I was scared of roller coasters, so instead I motioned to its rickety structure and said, "It looks like it's about to fall into the ground."

"OK," he replied, "how's your aim then?"

"Better than yours," I said, provoking him. So we walked over to the stall with the darts and the balloons. Jack gave me a mocking look as he handed me my darts. I bit my lip with concentration. I'd barely ever played darts before, but it couldn't be that hard, right? Aim, throw, pop the balloon, try not to hit the wall. Easy, right?

I threw my first one and hit the wall.

"Tough luck," the guy running the stall said. Jack smirked, and I told him not to look at me that way. I still had four darts left. I squinted, staring at the balloons like they were my mortal enemy. And…I missed three more times. I was terrible. Worse than I could ever have imagined. As Jack laughed maliciously, I passed him my final dart, warning him, "If you don't pop one of the balloons, I'll remind you of it for the rest of your life."

He asked the guy what he'd get if he hit one balloon. The guy told him he could have a stuffed unicorn or a bubble blower. "You got a preference?" Jack asked.

"I guess the bubbles…"

Before I could finish my phrase, Jack had popped a balloon.

"I always believed in you," I told him and giggled. I grabbed his hand and tugged him toward the photo booth. He couldn't help making a dirty joke and told me he didn't know I was kinky like that: doing it in public *and* documenting it?

"Idiot," I replied. "We don't have a single photo together."

"You're right," he said.

"So let's solve that now."

Before I could open my change purse, he had slipped three dollars into the machine. I tucked the bottle of bubble soap in my bag and hurried in with him, trying to arrange my hair and look at least somewhat pretty as the countdown started.

Jack looked straight at the camera and grinned as I kissed him on the cheek, then we stared into each other's eyes, then he leaned his head on my shoulders, then I grabbed his collar and kissed him on the lips. It was cheesy, I know, but it was something I'd always wanted to do with someone, and I wasn't going to miss the opportunity with him now.

He looked meditatively at our photos while I bought tickets to get on the Ferris wheel. That had always been my favorite ride. The carriage swayed a little as we got in, and then we were set in motion with a creak and clang.

"You do realize you've picked the lamest ride in the whole park," Jack said.

Offended, I replied, "Sorry, I think you mean the best one."

Rising into the sky, I asked him about my family again, how he liked them, if he felt comfortable around them. He reminded me we'd already talked about it and asked me what I was afraid of, and I realized I didn't really know, and that with Jack, I didn't need to worry. He was one of those guys everybody just naturally liked. He told me, "I don't know what you're afraid of, Jen, but I like them. They're great. Now chill out and enjoy the view."

I could feel relaxation spreading through my chest as we reached the top. I gazed out at the city entranced, as though I'd never seen it before, as though I hadn't come to this penny-ante fair once a year for as long as I could remember. I told Jack how when I was little I had been on this same Ferris wheel and my friends had tried to rock the carriage back and forth and I'd been scared we'd fall. Of course, he started doing the same. I panicked, and he laughed at my terrified expression. Even people in the other cars looked at us, and we noticed we weren't alone. A few feet below us, a teenager was trying to frighten his friends. I guess the urge to annoy people was like a virus.

"I hate you," I said.

"Sure you do." He stopped, and I leaned back and curled up against him when a gust of cold air struck me.

"You know, it feels like an eternity since I was last here," I murmured.

"Do you miss it?"

"I don't know. It feels different now. Like everything here happens so slow. As if time didn't move at the same speed here, or like it didn't move at all, maybe. The places don't change, the people don't change, even the dumb jokes don't change. I loved it here when I was little, but I don't think I could spend the rest of my life here anymore. I'm not sure it was ever really the right place for me, and it definitely isn't now. That makes me feel bad for my family, because I know they're scared of me ever going somewhere else, they're scared they couldn't protect me, and they need me and I guess I need them, too, in a way, but…it's my life, right? And I need to be able to decide who I want to be, and I could never do that here."

"You could just live with me," he said.

"I already live with you, Jack. I've been living with you for three months, in case you didn't notice. We literally share the same bed."

"What about your plan to move back to the dorms, though. Is that still a thing?"

"I don't know," I said. It had been so long since I'd said that, and I'd almost forgotten about it.

"You know you don't have to. You can stay in the apartment. Consider it yours. I mean, I'd love that, honestly. I love you, Jen. I love spending time with you. So much that it's kind of starting to worry me, but I'll deal with it, you know. So what do you say? Should we drop the pretense that this is just until your parents get on their feet and admit we officially live together?"

So he'd done it.

He'd dropped the bomb on me.

And he was cool as a cucumber.

Unlike me.

I was tense, and I knew he was waiting for me to say something.

"With a room of my own, you mean?"

"I'm sorry, do you have any complaints about sleeping with me?" he asked.

"I'm not sure if I should be sleeping with my landlord."

"Your landlord is sure you should be," he said.

"Yeah, my landlord is a perv, though," I replied.

As I smiled nervously, trying to be serious, he interrupted my thoughts. "You don't have to say anything right now. You've got the whole Christmas break to think it over. No rush."

But I knew what I wanted to say. What I would say. We kissed, and when the ride let us off, we joined my family again. Everything was fine until we got home. Spencer was a little drunk—he had run into some friends at the fair and had downed a few beers with them—and he was chatty, while the twins hurried off up the stairs. I was trying to guide Jack to my bedroom when Spencer stopped us, hugging us both, and said, "Kids, I want y'all to behave tonight."

"Spencer!" I said.

"Jenna, it's fine. It's natural. Just be quiet, OK? Some of us have to get up in the morning."

"You don't," I told him.

"Just listen to me," he said. "Don't scream and moan. And use protection. I've got all the nephews I want for now."

Jack was amused. I felt like I was dying inside, and as Spencer slunk off, I told him, "We're going to pretend that never happened, all right?"

In my room, I put on the pajamas with the little sheep on them that Jack had laughed at so many times and took out my contact lenses. I couldn't believe how small my bed looked. We were going to have to sleep on top of each other, almost. Not that I saw that as a problem. We lay down, and I got close to him, intertwining my legs with his.

"I can't believe Mom and Dad will be here tomorrow," he murmured.

"And your brother," I reminded him.

"And my grandmother. It's going to be interesting."

Toying with his collar, I told him, "You know, I've never had a guy up here before."

"I feel honored."

"I've never introduced a guy to my family, either."

"Not even Monty?"

"Not formally," I said, shaking my head. "Of course, they know him. Everyone here knows him, everyone here knows everyone. But I only ever brought him over when I had the house to myself. And I never let him off the couch. Romantic, I know."

"So I'm the first guy to be in your bed," Jack murmured with satisfaction. "I hope I'm the last, too."

"You wish," I said, and he turned over and kissed me.

Do I need to say I was nervous? At this point, that's the story of my life. But family introductions—that was a whole new level of potential catastrophe. Before they arrived, I sat up in my room breathing and trying to visualize everything going well. When we finally went down, Jack's family was already there. Talking. Apparently relaxed. I could hear them in the kitchen with Mom, Dad, and Shannon. Mike and Owen were in the living room playing video games.

"Auntie!" Owen shouted when he saw me, dropping the controller and running over for a hug.

"How are you, buddy?" I asked, and he burbled that he was great, and he was so happy I was home, and he was beating the tar out of Mike, and so on and so forth, until he saw Jack, and then he turned wary, asking, "Who are you?"

"I'm Jack. Nice to meet you, Owen."

Like a little tough guy, Owen warned him, "Just be careful. She's mine."

"Owen!" I shouted. Jack told me to let it go, but I wanted to know where he'd learned to treat strangers like that. It was funny, but he needed to mind his manners, and I tried to tell him so as Jack butted in, "Yeah, I've heard of you. Jenna told me how strong you are. Trust me, I don't want to get in your way. I'm just here to take care of your aunt when you're not around."

"Fine," Owen said, crossing his arms. Jack asked him if they could be friends, and after a moment's consideration, Owen said, "Friends," and they gave each other a fist bump.

Mary and Agnes looked overjoyed to see us, while Mr. Ross was his usual cool self. But there was less tension than last time. That was something, at least. I don't think my mother even noticed the friction, and that was strange, because she usually picked up on those things. So things were as good as we could have hoped.

We had lunch together, and the entertainment consisted mainly of my brothers and Dad making fun of me, which everyone else enjoyed it. I got upset and ran out in the backyard, and Jack had to come get me like a little girl and convince me to come back inside. In the afternoon, the parents left, and we had a snowball fight in the backyard. I wound up soaked and Spencer and Jack won, of course. What did I expect, having to team up with Mike? Sonny and Steve were renegades who joined us briefly only to turn on us at the last minute.

After that, I needed a shower and some relaxation, and we each did our own thing until dinnertime, when Jack decided to stay in the living room with the guys while I sat at the kitchen table with both groups of parents. They were talking about some series they had seen. I'd never heard of it, and I didn't really care. I stood and walked outside at some point and found Owen and Mike making a snowman. It was strange: I wouldn't have figured Mike would be so good with kids. They were far enough off that they didn't notice me sitting on the porch and watching them.

A few minutes later, Mr. Ross came outside and sat next to me. It was strange, especially that he would sit on our not-exactly-immaculate porch in his expensive designer trousers. He looked out and said, "Those two are like peas in a pod." Mike was gathering the snow into a bigger and bigger ball while Owen ordered him around.

"Yeah, everyone seems to be getting along great," I said, smiling.

"Yes, it really does seem wonderful," he replied, putting a hand on my shoulder. "And it really is all thanks to you, Jenna. If you hadn't helped with my son, this never could have happened."

I smiled shyly. He actually seemed sincere.

"All I did is come talk to you," I told him.

"It's not just that. It's everything. You don't know what Jack was like a few months ago. How he's changed. I'm sure I'm not the first person to tell you."

I nodded as he continued. "There was a time in my life when I thought he was truly lost. Jack is hardheaded, you know. He won't stop doing something once he's set his mind to it, even if it's blowing up in his face. And his girlfriends…my lord. Suffice it to say I wasn't crazy about them. Not that I really knew them, and I realize that means I shouldn't judge them, but you can tell when someone is good for your child and when they're not. You'll understand what I mean if you ever decide to have kids. You two, though—I can tell this isn't just some adolescent crush."

He was so serious that I hesitated a moment before saying, "No, it's not."

"It's more than that, Jenna. I can tell. I wish you knew how happy I am for the two of you. You're everything my son didn't know he was looking for."

I grinned awkwardly, but I couldn't really think of what to say. I hadn't expected this conversation, and I wasn't ready for it. I hugged my knees, watching Mike and Owen, who seemed to be having a ball.

"I should inform you, Jenna, that Jack is planning on sending a letter to the program in France letting them know he won't be attending," Mr. Ross said. "It's funny, isn't it, how a person's priorities can change. There was a time when he would have done anything to go there. And now... Well, you know."

"It makes me a little sad," I said. "He wants to be a director. If he went there, maybe it would help him be a success."

"There are other programs. This one is special, but it's not the only one."

I looked over after thinking a moment and asked him, "Do you think he'll have another opportunity in the future?"

"I doubt it. In his application essay, he wrote that going there was his life's dream. If he doesn't go now, I doubt they'll appreciate that kind of inconsistency. But as I said, there are other programs. It doesn't matter. He has serious feelings for you, Jenna. You're the truest thing he's ever had. That's why he's not leaving. And you can't blame him for it. It's normal, and he's of an age where he can make these kinds of choices."

None of what he was saying comforted me, nor did it put me at ease when he reached up and squeezed my shoulder. After a moment's thought, I asked him, "Do you think...if it were you... I mean, is Jack making a bad decision rejecting this offer? Be honest, please."

He waited a moment, then sighed. "I don't know," he responded.

"Sometimes we have to sacrifice things for love. Because we love the other person more than ourselves. Because we want the best for them. And once you find yourself in that situation, it's hard to turn back."

I nodded, a knot in my throat.

"He should have said yes," I told him. "Even if it meant having a long-distance relationship for however long. It would have been OK. We'd have gotten through it."

"I agree with you," Mr. Ross said. "But Jack doesn't."

"He needs to. And he needs to go."

"He won't, Jenna. He'll never go as long as you two are together."

He stood, and I watched him walk away, then turned back to Mike and Owen, who were still playing innocently in the snow.

27

THE RIGHT THING

Mom insisted Jack and I not leave so soon, so we ended up spending New Year's Eve at my parents' house, too. It was a good time, especially when my brothers got drunk and decided they could beat Jack at a snowball fight. I wished I could really enjoy it, but a part of me was unable. I was too worried about him giving up something that mattered so much to him for me. And I wondered if I'd have been able to do the same in his shoes. I thought so, but I wasn't sure, and that made me question again whether I was being selfish by accepting him staying there.

I even considered—not really, or not exactly—whether I should leave him so he would go. Because it was obvious that he wouldn't listen to me. I didn't even need to ask. I knew I shouldn't think that way, but I couldn't help it. Jack could tell something was up, of course. He always could. He tried to force me to talk to him, but eventually he figured out I never would, so he just kissed me, hoping that would comfort me until I got through whatever was bothering me.

How could he be so damn perfect?

It was New Year's Day, I think, at dawn, when I was finally able to admit what I really wanted.

And I wanted to stay with him.

I'd spent day after day thinking about it, and I knew: I didn't want to be apart from him.

Our last day there, as we packed our bags, I could feel him looking at me. Eventually he asked, "Are you OK?"

I nodded. He hadn't asked me for a few days. I tried to throw him off, saying, "I was wondering if I should grab anything else from here to take back."

With a sly smile, he told me, "I'm on the case. You just relax and let me look through your stuff. I'm dying to discover all your embarrassing secrets."

I told him I didn't think there was much there. "Challenge accepted," he replied.

I grabbed a few sweatshirts out of my closet and tossed them into my hot-pink backpack. Behind me, Ross was opening and closing drawers. He didn't seem too excited about what he was finding. He dug up a bracelet that I'd never worn, asked if I had any other jewelry, asked why not when I told him I never liked wearing jewelry. I had to disappoint him and tell him the notebook he found wasn't my diary, just a place where I wrote down lists of stupid stuff, lists of things I'd been happy to accomplish, like going to Disney World and passing calculus. Ross wanted to know where he was, and I told him to flip to the back, where all the things I was embarrassed about were. I wasn't worried. I'd told him about my failed attempt at sexting, and everything else in there was silly: the time I fell into a swimming pool fully clothed, taking a class I hated just to be with Nelle...

"Where's Monty?" he asked.

"Jack, I haven't written in that notebook in years."

"It's never too late..." he said before tossing the notebook back in the drawer.

When we were done, we said our goodbyes to my family. We had decided to catch an Uber to avoid all the tears at the airport. As my home disappeared behind me, I wondered whether I was doing the right thing. I could still change my mind. But…no. When I looked at him, I knew I couldn't. Being with him was right. I wanted to stay with him.

We didn't talk on the plane, or even on the ride home. I didn't want to, and I pretended to be asleep. I wasn't entirely faking. I was exhausted from the stress, and I'd been getting up every morning early to have a little alone time with my mother. I even threw on sunglasses, because the sun was bothering me, and that was something I never did.

When we were parked, Jack grabbed both our suitcases and dragged them to the elevator. As soon as we were upstairs, I smelled something burning. It was horrible. I could hear Naya shrieking through the door. We threw the door open and found her in the kitchen with the smoke alarm going off, holding open the oven door and letting out a black cloud of smoke. There was a tray inside, and on top of it, the black remains of what had once been a chicken.

Will, Mike, and Sue were leaning on the bar and cracking up as they watched her.

"See why I didn't want to cook!" Naya shouted. Then, when she noticed we'd arrived, she tried to cover for herself with the words, "Oh, hi, you guys!"

Jack asked, "Are you trying to burn down my home?"

"Some thanks I get," she replied. "I wanted to do something nice to welcome you home. There's ten bucks down the drain, I guess."

Honestly, the scene had put me in a better mood. I forgot my misgivings and told her, "Listen, if you haven't gotten tired of cooking, we could go get another chicken and I could give you a hand this time."

"See! This is why you're my best friend!" she shouted enthusiastically.

So we went to the grocery store, and then she and Will and I spent the rest of the afternoon cooking and trying not to cause another disaster. When the chicken was ready, we set it in the middle of the coffee table. Sue came in sniffing the air. Soon everyone else was gathered, and immediately Mike started complaining because the television was turned off.

"Mike," Naya upbraided him, "this is our Christmas dinner. We should talk, not look at the stupid TV."

"Christmas is over," I told her. "It's January now."

"Whatever," she said. "We didn't get to see each other for the holidays, so can't we just fake it for a day and try to be happy together?"

As everyone agreed, Mike butted in, "Where are my presents, then?"

Naya murmured with embarrassment that she didn't have any. Sue reminded him that he wasn't supposed to be living there and that he could consider not being homeless his Christmas present. Mike protested that we'd all be bored if he wasn't there to entertain us.

"Or happy," Jack said. "It's one or the other."

"Help me out, future sister-in-law," Mike pleaded, and I told them, "Leave the poor thing alone."

They did, but not because they felt bad for him or cared about my opinion. It was just that they were hungry. When we finished, we watched a terrible Christmas movie. Sue and Mike bitched about it the whole time, Will and Naya just made out, and Jack and I watched in silence. He was the only guy I'd ever met who actually tried to watch the movie when he told his girlfriend that was what he wanted to do. If I tried to distract him, he'd even get angry, which I have to admit I found hilarious. I couldn't help but grin as I stared at him.

"What?" he asked.

"Nothing. I don't want to distract you," I said.

"You're already distracting me."

"It's just…I've got a Christmas present for you."

"Give it," he said, eyes pinned to the screen.

"It's not exactly a conventional present." My cheeks got hot as I said that.

He smiled mischievously and responded, "I want to see it."

"What about the movie, though?"

"Screw the movie." He stood up and pulled me behind him into his bedroom, where he sat on the bed and said, "I've got something for you, too. It's a birthday present, but you can have it early."

"My birthday's in a month!"

"It's always better to be prepared," he replied. I was excited as he walked over to his dresser, opened a drawer, and tossed me a small package in wrapping paper.

"I don't know if you'll like it," he said as I tore off the paper. "This whole gift-giving thing is kind of new for me."

Inside was a small cardboard box, and inside that was an even smaller box made of blue velvet. I could see he was getting impatient, but I was so excited my fingers weren't working right. "Hurry up!" he said, and I was surprised to find inside a silver key.

"What is it?" I asked, confused.

"It's a key to the apartment."

"I don't get it. I already have a key."

"It's symbolic, dummy. Today marks three months since the first time we kissed. And I know I said on the Ferris wheel you didn't have to answer me right away, but you know, I got impatient. My idea was to wait to ask you if you'd make it official on your birthday, but I just couldn't."

He looked so nervous—I'd never seen him that way. It was cute, and I almost wanted to treasure it.

"I don't know what to say," I told him. "I think I hate you a little."

"Why?"

"Because my gift sucks compared to yours."

"I'll be the judge of that," he said. "Now hand it over!"

"Patience!" I told him. "Jeez. Go sit on the bed and behave. And turn your back to me." He did as I said, though he tried to turn his head once, and I had to tell him to stay still. I hurried to the closet as he hummed, pretending to be distracted. I kept glancing over to make sure he wasn't peeking. Thankfully he didn't. I found what I was looking for. He acted like a little kid the whole time, asking, *Can I turn around now? How about now? Now?* And I kept saying *No, no, no!* Finally I warned him that if he kept asking, I'd go even slower on purpose. I could tell by his voice how funny this was for him, and I saw him tapping his fingers on his knees. Once I was ready, I took a look at myself in the full-length mirror. I was blushing like crazy already.

I had put on the lingerie set Shannon bought me. It was all lace and satin, very sexy, and very weird, at least for me. Feigning annoyance, Jack called out, "I'm falling asleep!" and I said, "Just a little longer."

I let down my hair. But then I pulled it back and let it down again and pulled it back again before finally deciding to leave it down for good, though even then, I wasn't sure. I pulled my bangs behind my ear, wondering why the hell I was so nervous. It was just underwear. He'd already seen me with even less on.

I tossed the other clothes in the closet and closed it. Jack was lying down now, but he'd obediently kept his eyes shut. I tried a few different poses, but they were all awkward and uncomfortable. So I tried new ones and didn't like them any better. He told me he could hear me moving around the room, and that he wasn't sure how much longer his curiosity could hold out.

"Shut up and don't look," I told him.

"You're not preparing to murder me, are you?"

"Only if you keep talking."

He laughed. He was enjoying this. Finally I gave up and just stood there, arms slack at my sides, feeling incredibly uncomfortable. I took a deep breath and said, "OK, you can open your eyes."

He did, and turned. For a few horrible seconds that seemed like they would never end, he looked at me without uttering a word. I tried not to cover myself with my hands, but that got harder and harder for me the longer he stared. Never before had I felt so exposed.

"So…?" I asked.

With one last head-to-toe glance, he said, "Fuuuuck."

"Is that a good *fuck* or a bad *fuck*?" I asked.

"Just fuck…" he replied. When he'd recovered from the initial shock, he asked, "Can you please tell me how long you've had that and why it is you've never worn it before?"

"I was waiting for a special occasion!"

"Every day you put that on is a special occasion in my book," he said. "Now get over here."

I didn't dare to look at him as I approached. He sat me on his lap, touched my knee, touched the seam of my bra.

"New tradition," he said. "From now on, every year we're going to celebrate Christmas after New Year's, and it's always going to end like this."

After a week settled into the apartment, with everything back to normal, I'd completely forgotten about France. I was running in the mornings again, and Jack was complaining about Mike. It was almost as if we'd never left.

One night I was sitting on the sofa watching TV. Jack was out with some of his classmates, Sue was eating junk food and watching TV, and Will and Naya were being cheesy the way they always did. Mike supposedly had a new friend with benefits so he was out, and that meant I had a whole couch to myself.

Sue went to bed early, as did Will and Naya, and I decided to stay up watching TV so I wouldn't have to hear them moaning and groaning. When I thought the danger was past, I decided to go to the bedroom. I wasn't going to wait up for Jack. He'd wake me when he got in. But on my way, I saw a folded piece of paper on the counter covered up by a couple of notebooks. For some reason, I decided to pull it out, and my indifference gave way to intrigue as I saw it was Jack's letter to the program in France telling them he wouldn't be attending.

I couldn't help but read it. *While I appreciate the offer, for personal reasons I find myself unable to attend...* I frowned and put it back carefully, so no one would notice I'd touched it. And I almost had a heart attack when I looked up and saw Will standing there watching me.

"You're not supposed to go looking around in other people's things, Jenna," he said.

"Don't tell Jack, please."

"I won't. I'm assuming it's the letter to the French program."

I nodded, and he continued, "It's a hell of an offer he's turning down. Why do you look so sad?"

Instead of answering, I shook my head and wrapped my arms around myself. Everything I'd tried to ignore in recent days came crashing over me like a gigantic wave. I was sure Will was just making light of the situation when he called it a *hell of an offer*, but it made me feel like the worst person in the world. He came closer to me and asked, "Jenna, seriously, what's wrong?"

I sat on the couch, and he followed me and started rubbing my back. When I felt I could get the words out, I asked, "Do you think he's making a mistake?"

He hesitated. And as he waited to respond, his hand froze, and I knew that was exactly what he thought.

"Jenna, what do you want me to say? It's a massive opportunity, and his life's dream is to be a movie director."

"And it's my fault he said no."

"Jenna, you can't worry about it. Jack is the hardest-headed guy I know. He made his choice, and he's not changing his mind."

"But what if he's wrong?" I asked. "If I wasn't here, he'd go. There's no doubt about it, right?"

"I don't know what you're thinking," he said, "but I can promise you that the solution isn't…"

"Will!" I cut him off. "Look me in the eyes right now and swear to me that he can still live his dream if he doesn't go to that school."

"I can't do that, Jenna. I don't know. It's his dream, but there are lots of ways to fulfill your dream. I don't know how important it is, I don't know anything about film directing. All I can tell you is what Jack said, and before he met you, that program was an obsession for him. But he has you now, and if he's made the choice he's made, it's because you matter even more to him."

"But look at all he's done for me," I said. "He changed his whole life for me at the drop of a hat. He gave up so much already. Can I really just let him give up his dream, his childhood dream?"

"Jenna, what about all the things you've done for him?"

"What have I done for him, Will? What, exactly? Sure, maybe we have some laughs, maybe he got over whatever was wrong with him when he was with Lana, but you can't compare that. It took me months just to give up my stupid ex-boyfriend, and you're telling me I shouldn't worry about getting him to give up his life's dream?"

"But Jenna, the decision's been made. What are you going to do, leave him so he won't send the letter? He'd be destroyed."

"Maybe that is what I'm going to do," I said. "Maybe that's what's right."

"No, Jenna. You need to talk to him. He'll…"

"I know what he'll do. He'll say no. He'll say I'm all that matters, and he'll stay here."

"He loves you," Will said.

"You think I don't know that? And he means the world to me, and that's why I need him to do what's best for him. I'm his girlfriend, not his wife. And I'm eighteen years old. Imagine things go bad, imagine if we break up in a year or two, and then he's given up something that might have changed his entire life for nothing. For just another relationship."

"It's not nothing," Will protested. "It will never be nothing."

"You don't know that, Will."

"What if you went with him?"

This was ridiculous. He knew I couldn't just buy a plane ticket to France. How would I support myself? What would I do there? I'd been planning on looking for a job, trying to pay for painting lessons. If I went with Jack I'd just be in the way. And I couldn't owe him more money. I tried to tell Will all this, but I don't think he understood. I told him I had a job offer back home, that I could save up and pay for painting classes for myself. That if I went with him, I'd just be a bother. He tried to protest that we could find a way, but I didn't want to hear it so I told him not to say anything. He was about to fire back when we heard the keys in the lock, and Jack walked in with his usual, indomitable smile. "What are you two conspiring about?" he asked.

He didn't wait for an answer before kissing me, tossing his jacket into the armchair, and dropping his keys on the bar. I looked at Will again. His expression was somber.

As Jack announced he was going to change clothes, Will shook his head and told me, "You're going to destroy him."

"Maybe. But if I do it now, he might understand why."

"You're the one who doesn't understand," Will said. "You don't know him like I do. I'm not sure he'll be able to get over this. Please! What can I say to change your mind?"

When I didn't answer, he knew there were no options left, but still he begged me, "Just wait till tomorrow. Spend tonight with him. Maybe you'll reconsider. If you still feel like it tomorrow, fine, break up with him. But think about it first. Think long and hard about what the consequences could be."

"Fine," I said.

I stood up and walked down the hall. But I didn't make it far before I heard Will say, "Hey." I turned back. He was observing me with a sad smile, and he said, "You know you're the best thing that's ever happened to him, right? That's all. I just needed you to know that."

I walked to the bedroom. Jack was in there shirtless in a pair of sweatpants, lying on the bed and looking at his phone. He put it down when he saw me walk in. He could tell something was wrong, and his smile vanished as he asked, "What's up?"

"Naya put on that movie about the dog that stays there waiting for its dead owner and it made me sad," I lied. I'd been preparing myself for this moment mentally, but now I was flaking. I did learn one thing in that moment, though. I learned I really could lie to him if I needed to and not get caught.

"Well, come here. Let's make those bad feelings disappear."

I grinned and curled up next to him, and he turned off the light and slid down so my head was resting on his chest. As he stroked my back, he asked, "Better?" I nodded.

"We could adopt a little dog if you like," he said. "I've always wanted one. We could call him Biscuit Two. In honor of your dog at home."

"Biscuit's not dead, you know."

"It's not that. It's just like…you know how rich people keep a separate wardrobe in all their different homes? Same thing, he'll just be the Biscuit you have here."

I grinned, but I wanted to cry. He kept stroking my back.

"Or maybe a cat would be better. Cats are more independent. What do you say? Dog? Cat? Two-headed dragon?"

I sat up, and in the dark I could just barely see his eyebrow lifting as he waited for an answer. "A dragon sounds good," I said.

"Then a dragon it is. But let me warn you: you're the one who has to clean up after it."

"Sure," I said, staring up and opening his lips with mine. As our tongues touched, he reached up and felt my hair.

I let him lay me on my back. He could tell I was sad, but I think he still assumed it was the movie. He was calm and tender in a way he never had been. He kissed the tip of my nose, grinned, pulled up my shirt. I closed my eyes as our bodies touched. He was taking his time, and it was so soft, so caring, that I wished it would last forever.

We'd never shared a night like that. Our kisses, our caresses, our expressions, our whispers…all of it was surrounded by an aura of good-byes. I knew why, of course. I could feel myself trying to memorize every second of it in case it never happened again, but Jack… What was Jack sad about? Maybe he wasn't, maybe he was just so deeply in tune with me that he felt what I felt, and each of those kisses—on my eyelids, on my temples, on my breasts—was an attempt to wipe away my sorrow.

He knew I needed him to hold me, and when we were finished, he pulled me close, clutching me the exact same way he did the first time we'd ever shared a bed. My head lay on his chest as he slept, and after an hour passed, I knew I'd be awake till morning. I closed my eyes as I felt the tears emerge. He shifted only slightly, pinching the little space between his eyebrows, when I sat up. Then his forehead smoothed. He looked so calm when he slept…

I ran a hand over his stomach and up to his chest, felt his heart beating there, always steady. His skin was warm. His neck was warm, his lips were soft and perfect. He murmured something in the middle of his dreams.

And that was when I knew it.

It was as if that intuition had always been there, but I hadn't dared to think it. Because I was scared. Terrified. But that terror was stupid now.

"I love you," I whispered.

I'd never said it aloud to a guy, but then, I'd never felt it before. And it was like a stone being lifted off of me. I wiped away a tear and breathed in deeply. I loved him. I had loved him as long as I'd known him, and now it was more real than ever.

And that's why I had to do what I was going to do.

Again, I put a hand on his heart.

"I love you, Jack. So, so much," I whispered. "And a day will come when we'll look back on this and laugh. I know it. I just hope…that for now you can understand."

I lifted my hand, clenching it into a fist as though I had gathered some of his warmth and could trap it there, hold on to it, if only for a moment.

Then I stood and grabbed my phone, dialing Shannon's number as I left the room.

28

THE FINAL DECISION

I went to sleep in the dorm.

I had Naya's spare key and I'd managed to sneak past Chris, who was totally absorbed in some game on his phone. They hadn't placed anyone in Naya's room, so my bed was still free. It was cold and empty without him. I was. Everything was without Jack's warm body in my arms. And the worst thing was, I'd done this to myself.

When the sun rose, I looked at my suitcase. I'd been crying all night, and it was time for me to go. I looked at my phone. Shannon would be there in fifteen minutes. I'd go back home, the way Mom had wanted, the way I'd sworn to myself I wouldn't…and it would all be over.

It's not too late to go back, I told myself.

I shook my head and rubbed my face.

It was too late.

It's not too late. Maybe he hasn't woken up yet. Go back, go back while there's still time.

I stood, trying to turn off my brain and those thoughts, and walked to the bathroom, where I saw myself in the mirror looking like hell, eyes and lips swollen, pale. A walking corpse. I washed my face with cold water, thinking maybe I could make myself react. Was Jack up yet? Of course he was. Had he read the note I'd left him? Just the thought of it made me want to cry.

That damned note. I didn't even want to think about what I'd written. I was a coward. I couldn't bear to tell him what I had to say to his face. I prayed—the gutless part of me prayed—that he wouldn't see it till I was half-way home. I couldn't stand the thought of him showing up before I'd gone, of having to tell him everything to his face. And of course he'd know I was lying.

I rubbed my cheeks, trying to get some color in them, and looked back into the mirror.

You're an idiot, you know? my brain told me.

"Yes, I know," I murmured aloud.

Then I heard a knock. I froze. Could it be him?

I walked to the door with my heart in my throat, but before I could grab the knob, it flew open. My entire body tensed. It was Naya. OK. I was OK. I could breathe. Naya stared at me in shock and said, "What happened? Jesus, Jenna, what happened? Tell me!"

"Nothing," I said. "Is Jack up?"

"He wasn't when I left. But Will told me you were gone, and he wouldn't say any more. Why, Jenna? Why did you leave?"

I could have asked myself that same question. But what would I have answered? I tried to concentrate on the steps still to take. Ten minutes. In ten minutes Shannon would be there. I would walk downstairs, get in her car, and it would all be over.

"Jenna, are you going to talk to me?"

"I don't know, Naya. It's complicated."

"Are you going?" Her eyes filled with tears as I nodded, and she said, "No! You can't! I don't know what's going on, but there's got to be a solu-tion. I love you, Jenna! You're my best friend. You can't go!"

"I'm sorry," I said. She hugged me, and I hugged her back, just barely managing to hold myself together.

"Stay," she said. "These things, they always seem like such a big deal, but you get through them, you always do, and Jack's someone who..."

"Naya, it's not Jack. He didn't do anything. I'm just going home. I have to. I'm sorry I didn't tell you earlier."

"So fast, though? Did something happen last night?"

"I told you, it's complicated."

That wasn't going to work for her, and she started to argue with me, but a pounding on the door and Jack's voice calling my name startled both of us. "Open the door!" he shouted.

Oh no. Naya looked at me, I was literally shaking. "I can't see him," I told her.

Naya looked at me and nodded, and cracked the door, telling Jack, "She's not..."

But he warned her to stand back. It would have been useless for her to try to resist him. When he came in, he looked mad: breathing labored, hair sticking out in all directions, eyes lost. He looked at the bed and my suitcase, then at me, and in the dense silence, Naya said, "I'm going to go back downstairs. Will and Sue are waiting on me."

I felt my heart break as she shut the door. Jack struggled to find the words to express his shock: "What...what... I don't understand. You're going?"

I hesitated, then said, "Yes," in the firmest voice I could muster.

"Why? What happened?"

"I just need to."

"But last night...like...wasn't it good for you?"

I didn't answer. He ran a hand through his hair, his mind going a mile a minute, and then he continued, "No. You can't. I don't know what happened, but you can't just go like that. Why? What did I do wrong?"

He cupped my face, trying to see if I was lying to him. But I had thought this through, and I was determined to keep my feelings hidden.

"It's not you, Jack. I just want to go home."

"Whatever it is, Jen, I'll make it up to you, just tell me. Anything. I don't care…"

"Jack, I don't want to be with you anymore," I said, cutting him off.

He hesitated, then stepped back. "What?"

"I can't keep doing this." My voice was quivering. "I can't. I can't live with you, Jack. It's too much. I don't want to. I want to go home."

"This is your home."

"It's not. The apartment is your home. Not mine. None of this is me, Jack. None of this is my world."

"But you are my world," he told me.

That cut me like a knife, and I wasn't sure how much more I could take. I shook my head and said, "I need to go."

"You don't! Stay! Just stay awhile longer. I'll sleep on the couch. I don't care. Give me the chance to make it up to you."

"No. I had a deal with my mother. She told me if December came and I wanted to go back…"

"Jen, December's over."

"Exactly. And that means everything that happened before December is the past."

Silence. He tried to open his lips, closed them again, looked at me. His hands were shaking.

"Don't leave me," he begged.

Don't do this to me, Jack.

"Don't leave me," he said again, taking my hand. "I love you, Jen. I haven't been sure of too many things in my life, but I'm sure of this. Stay with me, please. If you want to come back to the dorm, do that. If you need space, I get it. You don't have to just walk out on me and disappear to…"

"Jack," I said, looking away, but he grabbed my chin and turned me back toward him.

"Is it something I said? Did I hurt you somehow? If I did, I swear I didn't know..."

He wouldn't stop, he kept asking what he'd done wrong, and seeing him so innocent, so ready to do everything for me, I could feel my resistance evaporating, and I had to do something. So I shouted before I could realize what I was doing, "I'm back with Monty!"

He froze, looking exactly like a statue, and only after a few seconds did he manage to ask, "What?"

"We were together before I even came here. And I've realized I miss him. And that's why I'm going back. I'll tell the police everything's OK. I'll get them to drop the restraining order. I know now he's the guy I'm meant to be with. I'm sorry, Jack."

"But you never said... I thought..."

"You must have realized something when you told me you loved me and I didn't say anything back."

He let my hand go, and my phone buzzed. My sister. She was waiting for me downstairs. Jack was staring at me, trying to see some hint that I was lying. But there were none. I had readied myself for this throughout my sleepless night.

"I've got to go," I told him. "I'm sorry."

He watched me as though he were looking at a stranger as I passed by him, grabbing my suitcase and wiping away a tear before he could notice. I took a deep breath and walked toward the door. Only then did he grab my wrist and force me to turn around.

"Are you in love with him?" he asked.

I swallowed and tried to get down the knot in my throat as I told the worst lie of my life: "I've always been in love with him."

He let me go and turned his back to me, and I turned my back to him. I didn't want to see him, and I didn't want him to see me cry. I wiped my face with my sweater and walked out the door. Each step was torture. My instincts were screaming at me to turn around, to run back to him. I didn't listen to them, and I didn't do it.

I walked downstairs and saw Chris staring at me. Neither of us said anything. I couldn't; I needed to get out of there as soon as possible. He looked down, and I turned quickly to make sure Jack hadn't followed me. Outside, I saw Shannon talking with Will, Sue, and Naya beside her car. They stared at me, my sister sighed. She knew everything.

She and Will were the only ones. Sue and Naya were completely in the dark.

"Oh, Jenna," Shannon said, "do you want...?"

"I just want to go."

She grabbed my suitcase and put it in the trunk of her car. I looked back at the dorm. Why did I keep turning around as if I wanted him to run out and stop me? I'd just broken his heart. Of course he wasn't coming out.

"I can't believe you're going," Naya said.

She hugged me, and I tried not to break down. Even Sue looked sad and confused, and asked, "Are you sure about this?" I nodded.

"Fuck," she murmured, and gave me a quick hug. I heard her sniffling and asked, "Sue, are you crying?"

"No, I'm not crying, you bitch. You think I care? I don't like you, I don't like any of you. Get lost and don't come back."

But when she separated from me, I saw her wiping her nose and looking away. I squeezed her shoulder and grinned as much as I could, telling her, "I'll miss you, too, Sue."

Will hugged me tight and whispered, "I sure as hell hope you're doing the right thing."

"Just make sure he goes to that school," I said softly.

He nodded and looked at me sadly. I don't think I'd ever seen him sad. "Take care of yourself," he told me, and I responded, "You take care of him."

And that was it. I looked back at the dorm. It looked like an empty shell. Shannon was already waiting for me in her car. As soon as I sat next to her and put on my seat belt, I knew the tears would start falling. I could feel her looking at me. I rubbed my eyes in frustration.

"Jenna..."

"Not now," I said softly.

"Yes, now," she said firmly. "Do you really know what you're doing?"

"I'm doing what I think is right," I mumbled.

"Listen," she said. "I always tell you the truth. Even when you don't want to hear it. And this time is no exception. You're making a mistake."

"I'm not."

"You are, Jenna. If you don't get out of this car right now, you're going to regret it. You and I both know it."

"And what if I get out and I still regret it?" I asked.

"I don't know," she confessed.

I tried to stop crying, but I couldn't.

Just then, I saw movement near the entrance to the dorm. It was Jack. He walked out with the saddest expression I'd ever seen. We looked at each other for a moment. I was far away, but I knew he knew I was looking at him.

"Jenna," Shannon said, "it's not too late yet. You can get out right now and tell him the truth. I'm sure he'll understand. You can act like this never happened."

I took a breath and grabbed the door handle. Jack was looking at me, imploring me with his eyes to stay with him. My heart was pounding, telling me he was right, telling me I needed to stay. I could even see myself getting out, running to him, telling him everything. Telling him I loved him. Telling him I'd never wanted to leave his side. Telling him that the months I'd spent with him had taught me things I'd never thought I'd learn.

But then I remembered I was doing this *because* I loved him. Because I needed him to do what I knew would make him happy, even if that meant that I wouldn't be a part of his life and that something would shatter inside me that I would never be able to repair.

Shannon looked at me. "Jenna, you know I'll support you in whatever you decide to do, but…don't do something you're going to regret. Please."

I looked at my hands. Shaking. My whole body was shaking.

But I couldn't.

I couldn't stay.

"Sometimes we have to sacrifice things for love. Because we love the other person more than ourselves. Because we want the best for them. And once you find yourselves in that situation, it's hard to turn back."

That was what Mr. Ross said. And he was right. It was hard.

I closed my eyes and let go of the door handle.

When I reopened them, I didn't dare to look at him. I couldn't. I just stared straight ahead.

Shannon watched me, then nodded, as though she understood everything in that moment.

"Ready to go home?" she asked softly.

I fought my impulse to turn away. With tears streaming down my cheeks, I took a deep breath and glanced over at her.

I nodded, certain.

"I'm ready."

One year and an avalanche of hurt later,
can Jenna and Jack save their damaged love?

READ ON FOR AN EXCERPT OF *AFTER DECEMBER*.

1

HEALING WOUNDS

They say time creeps by when things are going badly...and I couldn't agree more.

I'd suffered, and the worst part of all is I was the one to blame for it. I'd made a decision that had seemed like the right one, but it was difficult to live with. I'd abandoned the guy I loved.

Maybe *abandoned* is too strong a word. The guy in question still had his friends on his side: Will, Naya, even his brother Mike. They were with him. I was the one who'd stepped away, who'd gone back to stay with my parents, who'd left everything behind.

A year before that, I'd decided to go away to college and study a major that didn't interest me, just to get as far as possible from the life I'd lived before. That's where I met all the people I just mentioned, along with Jack Ross, who was something more complicated than just a *friend*.

He helped me understand that my relationship with Monty wasn't love, that I'd need to learn to think for myself, that I had devoted my entire life to pleasing others no matter whether they wanted to make me happy.

I don't think he realized that the first decision I'd make for myself would be leaving him. Jack needed to chase his dreams, and I wasn't ready to accompany him. I needed to find out what my own dreams were.

I'd like to take the credit for these insights, which sound like they came straight from a self-help book, but the truth is I'd learned them from the woman who had been my therapist for the last year. My big brother and big sister, Spencer and Shannon, had helped me pay for my sessions with her until I managed to scrape together money of my own.

In a single year, I'd worked as a cashier, a gas station attendant, a warehouse worker, and assistant phys ed teacher under Spencer. Some of these jobs had overlapped, and they'd taken up so much of my time that all I could ever think about was how tired I was. And funny enough, that helped me a lot.

The chance to do as I wanted, make my own money, decide things for myself…it was a huge change. One I hadn't known how to anticipate. Along with my therapy, it allowed me to see things from a different perspective.

And one of those things was my family.

What Jack had told me once, that they always managed to make me do whatever they wanted, had gotten stuck in my head. For a long time, I ignored the truth, the hundreds of signs that he'd been right. I kept pretending everything was OK…but then one night, it all exploded.

I was sitting at the kitchen table with Sonny and Steve, my parents, and Spencer. The only sound was the game on the little TV by the fridge. My brothers and my father had their eyes glued to the screen, and Mom and I were picking apathetically at our meal.

That was probably what started it—the fact that she and I didn't like sports and couldn't distract ourselves—because it gave us no choice but to interact.

"You're not hungry?" she asked me, watching me push around a brussels sprout with my fork.

I was too tired to deal with her. I'd worked five hours at the gas station and four out on the fields and I could hardly keep myself upright.

"Not really. I'll probably wrap this up and save it for tomorrow."

Mom glared at my basically untouched plate with resentment in her brown eyes, which looked almost exactly like mine. "Fine," she said after a moment. "I'm not hungry either. Maybe it's my cooking. Maybe it's just not good enough."

"Mom, I didn't say that," I responded.

"You don't have to. You never like anything lately."

"I'm tired."

"You always have an excuse."

She'd been snippy with me ever since I'd returned home, but this was the first time she'd just come out and attacked me, and I struggled to see why. Something was clearly up, but she wouldn't tell me what. And that meant I would have to be the one to pull it out of her.

"You want to tell me what's going on with you?" I asked. My tone was calm, but direct. *Assertive*, as my therapist called it. I had never spoken to my parents that way before, and everyone at the table turned to me with surprise.

My mother, of course, brought her hand to her heart. "What do you mean?"

"Mom," I told her, "you've been acting weird, anyone can see it. What I can't understand is why you won't tell me what's going on."

She and Dad exchanged glances. They'd been doing that a lot lately. I knew that they had talked about the situation, and it enraged me that they were both sitting there playing dumb.

"Well?" I insisted.

Dad warned me, "Don't talk to your mother like that."

"I haven't talked to her any way," I said, "I just asked what was going on and why you keep nitpicking at me."

Sonny and Steve burst out laughing, and I gripped my fork so tight in my fist, I was worried I'd bend it. Sonny told me I was out of my mind, and Steve added, "Yeah, since you came back, you think the whole world's against you."

"I don't *think* anything," I replied, "it's just that all of you are talking about me behind my back, and I'm over it."

"No one's talking about you," my father reassured me. He was lying, I could tell. He even blushed a little before he glanced over at Mom.

"Oh yeah?" I fired back. "Then why do you two keep looking back and forth like that?"

"We're not!" Mom shouted.

"You are!"

Steve pretended to cough, saying the word *psycho* as he and Sonny cracked up. I was furious and could feel the blood draining from my face, and that made me yell at my brothers for the first time in ages: "Can you shut up for once!"

"Jennifer!" my mother responded. "That's enough! No one's plotting against you! Stop being paranoid!"

"I'm not paranoid! Y'all are up to something!"

"Like what? Your brothers are laughing! What's wrong with that?" Mom asked.

"It's not that they're laughing," I told her, my voice getting louder, "it's that they're making fun of me! They've been making fun of me constantly, and you never say anything, and Dad doesn't either!"

My brothers turned irate, but Mom talked over them: "Where is all this coming from? Why now? When we're trying to have dinner in peace?"

I told her she'd started it, that she'd been acting weird with me ever since I'd returned home, and I didn't understand why. I asked whether she even wanted me back, or whether I was just extra now. She shouted back that I was pushing it, and I saw my father's back straighten as he got ready to intervene.

"You're taking it too far!" he screamed. That wasn't like him. But I stood my ground and asked if he was really going to deny that Sonny and Steve made fun of me all the time. Sonny jumped in to tell me to stop making everyone feel bad, and to top it off, he threw a napkin in my face.

At that point, I lost control: "Can you not just leave me alone? Do you two really have nothing better to do than mess with your little sister? Shouldn't you maybe try to drag your garage business out of debt for once! Focus on your own shit and stay out of my business!"

That was the first time in history I'd gotten them both to shut up. But Mom was fiery red, which meant I'd really gotten under her skin. She pointed at me and said, "You can't just go through life making everyone else feel miserable, Jennifer!"

"Everyone else? What about me?! Have you ever asked yourself how I feel, or does that just not matter to you?"

"When did you decide it was OK to talk to people that way?" she screamed, and started burbling something about how I'd changed since I'd gone away to college, and I must have picked up my bad behavior from my friends there and the guy I had gone out with.

For some reason, since my return, Mom had refused to call Jack by his name. He was always *that guy you were going out with*, and her tone, which had once been affectionate, was now totally disrespectful.

I agreed with her, though, and I let her know it, slamming my fork down on the table: "You're right! Jack opened my eyes to lots of things!"

"Exactly," Mom said, and I realized that was the answer she'd been looking for. "He got into your head and turned you against us! He even got your old boyfriend thrown in jail!"

I couldn't answer—her words had shocked me too much. Frozen, I noticed that Spencer, who hadn't yet said a word, stood and warned her in a steely tone, "Mom, no. Don't go there."

She wasn't used to people defending me, especially not against her, and she almost flinched as she said, "I'm just telling it like it is."

"He was an asshole, and he got what he deserved," Spencer said, and when Dad stood up and shouted at him, Spencer cut him off, "Stay out of it, Dad."

Mom yelled that getting Monty arrested had caused all sorts of problems for them: "Do you know how the rest of the neighborhood has looked at us since then? Do you know what they say about us? It's like we don't even exist anymore."

"He was hitting Jenny, Mom!" Spencer screamed.

"That's what she says!"

That made me react. I had been miffed before the subject of Monty came up, but now I saw what was really going on, and it shocked me. Mom wasn't mad that I was back home, she was mad because things had changed in her life. She wasn't worried about some maniac who might come stalking me, she was worried about the inconvenience it might cause her.

Before I realized it, I heard my chair sliding backward and found myself running toward the stairs. My movements were at once robotic and enraged. Enraged at my mother, at the twins… I couldn't believe a year had passed and people still didn't believe me.

Because most of them didn't. A few people in the neighborhood, maybe, but even then, they weren't brave enough to say anything. Monty just wasn't the kind of guy they looked at as an abuser. He was handsome, funny, and good at basketball. For many, he was the perfect man. And I was the weird girl who had insisted on going off to college, returned home without warning, and ruined a guy's life by turning him in to the cops.

Of course, people didn't believe me. How many people there even knew me, really? And despite the evidence, it wasn't in their interest to accept the truth. I could live with that, though. What hurt was my mother calling me a liar. She should have known better.

ABOUT THE AUTHOR

Joana Marcús, born in Mallorca in 2000, divides her time between her studies, her books, and her pets. Since she was little, she's loved writing. Her first compositions were short stories, and it wasn't until she was thirteen that she found the courage to publish her first complete story on Wattpad, where she is still writing today.

Instagram: @joanamarcusx